Praise for RUIN FALLS

"[Jenny] Milchman has a gift that allows her to delve deep into the mind and psyche of her characters, and fans of dark plots like the works of Gillian Flynn will find another author to savor."

—*RT Book Reviews*

"Essential for psychological thriller fanatics ... Extreme, heart-pounding action follows this determined mother as she risks everything to save her children."

—*Library Journal*

"[Milchman] carves out a new niche with this unusual mix of eco-thriller and family suspense drama."

—*Booklist* (starred review)

"Milchman weaves a complex and intriguing tale, adeptly pacing the narrative as danger escalates. ... Most impressive, though, is Liz's transformation from a meek wife [to] a strong, capable woman determined to rescue her children at any cost to herself."

—*Publishers Weekly*

"Milchman can evoke the shadows and fears of a rural community like no one else."

—*DuJour*

BY JENNY MILCHMAN

Cover of Snow

Ruin Falls

RUIN FALLS

RUIN FALLS

A NOVEL

Jenny Milchman

BALLANTINE BOOKS

NEW YORK

2015 Ballantine Books Trade Paperback Edition

Copyright © 2014 by Jenny Milchman

Published in the United States by Ballantine Books, an imprint of Random House, a division of Random House LLC, a Penguin Random House Company, New York.

BALLANTINE and the HOUSE colophon are registered trademarks of Random House LLC.

Originally published in hardcover in the United States by Ballantine, an imprint of Random House, a division of Random House LLC, in 2014.

LIBRARY OF CONGRESS CATALOGING-IN-PUBLICATION DATA
Milchman, Jenny.
Ruin Falls : a novel / Jenny Milchman.
p.   cm
ISBN 978-0-345-54909-9
eBook ISBN 978-0-345-54908-2
1. Parental kidnapping—Fiction.   2. Mothers of kidnapped children—Fiction.
3. Missing persons—Investigation—Fiction.   4. Family secrets—Fiction.
5. Psychological fiction.   I. Title.
PS3613.I47555R85 2014
813'.6—dc23   2014002240

Printed in the United States of America

www.ballantinebooks.com

2 4 6 8 9 7 5 3 1

Book design by Caroline Cunningham

This one is for my children, Sophie and Caleb,

who know all about dreams and have done so much for this one.

Here's to pine-bough eyelashes, Frank Automotive Corp. . . .

and cliff-jumping.

RUIN FALLS

CHAPTER ONE

The children had never been this far from home before. Liz had spent most of yesterday driving around, hunting for no-mess Crayola coloring books, praying they weren't too juvenile to keep a six- and eight-year-old occupied in the car, then running up and down the supermarket aisles in search of bars and snack pouches in case they couldn't find food on the road. Or in case they did find something, and Paul wouldn't allow the kids to eat it.

Now the hours had ticked by, four of them, and it seemed they were no closer to their destination than they had been when they left home. Descending from the mountains of Wedeskyull had presented a stark contrast and it felt like they were really traveling. But the view outside the windows ever since had been made up of little besides cornfields. Liz wouldn't have believed how bleak acres and acres of green could appear when the crop was so unvarying. The road they were driving on hadn't dipped or risen for thirty minutes. It was a flat length of asphalt, inky mirages always shimmering just ahead.

"Mommy?"

"Yes, sweetie?"

"I wish we could see some real trees."

As tired as she was—and they weren't even at the hardest part of this day yet—Liz smiled reflexively. Ally, her gardening partner, her green thumb girl. To say that their youngest had a desire to be out in nature was like saying she had a desire to breathe. Sometimes Liz looked into her little girl's eyes and saw a tiny version of herself in the serious brown lenses.

"Mom?"

Reid's turn now. Liz glanced in the rearview, but it wasn't angled to offer a glimpse of her son. "What is it, hon?"

"I'm bored."

"Me, too," Ally chimed in. "Everything looks the same out my window."

The flatness was getting to Liz, too. She looked over at Paul in the driver's seat.

"Another round of I Spy?" he suggested. "Or Ghost?"

Liz had already decided that car games must've been invented by some not-so-benevolent dictator masquerading as an elementary school teacher. For that matter, cars might've been invented by the same person, minus the schoolteacher part. She had no idea how people sat still for so long. Her body itched to be moving, knees sinking into the soil, hands digging in the ground. She had sympathy for both kids, who up till now had actually been pretty good.

"How about we sing?" she suggested, channeling the voice of that dictatorial teacher. Liz Daniels, schoolmarm.

Boos and groans from the backseat.

Paul responded belatedly. "I might have to let you out here if you do that."

Liz laughed.

"Mom? I'm hungry."

"Me, too!" Ally crowed.

Liz looked at Paul, but her husband had subsided into silence, eyes fixed on the long, blank road. "Bored and hungry, huh?" she said, twisting to peer into the backseat. A sight through the back window made her frown for a moment, but then the unhappy faces distracted her. She reached for a light tone. "Boy, you guys are really a mess."

"Mom!"

"Mommy!"

The protests were fast approaching a whine.

"Paul?" Liz said, squinting at the back window again.

Her husband didn't answer. Liz's gaze darted to the rearview.

"Paul," she said more urgently.

He looked at her.

"I think that truck has been behind us for a long time," she said.

Her husband reached up and tilted the mirror to get a better look. "It's just a pickup truck," he said, his tone a shrug.

"I know," Liz said. "But look how closely it's trailing us."

She made sure to pitch her voice low so as not to alert the children. Reid, especially, had a tendency to get scared. His fear of death belied both his age and understanding. When Liz's great-aunt had died last year, they took Ally to the funeral, but left Reid behind. No low-impact introduction to the subject, such as a children's storybook or short-lived pet hermit crab, enabled Reid to cope. They even skirted cemeteries in case Reid caught a glimpse of a gravestone. Liz actually mapped out alternate routes to school or the grocery store or seed depot, aware of where Wedeskyull's dead were laid. And although she occasionally dragged the whole family to church, hoping a religious connection might provide some sort of framework for Reid's fears, she usually regretted it. The sermons about heaven terrified him, and Liz had to work to steer clear of the tilting rows of headstones in the churchyard.

She wondered whether this boycott approach to death was really wise. The ban would have to end sometime, and then what?

The pickup had drawn even closer, but Paul's glance didn't shift from the road in front of them. Liz had the idea to try and identify the model, but it was impossible to make out the front grille, so close was it to their car. They passed a farm, and a pungent, animal stink came in through the vents, the smell of portable potties and compost that needed turning.

"Mo-om!"

The whine had become a shriek. Reid, going right past Go without stopping to collect his two hundred dollars.

Then Ally joined in. "How much longer? I'm hungry! I'm super hungry!"

The pickup loomed above them now, filling the entire rear window.

The volume in the backseat died at the exact moment as the noise from the pickup exploded into a rattle and a roar. Liz glanced down to see that her pocketbook had vanished, unfelt, from its position in her lap. It was in the backseat, and the children had begun tearing into packets of fruit snacks, looking shocked and sugar-stung by their unexpected bounty. At home, Paul tended to limit even the natural brands of treats, but these had been for an emergency.

An emergency.

The pickup truck's engine growled, so close it would soon be touching them. Liz braced herself for the jolt, sending an alarmed look toward Paul. He seemed to have finally noticed the vehicle rearing up behind them, although he still appeared unperturbed. Their hybrid didn't even handle winters at home all that well, and it certainly wasn't built to go head-to-head with a truck. Liz closed her eyes against an image of the back of their car getting pleated, accordion-folded with Ally and Reid inside.

She suppressed a scream, willing her husband to floor it.

The truck swerved into the other lane. For just a moment it hovered beside them, holding even with their car. Liz caught a glimpse of the driver's furious face, his knotted eyebrows. Then the pickup rocketed by them at such high speed that their car swayed in its wake.

Paul tapped the brake, swiveling the steering wheel to straighten out. He gave a shake of his head. "What a jerk."

Liz's chest was heaving beneath her T-shirt.

"A jerk?" she repeated. "Honey, that guy—I think it was deliberate. He was trying to terrorize us. Or something."

The something was vague and unarticulated in her mind. It had to do with being away from home, as far away as they'd ventured since both kids were born. It might even have had to do with their destination, her husband's childhood home, a place Liz had never visited before. But the expression on the driver's face hadn't just been her imagination, or an artifact of Liz's sense of disjointedness. He had looked into her eyes with real rage.

Maybe they'd just been driving too slowly, Paul reluctant to get where they were going.

Her husband's gaze slipped past hers. More and more interactions between them were going this way: Paul imposing his vision, Liz protesting in a way that felt feeble. She wondered when they had fallen into these roles. It used to be that their differences balanced them, but lately it seemed they just kept them on opposite sides.

Opposite sides of what? Liz wondered.

She decided to try again. "Paul, he practically hit us."

Paul flicked the cruise control back on and spoke calmly. "Well, he's gone now."

The pickup had indeed shot ahead, not even its tail visible any longer in front of them. In the backseat, the kids were quietly eating gummies.

She recalled the rising fear that had filled her, like water coming in. Not like her at all; Liz considered herself the practical half of their pairing. Down there in the trenches of the day-to-day, making sure things stayed their course. The house, school, the kids' activities. While Paul painted lofty pictures of what could be, leading people along like a Pied Piper.

He had settled back against the seat.

Ever since she'd known him, her husband's customary capability, which he wore like thick tree bark, had been a source of comfort, allowing Liz to reach for things she never otherwise would have. Her business. The children even. But for one flickering moment, with the car gliding smoothly along, Paul's unruffled demeanor made her angry.

She spied the blue sign that signaled services ahead. Liz forced herself to reach over, touch her husband's arm.

"How about we stop?" she said, aware of the complexities such a pause would create, but not caring at the moment. "I think we could all use a break."

CHAPTER TWO

She was surprised when Paul swung off at the exit; then she noticed the tilt of the needle on the gas gauge. Paul pulled up at the pump.

"Honey?" she said. "The kids are really hungry. I think we should get them something to eat." *Super hungry*, she heard Ally say.

"I made some sandwiches," Paul said, indicating a small cooler at Liz's feet. "But if we dip into them now, dinner might get a little tight. I doubt there'll be a decent restaurant."

Paul got out to pump the gas, and Liz let down the window. She leaned over to talk, surprised by the sodden heat in the air. At some point during their entry into western New York, the whole climate had changed. "I'll take them in, okay?"

Paul looked at her as if she'd suggested bringing the children to Mars. "There's nothing here but fast food."

The kids seemed to be gearing up for a rare opportunity. In the backseat, Ally looked at Reid, and both kids unbuckled their belts.

Liz nodded quickly. "Just this once."

"You already gave them candy," he said.

"Not candy," Liz corrected. "Fruit snacks."

For a topic as inherently light and pleasing as sweets, this was actually dangerous territory for them. Liz knew that both kids secretly ate food Paul would've forbidden. Reid, as the older child and the one who tended toward self-assertion anyway, pilfered packs of gum from the knapsacks of seatmates. But if Paul had known that, he would've felt the need to enlighten them all about the history of gum, its origin as a natural component of the beech tree to today's manufacturing outrages, and by the end none of them would be able to split open a package of Trident without worrying that they were ingesting something akin to cyanide, not to mention contributing to the exploitation of the working class.

And the thing was, by the time Paul had finished, Reid and Ally and Liz herself would all be left feeling grateful they'd gotten a chance to join his crusade.

Her husband shook his head. "Fruit snacks aren't much better than candy. You may as well just go ahead and have them chew gum."

Liz hid her smile.

"What's funny?" Paul asked, and Liz smiled again.

"Just thinking that you can be very convincing."

The pump clicked off.

"Dad?" Reid said, leaning over the front seat to talk through the open window. "We're hot."

"Yeah," Ally said. "Super hot. Look, Daddy. I feel like one of those pansies."

Liz looked when Paul didn't. There were planters here, someone's nod to beautification, but they'd been filled without a care to conditions, and the blotches of color were shriveled and blistered. Liz's fingers itched to uproot the bedraggled clumps, offer the dirt a mix of zinnia, snapdragon, and rudbeckia instead, blooms that could withstand the assault of the sun.

"Can we get something to drink?"

"And eat?"

Paul replaced the pump in its slot, studying the array of signs on the building behind them. "You might be able to find some fruit at the Starbucks," he said to Liz. "Fill the water bottle. I'll park the car."

Liz hustled the kids away from the car, thinking, Muffins. Muffins for Reid and Ally, and a grande for me, and Paul would have to be satisfied with that.

She was standing on a long, snaking line, welcoming the air-conditioned cool and watching for Paul, when she realized that while one kid still hovered right beside her, the other didn't.

"Al?" she said. "Where's your brother?"

She'd gotten used to the fact that the kids kept better track of each other than she ever could, unless she wanted to be one of those gluey moms who never let her children out of her sight. The teachers told her that even at school, Reid checked up on Ally and vice versa.

Liz took hold of Ally's hand and began looking around. People pricked the soaring, two-storied space; it was difficult to make out the head of an eight-year-old. Paul entered the building and she called out to get his attention. She didn't want to stray too far in case Reid came back to find her.

Ally gave a little yelp and Liz realized how hard she was squeezing her daughter's hand. She wasn't all the way to worried yet—the kids had plenty of independence on the farm—but this cavernous network of fast food offerings presented all too much temptation to a kid unused to them. Plus Liz's nerves were still jangled by their near miss on the highway.

"Christ," Paul said, as soon as he understood the situation. He scrubbed his face. "I'm tired. Reid!"

People in the crowd began to take notice, pulling their own kids close.

"I'll check the bathroom," Paul said, scooping Ally up.

It hit her like an *aha*. How had Liz been annoyed earlier by Paul's sensibility and competence? Her husband leveled her out every time. The restroom was where Reid had to be. After all, it was the kids who had polished off all the water, those sugary fruit things making them thirsty.

But a few seconds later, Paul was headed back from the men's room, Ally still hooked to his hip. He didn't have Reid.

Just then Liz's peripheral vision caught sight of a man's face, plum-colored and angry. The irate sound of his voice followed a second later. The man held Reid by one bony wrist, and Liz felt her own instinctual surge of outrage along with relief.

"Hey!" she cried. "Let go of my—"

The crowd was parting now, some studiedly ignoring whatever situation had developed, others observing it avidly.

"He yours?" the man called out to Liz.

She suddenly felt hollowed out and weary, spotting the fat leather wallet the man held in the hand he wasn't using to grasp Reid. Papers bulged out; the wallet's contents were disarrayed.

"I'm so sorry," Liz said, walking forward, knowing what must have happened, but feeling no ability to deal with it. "If you look, I think you'll find that nothing's missing."

The man let go of Reid, who shuffled in Liz's direction, eyes downcast. The man's frown appeared less angry now than bewildered.

"He likes to see if he can take them," Liz tried to explain. There was no good explanation, of course, although she had often been compelled to give one. "He's not actually trying to steal anything." She paused. "He always gives it right back."

The man kept silent for a beat. "Boys will be boys," he said at last.

Liz secured Reid by the arm, imprisoning him only a little less tightly than the man just had. They went to join Paul, who had come to a resigned halt a few feet away.

CHAPTER THREE

"One near car crash, one child almost arrested," Liz said, a parody of a checklist. "I'd say we're on vacation."

The Starbucks seemed less tempting behind her, its aroma slightly sickening. The children were standing in front of a machine that dispensed toys in plastic bubbles. Their expressions looked both dazed and dazzled by the unfamiliar carnival wares, but any minute now they were going to run back, asking for quarters.

Paul was distracted. He looked at her, and when his reply came, it was half-scoffing, half-joking. "Come on. That driver was just a little reckless. And Reid is still a free man."

But Liz felt too tense to laugh.

When Reid was two years old, he'd begun taking things out of Ally's nursery. They'd chalked it up to jealousy over the new baby, but the practice hadn't stopped with time. In fact, it'd gotten worse, or perhaps a more accurate way of putting it was to say that Reid had gotten better. Instead of impossible-to-conceal stuffed animals and blankies, an ear or corner of which always protruded from wherever Reid stowed his booty, small objects such as bracelets and billfolds started disappearing. He had a gift for sleight of hand. He'd once removed his teacher's earring as she bent down to grade his test.

The littlest pickpocket, they called him, during the time when all this seemed funny.

Liz and Paul had taken their son to a psychologist, and then a psychiatrist. Both doctors terrified them with a list of warning signs to look out for: fire-setting, cruelty to animals. They didn't seem to grasp, even after observation, that Reid was basically a sweet boy, protective of his sister, still innocent himself. The professionals seemed to regard Liz and Paul with a mute sort of pity whenever they sought to describe their son.

But Reid honestly seemed more gifted than sociopathic to Liz. She supposed anyone would say the same of their child. Everybody had a gift these days; no one was average. Well, Reid had his problems, and he certainly wasn't on top of his compulsion to relieve objects from their owners. But he never kept the things he stole, save for the occasional stick of gum, or the fruit snacks he'd swiped from Liz's purse earlier that day. Reid seemed more interested in practice, in diligently perfecting his craft.

Liz made a mental note to propose magic again. It had been the therapist's suggestion—a way to channel Reid's passion into something a little more appropriate. In the past, Reid had dismissed the idea with a decidedly teenaged snort. *Magic isn't real*, he'd said. *You just make things disappear for pretend.*

The return trip across the parking lot felt like an Olympic sport given the completely unanticipated heat. The air was like wet towels upon them, and the kids dragged their feet. Only the promise of turning on the air-conditioning, an oddity where they came from, got Reid and Ally to move. At home, Liz worked outside all summer long. She was unprepared for how a thirty degree leap in temperature, going from indoors to out, could make your body instantly sag.

Their car gave off a baking heat despite having rested for only ten minutes under the sun. Liz dabbed her forehead and vented her underarms in her tee. The kids looked flushed and overheated.

When she opened the door, Ally let out a little shriek, dropping her seatbelt buckle, and Liz took over so that the children didn't burn their fingers. She pulled spare shirts out of the suitcase and placed them behind each child on the blistering seats. Then she sat down herself.

Paul got in without making a move to turn on the engine.

"Paul?" Liz said. "It's pretty hot in here."

Her husband didn't reply.

"You tense, honey?" Liz asked. "Nervous about seeing your father?" She reached across the seat to touch her husband's shoulders, then started. "My God. Your back is like an iron rod." She began to rub.

Paul's face had gone similarly steely. Liz continued to compress the flesh by his neck, although his expression made her hand falter.

He seemed to sense it, deliberately softening his gaze. "I'm sorry." The two words sounded strange, as if he had pills in his mouth. "Maybe I'm feeling like I guilted you into this trip. Played the parents-getting-old card."

"No, honey." Liz shook her head. "You didn't. I've never gotten to see where you grew up. And it will be good for the kids to see another kind of farming." She didn't often think of what she did as farming, but the goods grown in her gardens had acquired a unique value compared to what she was seeing on this drive.

"A crueler kind," Paul said ruefully. "The rainbow chard you put in at Roots dies a lot more peacefully than my father's cattle." His mouth twisted, a sudden spasm.

Paul almost never talked about his father. They rarely saw the man, and the times they had, he and Paul didn't speak. It was going to be a strange vacation, although Liz imagined the children would run interference, along with Paul's mother.

"Swiss chard," Liz corrected gently. "I didn't put any rainbow in this year. Remember what happened last fall?"

Paul was quiet.

"Paul?"

"Ah yes," he said. "It wasn't much of a rainbow. More like monochrome chard."

Liz laughed. It had been a while since her husband had made her laugh, but this was now twice in one day. Her earlier flash of anger began to ebb away.

"I have an idea," he said.

"All ears," Liz said.

She turned around, surprised they hadn't been asked yet why they weren't moving, or pelted by demands for the promised air-conditioning. Both kids were woozy and drifting toward sleep. Liz tipped her head back, but the upholstery produced an instant slick of sweat. She leaned forward, fanning her neck.

"We got a late start. The kids are going to be cranky, and I don't want them to greet their grandparents that way."

Unspoken was the fact that neither child had seen Paul's parents for years.

"Okay . . ." Liz said.

"Why don't we drive a little while longer, then get a hotel room? We'll have one less day at the farm, but everyone will arrive in better shape."

Paul typically railed against the environmental impact of hotels. All that laundry, the waste involved in the free breakfasts he wouldn't eat anyway. His making such a suggestion had to be a sign of how the prospect of seeing his parents was throwing him.

He placed a hand suggestively on her leg. "We could even get a suite."

Something else they hadn't done much of lately.

Liz lifted her head. "That would be nice."

"Nice?" Paul finally started the engine. Baked air gusted through the vents. "What is that, monochrome wife?"

She laughed again. Three for three. "Okay, okay. That would be loin-stirringly good. Let's do it. Let's go to a hotel."

CHAPTER FOUR

Paul made the reservation from the car. A chain hotel, whose name appeared on yet another of those blue signs, and thus wasn't far off the road. The parking lot shimmered with heat, and light glared off the windows as the building rose, but there was welcome shade under an overhang at the entrance.

They let the kids sleep a few extra minutes, engine running, air on, while Liz fetched a trolley from the vestibule, and Paul got their bags out of the trunk. Perspiration appeared on his brow and in ovals under his arms as he worked; Liz leaned limply against the car, chiding herself for the position of ease when there was much to be done.

The temperature hardly seemed to drop despite the dying sun in the sky.

Paul squinted into it, slamming the trunk shut, and Liz went to nudge Ally awake. Her daughter's eyelids shot up like shades; Ally had this way of reentering the world from sleep as if she had never left it. She would slip into conversations mid-breath.

"Mommy?"

"Yes, sweetie?" Liz stroked Ally's feathery hair out of her eyes. Her daughter's scalp was sweaty.

"Sometimes I worry about Reid."

"About Reid?" Liz glanced across the seat. Reid's head lolled back, his sleeping face so open and revealed that it seemed her son could hide nothing. Not the objects he took, nor the source of his sadness about the end of life. "Why are you worried about Reid, sweetie?"

Ally took in a rippling breath. "I don't know."

It was clear she knew something, though.

Paul made an impatient gesture, swiping his brow with the back of one hand. "Hey. I'm dying out here. I forgot what this felt like."

Liz nodded quickly, holding up one finger. The car was heating up; they couldn't stay long. She looked down at Ally.

"Maybe he'll get into trouble. Like with that man in the—the place where you buy food that's bad for you. Or for some other reason."

Liz felt a flick of relief that she couldn't identify. "Oh, sweetie. I don't think you have to worry about that. Really. I think Reid will be fine."

Paul opened the door on the other side of the car. He woke Reid, trundling the boy forward, while Liz got out the cooler. They could eat dinner in their room. Liz half carried, half marched Ally across the parking lot. The doors to the hotel slid open, air-conditioning a welcome reprieve. The kids came to life, and began running laps around the lobby while Liz handled the process of checking in.

"Look, Mommy, there's candy machines!" Ally said.

"I bet I could get something out of one of those," Reid mused, a few feet away.

"Come on!" Liz heard Ally say behind her. "Let's go!"

"Reid?" Paul was rearranging things on the trolley. "No taking any—"

"I was just joking, Dad."

The two kids walked off. Liz allowed herself the indulgence of watching them for a moment, feeling the trace of a smile. Ally reached out and fingered the leaves of a potted plant, which even from here Liz could tell was fake. Her daughter looked dismayed by her finding, before hurrying to catch up with her brother.

"Sir?" A bellhop came up to Paul. "May I bring that upstairs for you?"

The woman behind the front desk slid Liz's credit card back, along with a little envelope with two key cards in it. "This is your room number," the woman said, pointing to the digits on the envelope without saying them aloud. A security measure, Liz realized.

Paul turned to round up Reid and Ally, forgetting to respond to the bellhop.

"Thank you," Liz said. "That'd be——" And then she paused.

"This way, ma'am," the bellhop said.

Liz had the sudden, purest desire to send this man away. She didn't want him handling their things, and she didn't want him to see their room, let alone their children. He was a nondescript man, in the flat expanse of middle age, with eyes of neutral blue, and a thinning cap of hair. The uniform he wore was a little dingy, as if the hotel didn't bother to replace them as often as they might. The bellhop's only notable feature was a thread-thin mustache.

"We can take care of it," she said. "Thank you, we're fine."

She glanced around for her husband, who was answering a text as he ushered the children back from the vending area. Probably one of his students. Even on vacation, Paul's students—disciples was more like it—couldn't leave their guru alone. Paul drew closer, sliding his phone back into its clip. He wore his connection to the rest of the world as if he were a surgeon or a cop instead of a college professor in a rural agricultural school.

Liz started to push the trolley forward. It was awkward and un-wieldy, the wheels swiveling instead of straightening out.

"Ma'am?" the bellhop said. "Let me."

Paranoid, Liz told herself. *This day has made me crazy.*

A long drive with two children, that near miss on the highway, Reid's episode of thievery. The heavy wet heat of a summer spent anywhere outside the Adirondacks. It was ridiculous to worry about a bellhop in a chain hotel. Liz fell into step behind the man, tugging Ally along with her, and pretending not to see the glimmer of wrap-per sticking out of Reid's back pocket. How had he done it? Neither child had any money on them. Then the elevator arrived, and the kids were excited enough by the ride that both stolen candy bars and strange-looking bellhops were forgotten.

THE COURT ORDER

Abby Harmon sat at her kitchen table, staring down at two things. The envelope that had arrived today, hidden between the usual sliding pile of junk, like a snake in a thicket of grass. And the text message she'd just received.

Envelope.

Text.

Two very different roads, each wending away into a thicket of its own.

If she did what the letter inside the envelope compelled her to do, Abby could envision the next several years of her life, and the prospect made her cringe. The next several years of Cody's life, actually. How old would he be when they finally emerged? Eight? Nine? Half again as old as he was now, years lost, and that was presuming a happy ending.

If there wasn't a happy ending, then they would lose a lot more than years.

A fan rattled on the counter, coming around again to unleash its hot breath upon her. Hot air that moved was hardly better than hot, still air. It wasn't supposed to hit temperatures this high up here, certainly not at night. The person who had just messaged her was right—things really were getting apocalyptic. Abby blinked sweat from her eyes.

She looked down at the sheet of paper. An ounce of wood pulp. Such a light, ephemeral medium—a match would turn it to curled, gray shreds inside of a second—to be the bearer of a blow that could destroy her whole life.

And then the text on her phone. Which would bring about an end even less predictable.

"Mama?"

Abby jumped in her chair, a flimsy metal thing that rocked back under the force of her sudden movement. She'd had to look for a furnished rental since she couldn't take any of her own things, stealing away like a captive during the brief hour Bill spent at the gym. They'd left the city when he got a job that allowed him to work from home— just one more way to keep an eye on her and Cody. And going back for her stuff was an encounter that she couldn't risk.

Even this letter, written by a third party, was too close to her husband for comfort.

Abby steadied the chair, and brushed her hair out of her eyes. How long had it been since she'd styled it? She used to give herself a blow-out every other day like clockwork, even after they moved. None of the women did that here, but Bill had insisted. Now Abby couldn't recall the last time she'd washed it, and the strands hung lank and deflated against her sweaty face.

"Mama?" Cody said again.

"Yes, Bun?" She had no idea where the pet name had come from. She only knew that it seemed to soothe Cody, and that Bill didn't use it. He preferred real titles to endearments.

"I had a bad dream again."

Her little boy's face withered, as wrinkly as an old man's. Abby had a vision of years passing while she and Bill wrangled things out in court, Cody's story changing in the telling as his perspective broadened with time.

She held out her arms, and he ran to her. His back was sweaty through the polyester of his pajamas. They had to make them flame-retardant, as if fire were the danger children were most likely to run into. This pair was a size 3T, bought over a year ago, then. Which Pixar movie had been available for streaming, and consequently

Cody's favorite film of all time? Abby looked down at her silently stroking hand. Lightning McQueen. She couldn't even remember seeing the second *Cars* movie. So many elements of your child's life were lost. Who recalled why one particular pair of pajamas hanging on a rack at The Children's Place had to be purchased, just *had* to be, to a tune of jumping up and down and long, drawn-out pleases? And yet those things made up a childhood. Abby shivered, right there in the stifling kitchen, and squeezed her son to her.

"You're warm," Cody murmured, an echo of Abby's tone whenever he ran a fever.

Abby released him. "Feel better now? Dream all gone?" Better not to ask who—or what—had visited Cody in his sleep. They had learned not to talk about the dreams.

Cody's damp head nodded against her.

She glanced down again. The letter with its declarative, impossible to ignore injunction. And the phone with its invisible, intangible connection to a whole other world.

Abby rose with her little boy in her arms. "I'll tuck you back in."

After laying him down on top of the limp, creased sheet—how she wished that sheet were crisp and cool, that Cody might need a light blanket as the night hours wore on—Abby drew the hollow door shut. Another thing she had learned: not to pull too hard on the weightless doors in this place. They splintered.

A few short weeks and a lifetime ago, she'd had rough-hewn beams and wood paneling in the house that they'd built.

Abby walked back to the kitchen, thinking about a frost-beaded glass of iced tea. There were a couple of bottles in the fridge, kept for nights such as this when she couldn't sleep anyway and the caffeine wouldn't be a problem. It would've been chilled white wine back in the days when Abby would never have dared to stay up all night. When she had plenty of wine and crystal to drink it from, but sleep was her only escape.

She had escaped for real now; she and Cody both had. Bill was a buttoned-up type who played by the rules. But rules wouldn't keep Bill from making her life hell, and Cody's, too. In fact, as this letter proved, they would enable him to.

Dear Ms. Harmon:

You are hereby ordered to submit to two (2) supervised visitation sessions weekly to be held at . . .

Abby put the letter down and twisted the cap on her iced tea, drinking deeply from the bottle. Frost-beaded glass indeed. Who was she kidding? There were sippy cups in the cabinet, some paper plates, and that was about it.

Abby felt a small poof of air upon her, even hotter than the enclosed heat of the condo. She went to turn off the fan, which was useless anyway. There was no air-conditioning in this place, even if she had been able to afford the utility bill.

She couldn't be sure, but she didn't think the air had come from the direction of the fan. Abby let the swallow of iced tea that had gone warm in her mouth trickle down her throat. She took a long look around the empty apartment.

In the room that was intended for living, but invited no such sort of activity, there was a pair of cheap club chairs, so small they almost fit Cody. They were upholstered in some nubbly white fabric whose nubs had long since worn off.

White. What a stupid choice in a place where people came, waited for their luck to change, and went. The cloth had grayed in spots where elbows and bottoms rubbed. The chairs' sole claim to fame was that they rotated; Cody loved to spin in them.

It was so hot. Maybe Abby would wash her hair just for an excuse to stand beneath a cold stream of water. She didn't like to be out of earshot of Cody, though. Not with his dreams.

Abby went to peer out into the starless night. A trident of heat lightning forked, and the window stared back at her like a lidless eye. She squinted, trying to make out something besides her own dark reflection. Then she turned around, and everything inside her folded. Abby felt her heart stop pumping, the blood cease its flow in her veins.

Bill sat in one of the club chairs in the living room.

His long body dwarfed the wheeling thing. He was a not-handsome man who spent regular time at the gym to compensate. Even through a shirt and suit pants, muscles could be detected. Bill rose from the ridiculous chair. His thinning hair was shaved close, and his face still bore the ravages of adolescent acne. He nodded at her, all business.

"I wanted to make sure that you received the letter."

Autonomic function had come to a halt as soon as she'd seen him. Abby couldn't catch her breath.

Bill took two long strides; they covered the cramped room. "And that you planned to obey it."

She felt the chill of wherever he'd come from.

"I always thought you were a team player, Abigail."

Abby stared down at the floor. The worn, scuffed floor, grouted with dirt. She'd been demoted; Bill used to address her, only her, by her nickname.

"But if you're not on my team any longer, you had better follow the laws of the land." Bill paused, taking a look around, and the sparse meanness of the place she'd come to live in was mirrored in his gaze. "You've probably already guessed that I entered this shithole through Cody's room."

He walked past Abby without so much as grazing her body. Bill's tactics had never been crude. Rather, he was like the very air around her: invisible, oppressive, impossible to escape.

After he left, Abby went back to the light, wobbly kitchen table and picked up her phone. Without a pause, she typed a curt reply in the text box.

OK. We'll come. What next?

CHAPTER FIVE

Liz woke the next morning under a dome of white comforter. She stretched luxuriantly, trying not to disturb the still-pristine sheets, or the duvet that lay over them light as a cloud. They must have both slept solidly, hardly tossing or moving. The promised romantic interlude hadn't come to pass before they'd collapsed. Liz remembered stirring once in the middle of the night, and shifting to reach for her husband as she hadn't done in more nights than she could remember. But the bed had been too delicious to do anything besides sink right back into sleep.

Next to her, Paul lay on his back, eyelids trembling as he slept on. A bad dream? It shouldn't be possible to have nightmares in such a sumptuous bed. Liz yawned widely, managing to extricate her hand from the material draping it so that she could reach for the clock. The temperature outside the bedclothes was pleasantly cool.

Eight o'clock. Even the kids had slept in.

Liz got up, trying not to wake Paul, whose body twitched as she rose. He'd done most of the heavy lifting yesterday with the bags, although getting Reid and Ally settled after the elevator ride had been no walk in the park for Liz.

She sleep-stumbled into the outer room of the suite. It was dark enough to be disorienting, but Liz didn't want to turn on a light. The more sleep the kids got, the better impression they'd make on their grandparents. She tiptoed over to the pullout sofa, squinting at the twin humps the children made under their blankets.

Liz stepped closer, rubbing grit from her eyes. Humps, but where were the kids' heads? She saw no hand or foot poking out from quarters that were snug for two kids sleeping together.

Liz threw back the blankets.

The sofa bed was empty.

She remembered the trio of false scares yesterday, her own uncharacteristic response to them, and took a deep breath. She flicked on a floor lamp as she strode past it en route to the bathroom. One of Reid and Ally's favorite games was filling up the bathtub to make potions. The prospect of a brand-new tub surely held an irresistible allure, and Liz should've known the kids would never sleep till eight o'clock.

She paused for a moment, the hotel carpet rough against the soles of her feet.

She didn't hear water running in the bathroom.

Because the tub was already full, she told herself.

Then where were the squeals, the screeches of laughter that the kids would never be able to contain, impervious to the needs of exhausted parents?

Liz pulled open the bathroom door.

It was dark in there, and empty. She smacked the light switch up, flooding the room with blue fluorescent glare, and yanked back the shower curtain. It felt plastic and stiff in her hand, and the tub was dry as silt.

Liz ran for the door, shouting to Paul.

She flipped the bar lock at the top of the door and peered out into the hall. Also empty, although a bustle of travelers could be heard below. The run of loudly patterned carpet wound along a wall that guarded a drop four floors down to the lobby. Heart pulsing in her throat, Liz reached the barrier in a single step and looked over. Her stomach did a slow, sick roll, but everything was quiet down there, save for a scatter of people wheeling suitcases.

A fall would've produced pandemonium, not this orderly buzz of the workaday starting. Liz looked in every direction, willing some nook or hidey-hole to reveal her kids.

Paul dashed out into the hall behind her, his chest bare, wearing only pajama bottoms.

"Liz?"

She turned to him, shaking her head back and forth, unable to summon a word.

"Take it easy," Paul commanded, instantly making sense of things. "We had two episodes of wolf crying yesterday."

Paul didn't even know about the third episode: Liz's irrational reaction to the bellhop.

The bellhop, she thought.

"Reid's probably got someone else in his sights, and Ally's trying to keep him from getting arrested," Paul added.

The likelihood of that scenario soothed Liz a little. Surely this would again turn out to be nothing, as fleeting a scare as the pickup truck. But as Paul walked Liz back into the hotel room, picking up the phone to call security before tossing clothes out of the suitcase for both of them, the order of his actions belied his seeming calm.

Hotel security arrived within what felt like seconds, although Liz didn't have a good handle on time by then. Either hours had passed—days—or else no time at all. She looked at the men who had come into their suite, and found herself utterly unable to command speech. A helpless spill of tears left her eyes, and she pressed her hand brutally against her face. It throbbed from the pressure she was applying, and she felt Paul remove it, heard him offering a description of the children's ages and looks.

Two men in uniform left the room, talking into radios.

The head of security was dressed in a suit. He informed them that all access points to the hotel—automatic entrance doors, side doors, kitchen, even the overhead riser in the supply area—now either had a guard stationed beside them or had been locked.

It came to Liz as soon as the head of security mentioned the kitchen. How hungry two kids who'd eaten mostly snacks and some candy all day would be. And suddenly her usual persona of practicality and acceptance reasserted itself. There was no reason to panic. Reid and Ally were used to going off by themselves, and they had found this hotel a wonderland last night. They had simply chosen to do some exploring on their own this morning.

"You serve breakfast, right?" she asked. "Downstairs?"

She didn't wait for the man to nod before opening the door. She already recalled being given four tickets for a complimentary meal, which the kids had used to play carnival before Liz finally got them to bed last night.

She covered the length of hotel hallway, then banged open the fire exit at one end and took the four flights of stairs at a run.

Paul arrived beside her as she was trying to parse the chaos of the dining room. Her eyes felt like laser beams programmed to identify her children, and yet the clumps and clusters of people eating at tables, or waiting in the waffle and juice and coffee lines overwhelmed her. The combination of smells brought on a nauseating pang. Liz shoved hair away from her face, then spun in Paul's direction.

"I'll look here," he told her. "You check the lobby."

Liz turned, biting back a sob. All thoughts of playful exploration had been snatched away. Reid and Ally were children—country kids at that—in a hotel in an unknown town. They had hardly ever left home before. Who could say how many people passed through here, and what they might make of two children alone? A parade of strangers marched through her mind, and she brought hooked fingers up to her face as if she could claw them away.

Stop it.

Liz must've hissed the words aloud; she heard their reverberation in her ears. But she couldn't halt the flood of fear. What if Reid and Ally weren't still in the hotel? They might be outside amongst the long asphalt stream of road or in a big box store or in somebody's car—

Her legs began to fold.

"And the gift shop!"

Paul's order saved her. How long had it taken her to think all that, conjure up nightmare scenarios no parent could survive? No time at

all. Paul hadn't even begun his search; he was still issuing instructions. She turned a tear-ravaged face toward her husband. Every moment that passed was a dangerous one; she knew that.

Paul began to approach the lines of breakfasting guests. He turned
one person around with a clap to the shoulder and a question, got a
head shake in response, and moved on to the next. Liz took off, following a blur of signs.

The gift shop, when Liz reached it, was tiny.

One of the security guards had clearly already had the same idea;
he was talking to the perky girl behind the counter. Liz dashed down
a row of toys, then over to a corner where goggles and bathing caps
were displayed.

The pool.

CHAPTER SIX

A memory had her in its grips as she began to run again, seeking pictures of a stick figure stroking through the water, indicating the location of the hotel pool. She felt as if she were moving in slow-motion, that sticky dream state from which you could never get free.

When Liz had been pregnant with Ally, and Reid was under two, her parents had invited them to their condo, which had the luxury of a pool. Reid had worn one of those floaty vests and the effect had been to make him top-heavy. Liz kept having to tilt the little boy back as she bobbed with him in the water. She hadn't taken her eyes off him for more than a second, only pausing to wipe some water from her face, when he went over. She'd blinked open her eyes to see Reid floating facedown on the shimmery blue surface of the water. Liz's father snatched him up by the back of his vest like a kitten. It'd been such a short time that Reid hadn't even gotten water up his nose. He had no idea how much danger he'd been in. But if her father hadn't gotten to him, Reid wouldn't have been able to raise his face, much less flip himself over. The precariousness, Reid's utterly helpless condition, had stayed with Liz ever since.

Maybe that was where Reid's fear of death stemmed from. Maybe some visceral part of him remembered the closely averted tragedy.

She swerved to see the security guard beside her.

He had intuited the same scenario. "Do you have both your room keys, ma'am? The pool and spa are accessible only with a keycard."

Ice water was filling her as if she had suddenly been thrown into a body of water herself. Her words came out stutter-stitched together. "I—I don't know."

Reid and Ally had loved swiping the keycard last night. If they'd gotten hold of one, they might be trying it in every door. She didn't think they'd dare to swim alone—the rule that an adult had to be present before you went into the water was impressed at a young age when you lived near ponds and rivers and quarries—but an accidental slip was always possible.

"Where is it?" Liz asked, words still slurry, hunting another sign.

They came to the end of the hall.

She didn't have her own keycard, she realized, skidding to a stop before the glass door. It didn't matter, though. She could see into the pool room and the gym beside it, and both were almost empty, devoid of people save for one lone guest, walking fast upon a treadmill. The water was a flat stretch, unbroken by any recent entry, without so much as a shadow beneath.

"Ma'am?" said the security guard from behind. "The police have been called."

The police assembling in the lobby made everything seem as real as a slice to the skin. Terror slicked her. No more could they pretend that Reid might be off harassing some guest. And Ally was a homebody, tending to the earth around her just as Liz did. Even if Reid had been up to his usual, Ally never would've stayed away this long.

With the arrival of the police, the hotel security staff stepped back, respectful, or maybe just cognizant of their place. Liz longed for the uniformed man who'd accompanied her between the gift shop and the pool. He'd seemed able to anticipate her thoughts, and his presence had served to ward off the assault of panic.

"I'm Detective Bissell." A plainclothes officer introduced himself to Liz and Paul. "We want you to know that we were on this the minute the hotel administrator made the report. We have police officers physically checking every room in the hotel. And two cars are searching the immediate area. An Amber Alert has gone out as well."

Liz's knees jogged. Paul slid a chair up behind her, and Liz sat down heavily. An Amber Alert didn't belong in their lives. They were for movies, or other people's stories, as cruel as that made Liz sound to herself. But she could stand to be cruel. She could stand to be anything, if only Reid and Ally were returned.

Her lips felt puffy, unable to make clear sounds. "Ally," she said, the word breaking into particles on her tongue. "Reid."

Paul patted her shoulder, a rhythmic, unfeeling touch, like the hand of a metronome.

"Ma'am," the detective said to her. "We need to speak to you and your husband."

"Yes, of course," Paul said.

Liz looked up blindly.

"The hotel staff has made this room available to us," the detective said, gesturing. "Would you like to step inside?"

Like, Liz heard. What does *like* have to do with any of this? How could they have traveled, even just to Paul's childhood home? They'd managed without a vacation for years.

She made her way into the darkened room behind Paul. The detective flipped on a bank of lights, and a table with chairs around it was cast into bold relief. At the back of the room another table held water bottles and a carafe. In different times, maybe even later today, conferences were held in this room.

The detective indicated two seats. "Can you tell me what brought you to this part of New York?"

Liz looked at Paul.

"I'm from Junction Bridge originally," her husband said. "We came to visit my parents. On the farm where I grew up."

The detective jotted something down. "Have you been in touch with your parents this morning?"

"Not yet," Paul said. "I—this just happened."

Liz pressed her lips and looked away. Paul's words cemented things somehow. Something had happened. They were different now than they had been before, and different, no matter how things turned out, from the way they would ever be again.

A sob crawled up her throat. She wanted to hold her children. It seemed impossible that they were gone. She still felt them, like a phantom limb.

She turned to her husband, whose gaze went bleak as he looked away. His words came from very far off, as if he were underwater, or she was.

"But I don't see why contacting my parents would matter," Paul was saying. "The farm is still almost an hour from here. It's not like the kids could've hitchhiked."

Liz sucked in a breath, and the detective looked at her.

Paul's shoulders dropped. "Sorry," he said. "I'm—a little tense."

"Perfectly understandable," the detective said without emotion. "I'm just trying to put a preliminary picture together."

Liz hardly heard the explanation, nor did she detect Paul's response. She was remembering something, and the realization occupied her whole mind, a storm blotting out the sky.

There was another person who had seen the children, one night and a lifetime before.

She rose, moving into the space between the two men.

CHAPTER SEVEN

At the front desk, everything was in a frenetic swirl. A busload of kids had just checked in, part of some field trip or school competition. They were older than Reid and Ally—teenagers really—but still, the sight of them made Liz feel light-headed, as if she had just stepped onto the moon. She came to a stop and leaned down, one hand on each knee.

It took a while for the person she was hunting to rise from the melee, but when he finally did, Liz launched herself at him.

Blood-colored uniform swam before her eyes. The fabric felt rough as she grabbed a fistful. The bellhop moved like a startled horse, up and away, rearing back. His refusal to meet her eyes only corroborated Liz's suspicions, and she held on even tighter.

A thought speared her—if the bellhop had been involved with whatever happened to Reid and Ally, he wouldn't just be hanging around the hotel lobby right now—but it was too late for logic to impact her actions. Liz was some kind of creature, small and stooped, or like a child herself, hunched over and shrieking out the sheer primitive scope of her need.

"Give me!" she demanded. "Give me back my children!"

The students began to form an uneven, ragged clump as their teacher corralled them, shielding them from Liz.

Paul arrived, and the detective, too. Liz heard them making

some sort of apology. To the kids, or their teacher? Surely not the bellhop?

The bellhop's gaze skirted past the detective before he looked imploringly at Paul.

One of the men—Liz couldn't tell which—unhooked her fingers from a swath of burgundy cloth. And while the schoolchildren looked scared, and their teacher alarmed, the bellhop's face was contorted by a frown.

Paul called his parents from his cell phone. Liz had to cover her ears when the initial announcement was made, but after that she listened to her husband's side of the conversation, aware that she was pinning hope on every word.

"I know," Paul said. And then, "No. No, not yet. Nothing yet."

A long pause to allow for what Liz imagined to be a horrified sort of taking in.

"Okay, Mom," Paul said. "Yes. All right."

He slid his thumb across the screen, ending the call.

Liz couldn't help but look up at him questioningly. She needed him to shake his head, needed to be told.

"They haven't heard anything."

And why would they? Paul himself had been in only infrequent contact with his folks. He and Liz were alike in this; distance from their families had been one of the less-lovely things that drew them together, which they bonded over, half regretful, half accepting, on early dates.

Her husband sat down beside her. At some point, they'd been moved to another identical room, their own cordoned off, Liz supposed. All the guest rooms contained the exact same appointments, and Liz's skin fired each time she chanced to catch a glimpse of something the kids had touched or played with or remarked upon last night. The tray of coffee Ally had pretended to serve. The safe Reid had fiddled with.

Liz felt her back curl, huddling over. Paul began to stroke her, but the touch felt mindless again. He couldn't be here for her now. Neither of them could be there for each other.

Suddenly Paul removed his hand from her back. "I have to do something."

Liz looked at him.

"I—we can't just leave this to the cops."

"What do you want to do?" she asked raggedly.

"We have a car," Paul said. "Let me get out there and look."

This disaster had jogged them from their normal roles. Always before, Liz had taken care of things on the ground, while allowing Paul to set the higher course of their lives. But in this instance he had seemed at least as paralyzed as she, possibly more so.

"Where do we start?" she said, glad to be asking, even as the enormity of the possibilities crashed down around her.

How would they whittle them down? Should they look in the stores and restaurants that populated the strip malls? Liz closed her eyes against an image of the roads that would take them there. She couldn't let herself think of the roads, how swiftly they carried people away.

Paul was moving toward the door. "I'll go," he said. "You stay here."

Because the children might come back. Liz allowed a lift of hope inside her before another possibility occurred. The police might learn something that she would have to be told.

Reid could've encountered anyone out there. Reid, and the way he walked up to people, viewing them as marks. Reid, and his fears of death. Last night, Ally had said she was worried about her brother.

Something filled Liz's throat, solid, choking.

Paul was met at the door by a uniformed officer. "Did you need something, sir?"

Liz stared down at her flayed hands. Sickles of dirt showed under her nails, flecks that even a good scrubbing couldn't reach. The beds were raw and bleeding now, too. She'd been digging at them without even realizing it.

"I'm going out for a few minutes," Paul said.

"Did you need something?" the policeman repeated. "I'd be happy to get—"

"Just some air," Paul said. He made a move to step into the hall.

"Sir?" the policeman said.

Liz glanced at him, then returned to regarding her ruined fingers.

The officer wasn't quite blocking Paul's way, but he wasn't moving out of it either.

"It'd be best if you and your wife left the search to us," he said. "Believe me, we know what we're doing. We're covering all the bases."

"Yeah?" Paul said, so roughly that Liz's gaze was yanked back up. "If you know what you're doing, then why the hell are my kids still missing?"

Liz got up and crossed to the door. Her husband was able to over-power almost anyone with words. Paul was part professor, part preacher, part psychic even, and people seemed to sense it. But worry and despair were tearing holes in him. He was facing the policeman, fists balled, as if he might throw him to the ground in an effort to get past. And what would that do, except distract everyone's efforts, take attention away from Reid and Ally?

"Where the hell are my kids?"

"Shhh," Liz said, arms around Paul from behind. "Come on. Let them do what they—"

Paul twisted in her grasp. He walked away from her, three long strides that took him to the window. He stood, visoring his eyes with his hand, staring out bleakly at the parking lot and all the vast acres of space that might contain their children.

The hours wore on and at the same time seemed to be hurtling away. Fear surged and Liz fought to suppress it. She knew what the passage of time meant. Paul, too, kept checking the clock as if willing it to stand still, a mask of desperation transforming his face each time the numbers advanced. Liz made herself focus on the presence of the policeman who had been assigned to babysit them, and Detective Bissell, who returned not infrequently to ask them more questions.

He wanted to know about their lives in Wedeskyull, about Paul's parents, as well as anyone Paul still knew downstate. When Bissell finished with background, he moved on to their trip yesterday, whom they might've encountered on the road, at the rest stop, anywhere en route.

"No one!" Paul cried. "It was just the four of us. Who could've seen anything?"

There was the man whose wallet Reid had pinched, but even Liz couldn't come up with a way to connect him to this. How would he have known where they were going, or gotten into their room? And how angry could he have been over having his intact wallet returned? She shut her eyes, other scenarios sparking in her mind. A small sound left her lips, and both men looked up. Liz found herself telling the detective about the pickup truck, as if one crazy driver might have something to do with the catastrophe they were facing now. She mentioned Reid's penchant for thievery, seeing Paul close his eyes.

Bissell listened, jotting notes.

Paul appeared to be migrating into a near-catatonic state, some kind of waking coma that severed the connections he was usually able to make, and his ability to piece things together. Liz felt a splinter of anger in her husband's direction. If ever she needed Paul to take charge, it was now, but the weight of crisis had robbed him of the ability. The monosyllabic responses he was offering the detective were nothing like his usual thoughtful elaborations.

No, he hadn't gone to his recent twenty-year high school reunion.

No, he wasn't in touch with anyone from home.

Yes, he was aware that his father's farm was in trouble.

Liz looked up at that. She hadn't known. And although her mind didn't seem to be operating as sluggishly as Paul's, she couldn't make out what difference it made.

What was the state of the children's possessions?

The word registered late, too awful to take in right away. Ally's favorite T-shirt, which Liz had to wash at the last minute back in Wedeskyull because it was dirty, and Ally refused to leave without it. Reid's new bathing suit, which was so big around the waist that it fell down to his ankles the first time he tried it on.

Had anything been taken or disturbed?

Detective Bissell was still firing away.

Liz couldn't bear to answer, let alone look. Paul offered to attend to the task. Liz watched as he headed off to the room they had checked into only last night.

The kids' clothing all seemed to be there, he reported back. The only thing that was missing was Izzy, a doll of Ally's.

Liz's gaze shot to Paul.

"Would your daughter have had the doll outside the room?" asked Bissell.

Paul coughed, and Liz realized that her husband was looking her way because he didn't know the answer. She blinked to clear her eyes. "She might've," she said dully. "Ally takes that doll everywhere still."

Bissell made another note.

At eleven o'clock, he finally began winding down. Bissell returned them to the care of the policeman who had stopped Paul from going out, and at noon that cop insisted they accompany him downstairs for some food.

"Trust me," he told them. "You won't be able to do what you need to if you're running on fumes."

The experience that must have lent the officer this perspective—not to mention the prospect of whatever he might mean for them to *do*—was something Liz couldn't consider. She followed the cop rotely out into the hall, reaching for Paul's hand when she sensed him beside her. They stayed that way, joined, until the policeman rang for the elevator.

It rose at a slow, stately pace, making its way upstairs. The door slid open and the sight brought a chorus of squealing children to life in Liz's head. How ashamed she was now to remember the faint annoyance she'd felt at Reid and Ally's pleasure last night, thinking only about quelling their giddiness so that she would be able to get them to focus on eating and then down to sleep.

Liz fell against the steel wall, not seeing the floors flash by, instead only the darting, sprite-like images of her children. She twisted around, unable to look a second longer, and slammed into a body she hardly recognized as Paul's.

Her husband allowed Liz to collapse in his arms, hissing in her ear, "It's all right! You hear me? The kids are going to be fine!"

The cop braced his arms across his chest, shuffling his boots in silence.

Liz felt her weeping taper off at her husband's words, barked as if he were giving orders. She allowed herself to bury the place that understood that Paul couldn't possibly know.

CHAPTER EIGHT

Morning became afternoon without the kids being found, which meant a whole other level of search. Perhaps even one involving the FBI, if the police turned up any suggestion that Reid and Ally might've been taken across state lines. Liz would have to be fully functioning if new officials were brought in, and if they weren't, she had to work alongside the men already helping. Had to conceive of possible reasons for this. Because the alternative—that it was random and her children had stepped into the path of a madman—made Liz's hold on sanity seem to flicker and go out.

As always, Paul talked her down, throwing out life rafts in a terrible sea. Two things counted against the possibility of an encounter with a stranger, he reminded her. First, such criminals were far more likely to go for a child alone than one in a pair. Bissell had said so. And second, Reid and Ally were farm kids.

Liz stared up at her husband, mesmerized by the conviction he was trying to impart.

Theirs wasn't the kind of spread where heavy machinery necessitated a deep knowledge of risks, or where an unremitting stream of death exposed Reid and Ally to its reality, but it was true that both kids had had to attain a degree of self-reliance. Neither would've been naïve enough to go with someone who approached, let alone the two of them together. They'd been warned about strangers, even if there weren't that many opportunities for chance meetings in Wedeskyull.

Liz left Paul to walk into the outer room of the suite, where Bissell and the other cop were talking in low, ruminative voices.

"Gentlemen," Liz said. Her mouth was trembling. "Please don't bullshit me." She took a breath. "I'm not some frail flower."

But suddenly that's exactly what she was. A woman who'd turned to other people all her life for sustenance and direction. A fake farmer, whose crops if they failed didn't spell starvation or death, but a lack of restaurant orders filled, a few fewer pretty jars at the weekend markets.

The cops looked up, appraising her.

"I come from wild country, and we're in another sort of country here. I have some idea what you're facing. What are you doing now? What's the next step?"

Paul had come up behind her, placing a solid, restraining hand on her shoulder. For a moment she welcomed its feel.

The policemen exchanged glances before Bissell spoke.

"I think our next move will be to speak with each of you separately. Sometimes one person remembers something alone that they wouldn't with the other present."

Liz felt her shoulders drop, aware that the added weight of Paul's hand was gone. He had stepped away from her toward the door.

Talk to them alone? That was all they had?

She agreed to stay in the hotel room with the babysitting cop, while Paul went with Bissell. She summoned strength, and began, again, to recount the events of the last twenty-four hours, and then the days that had come before.

"I know this might be hard, ma'am," the cop said, once Liz's answers had begun to trail off. "But do you think you can take me through the time when you discovered the children were missing once more? Just briefly."

Liz stared down at her lap.

The cop got up and entered the adjoining bathroom. Liz watched him remove the fluted paper top from a glass. She heard the tap running, then the cop returned with a drink of water.

Liz drained it. "I woke up, and it was late," she began. "Eight o'clock."

The cop nodded.

"At first I thought I saw the children underneath the blankets." She indicated the couch they were sitting on, and although this one wasn't dismantled, she saw a sofa bed, its thin mattress and ill-fitting tangle of sheets. "But when I pulled them back—the blankets—nobody was there."

The cop nodded again.

"So then I checked the bathroom because the kids love water games—" Splinters seemed to sit on her tongue and she worked to speak around them.

The cop sat silently, legs spread, palms resting on his thighs.

"But they weren't in the bathroom either."

The cop tracked her gaze across the new suite.

"So I opened up the door, the one to the room, and . . ." Liz stopped.

The cop gestured her wordlessly on.

" . . . I looked out by that low wall in the hall. I was afraid that they had fallen."

But she was remembering now, recalling exactly what she had done, and she suddenly couldn't speak. Words shriveled in her throat. She looked down into her glass, which was empty.

The door to the suite they were occupying swung open, and Bissell stood there. His gaze slid past Liz's; he wouldn't look at her.

Liz spoke to the other cop; she spoke to no one at all. Her voice sounded stunned and airless in her ears. "I flipped the lock at the top of the door."

The cop frowned.

Bissell summoned him forward, still not looking in Liz's direction.

Liz understood the reason for his change in demeanor, how her status had altered abruptly from victim to something much more murky.

When she had opened the door to look out in the hall for the kids, the bar lock at the top had been secured.

Which meant that whoever had taken the children had to have reentered the room.

Maybe she'd begun to figure it out even earlier, when she felt pinpricks of anger pierce her ability to cleave to her husband. Or upon reflecting during the drive out on the revised roles in their marriage. And if she was right about this, then she was right about what must have happened next, the reason Bissell had gone so chilly and distant.

Liz stood and faced the detective, forcing him to meet her stare.

"Paul is gone, too," she said.

THE BOY

Kurt Pierson sat in his car with his fists wrapped around the steering wheel as if he were trying to compress the plastic into a narrower ring. Blue, snaky veins stood out on the tops of his hands. It was his first day alone with his son, and the boy was about to wreck it. Kurt could sense a point not too far off, like the thin gray line of a horizon. He could see himself reaching it, and after that no attempt to salvage this day would work.

"I said be quiet," Kurt said from the front of the car.

"Why?" the boy asked. "How come?"

Kurt clenched the wheel. He didn't understand how an instruction to be quiet could generate not silence, but instead an instantaneous response. He wouldn't have believed that he could have a stupid child—Kurt himself was the son of two doctors—but after less than an hour spent taking care of the boy, he was beginning to wonder.

He had been a lot smarter at eleven than Tom.

Kurt had always hated the boy's name—the boy's mother had chosen it—and he avoided addressing his son directly as much as possible. But if the boy was to be in Kurt's care now, then Kurt would need to start using a proper designation.

"Why do we have to go on a drive?" the boy said.

Tom, Kurt bade himself.

"Where are we going? Why isn't Mom bringing me to school? Where's Mom?"

The questions swarmed around Kurt's head like insects. The boy had an entitled tone, almost as if he were jeering, which made Kurt want to show him how lucky he was. How little the boy or any child was in fact entitled to, and how much they had by sheer accident of birth.

Kurt had made do with far less.

He let go of the wheel, but the sight of his hands rolling into fists gave him pause. He didn't want to do this now, and he took a quick, furtive look around. No one was there, observing a man alone with a boy in a car. That part was working out at least. Not that a father being out with his son in the morning should've attracted any attention, but Kurt believed in keeping a low profile. Until the time came to have a high one.

He glanced at the clock on the dashboard. Fifty-five minutes before they were scheduled to meet in person for the first time. Presuming he could get the boy to go.

"Guess what?" he said, forcing an upbeat note.

A huff of breath. "What?"

Still, it was a much more appropriate mode for a response. Father poses a question, son inquires in return. Kurt felt his mood brightening along with his tone. If he could just get rid of the skeptical note in the boy's voice, he might have the son he'd always hoped for. A smart one, giving pleasure to his parents as soon as his intellect started to become apparent in childhood. The truth was, Kurt's parents hadn't exactly seemed to take joy in Kurt's accomplishments, but that was because both were psychiatrists, trained to be judicious with their emotions, to observe with distance. It hadn't bothered Kurt; he knew that they felt all the same things regular parents did. They just exhibited what they felt—*exhibited*, a psychiatric term—in different ways.

"Well, Tom," Kurt said, the name stiff as a piece of glass on his tongue, "we get to go on a trip today."

Now, when he didn't want it, there was silence from the back of the car.

"Did you hear me?"

"A trip," Tom repeated, as if the term had gone out of fashion.

"That's right. Isn't that great?"

Silence again. Kurt unclasped one hand from the steering wheel and turned around, laying his arm along the back of the seat.

Tom straightened from his slouch. His seat belt cinched his neck.

"It's something," he said. "What about Mom?"

It occurred to Kurt to lie. It would've been easier that way. Just say, *Mom will meet us there,* and no more of the mosquitoey drone from the backseat that made Kurt want to bang the boy's head into the windshield.

But Kurt was smarter than that. He'd gotten into a top liberal arts college, and even if his time there hadn't ended so well, the admission had been a point of pride for Kurt's parents. He could remember how they told their fellow physicians, unsmiling, but noting the name of the school and its proclivity for producing people of importance: lawyers, politicians, doctors like themselves. Kurt hadn't wound up in any of those professions, waylaid by the abrupt end to his school career, but that only meant that his intelligence had never gotten channeled, was still unspent. He could apply it to the challenge of child-rearing, which was turning out to be quite a challenge indeed.

But perhaps he had an aptitude for it, for Kurt intuited, as surely as if he'd been given predictive charts, that if he lied to the boy now, it would only provoke a crisis on the other end.

He kept his gaze fixed on the backseat. "Mom will be staying here."

Tom's face popped like a balloon.

Kurt couldn't deny the small lick of pleasure that gave him. "That's right," he said, as remote and detached as his own parents had been. Maybe they too had felt charges of emotion inside. Maybe they had just kept them hidden.

Kurt's mother had been addicted to true crime novels throughout his childhood. They were the one thing he could recall provoking any sort of light or heat from her. He could still see his mother, sitting in her chair by the living room window, lips slightly parted and breath coming fast as she turned each page. After his mother had gone up to bed, Kurt would look at these books, reading with a blend of fascination and disgust. There was a man called the Shoemaker who had gone on killing sprees, taking along his own son to help massacre the women.

Kurt refocused on the boy in back. His eyes were very wide, though dry.

"Your mother has been in charge for a long time," Kurt said, still in that tone of cool remove, whose effectiveness he now understood. The boy was docile, no longer making demands, nor even asking any questions. Tom. The name was growing on Kurt.

He reached out and chucked his son under the chin, choosing to ignore it when Tom flinched. "Now it's my turn."

CHAPTER NINE

He had made his escape after asking Bissell to wait while he used the bathroom, the cop who had babysat Liz all day explained, walking the two of them down to the lobby. Liz was having trouble catching her breath. She felt as if she had been plunged into a cold, depthless sea. She kept stopping, putting a hand on her chest, or the inside of the elevator, even just the wall to steady herself. Then she would bend over, trying to see if that brought air down into her lungs.

"Ma'am?"

She was a ma'am now.

"Do you need me to call someone?"

Who was there to call? Her husband? High, hysterical laughter frothed, which Liz squelched. If she allowed herself to feel all that she was feeling now, she would be no use to anyone, certainly not her missing children.

How could Paul have done this to her? Taken the children she had loved, and cared for, and nurtured every day, starting even before they were born. Not to mention the fact that the terror had nearly killed her. Was still killing her, although now she could at least tell herself that as horrible as things were, they didn't amount to the one case she had been trying to run from all day, ever since the moment she had woken to find Reid and Ally gone.

Paul had tried to prevent her from envisioning such a terrifyingly lethal scenario. But rather than easing any small part of her fury, this recollection only heightened it. The fact that he had offered assurance as if it were a hypothetical, when all along he knew he was speaking the truth, struck her as hideously cruel.

Bissell was waiting downstairs. Locating Paul shouldn't take long, he said to the other cop. There was an APB out for their car. His voice seemed to come from many yards away; Liz could barely make out what he said. But she focused on the part about finding Paul. Because once they did that, Liz wasn't sure if she'd fall upon her husband in fury or relief.

Another of the local police force, a policewoman with a take-charge frown, entered through the sliding doors. She let in a spongy rush of heat, and also something else. The realization that this wasn't going to be so easy.

Rage crested inside Liz again.

"That green Altima you wanted a BOLO on," the female cop announced.

Bissell emerged from his corner to gesture the policewoman on.

"It's still in the lot."

Liz stood with the babysitting cop in the conference room where she and Paul had first been questioned. Water bottles, coffee carafe, chairs, all still waiting to be used by phantom attendees. Also missing was Bissell, who didn't seem to be involved with their case anymore.

There was no case.

Liz could hardly believe it. "My husband kidnapping my children isn't a case?" she demanded. "Isn't a *crime*?"

The babysitting cop pulled a chair into place and took a seat, indicating that Liz should do the same. "This isn't a kidnapping," he told her. "Some states might handle it differently, but in New York we don't get involved in domestic disputes."

Liz heard the hiss of the words as she took in their meaning. There was no one to help.

"There's nothing more we can do." The cop had the grace to look away. "It's not even a custody situation, in which case there's a protocol in place. You and your husband are still married, not even separated."

A taut, tense silence drew out.

The cop turned back toward her. "Was there anything?"

Liz frowned.

"Anything to make you think . . ." He paused. "Even something small that may've passed unnoticed at the time. But now, in hindsight, might occur to you." He looked more closely at her. "Something that could've made your husband want to take away your children."

The words hit her like single, small blows.

The cop seemed to subside. "Listen, I contacted a buddy of mine on the Junction Bridge force."

She recognized it as the name of the town they'd been headed to.

"As a favor to me, he's gonna take a drive up. Look around. Maybe have a talk with Mr. and Mrs. Daniels."

Her in-laws. It took Liz a beat to realize what was called for.

"Thank you," she said. "I appreciate that."

The cop withdrew a card from his wallet. "I'll call you if anything comes up. And you feel free to check in, too."

"Thank you," Liz said again. "I will."

She rose. Her legs felt rigid, and she had to flex her fingers. Too many days not spent crouching over the soil had a way of making her stiff. She'd always preferred squatting to sitting.

Which was lucky because she had the feeling that she wouldn't be sitting still anytime soon. Liz waited until the cop left before plunging into the steamy cauldron outside, sky an electric blue sheet overhead. She got into their car and drove off.

CHAPTER TEN

Imagining the level of cold, pure calculation that had driven Paul all morning—complacent in the knowledge of their children's safety while terror beat circles around Liz—made her insides flare with fury.

Who was this man she'd married? Liz couldn't comprehend him, a person who'd been like a part of her, who had in fact become a physical part of her. It was like looking into a mirror and seeing a stranger stare back. Or a monster.

The food the cop had coaxed her to eat a thousand hours ago threatened to come back up. She lowered the car window and spat out bitter-tasting fluid. The afternoon air wrapped itself around her face like a terrycloth turban. She couldn't hear anything for the buzzing hive in her head, and she wrestled the car over to the side of the road. An accident now would slow her down. And if something happened to her, Reid and Ally would be left forever in Paul's care.

His care.

What had he whispered in her ear?

The kids are going to be fine.

Liz's nails dug into the steering wheel with such force that they made dimples in the plastic. She forced herself to unhook her fingers, and they ached in the relaxing.

She recalled the paranoia she had felt as they had left to come here;

that pickup truck driver, and even her sparking fear when Reid wandered off. It was almost as if she'd known disaster was coming, but just hadn't had any idea where to look for it.

Because who would think to look right next to them?

Paul had been trying to get away the whole morning, Liz realized. He had kept checking the clock. Paul wanted to go out—search while she waited back at the hotel in an increasing paralysis of unknowing—so he could do whatever it was he was up to right now.

How had he arranged it? Had his parents come and gotten the children sometime in the night, harboring them till one of them could come back and pick up Paul? It was the most likely order of events Liz could think of.

Other interpretations of her husband's behavior were coming to her, too.

The way he had lain beside her when Liz woke up in the morning.

She had thought he must be having a bad dream from the way his body twitched and tremored. But now it seemed that he'd been trying to feign sleep, nervous, wondering how this would play out, just waiting for her to stir to consciousness.

Waking her would've been suspicious; she would've wondered why he had done that when they were finally on vacation and the biorhythms of outdoor life didn't force an early rise. He would've had to lie, make something up about wanting to get on the road, and Paul wasn't a good liar.

She hadn't thought he was anyway.

Rage rocked her again.

Another question had taken her up in its hands and was shaking her back and forth.

Not how Paul had done it.

But why?

Before she could pull onto the road again, Liz pawed her cell phone out of her bag.

This wouldn't come to anything, she knew that, but she was unprepared for just how dead an end she would reach.

Liz dialed Paul's number, waiting for his message. She heard a robotic voice instead, nothing like the kind, patient voicemail lady's. It intoned eight words, the last so unfamiliar that Liz had to call again to be sure she had heard correctly.

You have reached a number that is unallocated.

It wasn't as if she'd expected Paul to pick up. After all this, he wasn't going to just take her call. *Can't talk now, honey, I've kidnapped the kids.* But shutting down all service on this number? It wasn't only Liz—nobody would be able to reach her husband.

There were a hundred necessary things a cell phone was used for each day.

Paul must know that he wasn't going to have to worry about any of them.

Dear God, what was he planning to do?

CHAPTER ELEVEN

Liz programmed the town of Junction Bridge into her GPS. Most of the miles were covered by flat, level highway, but she was grateful for the visual of the twisting purple length once she reached the low-lying roads at the edge of the state. They had left the pretty parts of New York behind, not only the mountains, but also the orchards and vineyards and lakes. This was featureless country, consisting of farms that were the cogs and working mechanisms of the country, the inner backbone without which America couldn't function, but that nobody wanted to examine too closely.

Liz had always been as connected to the land as she was to her own skin, and perhaps because the GPS told her she was getting close to her children and the end of this nightmare, she was able to register a pang of pity as she drove. A few hundred miles to the southeast, and Paul would've grown up cradled by lakes; his father would've farmed on land that was threaded by vines. A few hundred miles in the other direction, and he would've wound up in the mountains where they now lived, endless spires of trees piercing the sky.

Instead he'd been raised in this far corner where a bleakness had settled in, borne of being at the flat, unmarked end of the state. These farms didn't produce the fruits and frippery that Liz's gardens did. They supplied the endless rivers of grain that were churned into the products Americans subsisted upon, or went into the bellies of the animals they ate. Not a pretty business, but an essential one. Liz heard Paul's voice in her head.

A crueler kind.

What cruelty lived here? How had Paul become part of it?

A faded sign welcomed travelers to Junction Bridge, a good place to live, work, and play. Liz couldn't imagine what kinds of play took place here, and there didn't seem to be a whole lot of living either. She passed a Laundromat, a boarded-up diner, and a hair salon that operated out of someone's run-down house, before coming to a gas and repair shop on a lone stretch of road. Liz pulled into the dirt lot and got out of her car. Humidity instantly coated her skin and thickened her throat. Birds wheeled in slow circles, their speed belying the intentness of their flight as they searched for prey amongst the cornstalks.

Liz filled up the car at the pump, then turned to see a man coming out of the garage, wiping his hands on a grease-streaked rag.

"Help you with anything else today?" he asked.

Liz shielded her eyes from the sun. Sweat prickled under her arms, and a hot wind made the sheaves of corn rustle. "I was wondering if you could tell me how to find the Daniels place."

For a moment, it didn't seem as if the man was going to answer. Perspiration had darkened the bandanna on his head, which he pulled off and wrung out before nodding. "Got a pen?" He was looking into her car now, at the GPS that continued to display its silly purple line. "That thing isn't going to be much help out there."

Liz was grateful for the scrawled list of directions as she drove into a tangle of roads even more undistinguished than the ones that had brought her here. She was getting close to her children now; she had to be. It felt as if they'd been parted for nine years instead of nine hours. Sweat ran down her back, tickling, itchy, and she lowered the temperature in the car.

Look for three red flower buckets.

Liz spotted them, filled with a sun-scorched grouping of blossoms, some farmwoman's attempt to add a carefree note to her husband's hardworking spread. Rudbeckia, Liz thought for the second time in as many days. How did a farmwoman not know that black-eyed Susans could withstand almost anything so long as they had a regular sprinkling of water?

Then take Yarrows Road on your right.

Liz turned.

It'll be the fourth dirt road you come to after that.

The car was engulfed in a plume of dust. Liz nearly spun out as the road jogged, but she fought to correct, unwilling to lose even scant seconds making it back from the flattened grasses at the shoulder. Despite the sealed cabin of the car, Liz could detect a bestial odor outside. She spotted spindly-legged cows in a picked-over field, their coats patchy and thin.

The farmhouse appeared on a rise, and Liz braked. She parked the car on a slope in front of the house and got out amidst a wake of dust, which as it settled gave rise to a man's form. Not Paul, but an older, hardened version of him.

Paul exuded competence and reliability; he was someone you wanted to trust, believe in. At least he had been, Liz thought, with a sharp crimp in her throat. This man also had a mane of forcefulness about him, but you didn't so much want to obey him as feel compelled to. Her father-in-law seemed to dominate without moving a muscle.

He wore jeans and a checked shirt whose color had long since been lost. His arms were folded across his chest.

The fact that he was out here, waiting, proved her hunch—her one and only lead—and Liz went almost faint with relief. The air that entered her lungs felt like it came out of a steam room, and still it was the most refreshing elixir she'd ever sampled.

"Elizabeth," her father-in-law said. "They're not here."

"No," Liz said. "I mean, yes. Yes, they are."

Silence.

"They have to be."

Still nothing, and Liz was filled with a howling fury.

"They have to be!"

She rushed her father-in-law, who held her back with the palm of one hand.

"I said they're not here," he repeated.

"But you knew I'd come!" Liz cried. "You're not surprised to see me! So you must know what Paul has done!"

The logic of it seemed impeccable, even to her fevered mind.

Her father-in-law stared down into her eyes with his own flinty ones. "You'll do best now to leave," he said.

He took three long strides away from her, mounting the steps of his porch.

"Matthew!" She'd spoken her father-in-law's name on only a hand-ful of occasions. At their wedding. The few times he'd seen the kids.

The kids.

Rage that had plumed inside her began receding, leaving a solid, leaden weight as heavy as the saturated air. Sweat and tears bathed her eyes, stinging like needles. She'd been so sure. Certainty had been the only thing enabling her to keep going these last couple of hours; keeping her tethered to the earth at all. Why would Paul have sug-gested this trip if not to bring Reid and Ally to his childhood home, at least use his parents as allies in his desertion? Theories had begun to take shape in her mind during the drive: loosely formed, unarticu-lated. Paul had decided that living away from his roots amounted to depriving the children of something, but didn't believe Liz would allow them to leave Wedeskyull. Or else her husband's interest in survivalism had gone further than Liz ever suspected, and the cul-ture out here was a better fit, as was the broader breadth of the land.

But if Paul wasn't on the farm? Then where in this whole world could he be?

Breath escaped her, a slow, unstoppable leak. Liz sagged onto the dirt, pebbles beneath her knees, her hands splayed out on the gritty ground. Her body grew moist, lathered all over from the heat. With her children gone, all law had ceased to apply. The planetary spin could reverse; the earth might come loose from its moorings and simply float away. Reid and Ally were out there somewhere, and it was an upheaval so complete that Liz couldn't imagine ever standing upright again.

Matthew reached for the handle of the screen door. It gave off a dull metal glare under the punishing sun, and Liz squinted at it, bleary-eyed and lost.

What next? She couldn't formulate so much as a step.

The door opened, and a woman stepped onto the sun-faded slats of the porch. It was hard to make her out at first, so well did she blend in with the rest of the landscape. Her hair and skin were dusted and worn; she looked like a small, furred creature.

"Matthew?" Her voice, when it emerged, was timorous.

Liz was still on her hands and knees on the ground. Her father-in-law kept her in his sights without making a move to help her.

"Please," Liz's mother-in-law said. "Let her come in."

Liz's eyes were arid, unblinking as she followed Matthew's broad back into the sun-blasted farmhouse. Almost five o'clock, and the yellow orb hardly seemed to be sinking. At least the humidity was starting to lift, taking with it a low, level bank of clouds. Inside, the house felt close, fans stirring the air listlessly. The house was as spotless as picked-clean bones. Not an object out of place, nor a single dust mote floating in the shafts of sun. The floorboards were bleached bare, the walls washed in light.

Liz took a seat on a faded sofa. The sheers on the window offered little screen from the scalding light. After a few minutes the aroma of coffee arose, and Liz's mother-in-law returned, head lowered, holding two cups. She offered the first to Matthew, who accepted it without a word, regarding Liz as he drank.

"I didn't know how you took it," her mother-in-law said, a note of apology in her tone as she held out a cup to Liz.

Liz set it aside, untouched. "Where are they?"

Her mother-in-law looked at her.

Matthew placed a hand on his wife's arm. "Mary."

Liz's gaze shot from one to the other. "What aren't you telling me?" She was aware of how suspicious she sounded, almost paranoid. On the other hand, her in-laws had to be keeping something from her. There was a reason Paul had chosen to come to Junction Bridge.

Had he been back to this place at all? Was the hotel the closest he'd actually come?

Neither of her in-laws spoke.

There was a low, loose terror inside Liz, like an animal that had escaped. If she couldn't lasso it, get it under control, she would be clawed to pieces. She needed direction, someone to tell her what to do. But she had no idea who that would be.

She cursed Paul for putting her into this state. He'd always been the man with the answers, but the flip side of that meant that he had the power to cast her into total darkness.

The brilliant light in here hurt her eyes, and she blinked. Liz had made the extent of her helplessness clear without mustering any sympathy from Matthew. If being at the farm was to yield anything, it would have to be because Liz accomplished it herself.

Paul had never been close to his parents. He'd moved away after high school, wound up attending the same college where he now taught, and as far as Liz had known, never looked back.

Until planning this vacation.

Her gaze roved around, hunted, hungry, and her nose tickled at the blend of scents. Coffee, the slightly stale odors of an old house, and something fresher, like wood. Liz sneezed, blocking her face, and when she opened her eyes, the front door came into sight. It had been left open, the screen door the only barricade against the heat.

Liz's words pierced the hush of the room. "What's that?"

CHAPTER TWELVE

Liz got up, trance-like, to drift across the floor. Whatever she'd seen, or thought she had seen, wasn't obvious. It wavered in and out of clarity as she walked. But when Liz arrived at the entrance to the farmhouse and slid her hand down the doorjamb, she knew that she'd been right.

There was a dark scuff mark, a bruise on the otherwise pristine paint. And underneath it was a gouge in the surface, explaining the smell of newly exposed wood. There had been a disturbance in this aged home, every other inch of it smoothed and worn over, and a recent one at that.

"What happened?" Liz asked.

Matthew remained in the spot he had occupied when they first entered the house. One look at the hewn carving of his face told Liz that her question wouldn't be answered.

Paul had been here. She knew it. And from Matthew's fierce expression, which looked capable of shattering the window he was staring at, and Mary's meek, huddled demeanor, it seemed possible that he still was.

Liz started for the stairs, running as if she might be chased.

In the second-floor hallway there were two doors, one open, one shut. Sunlight shot through windows on either end of the hall. This close to the roof, the house felt like a sauna.

The open door revealed Matthew and Mary's room. A queen-sized bed was adorned by a single flocked pillow, and the blades of a window fan cycled.

Liz placed her hand on the closed door, picturing Reid and Ally huddled together, and quashing the knowledge that her children would never be able to keep quiet for this long.

The second bedroom was still and bare. A lifeless drape at the window couldn't entirely keep out the light, and starry bursts of dust danced in its stream, as if this room was infrequently aired. Liz shielded her eyes, squinting.

"Satisfied?" Matthew said from behind.

Liz suppressed a start at the sound of his voice, turning around unsteadily.

Mary stood silently in the shadow made by her husband's body.

Liz peered back into the room. There was a twin bed, made up flat with a blue sheet. The dresser was devoid of anything besides a few books. A stand of shelves mocked her with its emptiness.

Downstairs an old-fashioned phone let out a squawk.

Liz elbowed in front of Mary, then Matthew, beating them both down the stairs to a small table in the sitting room. She snatched up the receiver, its cord hitting her neck as she answered.

"Hello? Hello? Paul?"

There was an audible pause on the line, a sound like rushing. Then someone spoke.

"This is Frank Mercy. I live down the road. I'm looking for Matthew."

Liz's in-laws stood before her in the parlor.

"That'll be my neighbor," Matthew said. "Wanting to talk to me about fencing."

Liz wasn't sure which posed more of a dead end: Matthew's stony implacability or his wife's timid refusal to talk. She was about to hand over the phone when something occurred to her, and she quietly pressed the button to end the call.

Matthew frowned. "You had no right to do—"

Liz's voice trembled. "My children are missing. I have a right to do anything."

Mary winced, but Matthew's eyebrows knit, not an ounce of sympathy in the stormy expression.

"Paul called here today," Liz said. "At least he said he did, when we were with the cops. Was he lying? Or did you receive a phone call from him?"

Maybe, just possibly, Paul had dialed his mother from a new phone. His old one was obsolete not because he wouldn't have any use for a cell phone—*everybody* needed a cell phone—but because he wanted to hide from Liz. She looked down at the receiver in her hand, trying to make sense of the archaic technology, how you would access a call list.

"We don't have any of that," Mary said, all but whispering. "Caller ID. Missed calls."

Liz pounced on the moment of communication. "Not missed. Paul spoke to you."

Matthew took the phone out of Liz's hand. His fingers were as hot as soldering irons, and Liz recoiled from their touch. A rivulet of sweat ran down each of her father-in-law's temples.

"I didn't hear from Paul. He didn't come here for a visit or to mess up my front door," Matthew added, eyes eagle-bright. How could Liz have imagined her father-in-law failing to notice any detail she herself was able to spot? "Now," he concluded, "I'll thank you to leave."

Liz dropped her head, beaten. Racing down the stairs, she had seen herself besting the likes of Matthew Daniels, rendered somehow strong, smarter than she had been, as any female became when her children were threatened. But Liz was in no shape to wage a fight. She was a mother without a clue how to find her children.

A mother who had lost them in the first place.

Heated tears traced their course, and Liz felt disgust like a boil upon her.

Surprisingly, it was Mary who spoke.

"It's too close to nightfall to let her drive out," she said in a gentle tone. "Elizabeth will have to spend the night."

"Fine." Matthew spoke in a tone hard enough to split wood. "But if you sleep under my roof, if you eat under my roof, if you so much as make water under my roof, then you are obliged to follow one rule. And that is that you do not mention the son who will never do any of those things here again for as long as I live!"

The floorboards reverberated beneath the thud of his boots as Matthew stalked off.

CHAPTER THIRTEEN

It was as automatic as a homing pigeon's flight. Liz went upstairs to the room that must've been Paul's and plugged her cell phone in to charge. No way was she going to be without the use of it right now. The lit-up screen drew Liz's finger, and she hit the button to speed-dial Jill without even having to look.

When her best friend answered, Liz couldn't speak. She sank down onto the floor, phone pressed to her ear. Perspiration pooled between her skin and the plastic backing.

It took Jill only a second to enter the silence. "What's going on? Where are you?"

Still nothing from Liz. Her lips felt thick and numb, unworkable.

"It's something bad?" Jill said, an interpreter for the unseen.

Always, since they had met as kindergarteners at Wedeskyull Consolidated, Liz and Jill had been able to communicate wordlessly. On that first day of school, it had been a shared fear of the bus, their entangled hands enabling them to climb the towering steps. After that, a flashed look, raised brow, or traded snort signaled anything from needed distraction when a teacher posed too challenging a question to a *Get me out of here* when last year's discarded boyfriend came around again. But this went beyond words in a whole other way.

As soon as Liz said what she had to say to Jill, it was going to become real.

Her best friend's voice was a soothing hum in the overheated room. "I'm not going to say something asinine like *It's all right.* I'm here, if you can talk. Whenever you want to talk."

"Oh, Jill." Liz began to sob.

"Shhh, shhh," Jill murmured.

"Oh no. Oh, Jill. Oh no!"

"Liz!" Jill was crying, too. "Liz, shit, you're really scaring me. It's okay. It's okay. Where are you? Are you all right?"

Liz couldn't reply.

"Dammit. I said the asinine thing. Liz!" Her voice hit a high note. "Elizabeth Burke Daniels, you tell me what's wrong right now!"

"It's Paul," Liz sobbed. "Paul. He's taken the kids."

Silence pulsed over the connection in the wake of Liz's statement.

"What the what?" Jill said at last. "I don't even know what that means."

Maybe it was hearing her friend talk in something approaching her usual tone. It jogged Liz back into a semblance of normalcy herself.

"Neither do I," she muttered.

"That is not what I was—expecting. I don't know what I was expecting. I'm sorry, but what the hell are you talking about?"

Liz relayed her dire discovery, each unfolding turn that led to Paul's act, in as clear a stream of words as she could muster. The rug felt like burrs against her thighs, and she separated herself stickily from its weave. The act of telling had amounted to exertion. Liz was perspiring and out of breath, panting a bit as the story finally wound down.

Jill sounded blank. "But—how do you know what that means? How do you know Paul's not—I don't know, pissed at you, he's seemed kind of pissy lately—and they just came back here?"

Something let loose inside Liz. There was the matter of the disconnected cell phone, but she ignored that for now. She wiped dampness off her face and arms and neck, words tumbling out. "I—well—maybe I don't. Oh my God. Jill, can you—"

"You don't have to say it." There were fluttery sounds in the background, Jill rising, looking around. "Andy!" she called out, causing a brief ping of recrimination in Liz.

Andy shouldn't be disturbed at this hour, not in his current state, and not for what was surely going to turn out to be a wild goose chase.

But what if it wasn't?

"It's fine, Andy will be fine," Jill shouted, reading her, somewhere away from the phone. "I'll call you as soon as I get there," she added, and ended the call.

For a few minutes, Liz switched between staring down at the phone's blank face, willing it to light up, and forcing herself to walk back and forth across the room, saying things inside her head about watched pots. Finally she acknowledged two things. First, that it would take Jill at least twenty minutes to get to Liz's house, even if she tore down the road that left town and snaked out to the valley, and second that Liz could smell the acrid stink of her own body, an accumulation of sweat and fear and at least one missed shower.

She had left all her clothes in her suitcase back in the hotel; the idea of going anywhere near the fourth floor again had been anathema to her. The ones she was wearing would have to do, slack and wrinkled as they were. They felt a little fresher once Liz had located the tiny bathroom and sluiced off her skin under an icy rush of water, turning no hot on at all.

Dressed again, hair wet upon her back, Liz stepped out into the hall. There was a harsh, rasping sound coming from downstairs, and she followed it. Her father-in-law's form blocked sight, but the motions he was making were unmistakable. His big hand concealed a square of sandpaper, and the other held a brush that began to stroke on a fresh layer of paint.

Mary emerged from the kitchen, twisting the hem of her apron between her hands. "It's too hot to eat," she said, as if she were to blame for the weather. "But suppertime has come and gone, so I fixed us all a little something. Come in."

The kitchen was at the back of the house, where the sun had long since passed overhead, making the temperature marginally cooler. Matthew sat at the head of the table, and Liz took a seat on the opposite side, vinyl chair cushion sticking to her thighs. A bowl of chicken salad and another of cut-up fruit sat on the speckled surface. Mary poured cold tea, and Liz, who couldn't have taken a bite of anything solid, downed a glass gratefully.

Only Matthew's appetite appeared to be intact. He shoveled chunks of chicken onto his fork, using one finger to push.

"I put my purse in Paul's old bedroom," Liz said. "Is that where you'd like me to sleep?"

Matthew and Mary exchanged glances.

"Don't see as there's much choice," Matthew said.

"We only have the one spare," Mary apologized. "Paul was our only."

Liz looked up.

"Is our only," Mary corrected hurriedly.

Matthew's eyebrows intersected in a frown. "We're modest people, and it's served us well. I tried to teach my son to live that way, too." His own tone contained no note of apology. Rather, his implication seemed to be that Paul had strayed from the family tradition.

"I think we've done the same," Liz retorted.

But she couldn't keep up any sort of bold front. Thinking of the ways they'd tried to connect both children to nature and the earth, to help them understand where their sustenance came from and what went into its creation, made Liz long with a dizzying pang for Ally's eager affinity. She even missed the constant squabbles required to stop Reid from forming a Jenga pile with rocks, or making him weed in the gardens as opposed to locating buried seeds with fingers that seemed able to see beneath dirt.

She fingered the slick oilcloth on the table. "Why has Paul done this? You must know something. It was like you were expecting me when I arrived."

Matthew's gaze fell hot upon her. "We figured you'd be coming because a cop paid a visit before you got here. It wasn't any surprise to see you after that."

The piece of chicken that Liz had been trying to chew turned to paste in her mouth as understanding finally dawned. The babysitting cop's friend on the Junction Bridge force. He had delivered on his promise.

Liz brought her napkin up and spat out the lump.

"The policeman asked some questions," Mary said quietly. "Whether Paul had been here with the children, things like that."

Liz stood and pushed back her chair, its legs grinding across the wooden floor.

"I see. That does explain things." She paused to take a breath. "Thank you for dinner. I'll be sure to leave first thing in the morning."

Upstairs her phone began to ring.

Her in-laws looked up, their faces startled by the sound. It occurred to Liz how quiet and muted this place must be most of the time.

When Liz finally reached the phone, Jill delivered the news as any good doctor knew to: swiftly, definitively, leaving no room for false hope.

"They're not here, Lizzie. It doesn't look as if anyone has been inside since you packed up the place."

In the background there came a faint mew of bewilderment, one of Andy's noises. Jill's voice grew distant as she sought to comfort her son.

"Andy, sweetheart, come here, no, not over there . . ."

Liz's cell phone had been plugged into the sole electrical outlet in the room; it sat in the wall beneath a window. Liz heard a smart *thwack* as her forehead hit the glass. Outside, night had finally fallen and everything was dark, as wide and empty a blank as all that lay before her now.

CHAPTER FOURTEEN

Liz lay on top of a thin sheet, blanket puddled on the floor below, too hot to sleep although exhaustion pulled at her like weights. Whatever adrenaline had driven her here, prompting her crazed rush at Matthew in the yard and subsequent confrontation with him by the phone, was now drained. Time spent in this house had come to nothing, and the recession of hope left Liz limp and helpless.

The cattle lowed miserably from the fields or their stalls; they were uncomfortable, too. A faint breeze stirred the curtains at the windows, but the temperature was so hot that the current of air provided no relief. Every now and then the sky lit greenly, casting an eerie glow over the room: somewhere far off, heat lightning was spiking. Liz got up and shoved the splintering frame of the window another inch or two higher. She turned around beneath the sloping eaves.

Clues that at some point this room had been inhabited did exist, although they were hard to discern. There were a few lighter rectangles on the wall, where poster-shaped outlines hadn't faded in lockstep with the rest of the paint. And the closet door was slightly ajar.

Liz wondered which bands her husband had liked, the actresses he'd stared at. Why had Paul never wanted to bring her back to this place? It'd been easy for Liz to go along with her husband's reticence, caught in the drift of his current. Paul had a charisma about him, a magnetic draw. That much knowledge was potent in a man. His students were compelled by it, too; Liz used to worry about Paul having an affair with one of his female acolytes, not that the males were any less adoring. The thought made her tremble with rage. She'd worried he would cheat on her; instead he had robbed her of their children.

She was squeezing her hands so hard that they throbbed. Liz forced her palms to unclench. She walked across the floor, skin sticky, chafing. The backs of her knees were slick, and her upper lip tasted salty.

Liz drew open the dresser drawers. They were empty, giving off the sharp, clean tang of pine. Liz closed her eyes and pictured herself amongst a stand of trees. Cool, shadowed. The press of desolation would be easier to bear in the forest, anywhere green and growing. She crossed to the closet, and there she finally got a hint of former life.

The metal rod was devoid of clothes, just a few hangers, but high on a shelf sat a football helmet, its green dome visible from below. When Liz pulled it down, a jersey came with it. Eastern Agricultural College in gold letters and a gold number twelve. It was the school Paul had graduated from and now taught at. She hadn't known that Paul had played college ball, which seemed a strange omission on her husband's part.

There was nothing else on the shelf.

Frustrated, Liz walked back to the bed and sat down, the sheet clammy, clinging when she tried to shift around. Sleep felt as far away as another planet. She reached for one of the books on the bedside table. *Lord of the Flies.* Next to it, two tomes of Shakespeare, then *1984* and *Of Mice and Men.* Books from a high school English curriculum. Only one volume didn't seem to fit. Liz had read it a long time ago, but couldn't imagine this would've been assigned in any class. *Johnny Got His Gun.* A gruesome tale, as she recalled, a war protest about a man so mangled, he became a prisoner in his own body. Liz removed the book from the row and flipped it open. Before she could start to read, a sheet of paper fell out.

It was a letter of some sort, a note. The page had been torn from a spiral-edged notebook, and the words were like slashes across it, dark as daggers.

I cannot forgive the unforgivable, and in any case, you don't appear to be seeking forgiveness. I raised you to the straight and narrow, but you have shunned my teachings. From this day forward, you are no son to me.

Despite her own fury, Liz blanched at this display of hardness and rage. Matthew wore righteousness like a king's mantle, and it had led him to cut off his child.

What had Paul done? Left home, and the family farm? This note seemed to hint at something more dire. *I cannot forgive the unforgivable.* What awful act had been carried out, and could Liz uncover it?

She folded the sheet of paper until it was small enough to tuck into the pocket of her shorts. Then she replaced the book on the nightstand.

In the minuscule box of a bathroom, Liz let cold water run over her wrists before soaking her hair for the second time that night. She placed a wrung-out towel upon her pillow, and with those moves completed, finally fell into a fitful sleep.

She woke when a rim of gray lightened the sky. Even before a farmer's day began. Liz dressed soundlessly in the clothes she'd been wearing, then drew the bedroom door shut, hoping Matthew and Mary would assume she was still asleep while she took a look around.

CHAPTER FIFTEEN

Liz had left her boots back at the hotel. Before leaving home, she'd wrapped them in plastic and crammed them into her suitcase, knowing she'd be on a farm soon enough. But in the car she'd worn sandals, nice shoes for travel. Now clods of dirt ruptured beneath the soles, sanding her feet. Matthew and Mary probably had extra pairs of boots stationed in the mudroom, but Liz didn't want to make any noise that would alert them to her exit.

It was a little cooler outside, but the air still felt solid as she passed through it. Liz scrubbed back her hair, already beaded with dampness, or perhaps it had never fully dried out from last night. She paused, fists on her hips. It was growing less gray out here, daylight fast approaching, and with it another sweltering sun.

She'd walked a half mile from the farmhouse, steering clear of the stink that fumed the cow enclosure. The acres down here were devoted to feed, but not anything her father-in-law was growing. Instead, the bushy rows were flagged by miniature pennants.

Liz squatted, aware of the passing time.

The codes on the pennants signified this or that trial variety belonging to the big agribusinesses. They were created in labs, but tested on farms and ranchlands whose owners could earn more renting out their land than working it. So much endless green, even under the scorching August sky. Liz plucked off a leaf, and tasted it tentatively. Some breed of alfalfa, and over there was soy. The number of rows offering up so much uninterrupted abundance was staggering. Liz flashed to her own plots back home, the occasional dried-out husk, or failed exotic. The lack of variety, wrinkle, or mishap on these acres was creepy. The plants reminded her of the placid-faced wives of Stepford who blinked at everyone with identical looks of contentment.

She spat out the leaf, brushed off her hands, and set out for a series of cornfields. The heat fought her every step of the way, pushing her back.

If Liz hadn't been someone who spent almost all of her days outside—in cold frames during the brutal Adirondack winters, but still, surrounded by earth—she might never have spotted the break in the acreage. Row upon row of vegetation, but here was one aisle that stood a little farther apart from its neighbors, a break in the monotony of spacing.

Liz ducked between the high stalks, corn nodding heavy upon them. Soon this whole area would be swept bare by a combine, nothing left to dry to a parched beige, withering in the wintered-over fields. All that vegetation would be destroyed to make way for a new season's identical planting, the old put to no use, not even made into compost. This was the type of farming Paul called quick and clean: everything cleared to make way for the next money crop, instead of circulated to replenish the land.

Liz moved forward along the corridor of corn, trying to catch a glimpse of light at the end. The patch she was in appeared endless, green walls rising up on either side. It was so dense and close that her feet kept getting twisted up in leaves. Missed corn pods lay on the ground, their rows of kernels exposed like teeth. The sun had finally appeared in the sky, and Liz felt as if she were in a lidded pot. She didn't bother to swipe greenery away from her face; the motion only made her hotter. The oversweet scent of fallen fruit filled her nose, and Liz sneezed. Then the row finally came to an end, and she found herself at the rim of a woods.

Liz glanced down, registering the soft give of the earth beneath her feet. Dirt wasn't supposed to be so buoyant and spongy by this time of year. Something was being added to the soil here, and the effect was that of an alien spring, the year's most fecund time, unnaturally prolonged almost into autumn. Liz wondered how Pervadon or whoever owned these rows was accomplishing it.

And then she spied a bright spot of color amongst the moldering pods.

Not green.

Pink, and purple, and some peach.

It was Izzy.

THE APPOINTMENT

Abby spent at least a couple of days wondering what she had gotten herself into. Even worse, she wondered whom she had gotten into it with. She'd only met these people online, which basically amounted to not knowing them at all. Could she trust them any more than her soon-to-be ex-husband?

She felt as if she were filling a role similar to the one she had held in her overlarge family: that of the forgotten little sister. For a long time, Bill's constant contact and oversight had been a welcome change.

But this was like a reversion to childhood. Since she'd sent that text, days had gone by when she didn't receive a message with further instructions. There was no one to call, at least no one who routinely answered their phone. The thread on the website was basically moribund; nobody posted anymore. Meanwhile Abby was trying to obey the set of directions she had received; packing and preparing, while simultaneously having to go along with a life she didn't expect to be living much longer.

But for now there were tasks to be fulfilled. Enormous ones.

Cody was to start kindergarten this year.

The day of the first supervised visit with Bill arrived.

If Abby didn't keep the appointment, Cody would be taken into protective custody. A foster family would be responsible for making the sessions. Period, end of story.

It was still hot out as Abby buckled her son into his booster. Back in the city, this would've been par for the course, but up here it was irregular, unprecedented weather. And Abby had dressed nicely—who knew what the court-appointed counselor might put in her custody report—although she was already regretting the sleeveless white dress, a relic from another age. The cloth was see-through with moisture.

She turned the engine on, willing the vents to send cool air through fast.

"Mama?"

"Yes?"

"When I lick my booster strap, it tastes yucky."

Even at a time like this, Cody could make her smile. "Well, maybe you shouldn't lick your booster strap, Bun."

"Oh yeah!"

Abby smothered a laugh. But forty minutes later, as they were nearing the address, laughter seemed far away. The one-story building, which housed a couple of medical offices, seemed too bland and innocuous to fill Abby with this much dread.

She parked and got out, walking around to Cody's side. She glanced over her shoulder, expecting Bill to be there. She could feel him—smell him almost—and she yanked Cody to her, just as if he really had been about to be pulled away.

"Mama, ow!"

Abby forced her grip to loosen. "Stay close," she said, too sharply, to Cody.

She looked around guiltily as she tugged him along. If the counselor cared about the dress Abby wore, surely her harsh voice, or how the stress of the situation was wearing fault lines in her demeanor, would be worthy of mention.

Oh, how Abby longed to be away from here.

She saw Bill inside every car, was afraid to tug the door open lest her husband be lurking behind it, a blameless leer of greeting on his face as he reached for their son.

Instead the counselor stood in the waiting room, divided from the one where Cody was to be taken. Abby had only to sit in the chilly space, try to get her heartbeat to stop ramping up before suddenly diving, and wait for her son to return.

She never saw Bill.

But the anticipation that she might turned out to be even worse.

Even though the counselor had warned Abby not to talk to Cody about the session, lest he feel pressure to respond in one way or another, she couldn't keep one little how-was-it from slipping out as she unlocked the car.

"Good," Cody said. Then, "Ow!"

He had tried to pick up his DS, and the black box must've been burning hot.

Abby felt as if she were holding a flood back with her teeth. "Let me turn on the air, Bun."

They waited a moment for the seat belts to be cool enough to touch. Abby held the DS in front of one of the vents. Then she pointed the car north toward Wedeskyull.

"You know what's next on the agenda?" She glanced in the rearview. "Cody? Look up from your game."

"What's next on the agenda?" A beat. "What's a agenda?"

Abby smiled. "The visit with your new teacher."

She had thought it both odd and inspiring that Cody's teacher had scheduled new student meetings on a Saturday. The teacher had said that she would be in school that day anyway, setting up. And what did Abby know? She'd never had a school-age child.

"So we'll go do that now, okay?" Abby said. "And then pick up some groceries for dinner. What are you in the mood for?"

Again, Cody didn't reply, but the normalcy was beginning to strike Abby as reassuring.

The Consolidated School sat in a valley. It held all the grades, kindergarten through twelfth, in a brick building whose roof was pitched steeply enough to throw off all but a skin of snow, and thus was mostly impervious to winter's battering. The kindergarten classroom was so bright and welcoming that it distracted Cody from his device, which Abby had forgotten to make him leave in the car. She dropped the DS into her purse with a guilty flush, then faced the teacher.

"Hello, Mrs. Harmon," the teacher said.

"Ms.," Abby corrected. "I'm not married. Or I won't be soon."

"I'm sorry, Ms. Harmon. It's nice to meet you." The teacher crouched down. "And you must be Cody."

Abby watched while Cody toured the classroom with his new teacher, gratified to see how comfortable he seemed to be. Things couldn't be in that great a state of upheaval, bad dreams notwithstanding, if Cody was able to adapt so quickly to a new situation.

After the teacher had finished asking Cody his letters and numbers, then given him some worksheets to fill out during the last week of summer vacation, Abby asked if she could have an extra minute of her time.

"Of course," the teacher said.

Abby set Cody up on the floor of the hallway outside, giving him back his game. Then she closed the door behind her and met the teacher by her desk.

"What a sweet boy," the teacher said. "He certainly seems compliant and eager to please."

Abby smiled briefly. "Thank you." Then she wondered if the words had been meant as praise.

"What can I help you with, Ms. Harmon?"

Abby hesitated. "I'm in the process of getting divorced," she said, feeling the need to say it again. "Cody's father has supervised visitation," Abby went on. "He's not supposed to see him alone. So if he were to show up here . . ." Abby trailed off, trying to suppress the Lifetime movie images conjured up by that scenario.

The teacher took in Abby's story. "Don't worry, Ms. Harmon. The only name or names that go on Cody's pickup card will be ones you approve. And no one who isn't on that card is getting access to one of my kids."

She seemed duly focused, intent as she said it, but also very young to Abby.

Worry must've continued to reflect on her face, because the teacher went on. "One other person you might want to reach out to?"

Abby nodded quickly.

"The school bus driver. I can keep my eyes on things in here. But that still leaves two hours a day when your son is in transit and not in our care."

CHAPTER SIXTEEN

Liz snatched up the doll from the ground and ran. The temperature was momentarily forgotten, although Liz sensed its effect in the ragged thump of her heart. But she wouldn't be slowed, even though she was soon gasping for breath.

She kept to the path where Izzy had been found, then began to mount a hill. The slope was steep: black, porous-looking stone capped by a coral reef of lichen, and Liz tripped, the palms of her hands skidding painfully. But she rose and kept going until she reached a ridge of trees at the top. She was breathing even harder now, so slick with sweat that her feet slid inside her sandals. A low, orchestral thrum of insects filled the air.

Liz peered down. She'd been clutching Izzy in one hand; now she wedged the doll into her pocket. The other side of the hill was just as sharply pitched. Liz turned around, trying to get a sense of her bearings. No hint of the farmhouse. Even the inland sea of corn seemed far off. There was no direction that looked more promising than over this edge.

She was soon slipping, bracing herself with one hand to try and keep from careening out of control, when the sun struck something silver. Liz rotated slightly, turning toward it, as she kept on maneuvering vertically. She lost sight of whatever metallic glimmer had been exposed, and ground to a halt, letting out a grunt of frustration as she held herself in place. What had she seen? She scoured the earth around her, willing it to give up its secrets. There was some sort of cleft over there in the ground. Liz half slid, half scooted over to it, before getting to her feet. The soil here was too even, as if it had been smoothed into place. She began kicking clods of dirt away until it hit her that she was standing on something solid.

A plane of steel so thick that it didn't shift when she stamped on it. Liz dropped to her knees, banging with both fists and screaming.

"Ally! Reid! Where are you?"

Only the concert of sounds from the woods. Nothing human answered.

"Paul! Damn you! Paul!"

Someone caught her from behind and yanked her to her feet.

It was her father-in-law, his face red and shiny.

"What is this place?" Liz cried. "Open it. Please. Let me inside!"

"They're not here," Matthew said. "I wasn't lying about that."

"No," Liz said, withdrawing Izzy and wielding her like a weapon. "You were just lying about everything else."

If Matthew had the grace to flush, it wasn't detectable. "I don't lie," he intoned. "I have no idea how that toy got here."

"I don't care if you do or don't," Liz said roughly. "All I care about is where Paul and the kids went from here." Suddenly she seized his arm. "Please tell me. Are the children all right?"

Matthew stared at her wordlessly.

"Did something happen? Why would Ally leave Izzy behind?"

At last her father-in-law seemed to take pity on her. "I told you, I didn't see them. Maybe they were chased off by that cop calling."

But the babysitting cop's friend hadn't even come until yesterday afternoon. Where had her children spent the night before last, if not here at the farmhouse? Matthew's suggestion diminished clarity instead of adding it.

Liz's skin prickled with dirt and evaporating sweat. She felt desperate, unable to reach this implacable man. "Smart move with the rows," she said, speaking into the oppressive heat and silence. "The spacing. Be hard to find this spot without some sort of sign. But you wouldn't want to flag it."

Her father-in-law looked at her with faint surprise.

"I'm surprised Pervadon let you do it. Challenge to their uniformity."

"That section is mine."

"Oh, right," Liz said cruelly. "You're renting back some of your own land."

Matthew crushed his hand into a fist. "You think you're pretty smart, hah? How many people lived off what you grew last year?" He barked a laugh. "Or did they just have some condiments for their sandwiches?"

Touché, Liz thought. She touched the square of paper she'd put into her pocket. "What did Paul do that required forgiveness?"

Her father-in-law studied her for a moment. Pearls of perspiration had collected on his temples; now they began to dissolve and trickle down.

"I would think you'd know that," he said.

Liz searched her memory, but it was hard to find even the mildest reports of indiscretion. Paul thought that he knew the best way, the right way, to live. He kept a stranglehold on virtue. He'd even been reluctant to join in on frat-boy pranks, although he'd once stolen the rival fraternity's pig. That used to make them joke that Reid came by his talent genetically.

Reid. And Ally. None of this was getting her any closer to her kids.

"No," she said in a small voice. "I have no idea. Please tell me."

"That isn't my place," Matthew said with such a note of finality in his voice that Liz knew even hysterical begging would get her nowhere.

She kicked at the roof of the bunker that lay belowground. "Seems like you're preparing for a war out here."

"A war's coming," Matthew responded, studying her with brute disregard. "And if most folks are too ignorant to notice, I don't see why I should have to sacrifice my grandkids to their stupidity."

"Your grandkids?" Liz shot back. "The ones you've seen three times in their lives?"

Again Matthew subsided into silence, but it seemed less concession than obstruction.

"So that's what this is about?" Liz said. "Paul thinks he has to take the kids and—what, build a bunker of his own somewhere? This one wasn't good enough?" She let out a sharp peal of laughter, and a rattle of birds disturbed the high canopy of leaves.

Matthew looked away.

"I think my kids are in there," Liz said. "I think you're lying to me now."

Her father-in-law let out a huff of breath. He walked the length of dirt, which shrouded metal beneath. When he came to the end of the run, he kicked aside some sticks, pulled up hard on a handle, and disappeared into the ground. After a few seconds—too little time to have done anything beneath—Matthew hoisted himself back up, indicating the inside of the cavity with a gesture whose gallantry looked misplaced.

Liz walked to the edge and squatted down. She leaned over, trying to peer into the depths. The capsule appeared to go on for a while underground. The buried breadth was daunting, and Liz felt her chest clutch.

"Go on," Matthew said. "See for yourself."

Liz sat, then lowered her legs over the side.

"Feel for the steps," Matthew instructed. "They're built in."

Liz's shoe caught the lip. Bracing her hands against smooth steel walls, Liz strained for the next step, before getting the idea and turning her body around, climbing down as if she were on a ladder.

It was blessedly cool below; she took a second to bask in the sensation. How much warmer this place would be come wintertime, insulated by its many feet of dirt. Liz registered dimly how Matthew had fitted the place out—rows of canned goods, a rack of guns, a pipeline that must lead to a spring—but the only really important thing she sensed was that the capsule indeed appeared to be empty, devoid of human life.

She began walking its length.

Then the lid swung down.

CHAPTER SEVENTEEN

A caul of panic descended along with the roof.

She was in a steel trap, caught as surely as if metal claws had sunk into one of her limbs. It was utterly lightless. Liz's eyes blinked crazily, trying to adjust, but she couldn't see a thing, not even herself. The dark was as thick as paste, filling her eye sockets, her lungs. She fought for a breath, but couldn't get any air.

She leaned over, feeling for her knees, some sense of tactile connection to keep from passing out. Her voice rose and teetered, but at first she couldn't form coherent words. Then her shout drilled up to the ceiling, to the stolen sky.

"Matthew! *Matthew!* Let me out!"

Was her father-in-law still up there? Had this happened by accident? Or had he purposely locked her in while he went off to—what? Locate her children and usher them yet farther away?

"Matthew! Matthew, please!"

Her voice was ragged now, hoarse. Soon it wouldn't work at all.

Darkness straitjacketed her and she fought against it, flinging her hands out in the hopes of touching something, anything to hold on to. But her fingers located nothing besides empty air, and Liz realized she was in a blind spin.

She bent down again, disoriented. A completely futile hope, near-delusional in quality, assailed her. Paul was in here too, hidden away in some compartment she hadn't yet come to. If she could only find him, he would tell her what to do.

She crouched down farther, not entirely sure when it was that she fell to her knees. The darkness no longer felt so oppressive. Instead it was comforting, like a blanket.

"Paul?" she called out, her voice the only sign of life in the hollow space. "Are you here? Oh, Paul, where are our babies?"

The dark seemed friendlier now, a hand reaching blindly for her, and she began crawling toward it. She realized that for the first time in days she felt cold, but it wasn't a bad feeling; in fact, the relief of it made her want to lie down and stay put.

Her knee barked against something in the dark, and Liz felt for her leg, rubbing without being able to see.

If she did find Paul again, she would never be able to listen to what he had to say, and the loss of her reliance on him weighed as heavily as the dark.

You're smart, Jill used to say. *You can figure out whether or not to give the kids a Big Mac without Paul telling you the percentage of soy in the feed.*

How much of a puppet, a mouthpiece had she been for her husband's beliefs?

Liz forced her breathing to slow.

First light. Then the opening would be easy to find. The lid had to lift from the inside, requiring strength perhaps, but adrenaline would lend her that. She could feel it streaking through her like an electrical current, her heart pinging its beat. As if she were floating, Liz turned and began to feel for a wall.

The lid of the capsule swung open, and sunlight lit like a flare.

"Paul?" she shouted, voice crazed with reprieve.

"Elizabeth." It was Matthew's staid tone. "Get up here. I'm sorry. The hinges stick when they haven't been used in a while." He paused. "I told you, nobody's beneath."

He reached down, his hand a white, waving flag.

Liz refused it, climbing laboriously out on her own.

Aboveground, the temperature was like an assault.

But it didn't rob her of breath, not like that suffocating dark. When her voice emerged, it was steady. "You really don't know where they are?"

"I don't," Matthew said. "But it wouldn't matter if I did."

Liz hadn't let go of Izzy in the whole time she'd been sealed underground. She began stroking the doll's head, winding yarn hair around her fingers until they pulsed with constriction.

"Of course it would," she said. "If you knew what Paul was planning to do—"

Her father-in-law was shaking his head. "Whatever Paul is planning, he clearly has no intention of letting anyone else in on it."

Liz stared at him.

Matthew mopped his brow with his forearm, regarding her with what looked like a genuine sense of sorrow. It was the first spark of human connection she'd felt from her father-in-law, who seemed less man than monolith, something carved out of the hard, oaken land.

"Trust me, Elizabeth. I know all about losing a child."

CHAPTER EIGHTEEN

The car gave off a plume of heat as soon as she unlocked it. Liz welcomed the burn when she sat down inside. Sweat sizzled on her thighs, but she didn't turn on the engine. She deserved this punishment, this pain. She had lost her children.

Liz wrapped her hands around the steering wheel, letting the circle brand them.

From inside her purse, her cell phone let out a bleat of missed calls.

Liz's mother had left a message, and Jill had left three. It must've been Jill who sounded the alarm, since it was still days away from her mother's usual perfunctory check-in. Liz felt wisps of both gratitude and irritation at her friend.

A slip of paper tucked into her cell phone case snagged her attention. The babysitting cop's card.

He answered with, "This is Grayson," and Liz realized that in those desperate, frenetic eight hours at the hotel, she had never learned his name.

"This is Liz Daniels," she said. "I wanted to thank you—thank your friend—for going up to check the farm."

"I'm sorry it didn't lead to anything," Grayson said.

If only Grayson's friend had gotten there a little sooner.

"My children were there," she said. "I found—" She had to break off.

Grayson's reply was instant. "You found your kids?"

"They were gone by the time I arrived," Liz said. "But I found Ally's doll." She reached down to her pocket to touch it, the most tangible link she had to her children now.

Grayson didn't say anything.

"Can the Junction Bridge police do anything else?"

"I can't see that there's anything to do," Grayson replied. "There's the nature of the matter, for one thing. This is a family concern." As if sensing the understatement contained in that assessment, he went on. "Also, as you say, your kids are no longer there."

He was right. Liz stared out the windshield, which was coated with bug splatter and dust. The view to wherever her children might be seemed just as occluded.

"It seems almost cruel," Grayson said.

The word hit her like a hammer.

"Not only for your husband to plan some happy, jolly family trip in order to make off with your children. But also for him to have stuck around all morning. Stupid, too—we could easily have detained him." Grayson paused. "As a cop—if this were my case—I'd be asking why he did that. Because it might give you some idea where he wound up."

Liz felt baffled. Grayson was right, of course; those were bizarre moves on Paul's part. But she had no idea how to uncover their justification.

"Can I ask you a question?" she said after a moment.

"Sure, go ahead," Grayson said.

"How did you figure it out? That my husband . . ."

She didn't have to finish.

"Two things," Grayson said. "One took place that day, one a little later. First, when your husband went to check on the children's belongings—"

It was Liz's turn to break in. "He lied. He did take their things with him."

Of course he would have. Paul hated waste. Especially when the items to be squandered had been made by what he called overseas slave labor. Clothes so cheap they were painless to replace when outgrown or lost or their wearer just took a sudden dislike.

"No." Grayson spoke over the voice in her head. "He was smart enough not to do that. Everything was pretty much left intact, except the doll." He paused, as if aware that his words would cause pain. "It was that your husband didn't check in an authentic way. At least that's how it looked to the officer we sent to watch him. Your husband looked like he knew what he'd find before he went rifling through it."

Liz realized she hadn't blinked. The light blinded her, bringing on a sting of tears, and she forced herself to shut her eyes. "What was the other thing?"

Grayson hesitated. "An eyewitness came forward. Kind of a strange man; there was a delay before he reported what he'd seen. According to the hotel, he doesn't speak much outside of his required duties. But he observed your husband escorting the children out in the middle of the night."

"What?" Sunlight broke over her, a million flashing pieces. "Who did?"

Grayson's breath emerged audibly. "We've already checked him out, Mrs. Daniels. An employee of the hotel who was working the night shift."

Liz didn't have to speak; the pressure of her question ballooned in the air between them.

Grayson paused, checking his notes or maybe the report.

"His name is Larry Arnold," he said at last. "He's a bellhop."

CHAPTER NINETEEN

How stupid Paul had been to flip that lock on the top of the door. Liz had been thinking of the mistake as just an unthinking, automatic gesture, the act of a man who spent much of his life in books and research, in his head, rather than staging crime scenes. Or else it had been some kind of telltale-heart tic, an admission to the world of his guilt. But now she wondered if her husband hadn't in fact made several errors out of naiveté and lack of cunning, and if one of them might actually help her.

She started the car. The temperature inside had climbed to a broil during her conversation, and Liz's skin felt slick, her shirt wetted through. Praying she could find her way back along the tangle of roads, she left Matthew and Mary's farm behind in a yellow storm cloud of dust.

The hotel staff remembered her at first glance, and appeared both apologetic and relieved when they informed her that Larry Arnold wasn't scheduled to work that day.

Liz had dashed inside from the parking lot and her heart was beating fast enough to interrupt speech. "I don't suppose—would it be possible—can you give me his phone number?"

The woman behind the front desk traded looks with the man. "Larry doesn't really talk to strangers." She rolled her eyes, then seemed to remember why Liz was asking, and quickly looked away.

"I can call him," the male employee offered. He tapped a few keys on his computer. "No harm in trying. What do you want me to say?"

"Ask him—" Liz was attempting to catch her breath while wondering what it was about Larry Arnold that Grayson and the hotel staff all seemed to know. She supposed that she too had sensed something off about the man. "Please ask if he'd be willing to meet with me."

She registered the fact that the phone had been answered, and that this appeared to surprise the desk clerk. Also that Larry Arnold seemed to be agreeing to her request.

Starbucks, she mouthed to the clerk. As she started to run again, she called over her shoulder, "The one in the next mall over."

If Liz thought honestly about their lives, Paul had been preparing his family for something radical for years, getting them used to living without luxury or even the normal accoutrements of modern life— a constant stream of TV and Internet and video games—plus eating in a way that didn't depend on the factory system, while the rest of the world went merrily along, driving and flying and buying, all things whose imminent crash Paul constantly predicted.

Only why had he taken the children without bringing her? It made no sense.

The parking lot radiated heat more intense than any Liz had felt yet. The asphalt had softened, giving way beneath her shoes, and making it feel as if the very surface of the earth was unsteady. Liz had to separate her shirt from her skin, like pulling off plaster.

On the rare occasions when she'd had cause to leave the Adirondacks, it always struck her how homogeneous the rest of the world appeared to be. Here she was in western New York, and aside from the thick, wet air, she might as well have been in California. In any strip mall she could eat the same featureless Italian or Chinese, buy the same item of clothing, solve the same first-world emergency, such as replacing a cell phone or repairing a chipped nail.

The coffee in Starbucks smelled the same too, although the refrigerated chill as Liz pulled open the door felt wonderful. The iced version of whatever she ordered would do nothing for her racing nerves, so Liz decided to force down a bite to eat as well. It occurred to her how easy life was outside of Paul's reach. No scouting options for a healthier alternative, or asking what kind of oil was used for frying. What was the point of asking? It was always a bad kind. It could've been a Joni Mitchell song. Give me back my butter, lard, and suet. Assuming they came from a grass-fed, grass-finished animal, of course. All of the fats that scientists claimed were bad for you had turned out to be far more healthy than factory-bred canola or the toxic mélange that became vegetable oil.

Liz took a table looking out on the parking lot. Heat shimmered over the baking black expanse.

She recognized Larry Arnold as soon as he got out of his car, a midsize sedan Liz knew she wouldn't be able to describe five seconds after seeing it. The sight of the bellhop's wan face and sparse mustache still brought on a queasy pang. She half rose in her seat, then forced herself to sit back down until Larry Arnold entered the shop. He crossed to the table she occupied, hands fussing with something invisible on his slacks.

Liz stood up. "Thanks for meeting me. Can I buy you a coffee?"

"No, no," the bellhop said. He paused. "Or maybe you should. Or I can buy myself one. I always worry that the staff will feel taken advantage of by people who don't order anything. So many people do that these days. Plug their computers in, and *peck, peck, peck*, but never spend a penny. I suppose corporate is aware of this, of course. Figures it into their bottom line."

"Right," Liz said. She took a step toward the counter. "How do you take it?"

"Oh, you don't have to do that," Larry Arnold said. "Are you sure? There are so many choices. You can't just know how you take your coffee anymore, light, two sugars. The sizes are strange and there are all those syrups and toppings . . ."

"Sounds like a latte would do," Liz interrupted. She decided not to get into the complexities of iced versus hot.

She handed Larry his drink, warding off a meandering stream of thanks with one raised hand. Fear and stress had lent her a dreadful efficiency.

"The police said you saw my husband leave the hotel with our children."

Larry was rubbing that spot on his slacks. He looked up when Liz went silent, as if surprised she had finished speaking so quickly.

"Yes, I did," he replied. "I know I should've spoken up sooner. But I didn't understand how the children could be missing with your husband standing right there. It's like something on TV. Only on TV, the person who sees something—that's me—says so right away. But look what that leads to. Someone says something back. And then you have to—"

"It's all right," Liz said, in as soothing a tone as she could muster. She needed Larry calm and focused, but the man seemed likely to short out at any moment. "You did the right thing in the end. Can you just—can you tell me what happened?"

Larry didn't meet her eyes. "I was coming off my shift. The night shift isn't easy, but it lets me watch all my shows. I hear they have something that solves this problem now—you can watch when the show isn't even on . . ."

The man gave no sign of stopping, let alone proffering the information she needed. Liz understood the hotel staff's compunctions. She wondered how questioning could possibly have gone for the police.

"My husband," she prompted.

Larry looked up, lip puckered so that his wispy mustache drew down. "Oh yes," he said. "I thought it was strange because children aren't usually up so late. I don't have any children of my own—I was never even married—not because I wouldn't have liked to be, but because I never met anyone. Not that I didn't meet *anyone*, of course, just not the right—"

Liz's exhalation of breath must've been louder than she intended.

"But that's another story," Larry said with apparent effort. "What I meant to say is that it jumped out at me how sleepy those children looked and I also wondered why they were being taken outside through the side exit. Instead of through the automatic doors in front, I mean. I would've used the front ones myself, except that I was coming back from my last cigarette break and they don't like guests to see us smoking near the entrance."

His pause didn't give Liz time to interject.

"I know how unhealthy cigarettes are for you, but I don't have many bad habits. Well, sitting too close to the television and—"

Liz was starting to feel a little desperate. The coffee sizzled in her veins and she had the urge to grab Larry's thin arms and give them a shake. She might've done it, except that she suspected the act would only provide him more to chatter about.

She settled for speaking over him. "Mr. Arnold! Can you tell me anything else you saw? After my husband walked the kids out. Did you follow them to the parking lot?"

He stared at her blankly for enough time that his silence registered as alien.

"I might have," Larry said. "I might've done that, but only to ask if they needed any help. That's what I figured, you see. That they'd forgotten something in the car and were going out to get it. Maybe the man didn't want to leave the children alone in the room. Who knows what can happen these days, right?"

Oh yes, Liz thought with more than a shard of hysteria. *Anything can happen these days.*

"And it certainly would be my job to help them with their things, assuming they wanted help. That's what a customer associate does, you know, among other tasks, but you never want to be intrusive, people get annoyed—"

Again, Liz spoke loudly, trying to come up with a question that would corral the man, get him to stay on point. "But you didn't? Ask them if they needed help?"

"No," he said. "I assumed that was what the other person was there for."

Charges ignited all over Liz's body. She looked down at her skin. "Other person? Do you mean a woman?" Thinking, *You pathetic cliché. An affair? That's what this is all about?* And then, *Who the hell do you have caring for my kids?*

But Larry was shaking his head, and when he spoke, the information she needed came out before his slipstream of associated thoughts.

"No, not a woman. A man."

CHAPTER TWENTY

Larry Arnold's description of the man was too generic to mean anything. Tall, dark-haired. She wondered if the police had done anything with it despite knowing this could all be chalked up to a domestic dispute.

The two words were a hiss in her mind. *Domestic dispute.* How meaningless—utterly lacking in descriptive power—they were compared to the disaster that had befallen her.

It registered vaguely that Larry was talking again, and had been for some time.

" . . . better be getting home."

Liz blinked away a scrim of tears. "Yes. Thank you. I'm sorry I disturbed you on your day off."

"I'm lucky to have a house to go to. That hasn't always been the case. I used to be homeless, you see. As they say, we're only one paycheck away from—"

Perhaps he noted her tears for he seemed to forcibly wind himself down, wrapping his arms around his body and giving a shake of his head. "That doesn't matter right now. But I hope you get back to your house soon, too."

Liz looked up sharply, and Larry flinched. "Sometimes I say the wrong thing. My doctor says I talk too much because I'm afraid of saying the wrong thing. If I stuff all the words in there, he says, then at least some of them will be right—"

Liz rose abruptly from her seat, and the bellhop took a step back.

"I'm sorry," he said, voice rising. "My doctor says if I say I'm sorry, then nobody should take offense—"

Liz forced her voice down. "No, no, it's fine. I appreciate everything you've done."

He paused, his back to the counter. A few people looked up from their drinks and their Wi-Fi. Liz thought about how Larry Arnold merged topics, the silkworm threads of words he wove.

He was going home, he hoped she got back to her own house.

"Mr. Arnold?" she said suddenly. "Did you hear anything the children or those men said as they were walking out to the car?"

He was trying to meet her gaze.

"About where they were going maybe?"

He began shaking his head, slowly back and forth, and Liz let her head fall. "No," she said. "Okay. Thank you."

"They weren't talking." The direct reply came with obvious effort. "I've never heard any group of people be so quiet in my life."

Liz didn't respond.

"It was too quiet," the bellhop added. "I had to say something. I told them to have a nice trip. I love going on trips myself. I once went to—" He let out a ragged breath, cutting himself off. "And then the little girl did say something."

Liz kept herself from moving too fast, approaching him with urgency.

"She said she was going to be glad to see trees again."

In the bellhop's words, Liz found her daughter, and what she said indicated that Paul and the children were headed back to Wedeskyull. Where Paul lived, worked, made his life.

Trees were Ally's deepest association to home, the thing she loved best. For fruit-picking, climbing, and growing shade-loving plants. Ally had missed the trees as soon as they'd left.

It at least gave Liz a place to start.

Each passing mile was a relief, and Liz realized how much she also needed the Adirondacks, in all their towering glory and hidden pockets of land. The children, too; Ally wanted her trees. Please let Paul have understood that, and worked it into his thinking.

It occurred to Liz to call the police as she drove. Not Grayson, or anyone on the Junction Bridge force, who couldn't do anything anyway. But if this was a domestic dispute, then didn't Liz's hometown police force have jurisdiction? Shouldn't they at least be made aware of the trouble brewing within their mountain walls?

"Chief Lurcquer."

"Tim," Liz said. "It's Liz Daniels." After a moment she added, "Liz Burke."

The silence over the line went on longer than any official pause. Liz took the phone away from her ear, checking to see if the call had dropped.

Finally the chief spoke. "Liz. It's been a while."

She was blinking through tears again, the road blurring before her. Tim Lurcquer had never been an emotional guy—did any boys in high school have feelings?—but his voice brought her back to a different time, when she could rely on other people to take care of her, and also when there wasn't all that much to lose.

"Is everything all right?"

"No," Liz said. "It's not."

She pulled onto the sloping shoulder so that she didn't lose control of the car.

She reentered the road after finally reaching a break in her story, the jagged place she'd come to that had made her decide to return to Wedeskyull.

Tim's voice became brisk and businesslike. He asked if she was using a headset once the engine noise gave away the fact that she was driving. Then he said, "Nothing really seems to add up here, does it?"

"No," Liz said. Then she actually laughed. "I would say not."

"Cops tend to be masters of understatement."

Liz sniffed in raggedly, laughter evaporating. "I think that cart might've preceded the horse. You were understated long before you became a policeman."

Years disappeared between them, like the implosion of a building.

"Maybe I was," Tim said. "So your husband . . . what? Meets an old buddy from his hometown and . . ."

Tim trailed off at about the same point Liz's conjectures had. An old friend that Liz had never heard about? And why would Paul have left with him, much less taken the children with them?

"Seems a strange thing for two guys to do." Tim hesitated. "I hope you don't mind my asking, but could your husband be gay?"

Another of the increasingly far-fetched scenarios Liz had already come up with, although she had immediately dismissed the possibility. Of all the things Liz was doubting—whether Paul ever really loved her, what kind of world he intended to live in—the charge between them wasn't in question. Paul was an amorous man who demanded ardor in return.

It seemed odd to hear Tim raise the possibility; he had never been the most worldly of guys. Then again, Liz supposed she wouldn't want to be judged by her teenage self either.

"I don't think so," she said. "Partially because if he were, I doubt he would've felt the need to hide it, or do something this extreme. He probably would've expected me to . . . adjust . . . and we'd all be acting like one big blended family by now."

"Okay," Tim said. "What's the other part?"

"What?"

"You said Paul's assumption of tolerance was partially the reason. What's the rest?"

The road changed, swinging left into a cradle of low, huddled mountains. She was in the foothills now, and even though they made something inside her relax and give way, the words she was about to say imposed a totally different state. Liz felt suddenly chilled, and she let down the window so the air outside could warm her.

"The rest is that I went out to that farm, Tim. My father-in-law's place. And I saw things. It's not just business as usual there, Paul's boyhood home. It's—"

Sinister was the word that leapt to her lips, though she immediately quashed it as melodramatic and overblown. She didn't want to be that type of woman, scared of spiders and going out alone at night. But she could still feel the unnatural give of that earth beneath her feet, the cold, steely walls of the bunker.

She reached into her pocket and touched the folds of Matthew's note.

"There are things left unsaid there," Liz said at last. "Reasons for Paul's long absence—and for his coming back now—that no one would tell me."

"I see," Tim said, and she realized how useless what she was saying would be to any kind of investigation. "But you said your . . ." He cleared his throat. " . . . family isn't there."

She glanced at the clock on the dash, aware of how much time Tim was spending with her. "I can only imagine they went home. That's where I'm going to start."

"Seems a good bet." His agreement brought on a renewed flush of hope. Then Tim added, "I can think of one or two things to try on my end."

"Really? Like what?" Liz asked quickly.

"I don't want to get your hopes up. This is a strange situation, and anything I do is going to be after-hours, old friend to old friend."

"Thank you," Liz said. "I really appreciate that."

"Let me take down some information. And then give me a day, maybe two."

"Okay," Liz said. She rooted around for words. "Just you? I mean, we—you—couldn't get help from the FBI?"

"The feds step in if a kidnapping crosses state lines. But fortunately, there's no suggestion that's what you've got."

Liz was silent.

"Do you hear what I'm saying?" Tim said, his voice gruff. "Focus on that. You've got some time on your hands. I think it'll go down easier if you remember that hard as this is, your children are with someone who loves them."

CHAPTER TWENTY-ONE

A clogging sense of dread began to build in Liz the closer she got to home. After her children, it was the worst thing Paul could rob her of: her love of Wedeskyull. But as the road wound into the mountains, they seemed for the first time to present a barrier, six million acres of hiding spaces. Tree-studded walls enclosed her car, bearing down.

Liz found it hard to stop wrenching her hands on the wheel. She bent a fingernail back past the quick, and stared at the bead of blood that welled up.

Jill had checked the house, so Liz wasn't expecting to open the door and find Paul poring over journal articles in his study, the kids chasing each other around inside. But she still couldn't imagine facing the emptiness there.

It wasn't as cool in Wedeskyull as she'd been expecting. The spongy, wet heat from Junction Bridge had seeped out, infiltrating even this mountain refuge.

The turn into her drive came up suddenly, unexpected. Liz jerked the wheel, sliding across the seat. She braked to an abrupt halt, stumbling when she emerged from the car onto a half-moon of gravel in front of the porch. Her ankle bent sideways, and she had to sit down, rubbing it and trying to catch her breath.

When hotter temperatures did come to the mountains, they tended to stay there, unable to escape. Liz felt trembly all over with the need to cool down.

All around her were shouts—ghostly, yet real. A singsong of voices wrested back out of the past.

Mom! I took an egg from under the mommy bird! It didn't even break!

Look what's growing near the swing, Mommy! Alyssum!

Liz stood up.

The gardens beckoned, but no way could she go out to them now. Being amongst fronds and waving tendrils might keep her from ever moving again. The very vitality of the gardens would prove how dead she was. Liz could imagine lying down beneath their cool cover, digging herself an earthen grave.

Instead she approached the tire swing, which hung motionless on its rope. The roots of the tree it was attached to were as thick as a man's thighs.

Over there was the crater in the lawn where Ally had tried to display her own garden to Paul, before Liz had begun to take her daughter's calling seriously, and dug a separate plot. And there was the abandoned nest, one of whose eggs Reid had indeed addled, prompting Paul to come up with the rule that Reid could never pinch anything alive.

Another possible trigger for Reid's fear: when he found out the bird was dead in its shell.

I killed it? he'd asked, weeping.

The sound of their creek, a constant, white-noise rush, began to register.

Reid spent so much time intricately damming that creek. He didn't use his dexterous hands only to steal, he also built things. Suddenly Liz missed her son, with all his bumps and wounded spots, so white-hotly that she began to cry.

Eyes veiled by tears, she climbed the porch steps, ankle twanging as she unlocked the front door. It creaked, the noise jarring in the utterly still house. They never went in this way, choosing to use the mudroom instead. Liz entered the hall amidst a shaft of sunlight and spinning dust motes.

And then she broke into a run, ignoring her ankle as she took the stairs, flinging open the door to Reid's bedroom.

If anybody was unable to keep from disrupting a house—leave behind small giveaways of his presence—it would be Reid. A trail of objects he'd pilfered, scattered amongst the usual boy-mess of toys and sports equipment and discarded clothing.

Liz peered in from the hall.

The room was just as tidy as she'd left it. The bedclothes drawn flat, toys arranged on their chest. The spines of the books stood upright in a neat row. Even the closet door was shut.

In Ally's room, a bright cluster of VeggieTales sat on the floor, and only the gaping spot that belonged to Izzy revealed that somehow, entire worlds had changed.

Liz couldn't stay another second in this sad and haunted home.

CHAPTER TWENTY-TWO

Jill lived in a small house in town, which was why they'd had to base their business at Liz and Paul's place in the valley. Liz drove in her best friend's direction so unthinkingly and automatically that she was caught by surprise when she rolled up in front.

Jill came out on the stoop, her arms extended, before Liz had even opened the car door. She got out and stepped into her friend's embrace.

"Coffee," Jill said, as Liz cried against her. Then she murmured, "That was an asinine thing to say. But I can think of something a little better." She turned and led Liz inside.

Jill poured two glasses of whiskey as if she were serving iced tea. "Drink," she commanded, gesturing to Liz before knocking a couple of fingers back herself.

Liz obeyed. The whiskey heated her belly, and it struck her that the temperature outside wasn't much cooler. It was as if something foreign and terrible had come to blanket the whole land. She scrubbed damp strands of hair back from her face.

"I know," Jill said, watching her. "Awful, isn't it? It feels like we're in the jungle instead of the woods. I don't own a single fan, and they were all sold out in town."

Liz took another sip of her drink.

"Am I really talking about the weather?" Jill asked. "Have I mentioned the word *asinine*?"

"Jill," Liz whispered. "It's okay. You don't have to—try so hard."

Jill's eyes filled. "I want to try, Lizzie," she said. "I want to do something to make this all right."

Their gazes met across the kitchen table. Then they both drank at the same time.

It was Jill's turn to whisper in the hushed room. "I can't, can I?"

Liz shook her head and Jill copied the move, though she didn't seem aware of it.

"I can't," Jill repeated. "I should know better than anyone that I can't do a goddamned thing to make anything all right."

Liz looked away. A portable island was covered with rows of beribboned jars, Roots' newest product line.

"Those look good," she said.

Jill turned her own head and nodded. "Lia did a great job. That cloth is all hand-cut."

Lia was their intern, a student recommendation from Paul. Liz got up and lifted a jar of rhubarb compote. A piece of calico encircled its lid, tied off with a length of organza. The jar's heft was pleasingly solid. These would do well at the weekend markets, and there were other possibilities, too. Restaurants, B&Bs.

"Liz," Jill said from behind. "I know this isn't exactly comfortable territory for you, but can I ask what you're going to do?"

Liz walked back to the table. "What do you mean, not comfortable territory?"

Jill stared at her blankly. "I didn't think that was going to be the controversial part of the question."

Liz fisted her hands on her hips.

"Come on, Lizzie. You're great at putting the plants in, getting them to grow, but who came up with the financing, the client base? Who decided to open Roots as a business in the first place?"

"What's that got to do with anything?"

Jill dabbed off her forehead with a cloth. "I just mean that you're not exactly the decisive one. The doer."

Liz grabbed her glass and took another drink, aware that she was trying to disguise the flush rising on her face.

"Which is fine," Jill continued. "Except that now you've got a family to put back together again. And this time, you can't ask Paul."

No amount of alcohol could hide the stain now. The best friend she'd been hugging a few minutes ago suddenly seemed deserving of a slap. Liz would've delivered it—was stepping forward, feet a little loose from the whiskey—but then she realized she didn't have an answer to the question.

"I don't know," she said, turning around in the small space. She picked up a different jar. Pickled asparagus spears, and gingham instead of calico. "I have no idea what I'm going to do."

"Can I make a suggestion?" Jill asked, standing up also.

Liz looked at her and nodded.

"I know that nobody can understand a marriage from the outside. And it's not like I have any experience in the area anyway." Jill shrugged, then began to fan her underarms beneath the thin straps of her tank. "Man, is it hot."

"Yes?" Liz said, half-impatient, half-annoyed.

Jill looked at her.

"Marriage?" Liz prompted.

Jill stopped fanning. "You just never seemed to—know Paul all that well to me. He called the shots, and you either went along with them, or did your best to hide that you weren't going along with them."

Liz thought of the treats Reid lifted from other kids—how his sleight of hand might even be explained by all the things that were forbidden him and Ally—and what she herself kept hidden from Paul in the day-to-day. From sports the kids played that awarded meaningless, plastic trophies machined in China to the bottled water that was served at games.

"And Paul was kind of there, coming down every now and again, but otherwise not really all that available. At least, that's how it looked from where I sat."

Liz felt anger rise. From where Jill sat. They both knew where that was. "So?"

Jill lifted her shoulders. "So maybe a good place to start is by getting to know him, really know who he was. I guess that's what I'm saying."

Someone stepped into the room, and they both looked up.

"Do you need something, hon?" Jill asked.

Her son was a big, hulking boy, man-sized at not quite fourteen. He stared at Liz.

"Do you remember Aunt Liz?"

Liz had diapered this boy, and driven him to enough Cub Scout meetings, hockey practices, and church sermons on Sundays that he used to call her car the limo. *Lizomine* he'd said once as a preschooler, delighting both Jill and Liz, and the coinage had stuck.

Andy shook his head back and forth. "Hello," he said politely to Liz.

"Hi, And." Liz swallowed the nickname when he stared blankly. "Hello, Andy."

He walked over to the coffeepot.

Jill stood up. "Not at night. Remember? It keeps you awake."

After a slow beat, Andy stepped back. He opened the refrigerator and took out a carton of milk, which he seemed to drain in a swallow. Until six months ago, he used to access Liz's fridge in the same casual, unconsidered way.

"Goodnight." Andy turned and left the room, steps sounding deliberately outside.

Jill and Liz's replies echoed back.

"No change?" Liz asked quietly.

He had been injured during last year's hockey season. The team wasn't scrimmaging or even doing drills, just skating around after practice, when Andy tripped and went into the boards. Head injuries could be a freak thing. Jill—and Liz by trickle down—had learned enough about concussions by now that they could suggest changes to the NHL.

Jill shook her head. "He's still holding at seventy-five percent, which leaves holes. Newer stuff usually, but in Andy's case it's a mix." She spoke with clipped heat. "It's okay. We've got him on this new regime—massive doses of fish oil—and it really seems to be working."

Once Jill would've snorted over the idea of alternative medicine the way she laughed about mothers who wouldn't let their kids watch TV on a playdate. But desperation drove you to new places. Liz understood that now.

"Well, that's good," she said. Wondering darkly, as if tonguing a sore spot, who had it worse. Was it better to have your children in some unknown location, but presumably doing okay? Or some carved-out version of the child you'd raised?

Jill nodded, three rapid times.

Liz felt a surge of sorrow as she stood. "Andy looks good. Still growing like a weed."

Her best friend gave her a smile whose ingredients only Liz would have recognized. Love, and remembrance—for the days when his size was the one worrisome thing about Andy—and a bitter, jerking regret.

"Yes," Jill said. "He does keep doing that."

Liz hugged her before going out into the gathering dark.

CHAPTER TWENTY-THREE

This time when she got out of the car, Liz approached the house from the side instead of the front. As she walked, her nose filled with a peaty scent, and she caught a glimpse of curling leaves.

Something was overgrowing the fence. Liz walked over to take a look.

The farm occupied two acres at the rear of the house, signaled by a painted sign hanging from a fence post. *Roots.*

Before there was a business, this was just Liz's solitary garden, penned to keep out the deer. Then Jill had begun to help. She proved to have not only a thumb green enough that the plot had quadrupled in size, but also a head for business. Soon the two of them were producing small but viable crops never before seen in the brutally brief Adirondack growing season. Poona Kheera cukes and micro-greens like mizuna and tatsoi, papery-skinned tomatillos and mulched asparagus as pale as vanilla ice cream.

The pursuit had married well with Paul's knowledge about resilient ways of planting, methods that weren't dependent on commercial fertilizers, yet that extended the growing season to nearly year-round. Paul had consulted as two room-sized cold frames were built, and soon Liz and Jill had far more bounty than they were able to ply neighbors and parents and teachers with.

They began turning their extra wares into pickles and jams and spreads, jarring them prettily, and before long they needed Lia to help with the overload.

Liz unlatched the gate and stepped past the mesh fencing onto a winding path. She braced her hips with her hands and took a look around.

It was the height of the season, and she and Jill had been spending four hours a day just staying on top of the weeds. In Liz's absence they had proliferated; the crops would be impacted if this hogweed and loosestrife and bittersweet couldn't be beaten back. Liz made a mental note to charge Lia with the task. Their intern didn't come from a farming background as most of Eastern Ag's students did. Lia was part of a new wave of farming hopefuls, young people for whom the pursuit was part avocation, part art. And as such, she wasn't fully acculturated to the life; the constant, changing needs of its cycle; and its twenty-four/seven chokehold.

Aware of hunger for the first time all day, Liz reached down and peeled a leaf of sweet cabbage from a closely clustered head. She chewed as she walked down the rows, making sure vines wound upward, snapping off any withered or overlarge stems from the varieties of kale.

She brushed dirt from her hands. A pocked moon had risen in the sky.

She was avoiding going inside. Jill's words had left a harsh and bracing taste in the back of her throat, but they had also given Liz an idea.

In the mudroom, she stepped out of her shoes.

Then she climbed the stairs and went into her husband's office.

Paul was an academic and the spaces he occupied reflected the role. While Liz devoted most of her time to being outside, Paul spent the same stretches cooped up. That was why indoor spaces always felt cluttered; their occupants were trying to push against unnatural bounds. Outdoors there was an endless offering; here Paul had been constrained by a desk and shelves and some spillover onto the floor.

Liz crouched down, fanning through piles of journals before reaching for some more. They gave off a meteor shower of dust and she sneezed. *Journal of Independent Farming. Permaculture in the Larger*

Culture. Tracts on genetic modification—its potential risks—and lengthy exegeses about the misuse of corn in ruminants and fowl. There was a journal that focused solely on the process of making soy protein isolate.

Nothing Liz wasn't used to hearing about, so frequently that the words had turned into a vague background thrum. This had been the bread and butter—the sprouted wheat and flax oil—of Paul's daily life.

She made neat stacks out of the volumes she'd looked at, two or three towers, then rose and crossed to Paul's desk. He hadn't taken his laptop wherever he had gone. She flicked on the machine, removing a stack of books from the chair so that she could sit. The dark was growing oppressive, pressing in from the hall, and Liz turned on a lamp.

She watched the computer boot up. It was an older machine; Paul spurned the latest upgrades as he did most forms of consumerism. He believed that the endless succession of new products was worse than a mere play for money; he saw it as a way to acclimate people to a life of constant consumption.

Over the churning of the hard drive, Liz heard some sort of rapping, and went out into the hallway to check.

There were windows along the hall, but a tap on one of them wouldn't have been audible from the study. Liz went downstairs, pulled open the front door, and stepped onto the porch in her stocking feet. The moon gave a silvery glow to her car, but there was no other vehicle visible. Nobody was around. The evening had finally cooled off; the lighter air was a relief.

Liz went back inside, pulling the door shut behind her.

She peered into the living and dining rooms, then checked the kitchen and mudroom just to make sure, but they were each empty. Liz did something then that she couldn't recall doing in all the years she had lived and gardened and raised children here. She turned the lock on the mudroom door. It swiveled slowly, unused to movement, before settling into place with a decided *clack*. Liz went back to the hall and latched the front door as well.

She walked upstairs, feet padding. At the top, she turned and looked down, leveling her shoulders. She'd never been scared in her own home, scared anywhere really. But fear was a constant companion now, and the house's grasp around her suddenly felt suffocating. Liz couldn't escape the dread awareness of whatever might be happening to Reid and Ally, and even that was just a blind for the worst fear of all: that she would never see her children again.

Paul's machine had booted. She used the mouse to start surfing the web, clicking the History button as soon as it appeared. The column that came up was blank.

Liz closed the browser and tried again, frowning, but the same thing resulted.

Had Paul scrubbed his search history? She checked—all of his emails had been deleted. Fully deleted, not just sent to *Trash*.

Paul had flipped the interior security lock, failed to fool the police, and allowed himself and his companion to be seen by the bellhop. But in this sector at least—as with his cell phone—he'd evinced some shrewdness.

Which had to mean there was something on the computer he didn't want her to see.

A pall of hopelessness settled over Liz. For a man who spent his days immersed in text, a digital trail had seemed likely to point in some direction. If it was blank, Liz didn't know which way to turn.

And then she noticed an icon for another search engine. She clicked it, and a tab popped up on the screen.

WELL, THIS IS EMBARRASSING, it said. FIREFOX HAS CRASHED. WOULD YOU LIKE TO RESTORE YOUR LAST SESSION?

Paul hadn't cleared his history; he'd just been using a different browser. And deleted emails notwithstanding, his ambivalent relationship with technology had allowed him to miss the fact that the Internet had crashed while he was in the process of shutting down.

Whatever Paul was doing the last time he'd been at this computer could be resurrected.

Liz let the arrow float over the options.

Yes, she clicked.

THE CHAT ROOM USER

Madeline Jennings sat on a huge purple bouncy ball in the waiting room. This office was brand-new, a softer, kinder breed of doctoring, and Madeline had fallen in love with it at her first appointment. In addition to the balls, which were supposed to prepare you for labor, there were ergo-something chairs she could actually get out of on her own, even at thirty-six weeks, with her belly as big as one of these balls. Women who already had children could let them wander off to a dedicated play space, close enough to keep an eye on, far enough away that the moms would get a little break. Madeline could imagine how appreciated that must be.

Not that she herself ever intended to do this again.

Her mother wouldn't let her.

Cara Jennings sat beside her. She'd come to every appointment except for that first one. If her mother had come the first time, then Madeline wouldn't be a patient in this practice, which considered bouncy balls a reasonable means of seating, and set out a tray of whole-grain muffins for expectant moms to snack on. Cara prepared Madeline's meals with a ruthless sort of precision. Calories were carefully counted so that Madeline didn't gain too much weight, and her mother didn't believe in any of the health crazes that had hijacked pregnancy in recent years.

"My grandmother smoked every day when she was with child,"

Cara would say. "Babies are hardier than we think. Children, too. They don't need to be told that every single thing they do is wonderful. A little shaming goes a long way when they act up."

But Madeline loved how they did things at Every Woman's Care. She wanted her baby's start to be pure and bright and colorful. And she loved the idea behind this practice—that everyone was entitled to a gentler kind of life.

There was a cluster of women as big-bellied as she, sitting on balls in another corner of the room. Their voices flitted from low murmurs to laughter; despite their obviously uncomfortable bulk, they seemed to be enjoying themselves. The women reached down frequently to touch their bellies—something Madeline had to stop herself from doing since her mother didn't think it was acceptable to touch your body in public—and rolled back and forth, complaining about pains in their knees and their backs.

Cara Jennings didn't approve of complaining either. Mumping and grumping, she called it. Just get on with things and your day will pass before you know it.

But Madeline didn't want to kill time. She wanted to enjoy these days and the life growing inside her—a real life she'd created! It was a girl, she just knew it. But someone to moan with about the associated difficulties would've been nice, too.

Madeline took part in several pregnancy boards; they were the only place she could get any privacy from her mother. Online, she had a taste of the chat that the women here were indulging in. It could get a little grisly for her tastes—terms like *mucous plug* and *perineal massage* were bandied about as if people were talking about the weather—but Madeline still enjoyed the companionship. She made a mental note to ask about the topic she was now overhearing the flock of women discuss. Water birth. It sounded like such a peaceful way to enter the world. There was no sound under water. Madeline was fairly sure, though she'd been unable to bring herself to confirm this, that her mother intended to be in the delivery room with her. It would be nice to spare the baby a few extra seconds of hearing her grandmother's voice.

Madeline wished she could waddle over to the group of women, make herself part of their easy laughter and equally easy bemoaning, and ask if any of them was considering a water birth. Was it dangerous? That wouldn't be her mother's objection, though. Cara Jennings would simply think it was nuts, one more way to try and up the ante of living away from a brute, bare-bones, just-get-through approach.

What's wrong with a bed? Madeline could hear her mother say. Perhaps Cara would even make a rare joke, her flat lips forming a scythe. *You made the baby in a bed. So have him in it.*

You got through sex. You got through pregnancy. You got through life.

Madeline wanted more than that. The women over there seemed to have it. They even seemed to be enjoying their complaining.

"Madeline?"

The physician's assistants at Every Woman's wore colorful scrubs with pictures of ducks and balloons on them. The one who had just stepped into the waiting room—called the *rest area* here—was Madeline's favorite. She was pregnant herself, and constantly touching her stomach, only half-consciously. Madeline was sure the PA wasn't aware of the faint smile that bloomed on her face whenever she reached down to her round little bump.

Madeline got up awkwardly, feeling the ball slip away beneath her. It was headed right toward the clump of chattering women. One reached out and stopped its roll, giving Madeline a smile. Madeline flushed, and dropped her gaze. She looked at her mother, rising seamlessly from her chair.

The PA stopped Cara as she made her way to the door in front of Madeline.

"Mrs. Jennings, we spoke about this," the PA said. Brief pat to her stomach, causing Madeline's mother to frown. "Madeline is going to provide a urine sample and step on the scale. You don't need to be there for that."

Cara's frown turned furious. "I'll thank you to watch your language. Not because I give any truck to the notion that these babies can understand things in—what would you call it?—utero," she went on with an expression of distaste. "But because bodily functions are best left behind closed doors."

Madeline experienced a deep flush of empathy for this PA she so liked. Cara Jennings had made her seem as disgusting as if she'd given a sample herself, right here in front of everyone. But when Madeline caught a glimpse of the PA's face as she tried to squeeze past, she saw that the PA didn't look embarrassed at all. In fact, she was regarding Madeline's mother as if she were the one who should be ashamed.

In the doctor's office, Cara Jennings took a seat first. "Thank goodness," she said with a snort. "None of those ridiculous playthings in here."

It took Dr. Shelley a moment to get it. "Our offices don't have as much space as the rest area because of the examining tables."

Even those were extra padded, and had nice, soft blankets at the bottom. So you wouldn't feel cold or exposed, Dr. Shelley had explained during Madeline's first visit. Madeline curled her toes beneath the fleecy fabric now.

"But the balls are wonderful for pregnant women's backs," the doctor went on. "Are you keeping up with your exercises, Madeline? Kegels especially?"

Madeline nodded, feeling her cheeks stain. She glanced down at the globe of her belly, waiting for the reassuring moment when the ultrasound wand picked up the railroad beat of the baby's heart. Maybe because she didn't touch the baby all that often, Madeline had a hard time believing she was actually there. Cara spent so many hours overseeing things at home. Madeline had no trouble believing that she might come into Madeline's bedroom at night and do something to take away the one thing Madeline had ever made for herself.

Dr. Shelley helped Madeline slip out of her gown, and handed a ballooning shirt back to her. Cara had chosen all of Madeline's maternity wear. *I don't know where pregnant women got the idea that it was all right to let clothing cling to their bellies,* Cara had said in the store.

The doctor spoke in a low tone. "It's getting close enough that we really do need to come up with your birth plan."

Madeline had been avoiding this. She looked down at the tile floor.

Dr. Shelley switched her focus. "Mrs. Jennings?"

Madeline's mother looked up sharply.

"I'd like to spend a few moments with Madeline," Dr. Shelley said. "Alone."

"That won't be necessary," Cara Jennings replied.

The doctor gave Madeline a small, encouraging smile. "It may not be. But your daughter is eighteen years of age, so unless she objects, I would ask you to step outside into our rest area for a little while. There are muffins and tea there you can help yourself to."

Madeline continued to stare at the floor. Every row had forty-seven tiles, each speckled like an exotic bird's egg.

"That's quite all right," Cara said, taking two quick strides toward the door. "I won't be needing any tea."

The door closed with a decided *thunk*.

Once her mother was gone, the room seemed to inflate and expand. It wasn't cramped at all anymore; you could fit a million bouncy balls in here.

Madeline smiled at Dr. Shelley. "Do you think it's a girl?"

The doctor smiled back, but it was fleeting. "We can find out. I told you that, right?"

Madeline shook her head. "I want to be surprised." She allowed herself to touch her stomach lightly. "Besides, I already know."

"Madeline," the doctor said, "I was wondering if you had any sources of support besides your mother. Friends? Other parents-to-be you can talk to?"

Madeline thought about the women in the waiting room—the rest area—and shook her head again.

"How about the baby's father?" Dr. Shelley asked.

Madeline's face heated. "No. I don't see him at all. My mother won't let me."

Dr. Shelley was silent for a second. "I see."

Her face looked lined and drawn. Madeline would've done a lot to erase that expression.

"I go online," she offered. "To visit the pregnancy boards."

The doctor regarded her. "You have a computer? Of your own?"

Madeline nodded. After a moment she said, "My mother wouldn't know how to use it."

A look of such understanding passed between them that Madeline felt her eyes fill. She cried so easily these days. She reached down and patted the baby, letting her hand linger this time. The baby kicked, and Madeline's eyes spilled over.

The doctor's nails tapped out a percussive rhythm. She glanced away, then back at Madeline. Finally she located a Post-it pad and began writing something down. "You might want to reach out to these people the next time you're online. Tell them I sent you. I'm giving you a password, which I'd ask that you not share."

Madeline frowned, accepting the small slip of paper. "But I have plenty of places to go online. If anything, there are too many of them. I never know which to choose."

The doctor's face was grave. "I'm directing you to a particular thread on this site." She pointed to two scrawled words. "I promise you won't find anything else like it online."

Madeline looked at the note. The password caused her eyes to fill again. It read: *motherdoctor.*

But the website url was just plain confusing.

PEW.

CHAPTER TWENTY-FOUR

One by one, windows were opening on Paul's screen.

Come on, Liz thought, with a mental rub of her hands. *I hope you really did yourself in, you bastard. I'll hunt you down as if you left a road map.*

Outside it was now deep dark. Liz flicked on another lamp.

This was the third night in a row she hadn't kissed her babies goodnight.

She hated her husband with a lethal, hot fury.

The machine finally stopped churning.

There weren't as many windows as Liz would've liked—her husband's last session must have been brief—but she clicked on the first with a small lick of hope, as if she were rolling dice. What did the kids used to say, playing board games? *Mommy needs a new pair of shoes.*

Mommy needs her children back.

Tears sparked in Liz's eyes and she blinked.

It was a site about poly-culture farming. There was text and graphs explaining how the purchase of equipment invited debt and ultimate dependence on government subsidies, which in turn led to constriction of variety in crops. Pieces about how smaller yield paradoxically meant greater nourishment. The return of diverse small-scale farming for a new world order.

Liz had heard it all a thousand times before.

Her husband had been planning to bring the family to Junction

Bridge on a supposed vacation, then abscond with their kids. And the night before they'd left he'd been reading what he always did, as if he wasn't about to set off a nuclear bomb in their lives.

Liz clicked on the next window.

It was Eastern Ag's website. The fall course schedule had a ticker-tape roster of the season's football games scrolling along at the bottom.

One final window to open. Liz clicked on it.

Something fell over outdoors.

This time there could be no doubt, and Liz jumped in her seat. The hand she'd been holding the mouse with jogged, and Liz looked down in a panic, afraid that she had inadvertently closed the window.

She frowned at the banner at the top of the page. All capital letters spelling out one word. *PEW.* A password was required to get in.

Something else banged. The wind must be really picking up out there. Maybe it would finally cool off.

Liz Googled the three-letter term, getting links about a charitable trust. But those letters were in a different font, and not all in caps. It funded some sort of think tank, whose projects didn't seem relevant, although Liz bookmarked the page for later.

Another noise came from outside, this one even louder, a great clawing of wood.

Their nearest neighbor, splitting logs? His house was too far away. They'd never heard anything from any of the houses out this way.

The noise had come from the direction of the gardens.

Jill or Lia maybe, arrived to do some work?

Liz was used to hearing things outside. Deer nudged at the fencing, smaller rodents crawled beneath. Branches cracked when bats or owls flew. The country was never silent; nature presented a constant backdrop. But the sounds she'd been hearing tonight had a different tenor.

A human one.

Liz left Paul's computer behind, making sure the windows remained open.

In the midst of walking to the door, she began to run.

Outside, a child was crying.

The fields lay in shadows, gate securely fastened. The sign with *Roots* spelled out in twisting vines swayed back and forth, clattering in the rising wind. Liz jogged past it toward where she thought the crying had come from.

"Reid?" she called out, unable to help herself. "Ally?"

Clouds blew across the sky and suddenly it was as cold as autumn. Liz drew near the woods that bordered their house. She pushed branches back, trying to shield her face from the flutter of leaves. She needed a flashlight, and was cursing herself for her heedless rush outside. But what else could she have done? Even in the scant seconds that had passed, Reid or Ally—if that's who it had been—might've been taken away.

A twig snapped beneath her feet. Liz stared at the occluded moon, which didn't cast enough light to see into this tangle of woods, and bit back a sob of frustration.

"Reid!" she cried. "Ally! Are you there?"

There came a great leathery flap of wings, a bird taking off clumsily from the ground, disturbed by her presence. It wasn't as close as it sounded—noise traveled in the night—but still, Liz had to work to quiet her heart.

Then a hiss emerged from a stand of trees to her right, and Liz spun around. She squinted, trying to see between mossy trunks. She wedged herself past a tall oak, its branches laden with leaves. She stepped into a space on the left.

A few yards off, a spear of wood had broken off another tree, leaving raw, exposed wood. That must have made the sound she'd heard from Paul's study. Beneath the split, a child's small form huddled on the ground, and beside him crouched a woman, commanding the child to hush.

Liz walked in their direction, picking her way over clumps of forest debris. The night had lost all potential and all threat. She moved incautiously, not caring anymore if she was caught unaware by a stabbing twig.

"Are you all right?" Her tone sounded dull in her ears.

The woman got unsteadily to her feet. For a moment, Liz wondered if she might be drunk. She looked down at the boy, who was perhaps four, his face dirty and tear-streaked.

"I'm sorry," the woman said. "He fell."

She said it as if climbing trees on someone else's property was a perfectly reasonable thing to do in the night.

"Who are you?" Liz asked. "What are you doing here?"

"I'm sorry," the woman said again. "I suppose we're a bit lost. I must've had the wrong address."

"Do you live around here?"

Before the woman could respond, the little boy began to whimper. "Mommy, it hurts."

Liz took a look at the child through the penetrating dark. There was a blotchy, wet patch on the back of his head. Head wounds bled a lot, she knew, but still, this required treatment.

"You'd better come inside," she said.

Liz turned and led their small, injured caravan out of the woods.

She had locked the mudroom door, Liz recalled, ruing her earlier precaution. Had this been what she'd been hearing all night— a mother and child nosing around her house? Why would anybody do that? She left both of them waiting by the side so she could go in the front, then walked through the house to the mudroom. When she'd finally gotten the door unlocked, she opened it to find both of them gone.

Liz stepped onto the flagstone patio, looking around. A minivan was parked some ways down the road, and the mother was hurrying her child along to it.

"Cody! Come on!" she urged.

Liz ran after them. "Why don't you come in? I have first-aid stuff for his cut."

"I have a kit in the car!" the woman cried over her shoulder. "But thank you!"

"But—" Liz came to a helpless stop. "Who are you?" she called. "What were you doing on my property?"

The woman paused also. The two were almost at the car.

"I'm sorry—I don't think I was supposed to be here now!"

Then the woman tugged the boy forward, keying the automatic sliding door and hustling her child inside.

Where was she supposed to be? Liz thought, as she watched them drive off.

CHAPTER TWENTY-FIVE

Tim Lurcquer showed up on her porch the next morning, dressed in uniform. He had broadened since high school, and he somehow looked a little taller as well, as if his new position suited him. His eyes were the same dark, penetrating pools and his hair had lost nothing to time.

"I'm sorry to come so early," he said. "I have to be at the barracks in half an hour."

"I was awake," Liz said, stepping back to allow him inside. "Let me put on some coffee."

In the few moments she'd been able to attain unconsciousness last night, her rest had been overrun by what she'd learned on that website Paul had visited. Or what she hadn't learned. Letters danced through the shards of her dreams. Ps and Es and Ws.

She had been unable to guess Paul's password. It wasn't any of the ones they used for online banking, Internet shopping, or the private code the school wanted all children to have.

"Tim?" Liz said, pouring coffee. She had started to add milk—the way Paul took the one cup he allowed himself per day—when Tim put out a hand to stop her.

"Black is fine. Thanks."

Liz looked down at his hand on hers. She set the jug of milk on the counter.

"You were going to say something?" he asked, lifting his cup.

She gathered her thoughts. "Something strange happened last night."

He looked at her.

"A mother and her son were here in the woods near my house."

Tim put down his empty cup. "What happened?"

Liz described the brief encounter.

"Did you get the license plate of the van?"

It hadn't even occurred to her. She shook her head miserably.

"Hey, it's okay," Tim said. "Most people don't."

Liz turned around on a patch of kitchen floor. The one real lead she might've had and she hadn't even recognized it for what it was.

"I tend to distrust coincidences," Tim said, contradicting her thoughts. "Your kids disappear, another one shows up."

Liz looked at him.

"I'll ask the men who were on last night if anything matching the description of that vehicle came in. Tell me what the people looked like."

Liz did, still feeling sick inside. The license plate. It had been right there, hers for the taking. "More coffee?"

Tim shook his head. "Listen, I checked into a few things."

Liz set the coffeepot down on the counter with a brittle *thwack*. She'd been so consumed that she'd forgotten Tim must've had a reason for coming all the way out here.

"Your husband hasn't used any of the credit cards you gave me," Tim said. "There have been no withdrawals from either of your bank accounts."

Liz frowned, questions beginning to coalesce in her mind.

Tim was watching her. "It's pretty hard to hide these days," he said. "What this means is that your husband isn't leaving a record of his movements. And what that means is, he either prepared long and hard for this beforehand or he's gone someplace where there's no record to be left."

Liz told Tim about the site she had found, or almost found, and he promised to check out PEW on his end. "Unless you just want to find some kid with mad skills," he suggested lightly, brushing off the gray shirt of his uniform and straightening his hat as he left.

His comment gave Liz an idea. They probably couldn't help with her password woes, but Eastern Ag *was* a repository of kids with skills. And it was where Paul had spent most of his time.

Liz caught a glimpse of herself in the mirror as she was about to leave, and stopped short. How could she have allowed Tim to see her like this? Not Tim, that wasn't what she meant, but anyone? Her hair was matted and her skin pasty. Her eyes looked sunken into caves. The clothes she was wearing were the same ones she'd had on in Junction Bridge. The Eastern Ag students would never open up to this crazed hag, no matter whose wife she was. Maybe especially given whose wife she was.

Liz rubbed her face with one hand. She wouldn't have believed a transformation this complete could take place in a matter of days.

On the other hand, it had taken less time than that to rid her of everything.

She climbed laboriously into the shower and located a change of clothes before setting out on her day.

CHAPTER TWENTY-SIX

The students who worked most closely with Paul tended to congregate in a small office he'd procured for them. It used to be a supply closet, but Paul, the consummate recycler, had reallocated the space. Supplies that had mostly been gathering dust had been put to good use, and Paul had found some armchairs and a table destined for Wedeskyull's Share/Care program. The hot plate used to belong in Liz and Paul's own kitchen, as did many of the chipped mugs. Liz recognized them as she nudged the door farther open and walked inside.

Lia sat on one of the scruffy chairs. She was Paul's most advanced student, doing a thesis on micro-farming. Liz had been surprised when Paul suggested she intern for them; she and Jill jokingly called Roots the garden that had grown, and they certainly didn't consider it a farm.

Three students Liz didn't recognize occupied the other chairs. All of them were pecking or scrolling away on tablets, the modern-day equivalent of heads being buried in books. Liz gave a small cough and everyone looked up.

"Liz!" Lia said, startled. She set aside her tablet and rose in one fluid motion. The high blades of her cheekbones had taken on a guilty flush and Liz had to stop herself from rushing to the girl and grabbing her arms. Lia knew something—how could it have taken Liz so long to think of this? Paul's students, maybe her own intern, were going to lead Liz to her children.

"I'm sorry I haven't been out to the farm in a few days," Lia said. "The weeds must be getting out of control."

Liz looked at her, silently urging the girl on.

"That bad?" Lia said, fidgeting with her hair. "I'll be there today. Soon as I get done with a few things." She gestured to her tablet.

Liz felt everything inside her deflate. Lia had been feeling badly about not working her usual hours when Liz was gone. A little mice-play-while-the-cat-was-away. She looked around at the others. "Have you seen Paul?"

They tilted their heads in her direction, their expressions uncertain.

"Professor Daniels," Lia explained to the others, still winding spiky black hair around her fingers.

Understanding seemed to dawn among them. As if a reporter had called the president by his first name at a press conference.

"Right," Liz said, still holding her position by the door. "Professor Daniels."

"Classes don't start for six more days," Lia told her, speaking rather slowly and distinctly, as if Liz were unwell. "We thought he was away with you."

Nods from everyone in the small room.

Liz looked at their upturned, innocent expressions, and she couldn't deny a flick of anticipated pleasure. *You think your professor's so great? Well, let me tell you something.*

She pictured disgust crawling over their faces as they finally took in the truth, and wished that Paul were here to see it. But when she had finished telling them what their professor had done, their looks hadn't changed much.

"What do you mean, Professor Daniels went somewhere?" asked a boy slouching in his chair. He had a triangular scruff of beard on his chin that gave him a faintly vampiric appearance. "He's my thesis chair this semester."

A female student with long blond dreads nodded, her expression reflecting pride. "Jake's graduating early," she explained, gazing adoringly at the boy who had just spoken. "He scored a killer job down-state. With the government. Thanks mostly to Professor Daniels."

"Sara, enough." Jake appeared less embarrassed than annoyed by the girl's excessive praise. He looked down at his screen, fingers flicking rapidly. "I don't have any email from him," he said. "He'll be here. He has to review my methods section."

The certainty in his voice assailed Liz and she crossed the tiny space, looming over Jake in his chair.

He recoiled. The girl reached out and touched his arm, dropping her hand to rearrange the folds of her peasant skirt when Jake didn't acknowledge the gesture.

"Look," Liz said through gritted teeth. "You don't have any email from Paul because he's completely out of contact. He's not emailing—he doesn't even have his cell phone."

"That makes sense." A boy who hadn't spoken until now looked up. He was quintessentially Ag with his buzz cut and jeans, the type of student who had comprised the population before it was invaded by Lestat and his dreadlocked love. "Professor Daniels has such a love-hate relationship with tech. Remember when he made us go a week without using our phones?"

Nods and smiles of reminiscence.

Liz wanted to reach out and shake every single one of them. They were all so placid in their regard, so hopelessly clueless. But they spent as much time with Paul as she herself did. These kids might know something, even if they didn't know they knew it.

Lia came over to Liz and spoke gently. "Did you say he's taken Reid and Ally?"

Hearing her children's names brought on a crushing pressure behind Liz's eyes. She tried to nod, but her head felt like it was caught in a vise.

Lia was guiding her. "Liz. Here. Sit down."

Liz felt her legs give way. She sank onto a coarsely cushioned chair.

"That's impossible. Professor Daniels would never do something like that," said the girl who had the crush on Jake. Sara.

Liz closed her eyes against the nods and statements of assent that arose.

It hadn't always been like this for Paul at school. His unwillingness to be diplomatic had cost him friends and promotions until the collegiate culture began moving in his direction, almost as if he were the moon pulling the tide. Right up until the day he had squired her children away, Liz would've said that these kids were right. Her husband would be incapable of deception, of masking a single one of his many thoughts, beliefs, and convictions.

"Guys," she said, eyes still shut, "I know how much you love—admire—Professor Daniels. Believe me, I felt the same things for him for years." She took in a breath of air that tasted stale. "And he deserves it. Paul—Professor Daniels is capable of some remarkable things."

"*Extraordinary* things," Adoring Girl said.

"He's inspired me in a way nobody else ever did," said Jake.

"He's just so damn smart," added the second boy. He rubbed his head, trying to flatten the bristles. "Remember that whole unit on how water's going to be this century's oil?"

"Embargoes," Jake agreed. "Water cartels."

"But the really brilliant part is he knows what to do about it. That filtration system he found—"

"His desalination theory—"

Liz felt a scream building inside her. If she couldn't put a stop to this, she was going to do something a lot worse than desecrate their image of Paul.

"I know all of that," Liz said. "Most of it anyway."

Her words were lost in an excited brew of memories and ideas.

"Listen!" she cried.

The chatter continued.

"Goddamnit, I said listen!"

A shocked silence finally fell. Liz opened her eyes and took in the entire earnest ring of them. "I was there for all of that. And more."

They were looking at her now with a blend of fear and interest.

"I remember the good old days before global warming when the energy crisis was just about fuel shortages. Paul's father refused to wait on line, and Paul learned to run a car on ethanol they grew and distilled themselves. It was great. It's all just great." Liz held up a hand before the admiring clamor could begin again. "But Paul's done something a lot less noble now," she went on over the protests she could see mounting. "And it's deprived me of my children."

The faces that gazed back at her were as blank as a rolled-down shade. Even Lia refused to meet her eyes.

Liz felt the solid wall of their obstruction, and her body sagged in the chair. She knew this particular brand of unwillingness, borne of the disbelief that Paul could be anything besides the image he presented. She'd bought that image for the better part of two decades. Nobleman, thinker, provider, chief. A Robin Hood, taking bounty from the greedy lords of capitalism and spreading it out amongst the people. A visionary who would lead those people to a better day. These students weren't resisting her only because she threatened their idea of Paul. Liz was threatening the entire world they stood to inherit.

"Is there anything?" she asked in a whisper. "I know this must all seem hard to believe, but is there anything that Professor Daniels was teaching—or talking about—last year that might give you an idea of what he's doing now?"

Matching faces met her gaze. Heads shook at an identical pace.

"Sorry."

"No, nothing."

Liz dropped her head. Scuffmarks and scratches formed a frazzled pattern on the floor.

"Would you like some tea?" Sara asked. "It's herbal, from right around here. Professor Daniels doesn't allow coffee or real tea, of course. The miles traveled are far and away the worst. Except for maybe pineapples. Or non-hearty kiwis."

"The mix is made at Mrs. Daniels's farm," Lia said to the others. "She knows its carbon footprint." She turned to Liz, having the grace to look uncomfortable. "Would you like some?"

Liz's response emerged brokenly. "No. No tea."

She struggled to rise, but fell backward into the chair. Jake jumped up to help her, and she held out a hand, warding him off. He flinched, and Sara guided him into her reach while Liz finally got to her feet and pushed past all of them, feeling their breath and their heat and the pent-up energy inside them as she made her way out.

CHAPTER TWENTY-SEVEN

The students may not have known anything, but Liz had gotten something out of the time she spent in that small, airless space. Only Paul Daniels could stick a bunch of kids into a column of closet and make them think that he was Superman.

Still, the place had been a repository of password possibilities. Paul's students were the fastest ticket to whatever he was thinking about these days. *Water cartels, embargoes, filtration systems,* and *desalination.* Liz had glanced at the screens on each tablet to catch key words. *Closed-loop farming. Humanure. Rooftop-ready soil.*

Liz was headed down the hall when she noticed the secretary's door standing open. She backtracked to the department, then crossed the wide corridor.

"Marjorie. Hi."

Marjorie had filled this position since Paul had been a student himself, and she wore her seventy or so years well, mostly by not trying to hide them. Her steely hair fell in a neat bob, and her eyeglass frames were fashionable.

"Mrs. Daniels! I thought the family was on vacation," Marjorie cried, rising from her wooden seat. Paul imposed upgrade-free living on the department as a whole. Marjorie's desk was the same gunmetal gray as her hair, its gouges rusted, and whatever pattern had once been on the rug was no longer detectable.

Liz should've been used to the sinking feeling by now, the jolt her knees gave, her body loosening against the door frame. How did no one—no matter how close to them Paul had been—know anything about this? Tim's statement about it being hard to hide came back to her. Paul Daniels didn't do covert. He was in-your-face, larger-than-life. At least he was right up until the night he had vanished.

"Mrs. Daniels? Are you all right?"

"Paul isn't going to be here to teach," Liz said abruptly.

Marjorie frowned. "Oh no. Has he gotten sick?"

Liz barked a laugh. "I don't know. You tell me."

The secretary frowned.

Liz straightened from her slump. "I don't know where Paul is. He could be sick, but I rather doubt it. He's made off with our children. I'm guessing you don't know anything about that."

"Your children!" Marjorie's gasp was genuine. "Mrs. Daniels, that's—"

"Crazy. I know."

"I was going to say, not like Paul at all." Marjorie paused. "Here." She guided Liz into the office, shutting the door. "Now, what do you mean, he's made off?"

Liz recounted the story soliloquy-style. The horror was that she was growing used to her speech, like an actor who had learned her lines. Except that in reality, her whole life with Paul had been an act, and now she was *un*learning them.

Marjorie shook her head back and forth, tsking her tongue. "I don't know what to say. I just can't imagine Professor Daniels doing anything like this."

"I know," Liz said when the secretary fell silent. "I couldn't either. I suppose I've had a few days to wrap my head around the flip side to Paul's greatness."

The secretary looked up, and Liz waited for a display of outrage, the electrified defense. But perhaps Marjorie had also left the Church of Paul at some point because she didn't say anything. Her nails, polished clear, clicked against the surface of her desk.

"I wish I knew what to say, Mrs. Daniels."

"I wish you did, too," Liz said quietly. "Well, at least now you can make arrangements to cover his classes."

Marjorie was staring into the hall as Liz took her leave.

Liz wound down the halls, searching for the set of doors she'd come through, but she had gotten twisted around. There was a shortcut through the gym and Liz took it, coming out by the pool. The sight made her turn her head, seized by a surge of yearning. Reid had never looked back after his near-drowning in toddlerhood, and it was both children's favorite treat to come swim at the school. Ally also loved exploring the ornamental gardens, although she maintained that she preferred the naturalistic borders of Roots: its swaying meadow of wildflowers from which flower shops and event planners might one day purchase stock.

What were Reid and Ally doing now? Was being in Paul's comparatively rarefied care a bonus, or were they unhappy every day? Liz hoped fervently for the former. Please, let Paul be doing something that the kids would characterize as fun. And let him have come up with something to tell them, an explanation that made sense. The idea that Reid and Ally thought Liz wanted this—was okay being apart from them—turned her clutch of longing into a chokehold.

Shouts and jeers, boys trading insults amidst laughter, came from behind a locker room door. Liz swerved in the other direction, hunting an exit. Filtered sunlight shone down the hall, and the yellow bars glinted off a glass case along one wall. Liz paused. Inside the case were a few faded green pennants with gold lettering on them and twin trophies from back-to-back years. There was a row of newspaper articles, the usual rah-rah stuff about local boys, coach honored, money raised for new this or that. One story on faded paper was tacked up front and center, its headline blaring.

EASTERN AG SLATED TO TAKE DIVISION

Which division? Liz wondered wryly. Twenty?

Next to the piece was a slightly blurred photograph that erased all traces of wryness.

In addition to the older man beaming in the shot, probably the coach, there were two boys, arms slung around each other's bulked-up shoulders, grins as wide as their pads.

One of them was Paul.

CHAPTER TWENTY-EIGHT

The helmet and uniform in Paul's closet at home. Even the ticker-tape of games that had been scrolling along one of the last pages Paul had open on his computer. Liz had assumed he had been looking at course rosters, but what if the football schedule had been his focus?

Why had she never heard about Paul's football career?

Marjorie had worked at the college back when this photo was taken. The last time, it seemed, that Eastern Ag had had a winning season.

A couple of boys, wet from the shower, ran past her, sneakers drumming.

Liz quickly outpaced them.

The secretary was already gone for the day, the department door locked. These were the last meandering days of summer, and Marjorie had been good to come in to get things ready for Paul, but working long hours went above and beyond even that call.

A click of heels sounded along the adjacent hall, and Liz ran. Marjorie hadn't quite reached the exit yet. Liz called out, and the secretary turned, frowning as she headed back. The two of them met in the middle.

"I feel terrible about what's happened," Marjorie said.

It seemed a strange way to put it, as if Marjorie were somehow responsible.

"I hadn't realized that Paul played football," Liz said in reply.

Marjorie's back sagged, and she suddenly looked every one of her seven decades. "I hadn't realized that you didn't realize that."

Now it was Liz's turn to frown. "What do you mean?"

Marjorie checked her wristwatch. "Do you have a few minutes? The library should be open."

Liz felt her brow pucker again.

The secretary turned, leading the way.

It was Eastern Ag's oldest building, a noble stack of bricks. Marjorie pushed one of the heavy doors open, twisting a filigreed knob. The air inside was cool to the point of chilliness, and a deep hush lay over the space. Dust twirled in the sun shafts beneath a skylight, and shelves of books soared. Not even the dimly glowing bank of computers could detract from the sense that by walking through the doors, you had entered a bygone age.

Marjorie strode past the front desk, and a curving stone staircase. A couple of sharp turns brought them to a less majestic section of the library: vinyl tiles on a narrow flight of steps. Liz raised her eyebrows doubtfully, but Marjorie was already descending at a good clip. She waited for Liz at the bottom, then led the way between a narrow length of stacks. Marjorie came to a stop by a shelf that held a row of green volumes with letters stamped on them in gold.

Yearbooks.

After some study and running of fingers over dates, Marjorie pulled one out. The cover looked muted, a little less bright, compared to those from more recent years. Marjorie paged through the volume to the athletic team photos in back, then held the book out flat for Liz to see.

Liz was unprepared for the fury that settled over her as soon as she glimpsed Paul's face. Like a young buck he was, head-tossed and proud. Liz reached for the glossy sheet with his image on it. The edge of paper sliced the tip of her thumb and Liz sucked in a sharp, hissing breath. She had no idea why Marjorie had brought her down here. The list of names beneath the team photo didn't mean anything to her, aside from Paul's. The candid shots were equally lacking in information, besides the fact that Paul had been captured several times in concert with a teammate named Michael Brady.

Marjorie turned the page.

The next one was filled entirely with a photo of Michael Brady. *In Memoriam* read the words underneath.

Liz looked up, then down again.

Michael Brady had been a good-looking boy; a unique brand of fiery vigor had been preserved in the shot. The photo caught him leaping toward an opposing player, the look on his face like one you might see on a lion about to tear apart a gazelle.

"What a tragedy," Liz murmured. "He couldn't have been more than twenty-one or -two."

"He would've turned twenty that year," Marjorie said.

Liz shook her head. "Paul's teammate?"

"Paul's best friend."

"Oh no." Liz set the yearbook back on its shelf. "Best friends? Paul never mentioned him. He didn't even really tell me that he'd played football."

Marjorie peered at her. "He was the quarterback. You never knew that?"

Liz looked down. "You know, it's funny. As much a part of Paul's life as Eastern Ag is, he hates to talk about his connection to the school. I used to ask him sometimes how he could work here, yet not enjoy reminiscing, talking about the glory days. I never got a good answer."

Paul would change the subject to the here and now, something he was teaching, or doing in the department.

"He stayed because of Michael Brady," Marjorie said. "Because Michael never got to leave."

The skin on Liz's arms prickled. "What happened to him?"

Marjorie frowned, wrinkles appearing like canyons on her brow. "There was a car accident on Wicket Road. That's a mean road— curvy as the devil's tongue. Trees hang over it like beasts. Paul was driving, and he had been drinking some, according to the police."

"He *had*?" Liz could hardly imagine it. A carefree, irresponsible Paul who didn't always maintain his hold on the righteous position?

Was this what Matthew's note referred to, the drunk-driving accident that had killed Paul's best friend? Liz shivered again. The sun
was lost down here, and it was cold in the basement.

The secretary seemed to be following her thoughts. "Michael
didn't die in the crash."

Liz turned to her.

"He survived the accident. He might've survived indefinitely, or at
least for many years."

Liz nodded, although she wasn't sure how to parse the meaning.
"Well, that's better than what I was thinking," she began.

"It's worse than what you were thinking," Marjorie said sharply.
"Michael was paralyzed. Completely. He couldn't even blink. His eyes
ran and ran with tears. They gave him a drug to stop the flow, but
that caused terrible dryness. Eventually he had to be blindfolded."

Liz flinched at the image.

"And that was the least of the horrors he had to endure," Marjorie
went on. "Or would have had to endure if he had lived."

"What happened?"

The secretary took a breath. "Someone put him out of his misery.
Michael was smothered to death the day before he was to be moved
to a rehab unit."

"Oh my God. Oh no." What a cascade of tragedy to descend on
boys so young, kids really, just ready for the prime of their lives.

Marjorie's mouth compressed. "The team lost its star player that
year and also its coach."

"Why the coach?"

Marjorie reached out and took Liz's hand in her own papery one.
"This is why I felt the need to tell you this now."

Liz stared down at their entangled grips.

"It was Coach Allgood who supplied mercy, to the extent that
that's what it was. I suppose he felt responsible in some way." The
secretary gripped Liz's hand harder. "Coach killed Michael Brady. He
went to prison for it. And Mrs. Daniels, he was just released. His
sentence ended on August twenty-second."

Liz looked up and realized that Marjorie had also put it together.

August twenty-second was the day they had left on vacation.

CHAPTER TWENTY-NINE

"Do you have a little more time?" Marjorie asked. "There's something else I think you should see. The end of the story, so to speak."

But Liz had the feeling it would only be the beginning.

They climbed the stairs, Liz feeling the secretary's laborious step in her own tread, and went outside through the grand set of doors. The library lawn was lush, with a scattering of fallen leaves upon it. Students as bright as the leaves dotted the ground, plugged in to various degrees. Some hunched over laptops; others texted on phones; a few seemed to be doing nothing except enjoying the placid scene, until you noticed the tiny cones in their ears.

"Two hundred people and they're all completely alone," Marjorie observed.

It was true. The expected sound track when this many people were gathered in one place was damped. You heard more clicking and beeps than hellos or shouts of traded laughter.

A trio of boys came pushing and clobbering out of the library. They veered around Liz and Marjorie without so much as a glance. Liz wondered when she had crossed that valley, making the switch from college guys sizing her up to picturing Reid as one of them.

Reid. Ally.

Marjorie approached what looked like a solid barricade of trees, showing no intention of stopping. A small path became apparent at the last moment, threading its way through the woods. The sun-dappled column of greenery ended, and they came out in a shallow cup of meadow at the bottom of a hill.

How had Liz never discovered this part of campus? Ally would've loved it here, she thought with a pang. The grasses were wild and tangled, dotted all over with merrybells, Dutchman's breeches, and azure bluets. A veritable song of color of the sort that Liz and Jill had labored to duplicate at Roots. The perfection of blooms, the intensity of their tints, distracted Liz's eye for a moment.

Marjorie had come to a stop several yards ahead. A mixture of bluegrass and rye had been planted there, and mowed in a carefully kempt circle. The sight, amidst all this wildness, was like finding a gemstone in a bed of gravel. The secretary stood in the center of the greenery, her body arched over, and her head lowered. Liz crept closer, leaving the meadow behind to enter the emerald sphere.

In the middle of the green circle, a half-moon shaped piece of granite had been placed. Michael Brady's name had been carved into the stone. There was also a football helmet that matched the one in Paul's closet. It had been camouflaged momentarily by the intense green of the grass, but this too looked to be oft-tended, its dome pol-ished to a high shine.

Liz looked at Marjorie.

"Paul tended this memorial," the secretary explained. "Every year, week in and week out, since Michael Brady died."

For the first time since Paul had done what he did, drilling down and scooping everything inside her out, Liz felt a flicker of pity. The guilt Paul must have borne for what in the end was a terrible, tragic accident.

Riotous color blurred before her eyes. Liz wiped away a screen of tears.

The secretary spoke again. "Paul was driving Michael's car."

There was a shimmer of anger in the statement.

"I don't think anyone knows why they switched. If they hadn't, then perhaps they wouldn't have crashed. Or else..." Marjorie trailed off before mustering breath. "Perhaps Paul would've wound up in the condition poor Michael did."

It took a second for the horror of the alternative to unspool. Marjorie delivered a brief pat to Liz's shoulder, signaling goodbye. Liz watched her retreat into the woods.

The silence out here was pressing, intense. Through a barrier of trees lay a shaded grove in which older stones, gray and ivory rectangles, thrust themselves out of the ground like a ring of teeth. The faculty cemetery, where a few of Eastern Ag's somewhat illustrious members had been laid to rest.

Liz drifted in its direction, her footfalls quiet upon the soil. She slipped through a stand of knotty trees, making her way to the open maw of stones. Much of their lettering had been rubbed off, although some dates were still visible, along with names, even an epitaph or two. A few of these headstones dated back to the eighteen hundreds, sway-backed, leaning over.

Liz crouched and read the carving on one.

> To life's unending cry, I say
> There is no end but comes too soon
> When ruin falls
> The rest comes down
> We wish we could but weep again

A scrim of tears blocked her vision.

The cemetery felt unnaturally hushed. Liz squinted to try and catch a glimpse between rutted trunks, but she couldn't make out even a sliver of light, so closely crowded were the branches and undergrowth. The woods seemed to reach out, beckoning, their twigs like forked fingers. Liz stepped forward, curious to see the effect of so much darkness. It would be like entering a cave, or a mouth.

A hand settled around her wrist.

"Marjorie?" she cried out.

No one answered.

Liz sucked in her breath and whirled.

It wasn't a hand on her, but the soft and tender edge of a leaf. Liz should've been the last person to mistake plant life for a human touch, and she would've laughed at herself if she hadn't been so rattled. She drew air into her chest and turned away from the awful reach of the forest, which more than a century's worth of Ag students hadn't been able to tame, or even penetrate.

The word Liz had applied to Matthew and Mary's farm—*sinister*—arose in her mind like smoke. The harshness of the note Paul's father had written. But this place was spooked, too. Paul had concealed the fact that he'd played football from her for a reason. He had brought about his best friend's paralysis, caused Michael Brady's football career and ultimately his life to be snuffed out, in one moment of abandon. As far as Liz could tell, that night in the car had been the last time her husband had ever been carefree.

Of the cast of characters back then, the first was missing and the second was dead.

Which meant that Liz had better track down the third.

CHAPTER THIRTY

A text from Tim arrived as she hurried to her car.

that site u found is sealed like a grave. i know an IT guy i can call

A late summer wind was kicking up again. Humped mountains of clouds had gathered in the sky, and leaves slapped against one another, fleshy and thick.

Liz drove back to the house whose emptiness now cast such a pall.

Only it wasn't empty.

Liz caught a glimpse of the gate, swung partway open, and heard voices coming from the gardens. She nearly wept when she spotted Lia squatting beside the high-bush blues, and Jill checking on a cage of predatory mites, one of Paul's experimental pest-management strategies.

Liz headed over to both women, gladness pumping in her heart. The ground was a welcome cushion as she walked, a medley of earthworms and topsoil and newly deposited compost. Lia looked up as she drew near.

"Liz. Hi."

Would Jill detect any awkwardness in Lia's greeting? It wasn't really fair to blame the girl for how little help she had been. Paul kept his own counsel with Liz, with his students, with everyone.

"Thanks for getting on top of this." Liz gestured to the raised beds, now clear of weeds.

Jill began walking over, pulling off her pair of gloves. "We're not on top of it yet. At this rate, we'll be at it till after dark."

"It'll go faster with all of us working," Liz said. Then she added, "Andy?"

Taking care of her son since his injury had cut into the hours Jill was able to put in at Roots. It was one of the reasons Lia's assistance had been welcome.

Jill's face bloomed. "At a party. With lots of reminders to take things slow, and instructions for the chaperones. But he's going to try."

"Oh, Jill." Liz felt a terrible burst. Happiness streaked with envy, like dirt through a dish of food. "That is just great."

Jill was watching her carefully. "But what about you? What have you been up to?"

Liz looked over her shoulder at the house, recalling the task with which she'd left the students, and also the one Marjorie had inadvertently assigned her. Where had the old football coach gone after he left prison?

"Give me a few," she said. "Then I'll come back to help and I'll tell you."

Jill looked about to argue, but Liz was already walking off. "And watch out for that wind," she added, glancing skyward. High-up branches were twisting back and forth, their foliage getting snarled. The temperature was dropping. "There are jackets in the shed."

"Liz!" Jill called, and she turned. "You watch it, too. Okay? I mean it. You watch out."

Liz raised one hand in acknowledgment, but the wave felt more like dismissal. It was too late for her to watch out.

In the mudroom, she kicked off her shoes, then went upstairs to Paul's study. His machine exerted a magnetic pull, and Liz switched it on. The History button brought up the three preserved tabs, and Liz clicked the one with the letters *PEW*, getting that same blank homepage.

Only now she had passwords to try.

Paul's username was easy to figure; he always used the same one. She typed in *Professor*, then let her fingers hover over the keyboard. The cursor flicked in the second blank slot.

c-l-o-s-e-d-l-o-o-p Liz typed swiftly.

INCORRECT PASSWORD.

w-a-t-e-r-s-h-o-r-t-a-g-e

She hit Enter.

Same message.

What had Tim's text said? This site was sealed like a grave. The police worked with an IT guy, but that guy didn't know Paul, the esoteric bank he would draw on for a password.

t-o-p-g-r-o-w

It was a new system of raised beds for roofs, which Adoring Girl had been looking at on her tablet.

INCORRECT PASSWORD. YOU HAVE NO TRIES LEFT. PLEASE RETURN LATER.

Liz clenched her hand around the mouse and refreshed the screen. Paul's three tabs blinked, and for a moment, it wasn't PEW that drew her attention. She clicked on the page for Eastern Ag, letting her eyes drop from the fall course schedule to the scrolling line of this season's football games.

She skidded the mouse back over to the PEW page, and entered Paul's username in a series of rapid clicks.

In the password box she struck an entirely new series of keys.

m-i-c-h-a-e-l-b-r-a-d-y

The screen changed and she was in.

At first glance, PEW was organized in much the same way her gardening boards were. Whenever Liz had a question or just wanted to chat online she went to a site called The Thumb. Most people hung out in The Shed, and there were a few less frequently visited rooms: Exotics, Keeping It Real, The Last Layer.

She had no context to understand the titles of the PEW pages. Road Less Traveled had the most threads and posts, while ones like Playdate, Ingredients, and Pitchfork had fewer. There was a thread specifically for lurkers. Liz decided to start with Road Less Traveled, staring at a long, glowing chain of threads. Thousands of them. This site had to have been around since the Internet came into broad use.

She chose the most recent, which had the heading HOW ARE WE? Liz scrolled, looking for Paul's avatar and, when she didn't find it, trying to get a sense for the cast of characters who were here. But it was like arriving at a party where everybody else already knew one another. Liz couldn't make sense of statements that read: THIS ISN'T COMPARING BRANDS OF HUMMUS, PEOPLE. Or, SOME OF WHAT WE GIVE THEM AMOUNTS TO LIFE OR DEATH.

Give who? Liz rubbed a hand across her eyes, reopening them to see a stream of avid remarks. You couldn't start a chat with the most recent thread; you had to go back to the beginning. There Liz would find an appearance of the Professor, get to know the people Paul had been chatting with.

She screwed her fists into her eyes, willing an explosion of clarity along with the white stars that sparked. Liz scrolled through the array of dates, backward in time, until she came to the first few posts in Road Less Traveled.

PLEASE INTRODUCE YOURSELF and HAVE I GOT A PROBLEM FOR YOU.

Then she began to read.

The computer kept track of how much time had passed; other than that, Liz had lost all sense. She was gritty-eyed with tedium, her fingers numb on the mouse and her mind bleary.

Paul wasn't in any of these threads. No avatar seemed to be his; Liz didn't hear his voice. She had come to know a group of parents—moms mostly—concerned with how to cope on playdates when the other mom insisted on serving doughnuts or juice drink. Or at which point to email the school because the teacher incorporated screen time into her lesson plan. How to shield your child from the fact that the way of life he was living was destined to come to an end.

For the most part, Paul hadn't concerned himself with such minutiae of child-rearing, which was why Liz had been able to apply her own brand of moderation. But even if Liz were able to swallow the idea that Paul had decided to hang out in a chat room with a bunch of clucking moms, commanding power because he could back up his replies with science and research and theory, she couldn't find any evidence of his presence here. She continued to scroll and click and read, but it was no use.

Outside the wind was strong enough to bring down early leaves from the trees, send them scuttling across the ledge outside Paul's window. Liz got up to lower the sash. The sound of the wind quieted, although she could still hear its rasp.

And then she realized. She'd been wasting great gobs of time. She didn't have to go back to the inception of PEW. Whatever Paul was doing, he hadn't been planning it for decades. A few months—a year at most—should do.

The mouse overshot in Liz's haste to click on a more recent thread. She drew it back to the title, steadying her hand.

A great gust of wind sounded outside.

And then the fist-sized end of a branch crashed through the window, spraying a broken rain of glass out over Liz's arm, the desk, and everything on it.

CHAPTER THIRTY-ONE

Sheer instinct sent Liz shooting back across the room in Paul's chair. The chair hit a stack of books and tilted precariously, nearly tipping her over. She got it back onto its wheels, then stood up on trembling legs. She looked down, checking herself for damage. There was a dagger of glass lodged in her forearm.

"Liz!"

"Liz, are you all right?"

A paired beat of footsteps up the stairs, and Jill and Lia burst into the study.

"Oh God!" Lia cried when she saw the shattered window.

Jill reacted with brute efficiency. She marched Liz down the hall and into the bathroom, taking out alcohol and other supplies. When Lia appeared in the doorway, Jill ordered her to find a dustpan, some cardboard, and duct tape for the window. "Wear your gloves," she commanded, and Lia tugged on her thick canvas pair before disappearing.

Jill looked down at Liz's arm. "This is going to hurt a little, Lizzie," she said, and drew the blade of glass up and out. She slapped a gauze pad to the wound, pressing hard and switching it out as soon as blood soaked through the cotton. After a while, the bleeding slowed down. Jill cleaned the cut, then dressed it with a large, square bandage.

"Good job, Florence Nightingale," Liz said through clenched teeth. "I think you missed your calling."

"You should've seen how Andy's wound bled the first few days," Jill replied mildly, seeking no sympathy. "I've developed some skills."

Mad skills, Tim had said earlier. Look where Liz's had brought her. Where *had* hers brought her?

She frowned, feeling the movement all the way down in her forearm, which was beginning to throb. There was something wrong with what had just happened—beyond the obvious—but pain was keeping her from identifying it.

From down the hall came the whir of a vacuum. A few minutes later, the machine quieted and Lia came in holding a roll of silver tape and a leftover piece of cardboard.

"I blocked the window." She indicated her supplies. "It should hold for the night. But you're going to need to get a glass guy out here. Might be hard to find someone good, given the age of the house."

Artfully replacing the window was the last thing on Liz's mind. She trailed both women back to the study. The missing panes of the window were covered, and all the glass had been cleaned up.

"Nora Hamilton," Jill said suddenly. "The woman with the adorable baby who comes to the weekend markets? She has a big black dog?"

Liz nodded, though she wasn't sure she remembered.

"She does home renovation or restoration or something. I bet she'll know a glazier."

Liz gave another vague nod.

"I took a look outside as I taped things up," Lia remarked.

Liz and Jill both shifted in her direction.

"That branch had to have sheared right off the tree in order to hit this window."

"Branches coming off trees in a windstorm," Jill said in an imagine-that tone.

Liz sent Jill a sharp glance. And then she realized what she'd been trying to put her finger on.

A flush rose on Lia's elfin face. "I'd better be going. Hope everything works out, Liz."

The girl's footsteps tapped out a rhythm on the stairs, and Liz turned to Jill. "She's right, you know. How did a branch make it that far?"

"I don't like her," Jill said with a shrug. "Or maybe more accurate is that I don't trust her. I haven't ever since Paul made the suggestion that she intern for us."

"It sounds more like you didn't trust Paul."

Jill looked down. "Maybe that, too."

"Why?" Liz's gaze flicked to the computer screen, the pages and pages of chat. "Jill? Tell me. What did you see that I didn't?"

Jill lifted her eyes. "What have I always seen, Lizzie? Darkness? The flipped-over underbelly to things that would otherwise just slither away on their own?"

"Paul's not a snake."

Jill took a breath. "He's a compelling guy, mesmerizing even, and I can totally understand why you fell for him."

Had the people in the chat room done the same thing? Fallen for Paul? And if so, where had that led them?

"But I don't think he's a good man, if you know what I mean," Jill went on. "As strong a pull as Paul has, I guess I've always wondered why you chose to give so much to him."

There was a thousand years of understanding in the statement, the ageless calendar of best friends. But all it did was cause molten anger to bubble in Liz.

"Coming from the woman who never gave a guy more than a few days of her time," she snapped. "Including the father of her child."

Jill let out a shocked laugh. "That was low, Liz. Underbelly-of-the-snake low." She paused. "I'm sorry if I pushed. I guess I figured time might be a little short for tiptoeing."

Liz stared at her, unseeing.

"We're moms, Lizzie, and we're gardeners. We put seeds into the ground and hope that they grow. But children make you work harder than that. For that matter, gardens do, too."

The distance to where Jill stood felt endless, impassable.

"Our kids are in trouble. You don't even know where yours are. And I'm just saying that if you want to find them, then you have to start turning to yourself for some of those answers Paul used to provide." Jill took a breath. "You have to start digging."

THE MAN

"You won't have much time," Kurt had cautioned his son as soon as they'd arrived at the house and located the woman. A light was shining from a room on the second floor. Kurt scaled the clapboard side of the building to find her sitting at a desk.

He returned to the ground, feeling a surge of power so great, he could've jumped. But back on the grass, Tom stared at him with the bland gaze that Kurt was coming to loathe.

"You will need to get in, grab them, then get back out," Kurt told him.

Still that look. It said, *There's nothing you can do that would surprise me.*

Oh no? Kurt wanted to respond. *I'll bet I could come up with something that would provide a little zing.*

Tom's smaller size would be an advantage in making it through the window. Kurt explained the task, issuing instructions as they both climbed up to the flat stretch of roof that lay right below the pane of glass. He let Tom peek through so that he could see what he'd be going for. Kurt had volunteered the two of them for this task, claiming that he had the necessary skills, which was true. But what Kurt didn't say was that this was less a job to him than an indulgence. He could've come at any other time, in the middle of the night, or— given a little advance scouting—when the house was empty.

But that would've been far less gratifying.

Kurt had never been a collector of objects: rocks or action figures or cars. Instead, he collected observations. He lurked and listened, watched and took in. Kurt absorbed people's thoughts and behaviors in the same way that a cold-blooded creature soaked in sun.

Tom didn't seem to notice the woman sitting there, which strained Kurt's sense of credulity. The woman was in everything Kurt saw, a double negative over the reason they were really here. There was a light in her eyes, a crazed heat, which Kurt had never experienced before. Those kinds of things—engorged emotion, frenzied closeness—weren't for the likes of him or his. Kurt's wife, Tom's mother, was a reasonable sort, placid and unfazed by anything.

Of course, Tom's mother probably wasn't feeling quite so reasonable these days. The thought lit a charge in Kurt, and he turned to gaze at the woman again. It might've been reflected glow from the computer screen, but her face seemed wreathed in a halo of light. She was utterly unaware of Kurt's presence, focused and intent, which made things all the more exciting.

"How long are we going to stay up here?" Tom asked, not exactly complaining, sounding mostly just bored.

Kurt looked at him. The boy was sprawled a little too close to the edge. There was a smell of mildew, decay, coming from the piece of wood that Kurt gripped, and for a moment Kurt imagined giving one good swing and sending Tom flying down fifteen feet to the ground.

A piece splintered off, penetrating the webbing of Kurt's thumb. Kurt was able to make out the protruding wedge even in the low light. He drew it out, calmly placing his other hand over the blood that welled up.

Then he spoke to Tom. "Until the room is empty and I can allow you access."

Tom rolled his eyes, sprawling back on his elbows.

Again the piece of wood frayed in Kurt's grasp.

He wondered if the Shoemaker had taken his son along on killing sprees simply because he had no other choice. Finding a babysitter was risky when you planned to return with a body or two. Kurt felt rusty laughter build in his throat. He was with Tom all the time now.

He too had to make him his companion in everything. But that didn't mean he liked it.

Kurt had asked his mother about the Shoemaker once. He had come back for the weekend, just before everything imploded at college, and his mother was preparing the same tasteless, sterile offering she had served every night while he had been growing up. One of her paperbacks had been splayed open on the counter, commanding her attention as a pot of vegetables boiled down on the stove and the meat cooked through.

Something about the sight of the book emboldened Kurt. He was an adult now, away at college. His parents probably missed him and would welcome a little additional company. Even if they didn't, Kurt was old enough that they could move onto a more level plane of relating. His parents might not have been great with children, but children were a foreign species of sorts. As adults they could be equals.

"Do you need any help?"

His mother looked at him distantly, stirring the slurry of vegetables.

"With dinner?"

The spoon stilled in his mother's grasp. "No. I don't need any help," she said, as if the word tasted bad. The pot gave a thick, vegetative *blurp* and Kurt's mother wielded her spoon, sloshing the mixture around until it had cooled.

Kurt looked around the kitchen at the unset table, the roasting pan in the sink.

"Don't you have some studying to do?" his mother said.

"It's done," Kurt said, then waited for the praise, at least an acknowledgment. He could hear it in his head. *Do you ever give yourself a break, son? You're always so responsible.*

"Go let your father know dinner will be in fifteen minutes, then," his mother said. She removed an oven mitt from her hand before reaching for her book.

"Is that the one about the Shoemaker?"

His mother lifted her head slowly.

"The book," he said, pointing. "I used to like reading them, too—"

His mother looked down at the copy as if she'd never seen it before.

"Go tell your father to come," she repeated in the same tone of chilly disdain.

She inserted the paperback beneath the stove burner, moving the vegetable pot aside. The cover caught with a gentle *whuff*, edges of pages curling in, and his mother kept it there until all the charred bits had disappeared in a scurrying fleet.

Kurt smashed the glass with the branch, then lay down beneath the window frame. He listened for the beat of footsteps to recede before pointing his finger at Tom. The boy dove through the open space. It occurred to Kurt that Tom could get cut by the leftover fangs of glass. But there were leaves that would disinfect wounds. Kurt knew how to identify them now.

Tom seemed fine as he crawled back out, clutching his bounty. Kurt took the stack of dusty academic journals from him and they traded nods. There was something new in the boy's gaze, a pride that made Kurt blister.

The floor inside again shook with footsteps. In silent agreement, Kurt and Tom stayed put, lying flat against the tarpaper until the room had emptied. Then they lowered themselves to the ground. The van was parked a half mile away. As they began to walk, Kurt felt an altogether alien sensation on his back.

Tom's hand.

"Dad?" his son said softly in the dark.

An alien sound, too.

Kurt turned around slowly, precisely, on the spot of earth he inhabited.

"That was—kinda cool. Not something you get to do, you know, every day."

Heat surged inside Kurt like a lava flow. It was hard to see anything, but he sensed that the boy was staring up at him. Kurt reached out, his hand cupped, tender, and then he slapped Tom across his milky cheek.

The boy's face snapped back. He opened his mouth, yowl-shaped, but clamped it shut before any sound could emerge.

Kurt swiveled smartly. He hadn't expected to go back. Tom had fulfilled his part, and they could have left right then. They had what they needed without attempting what had essentially been a fallback, a far more risky Plan B.

But something was alive in Kurt, and he couldn't damp it. There was more here for him to mine.

His mother had never fully recovered from her destruction of the book; scaly scars grew to cover the narrow column of her wrist until it looked reptile-like, less than human.

"Conceal yourself," Kurt commanded Tom. "Here. And stay put no matter how long it takes for me to return. Do you understand?"

The boy's head nodded up and down, Kurt's handprint still flaring. He wore that look again. Utter boredom and disdain.

"Yeah. I think I got it."

Kurt would move the van a little closer. Make sure he had his supplies.

And then he would go inside.

CHAPTER THIRTY-TWO

It was long past dinnertime, although Liz had no appetite. The cut on her arm was making her queasy, and so was the exchange with Jill. They had never been that kind of friends, getting into girl-fights in high school or the earlier grades. Jill might have initiated a quarrel or two, but if she had, Liz had only a distant memory of it, and she herself wouldn't have fought back.

Another thing Liz couldn't remember was the last time she'd eaten. Meals seemed an artifact of a former life, when hungry voices would clamor, and she would delight in concocting rainbows from the garden and arranging them on plates.

She fixed herself a sandwich, then sat down at the table. The dressing Jill had applied caught her attention. A plum-colored shadow of blood had seeped through.

Someone knocked in the front hall, tapping on the screen part of the door.

Hope lit inside Liz. Maybe Tim had learned something about that website, or the mother and her son. Or else Jill had come back to apologize, and suggest a course of action.

Liz got up and went to the door. The man standing there wasn't the police chief.

He was tall and broad-chested, with a waving slick of hair, the color of coffee taken black, and worn in an old-fashioned pompadour.

His blue jumpsuit had the word *Crane's* embroidered above the pocket on the bib, and he carried a metal toolbox in one hand.

Liz peered around him and saw a panel van parked a little ways down the road.

"Hello," he said to her. "I hear that you have a broken window?"

Jill, Liz realized, with a prick of feeling. At war or not, her best friend had still managed to track down a referral for a glazier.

Liz stepped aside, letting the man in. "It's upstairs."

He took a few studied steps around her, giving her space. Liz noted the wide circle he made, as if aware of how she might feel, a woman alone at night with a strange man. Of course, he couldn't know that no one else was home, but still, she appreciated his discretion.

"It's a good thing we're having a slow night," he said as he trailed her upstairs, leaving two steps between them. "That wind is supposed to start picking up again."

"Is it?" Liz said. "I don't really know how this happened. I should go take a look at the branch."

The man set down his toolbox and began peeling off the pieces of duct tape Lia had applied. He whistled through his teeth upon exposing the damage. Night air entered through the missing panes. "Now, this is a fine mess."

"Bad?" said Liz.

He was frowning as he planed his hand around the empty mullions. "Someone didn't trouble to clear these shards out very well."

He spoke with a strange precision, and moved that way, too. When he drew his hand slowly back into the house, a bead of blood welled up on the palm.

"Oh no, you're cut!"

The man gazed down at his hand with an expression of distaste.

"I have first-aid stuff," Liz said. She extended her own arm ruefully. "You're not the only one this window attacked tonight."

The man took a step backward when she stretched out her arm. Frowning, he bent and unsnapped the clasps on his toolbox.

Liz's cheeks stained. She felt bad that the man had to come out at the last minute, then got hurt to boot. But she also felt embarrassed at how he had taken her reaction to his injury. This was a good-looking guy, probably used to attention from women, and now he thought she was some cougar whose husband left her alone for too long.

"Can I make you some coffee?" she asked, still feeling heat on her face.

The man straightened. Something caught his eye on Paul's bookshelf and he picked up a framed photo. "Are these your children?"

Liz had kept her back to that photo every time she'd been in this room, unable to bear looking at it—or worse, turning it facedown.

"Yes," she murmured. "Coffee?"

The man looked at her. "They're quite a pair. How old are they?"

Liz felt an odd prickle, the instinct any mother has when a grown man took perhaps too great an interest in her children. Good-looking, she'd just been thinking about him. Used to attention from women. Yet he sure had been keeping his distance from her since he'd arrived.

"Eight and six," she said. "Let me see to that coffee."

"Never drink it," the man responded. He was still looking at the picture. "No coffee, no alcohol, no medication."

"Wow," Liz said. "That's—strict."

"Oh yes," he said. "I run a tight ship." He finally set the photo down on the bookshelf again. "Eight and six, you said?"

"That's right," Liz replied. "Look, how long do you think it will take to replace the window? I'm going to be—I mean, my husband will be getting home soon, and—"

The man had taken a small tool from his box and was loosening errant pieces of glass, whisking each one into a pile on the sill. "Will he?"

"What?" Liz asked sharply.

"Silly," he grunted. He was straddling the desk in order to lean for the farthest square of open space. "I should have made sure I can match the glass before I started this. At least it will be in better shape now."

"Yes," Liz said quickly. "It looks great. You know—you don't even have to finish tonight. We could put the cardboard back. Or, it's pretty warm out, we don't even have to—"

He was studying her without quite meeting her gaze; his own eyes fixed on a point a little lower than her face. He got off the desk deliberately, planting first one foot, then the other.

"You'd like to just leave it alone, would you?"

"Well, it would be okay. One thing I do feel strongly about is matching the age of the glass—" Two hours ago, it'd been the last thing she cared about.

"Oh, I know you do," the man said. "I know how you historic homeowners feel. Let me see what I have out in the van."

Liz followed him downstairs. As soon as he was gone, she had the impulse to lock the front door, then all the other entrances to the house. Thank him politely through a window—an intact one—and say she'd suddenly remembered something she needed to do.

What could that possibly be?

And he'd left his toolbox upstairs.

The man reappeared with a stack of blue-tinted squares. Their edges looked sharp, dangerous. "Let's see how these will do."

"I'll just be . . ." Liz hesitated. " . . . seeing to things down here."

The man turned on the stairs. The glass caught bristles of light from the chandelier, striking Liz's face so that she had to block her eyes.

"You'd better come along," he said. "You were the one who cared about getting just the right match."

Liz looked over her shoulder. The front door was still open. She could say she had something to do in the garden, but if she went out there, she'd be in the worst possible spot, isolated and alone. And if instead she ran for her car, she would look ridiculous. Unless she was right—about what, she wasn't sure—in which case this man could easily beat her to the porch.

She imagined the pile of glass dropping in a tinkling shower. The sound of his shoes crunching it as he gave chase.

She took a step forward and followed the man to the second floor.

CHAPTER THIRTY-THREE

"I apologize if I sounded strange before," he said, heading over to the desk. He set the stack of glass down. "About your children."

"Oh," Liz said. "No, not at all."

"You don't have to be polite. I rattled you," he said. "And I didn't intend to."

"Well . . ." Liz hesitated, unsure how to proceed. "Maybe a little."

"I have a boy of my own," the man said. "He's eleven."

Liz waited for him to say something more, but he didn't. He turned and held one square up to the unbroken pane above, tsking his tongue.

Liz glanced into the open toolkit. She didn't see anything that looked capable of glazing a windowpane, although she supposed she wouldn't have any idea.

"Your children are happy," the man said suddenly. He laid the piece of glass he was holding aside. "They get along well."

Liz felt her eyebrows drawing together.

"You can tell from the picture."

"Oh," Liz said again. Her throat clutched. "Yes. I hope so."

It was a shot of Reid and Ally on a tree. Reid was straddling a high branch, and Ally was looking up at him, head thrown back so that her hair looked almost translucent, shot through with sun.

"My boy is happy," the man mused. He wasn't doing anything with the glass anymore. "Maybe you can't see it in pictures. But I still think that I'm right."

"I'm sure he is," Liz said softly. She had to get this man out of her house. How long did it take to replace a pane of shattered glass?

The man walked over to her in the oddest way, a forced slowness to his step, as if he were moving through mud. He leaned down and his gaze hooked hers. His eyes were strange: lushly lashed, beautiful orbs of color, but with no depth to them. They were as lifeless as beads.

"You couldn't have prevented it. There's nothing you could have done differently."

It was ridiculous to keep pretending this was just an ordinary home-repair mission.

"Prevented what?" Her voice reached a shrill note. "Do you know what's happened?"

He reached for her arm as if trying to pluck an electrified wire, fingers missing their mark before descending again. Liz recoiled, and for a moment the man seemed to regard her with understanding. He skated his thumb over the dressing Jill had applied. The cut was sore, and his touch probed it painfully. Liz tried to withdraw, but she'd have had to apply real strength to get free. Now that he had her in his grasp, the man didn't seem inclined to let go.

"Even if you were a person inclined to try and step in."

Liz went rigor mortis stiff in his hold. She felt as if she'd just discovered she wasn't wearing any clothes. "What the hell are you saying?"

"There's no need to get upset. I was only trying to reassure you." The man finally let go of her arm. "The wind kicked up. It was a force of nature."

She followed his gaze to the open panel of glass.

He picked up his toolkit, then turned and left the room.

Liz hurried after him, but he was down the stairs and out the front door before she could catch up.

He hadn't taken his glass.

An engine rumbled outside. Liz lifted the curtain and peered at the van as it drove off, trying to make out the plate. It was impossible to see at this distance. Shivers skittered over her skin. She got out her phone and scrolled for Jill's number. As furious as she still felt at her friend, she had to tell her this.

"That was the creepiest thing," she said. "Or maybe it was meaningful—I honestly can't tell. I'd better call Tim."

"What? Who?"

"Lurcquer," Liz replied absently. "He's been helping me."

"Well, well," Jill said. "Tim Lurcquer. There's a name I haven't heard in a while."

Liz ignored that. "I'm sorry about before. I still think you were out of line, but I shouldn't have lashed out like that." She felt the press of tears. "Some days I just hate everyone now. Most of all myself."

"Nobody could've seen this coming," Jill responded. "Don't blame yourself."

It was an eerie echo of the glazier's words, and Liz spoke abruptly.

"Jill? You didn't—call anyone to come out and fix my window, did you?"

She shuddered a little, recalling the way the man had trouble touching her, then wouldn't let go. Beneath the bandage, her cut pulsed rhythmically.

"Not yet," Jill replied. "I'll look for someone, I promise—"

"That's the problem," Liz interrupted, a series of shivers rippling up and down her spine. "Somebody already came looking for me."

CHAPTER THIRTY-FOUR

rane's, his overalls had said. Liz booted up Paul's machine again, Googling glaziers in Wedeskyull. She searched the whole Albany area, downstate as far as New York City. There wasn't any glass business called Crane's. Aside from a heating and cooling company in New Jersey, nothing by the name of Crane's came up for any household services.

The man hadn't been here about the window. He'd even left his pile of glass. Liz bet if she looked at those panes, they wouldn't be close to a fit for the one that had broken.

Liz phoned Tim at the station, but he wasn't on duty. Before she could try his cell, someone banged on the front door.

Liz ran downstairs, questions for the glass guy already coagulating. He'd come back, he wasn't a threatening presence at all, but here to help—

When she drew open the door, something painful gripped her chest.

"Mom," she said. "Dad."

Her mother looked at her, before switching her gaze to Liz's father.

"So you are back from out west," her father said, as if Liz had ventured to Wyoming with her family.

Liz didn't bother to ask how they had found out about her premature return. Jill had told them what happened when Liz was still in Junction Bridge, hadn't she? But the news could've been transmitted in any of a dozen small-town ways.

"Is it true?" her father asked. "Has Paul taken the children?"

Jill. Small-town ways. Liz nodded.

Her mother drew in an audible breath. "Oh, Elizabeth. Why would he do that?"

Liz stared at her mother. "I don't know, Mom. You make it sound like—there could be a good reason."

Again, her mother looked to her father.

Until a few years ago when they'd downsized, the Burkes had lived in the same house in Wedeskyull for four decades. Their people came from an Adirondack village a little farther north. The Burkes went to church every Sunday, visited their doctor twice a year, and worked on the other days. Liz's father considered himself a self-taught man, while Liz's mother was always busy, either in the house or the community. For them it was Paul who was the throwback to another era, not a visionary but a hippie. He came from away, even though his home was in the same state, and that factor also worked against him.

For a medley of these reasons, Liz and Paul had seen little of Liz's parents once they'd married. Ally and Reid had only slightly more contact with this pair of grandparents than they had with the other. Liz's mother contented herself with biweekly check-in calls, as regular as a metronome, and aside from the occasional summer barbeque, an hour or two stolen away from high season at Roots, or holiday suppers, the two families spent hardly any time together.

In retrospect, Liz realized that she hadn't been much closer to her parents even when they all shared the same house. Her father was the sun she and her mother orbited distantly around, never touching it or each other.

Still, in an emergency, her parents would step in, especially her father.

"All right," he said, clapping his hands together. "Here's what we're going to do."

Liz went light as a little girl. There was a relief in having her parents here, especially her dad, and knowing exactly which role to fill.

She stepped aside to let her father into the house, telling him about the strange glass guy's visit as she did.

"Well, I can't see a connection there," her father said. "Human beings tend to impose patterns. But you have enough on your plate right now without conspiracy theorizing."

Liz felt something in her subside as she began to follow her father up the stairs.

"Have you looked through Paul's closet?" he asked over his shoulder. "Itemized what was taken? That will give you some leads as to where they've gone."

Liz's foot faltered on the step. "What do you mean, Dad? Is Paul's winter coat missing? So I know whether they're in a warm or cold climate?"

If Jill were here, she'd tell my father that now we know which hemisphere to search.

Her father came to a stop at the top of the stairs, and Liz paused on the riser beneath. She could sense her mother from behind.

"We need lists of Paul's known contacts, the people he was spending time with," her father said. He began to open doors along the upstairs hallway, peering into Reid and Ally's rooms, which Liz had been avoiding. Her father stepped inside, and a host of noises ensued.

Liz was assailed by sudden clarity, as if she could see through walls. Her father was in there shuffling things around, looking at things, tugging open this, flicking shut that. Busy as a swarm, but Liz would never hear another word about this. Or rather, she might *hear* a lot. But that would be it. Talk that amounted to nothing.

Her father emerged from Reid's room.

Liz looked at him, the face and form that had always seemed mountainous to her, hewn out of the same earth she submerged her hands in every day.

"I already went to talk to some of his students," she said.

"That sounds like a good start. Is there anybody else?"

"I don't know," Liz began, her voice trailing off. There were other possibilities—the recently released coach, for instance—but she couldn't think straight right now. "I mean, yes. I think so."

Her father's eyes filled with the strangest blend of traits. Pity and love and just a trace of excitement. "I'll start brainstorming," he said. "Colleagues, your pastor, his doctor even."

Liz and Paul almost never went to church. Her parents knew that, even if they disapproved. And Paul shunned Western medicine. She couldn't think of the last time he had seen a doctor for anything.

"You'll see," her father said. "There are plenty of possibilities."

Liz's mother was nodding. "Don't worry, dear. In the worst case, even if you turn nothing up, I'm sure Paul will be back with the children. I'm going to hug those wee ones so tight the next time I see them ..."

The words sounded strange, artificial-tasting, as they left her mother's mouth.

Her father started to descend the stairs.

Liz had to shift to make room so that he could go by.

After her parents left, a dull, weighty paralysis settled into Liz's limbs. She was aware that she had to shake it, but she couldn't imagine anything to conjure up life or motion. Her father had said he would help, stepping in to take over as he always did, but Liz sensed the hollowness of what he had to offer. And she herself knew no more now than she had in Junction Bridge. All her attempts had come to nothing.

No. That wasn't true. She had discovered that website. Learned where Paul had been spending some of his time, even if she hadn't found him yet. Liz wandered back up to the study, lifted Paul's laptop with her good arm, and turned away from the sight of the ruined window.

On the floor in the hallway outside, she opened up a browser and typed in *PEW*. The Internet was slower out here, far away from the router, and it seemed to take forever for the page to load. Liz watched the tiny disk spinning. Once it stopped, lines of text blurred before Liz's eyes and she could hardly make sense of them. Her arm throbbed whenever she moved the mouse. There were avatars for people called *Pam's Mom* and *Processed* and *Enviro Pyro*. Faintly punny things or references to children from people who seemed to want to parent in a more responsible way. Threads about how to turn off the TV for good, nature-deprivation disorder, alternatives to foods with soy or corn in them. A *Motherdoctor* who offered tips for healthy pregnancies and alternative birthing. Liz might've been able to imagine Paul chatting about subjects such as these, but she couldn't find any instance of *Professor*, nor a single *Reid's Dad* or *Ally's Dad* on the off chance that Paul had decided to change handles.

And what did it matter if she did locate her husband in cold cyberspace? That wouldn't have anything to do with wherever Paul was now. Liz was looking for Paul on a blank screen, in a nest of wires, when what she needed to do was pound the earth, find her children amidst live, growing things, hold the warmth of their bodies.

The urge came at her like a gathering storm.

Liz rose and walked back into the study. She picked up one of the journals Paul subscribed to, knowing there wasn't likely to be useful information in it either, yet still leafing through, slowly at first, taking in passages, before starting to skim pages, flipping faster and faster until the type turned into skittering black beetles before her eyes.

The cover tore in her hand, and the sound was both sacrilege— Paul pored over these tracts with religious fervor—and so deeply satisfying that Liz hurled the book across the room. It hit the wall, dropping to the floor in a splayed-out position of ignominy. Liz was about to reach for another when she paused.

The first time she'd been in this study, she had built carefully segmented stacks of journals, sorting and grouping as she looked for anything that might contain a hint of meaning.

Some of those stacks were denuded now. There were fewer of them.

Liz looked around, nerve-endings alighting on her skin.

One stack of old journals remained, with a half stack, also dated, spilling over nearby. Liz went to straighten the slumping ones and an envelope fell from the center of one volume. A hard object slid around inside.

The edge of the envelope sliced her skin, and Liz let out a cry. Twin wounds on her hand and her arm pulsed in concert, but Liz ignored them, concentrating on slitting the seal.

A small, silver key dropped out, the kind that would open a lock-box.

Untold amounts of time passed—great, leaching stretches of it as Liz looked through Paul's study, then the rest of the house, searching for a lockbox she never knew her husband had. She opened every closet and cupboard, took out each drawer. She lifted the dust ruffle on their bed, then dared to look beneath Reid's and Ally's, trying not to focus on the childhood detritus under there: abandoned items that had once meant everything to their owners. Liz searched the dirt-floored base-ment; she even checked the attic crawlspace. Finally, dusty and rum-pled and disheveled, she had to give up.

There was no lockbox in the house.

Had Paul kept it in his office at school? Maybe Marjorie would know.

It was after midnight.

Liz trudged into the dining room, the room that had been left the most intact by her hunt. She curled into a ball on the floor next to the table, and fell asleep to the far-off lowing of a train, tiny key still gripped in her hand.

CHAPTER THIRTY-FIVE

By dawn Liz had combed the house again, still finding no sign of a box. She had neither the energy nor the will to put the house back to rights, and the siren's call of the garden was strong. Roots was a sprawling expanse, but once it had simply been the plot of soil into which Liz deposited seeds with cupped hands, watching fronds and shoots appear weeks or months later with a sense of wonder trumped only by the first times she'd felt Reid and Ally flutter-kick inside her body.

Liz pulled on her boots and a jacket against the pre-morning chill, then went outside into the fading moonlight.

She wove between overflowing rectangles of squash, checking their wrist-thick stems for signs of blight, until she came to the raised beds that lay adjacent to the wildflower meadow. It was almost impossible to keep on top of weeds here; often an utterly perfect dame's rocket or a spiky elecampane was discovered in a handful of bindweed that Liz or Jill had been just about to pull out.

Liz crouched down, feeling a sense of solace steal over her as she plunged her hands into the growth, separating strands. Leaves tickled her wrists above her gloves, and the loamy smell of earth filled her nostrils. Liz teased apart stalks of Indian paintbrush and corn-flowers, plucking the occasional interloper and bagging it carefully to prevent spores from dispersing.

She didn't realize how far she had migrated from her original spot, sidling on her knees deeper and deeper into the field of blossoms, until she felt a vibration of footsteps on the ground.

Liz looked up, blinking away an orangey afterglow from the flowers. The sun had risen in the sky and she had to block her eyes.

Tim spoke as she got to her feet. "This is some plot of land."

Liz nodded, tracking his gaze.

"I saw that you called," he said.

He was dressed in jeans; still off-duty, or just going off. Liz told Tim what had happened last night. The wind, the punching branch, the repairman who had come. Even her sense that journals might be missing from Paul's study, along with her realization that no branch could've flown that far by itself.

Tim's expression was implacable. He was no easier to read now than he had been as the completely alien species of teenage boy. Way back when, Liz and Jill had wiled away untold hours, trying to understand that species. Trying to understand Tim.

"Why don't we go take a look?"

Liz shucked off her muddy boots before leading Tim up to Paul's study. She flinched at the disarray, the journal she'd thrown, all the items moved in her search. But Tim appeared unfazed, taking the measure of the room. She supposed he had seen much worse.

He turned to face her. "Mind if I take a walk around outside?"

This time Liz followed.

From the ground Tim tilted his head up to the missing window, then walked a wide, looping circle toward the woods. "It came from one of these?"

Liz shook her head, the back of her neck prickling. "It was an oak branch. Not a fir."

Tim left the evergreens and counted out his paces forward. "Still couldn't have made it. You're right."

Liz nodded, tentacles of fear upon her. "The glass guy was up there," she said. "On my roof. He broke the glass himself."

"That'd be my guess," Tim agreed. "That's how he knew to come."

"Maybe he was trying to get those journals."

"Maybe," Tim said. "But it's not the biggest question I have right now."

Liz frowned.

"Liz," Tim said, and his tone contained an aching kindness, even if his next words penetrated like a spear. "Why were you in the yard when less than a week after your children were taken, two strangers showed up at your house?"

Liz's fingers hooked themselves into claws; she felt crumbly bits of soil beneath her nails. She'd been pulling up weeds. When her children were missing.

Everything Jill had said was true. Liz had always accorded Paul the power to figure things out. But he hadn't taken control—she'd ceded it. Given it up. And then her father showed up, and Liz was all set to do it again. Her terror-induced epiphany in the bunker at Matthew's farm, when she'd realized that she could get out by herself, had been just as short-lived as her time down there. Left to her own devices, Liz embarked on futile searches and met dead ends. She was waiting for someone not only to chart a course, but to navigate it for her.

Liz wandered blindly back into the house. Walked in circles until the smell of coffee lured her toward the kitchen. Tim was standing there, wiping his hands on a dishcloth and watching the dark brew drip.

He took a cup from a shelf and offered it to her.

Something in Liz seized up and she snatched the cup away. "Isn't this my job?" she snapped. "I can make coffee in my own damn house."

"Of course you can," Tim said, his voice hoarse. "You just looked as if you could use someone—"

"What?" Liz broke in. "To do it for me? Do I need everyone to do everything for me?"

"Just make you a cup of coffee once in a while."

Liz turned around, hunting milk and sugar, and Tim reached for her. She whirled. His fingers felt like brands upon her shoulder, and his eyes were dark coals.

"Liz," he said. "I've never been the one who doubted you."

Something in Liz began to move and break up. Portions of time, relationships shifting like tectonic plates. She was the one who had found PEW, even if the chance that it might contain any relevant information was uncertain. She'd discovered the tragedy that had assailed Paul long ago, and the link it might hold to today. She had a key now, a literal one.

Liz and Tim seemed to realize at the same moment that his hand was still gripping her. He let go, averting his gaze. Liz thought about the glass that had been punched in last night, and wondered why, of all people, Tim had been the one to open this window into herself.

"So you do think there's a connection," she said when she could trust herself to speak. "Between the things that happened here and Ally and Reid going missing."

Tim responded swiftly. "As I mentioned before, I don't trust coincidences."

Liz nodded toward the table. "Please. Have some coffee."

Tim took a seat and drank from his mug.

After a moment, Liz joined him.

"So, do you investigate?" she asked him.

Tim hesitated.

"I mean, this is criminal, right? Destruction of property? Trespassing?"

Tim tented his hands. "Normally I'd submit a report and we might have a man drive by your house a few times over the next couple of days. Make sure the guy doesn't come back."

Liz nodded. "And abnormally?"

Tim began drumming his fingers upon the surface of the table; they made a steady beat. She watched his hand move rhythmically.

"Look, I could do a more thorough search for a company called Crane's. If I come up with anything, I'll take a trip out to see if anyone matching your description works there." Tim paused. "This guy sounds like he'd stand out."

Liz could still see that sweeping wave of hair, the sheen over the man's eyes that masked any feeling. He'd spoken with exquisite precision, yet he'd just been crawling around on her roof in order to smash through the window while Liz sat at Paul's computer, blithely unaware. Jill and Lia had been working right nearby, also unwitting. Liz's insides gave a slow heave.

She fought to keep her voice level. Emotion still churned inside her, a mix of many things, only one of them her nightmarish last night. "Thanks, Tim. I really appreciate that."

He stood up, coffee cup empty, and came to a halt behind her chair. Liz closed her eyes, listening to the sound of Tim's breathing. It was slow and even, strangely comforting.

"I hope that I . . ." he said from above.

But his words tapered off, and Liz was left listening only to the firm retreat of Tim's boots and wondering what he had decided not to say.

CHAPTER THIRTY-SIX

She looked up a glazier, a real one, and arranged for an emergency appointment that morning. Liz tidied up the study, then the rest of the house. She stood by while the window was repaired, no word or notice paid to which glass was chosen.

There was only one place to go after that.

Liz drove through the gates and parked in Paul's faculty spot. Security wouldn't be too voracious about checking stickers before the start of the semester, and Liz wanted to get close to her husband's office. She was tired, sleep largely lost to her now.

Paul had gone to school here in the mid-nineties, coming up from Junction Bridge, while Liz herself had been downstate at SUNY Binghamton. Liz had once expected to be a Lit professor, or maybe a writer, and Binghamton had a great English department. Funny how things ended up. Liz had met Paul during their senior years while she was home on break. After they started dating, she'd seen the struggle he went through as academia began to close in on itself. Even after getting a master's degree—which Liz helped pay for, working mostly pointless admin jobs—Paul hadn't been able to find any position besides a non-tenure track at his alma mater. But those early years of their marriage had served a purpose. They'd exposed Liz to Paul's preoccupation with matters of the earth, and she had discovered a deep vein within herself that connected her to the outdoors. It made any life of the mind feel imprisoning.

She tried Paul's office door, not surprised to find it locked. Backtracking down the hall, she was relieved to see Marjorie at her desk.

The secretary looked up, such a light of hope in her eyes that Liz almost pitied her.

"He's not back," Liz said.

Marjorie closed a window on her computer. "I suppose you wouldn't be here if he were."

"No," Liz agreed. That had been the problem, hadn't it? Her willingness to let life proceed largely at Paul's direction, and unseen by her? She took a breath. "Marjorie, do you know if Paul kept a lockbox of some sort? Maybe in his office?"

"Not that I know of." Marjorie rose. "But you can certainly check."

The two of them walked down the hall so that Marjorie could unlock Paul's office door. This room was neater and more spare than his office at home. The bookshelves contained the popular texts that Paul used in his courses—*Bet the Farm, Garbology, The Humanure Handbook*—but no teetering rows of journals. The desk was bare; Paul had simply brought his one laptop back and forth. And most of the drawers were empty. Here at school, Paul had demonstrated his philosophy of small living. There certainly was no lockbox. Liz felt something inside her deflate. She reached into her purse, reassuring herself that she still had the key, even though there seemed no place to make it fit.

"Thanks, Marjorie," Liz said, watching the secretary read resignation in her eyes. "I think I'll go try to catch Lia."

She could thank their intern for her help last night, and apologize for the tension coming from Jill. Although part of her wondered what her best friend meant by *untrustworthy*. Jill had been right about the charges she leveled at Liz. Maybe she was on to something where Lia was concerned, too.

Liz steered toward the students' workspace. She got twisted around in the halls and had to walk through an adjoining department. Urban Planning and Design didn't seem to fit the scope of Ag, but as Liz walked, she realized that dividing walls were coming down. There were now farms on high-rise rooftops, and city dwellings had postage stamp–sized gardens. Liz's eye was drawn to the display of one student's work. Jeffrey Matters seemed to be interested in the transformation of gray water. His model contained a tiny stand of cattails: invasive phragmites that filtered contaminants so that only pure drinking water remained.

Liz could've remained there a while, studying the minuscule grouping of carp in a circle of glossy painted water and reading how they fed on shrimp the size of rice, but she wanted to try to catch Lia. She sorted out the skein of hallways, coming at last to the retrofitted closet. Liz knocked, but nobody answered. She tried to swivel the knob, but it was closed up tight, and she found herself backtracking to the football display case, staring at its sorrowful contents.

Liz turned at the sound of footsteps. Adoring Girl—Sara—wore a long, flowered dress, and was knotting a blond dreadlock around her finger as she meandered along.

Liz called out, and the girl stopped.

"Is Professor Daniels back?" Sara dropped her eyes, but couldn't hide a flush that deepened the color in her cheeks. "I mean, I just had a question to ask him. About getting into one of his classes." The flush had gone from a ruddy pink to something that looked almost blistered.

What kind of teacher had Paul been? Liz wondered for perhaps the first time. There seemed to be tiers between students, cosseted favorites who got to make use of that room, then further elevated ones, like Jake, whom this girl appeared to admire almost as much as she did Paul. As a teacher, Liz realized, Paul created the same structure as had arisen in his family. There was Ally, on the surface seeming to share Liz's love of the earth, but really putting her wares on display for her dad. Reid, taking anything, everything, he could for himself, and literally afraid of the ground, the final resting place it posed. And Paul, always, always at the center of everything.

"No," Liz said. "He isn't."

The girl began shuffling forward again, sandals flapping on her feet.

"Sara?"

She stopped.

"I came in through Urban studies," Liz said.

Sara nodded.

"There's a student in that department—Jeffrey Matters? He seems to be interested in some of the same things Paul is."

The blush, which had never entirely faded, flared again on Sara's cheeks. "Tree."

"He's interested in trees?"

She let out a snort. "Um, for sure. But also, he calls himself Tree."

"Really?" Liz said.

"I know," Sara replied. "Can you say *pretentious*?"

"Did he and Paul know each other?"

Sara's face went redder and angry. "*Know* isn't the right word. He was positively awful to Professor Daniels. Really made an ass of himself."

"What happened?" Liz said. "When?"

The girl faced her. "It was the night of the faculty dinner. This guy shouldn't even have been there, it's not like he's faculty. But he's sainted for whatever reason and so he came."

Liz nodded patiently. "What did he do?"

Sara gave a sharp thrust of her shoulders. "Said awful things. About how Professor Daniels should climb back into his ivory tower and let the real men climb trees."

"Real men climb trees?" Liz repeated, baffled.

"I told you he's an ass."

"But—" Liz broke off, knowing how Sara was likely to take this. "It sounds like it was Paul who was humiliated. It sounds like this guy made a fool of him."

"No one could humiliate Professor Daniels," Sara told her, eyes shining.

No one ever had, that was probably true. Paul had been in command when it came to environmental politics for as long as Liz could remember. The vacations they took, or didn't take. His desire to control waste and contaminants, even where the children were concerned. Especially where the children were concerned. For a long time, Liz had seen this as a result of Paul's need to be revered. But that wasn't entirely fair. Paul truly had an investment in more responsible living. How could this guy have said otherwise?

Sara was still speaking. "He thinks his department's so much better than ours, new and shiny, and Ag is for a prior century," she said. "Well, I don't see him making inroads in New York City either. We can't even start county-wide composting up here."

Liz nodded, distracted. "Do you know how I'd find him?"

"Not sure why you'd want to, but he lives right off campus. You know that road you come to if you don't turn in at the gates? But don't look for a house—he has a grant."

"A grant that allows him not to live in a house?"

Sara snorted again. "You'll see."

THE FIRST DAY OF SCHOOL

Abby woke before the sun came up. Finally, the heat had broken, and the bed she inhabited felt cool, not warmed even by a whole night's tossing and turning. Cold breaths of air emanated from the other, empty side of the bed.

She hadn't expected to be here still.

A text had arrived, giving an address where she and Cody would be met. Apparently their destination was all but impossible to access: a tangle of overgrown passages, hardly roads, led in. The only other way was more difficult yet and needed to be traversed on foot.

Abby had gone to the meeting point immediately. In hindsight, poring over the sparse words in the message while dark descended and she and Cody continued to wait, Abby realized that she hadn't been given a time or a date, just the place.

She had jumped the gun in her urgency to get away.

She texted, asking if there was any way they could be picked up that night, but no one was able to get away.

She and Cody were creeping around behind the house like characters in a spy movie. Then the owner had come out, clearly perplexed, distraught even, and Abby had really felt like someone in a movie, running away with her son.

She pulled the covers up to her throat.

This couldn't take too much longer. Bill was closing in. Abby knew it, like she'd always been able to intuit Bill's presence, his endless wants and needs and demands, even those he never made explicit.

Bill had never abused her physically; he was far too buttoned-up for that. But Abby had always sensed a potential for violence simmering like liquid beneath a lid. If a man like Bill—straitjacketed by regulation—ever blew, it would be a volcano. Even without physical force, Bill had made a zombie out of her, a reflection of his every vision. Abby had to dress as he demanded, keep her hair and face and body to standards he set, read about subjects he deemed worthy, fill her days with the activities he decreed, and worst of all, the camel-breaking straw, raise Cody as Bill dictated. Only in the lightness of her new state could Abby feel the full weight of the orders her husband had issued every day and the rules she'd had to follow.

Which brought her to the frigid state of this bed.

Abby kicked back the sheets and got up.

Today Cody was going to start school.

Abby decided to make French toast. Despite the fact that she lived at a slow boil of fear these days, Cody deserved to have his special day marked. Abby hurried with the mixture and the soaking, then fired up the stove. She flipped a piece over, slapping it back down in the pan. She should be dressed already, a dash of makeup on, smiling at Cody as he ate breakfast. She had fallen behind; the rigid schedule Bill set served some purpose. If Abby didn't hurry—*run around like a harridan*, she heard Bill accuse—Cody would be late his first day.

She set the plate down, noticing that although she'd remembered the syrup, the French toast was missing the fruit Bill insisted on and which Abby admitted did make for a pretty presentation. No time now. Leaving Cody in the kitchen to eat, she dashed upstairs for the outfit she'd at least had the forethought to lay out the night before.

She got Cody dressed, kneeling on the floor, and contemplating the next step: tooth brushing. Her son smelled yeasty and sweet, delightful to her mind. But the voice of Bill was loud in her head. Teeth had to be cleaned, the spaces between them flossed, after each and every meal.

She led him into the bathroom.

"Mama?" Cody asked through a mouthful of froth. "Am I going to have to do this every day?"

"Go to school, you mean? Every weekday," Abby confirmed as she worked the nylon thread up and down. Who knew what Bill would do if she stepped out of line? Cody had better be enrolled, present and accounted for in his new school, as long as they were here. She vowed that her son wouldn't come down with so much as a cold. "Why? Don't you like it so far?" Abby offered an encouraging smile. "French toast in the morning's pretty nice, right?"

Cody nodded.

Abby studied her son's small form. She didn't see the eagerness she'd hoped for, evidence that despite everything, Cody was ready to move on to this next stage. Instead her son looked a little lost; his face aimed down.

Abby's gaze sought out the clock. In just seven minutes her son would be on his own. She mounted a smile. "One sec, Bun." She had remembered the source of the nickname. Honey Bun, she used to call him as a baby.

Abby trotted up the stairs, returning with a small silver whistle on a string. She brought the loop down over Cody's tousled head, trying to smooth out his hair at the same time.

Cody touched the whistle in wonder, tilting his head down to see it. Folds of flesh compressed on his neck, a little leftover baby fat.

"That was mine," Abby told him. She'd had to blow the whistle when she came to the busy street that lay between her house and school. Other kids got driven, Abby walked. If one of her siblings was home when she reached the corner, and heard the whistle, they would help her cross. Otherwise she had to make her way between the whizzing cars herself.

"Can I blow it?"

It was a mark of Cody's earnest personality that he hadn't emitted a shrill note already. The whistle sat on his chest, its lump concealed beneath the new yellow shirt Abby had bought him, a size up in the hope that it would last throughout the year. Bill never allowed clothes to be bought big; they had to fit precisely. But Bill hadn't paid for this shirt. Also, where she and Cody were going, it would be necessary to hang on to clothes for as long as possible.

"Only blow the whistle if you need to," Abby replied, making her tone severe.

Cody mimicked her solemn nod.

"It's for emergencies," Abby said. "If you need to try and summon help. Or let somebody know you're nearby."

Even to her own ears, the words didn't quite make sense, and she knew Cody would be unlikely to apply them to any situation he might be in.

The whistle had been just for fun, really. A first-day-of-school present to jog Cody out of his apprehension.

"Come on," she said, taking her son's hand. "Let's walk down the hill."

Abby hadn't realized just how steep the hill in front of their new rental was, how far away its peak, until she stood at the bottom with Cody.

The bus appeared from around a bend, and Abby's heart seemed to lift and leave her body. She swallowed around an obstruction. Her stomach was pulsing and she could hardly hear when her son piped up.

"That's what I ride in?" Cody asked.

Abby tried to nod, but her head wouldn't obey the command. She was a marionette with no puppet-master. Cody's hand slipped from hers and she didn't recapture it.

"Mama?"

He was speaking through water. They both were. Abby couldn't answer her son.

The ancient bus pulled up, its yellow color faded and its brakes wheezing. A pair of accordion doors sighed open.

Abby had called the company after her meeting with Cody's teacher. She'd described her situation at length, and the dispatcher had dutifully taken a report, promising that the driver would be made aware.

Abby studied the man now as Cody hung back at her side.

"Good morning, Mrs. Harmon," said the bus driver from high up in his seat. He glanced down at a sheet of paper. "And this must be Cody."

"Ms.," Abby said rotely, or thought she did. "Yes. He is. Cody."

The bus driver didn't respond to her strange delivery, for which Abby felt grateful.

"My name is Earl. I'll be driving the steed this year. Does Cody like trucks?"

He was an old guy with steely hair and a sharp look behind his lenses. Not someone whom Abby would have chosen to transport her son. She worried that divorce and a custody battle would be a foreign language to a man of his generation.

He's experienced, Abby told herself. The dispatcher had said exactly that. *You have our most experienced driver.*

Earl leaned over, shifting so that the bus gave a heave. As it settled into place he stood up, turning and facing the students, who sat up straight in their first-day-of-school outfits and kept quiet, as if stunned by reimmersion into this routine.

"Hold on, kids."

The driver took a step down. His knees appeared to pain him; the three stairs were hard to traverse. After a moment he stood before them on the road.

"My dispatcher told me about your situation, ma'am."

At closer glance, she saw that his gaze was indeed sharp, but only in one sense of the word, not stern so much as probing, and alert.

He crouched down with a grunt of effort. "Cody?"

Abby was surprised to see her son nod. Usually he didn't respond to strangers, especially men.

"What do you think of my bus?"

Cody ducked his head.

The driver jerked a thumb toward the humped yellow hood. "Know what kind of engine I got under there?"

This time Cody spoke up. "Nuh-uh, sir."

The bus driver smiled at that. "A big one."

"Really?" Cody said. "Can I see it?"

"You can do better than that." The bus driver got to his feet, one leg at a time, and aimed a smile in Cody's direction. "You can hear it, and you can feel it working when the bus goes up that hill."

Abby felt her chest clutch upon being reminded of the distance. But Cody looked eager now, and some of her fear receded. She watched her son's slight body disappear behind the driver's bigger form as he helped Cody mount the steps. Dimly, she heard the man assigning another child the task of helping Cody buckle in. And then the bus was laboring to life, its body bucking as it made the arduous trip uphill and disappeared from view over the rise.

CHAPTER THIRTY-SEVEN

The road you came to if you didn't turn in at the gates, Sara had said.

Liz pulled over onto a piney shoulder, staring down at her phone, which wasn't any help out here. A dirt trail bisected the woods over there; from here it looked like more of a footpath than a road. Liz maneuvered her car onto it, driving beneath a high-slung canopy of trees.

The road narrowed further, imperceptibly at first, but by the time it dead-ended at a vast swath of land, branches fingered both sides of the car. Liz got out amidst a stand of trees, birch leaves shivering on their limbs. She began to walk up a hill.

The slope rose steeply and Liz was soon wiping sweat-glued strands of hair off her face. It looked as if she were climbing into the sky, a banner of cottony blue. She came to the crest, and the world opened up before her. Liz took in the sight with a feeling of wonder. Who knew this much open space existed less than a mile from campus?

She walked through a meadow, switchgrass and speargrass knifing her calves. Although she couldn't detect any hint of habitation, no house or driveway anyway, this place looked as if the model in the Urban Planning and Design department had come to life. Liz passed a pond densely surrounded by reeds—these were the phragmites—

and speckled with algae on the surface. When she bent down, she saw clouds of tiny shrimp rapaciously nibbling. The bodies of golden fish whisked back and forth in the murky depths. A creek led away from the pond, and Liz followed it to its source, where a crystalline stream of water was deposited into a pool.

Off in the distance, groves of fruit, hoop houses, and rectangles of crops sent out shoots toward Liz's own soul. She wandered toward the fecund acres, scenting ripeness in the air.

"Who goes?" The voice was earnest, without humor.

Liz turned.

He was a tall, rangy guy, with hair that fell past his shoulders and a cloud of beard that hid half his face. The facial hair made his age hard to determine, a contrasting blend of boyish eagerness in the eyes and sun-creased, leathery skin.

"Who goes?" he said again, like some medieval palace guard.

"Are you Jeffrey Matters?" Liz asked. She got no response. "Um, I mean Tree?"

"Sure am." A pause. "Hey, are you from *Global Living*? Or the *Today Show*?"

Liz frowned. "No."

Tree dropped his head for a moment. "Oh, shoot, thought I might've gotten a nibble." But then he took a look around, pride settling into his stance. "I've done all the local media, and the big guys should be interested now that I've converted the Experiment in Alternative Living dorm to humanure. But no one's been out yet."

Liz's head felt caught in a swirl. She could just about keep up with what this guy was saying—slips of things she'd caught over the years from Paul—but she was taken off guard by the disconnect from Sara's description. Liz had been anticipating an abrasive rub of arrogance, but this guy's worst trait seemed to be a youthful excitement not quite in keeping with his age.

"I'm not a reporter," Liz said. "Sorry."

A frown appeared above the beard. "I usually give tours on scheduled days, but I can show you around if you like."

Liz squared her shoulders. "I'm not here for a tour either. My name is Liz Daniels. I'm Professor Daniels's wife."

As soon as she said the name, the eagerness receded from his eyes. "What can I do for you? I imagine Paul didn't send you."

Anger at her husband had solidified into a small, hard stone inside Liz, but she still blanched at this guy's palpable dislike, mostly because she knew what it would've meant to Paul. As far as she knew, no one had ever felt that way about him.

"How do you and Paul know each other?"

Tree rolled his shoulders back and forth. "We don't really know each other."

Liz followed his gaze to a distant rim of forest. "But you've met?"

He hesitated. "Once. At a dinner. I don't come down from here very often, but I was—well, I was being honored."

Honored? Sara had made it sound as if the guy were an interloper at the faculty dinner.

"You're a professor here?"

"Not exactly. I have a DEC grant. And my father went to Eastern Ag."

Liz nodded uncertainly. Some environmental funding from the state, she figured.

Tree's expression darkened. "Farming nearly killed him. No, it did kill him. He died from a rare form of cancer caused by the pesticides he was using, though no one could prove it in court." Tree had fisted his hands; now he forced them to unroll. "That's what made me want to bring this work to Eastern Ag. And its time has come—even the administration knows it. So they gave me this piece of land, which no one was using. I have to reapply every year, but I've gotten it four years running now so I think I'm in pretty good shape."

Four years. To reach this point.

"Paul does, too," Liz said abruptly.

"What?"

"You said even the administration recognizes the value of this kind of work. So does Paul. So I don't understand . . ." She trailed off.

"I think I'm the one who doesn't understand," Tree said. "Why did you come out here to talk to me about Paul?"

"Because he's missing," Liz replied.

Tree's look of surprise was genuine.

"He's left and he's taken our children," Liz said, feeling faintly embarrassed by the pitch of her voice, but helpless to control it, "and I have no idea where he's gone!"

Tree frowned. "I didn't know. Sorry. But I still don't see what that has to do with me."

Liz turned away, the bright sky stinging her eyes. "Probably nothing."

Tree looked as if he had no idea what to do next. Liz felt almost sorry to have put him in this position. He was half hermit, half genius, and neither role was well suited to awkward social encounters. How had Paul never mentioned this guy or his work?

"Hey," Tree said. "Would you like to see where I live?"

The open space gave way to trees, and when they came to a particularly large one, an old-growth fir, Tree stopped. The majesty of the tree spoke to Liz; there weren't many of these left in the East, with trunks so big four men wouldn't span them. Liz heard herself gasping when she looked up. A structure was entwined in the thigh-thick branches toward the top. It was built of the same wood in which it resided, and its roof was composed of solar panels, high enough that nothing else competed for sun. There was one south-facing window, a long run of glass.

"Zero energy loss, net gain on heat, and best of all, zero waste," Tree recited. "The first year, I restricted my trash to a single mason jar. Now I don't even need that." His face shone. "Would you like to go up?"

Liz shook her head. Suddenly she had no idea what she was doing out here, viewing some experiment in sustainable living when her children were missing. Tim's voice—asking why she'd been out in the gardens—drifted back on a current of breeze. For a moment, Liz wished Tim were here to provide direction, but then realized she had one already.

The coach might know something about what Paul was doing. The timing was too coincidental: Paul's flight, Allgood's release from prison.

"Thank you," Liz said. "For the unscheduled tour."

Tree met her eyes. "I hope your husband comes back with your kids."

He began his climb up. No rungs had been mounted; there was no rope. Tree shimmied up the trunk as if he were some kind of long, snaking animal.

On a whim, Liz called out, "Do you happen to know a website named PEW?"

Tree held on with one arm. "Nope, sorry," he replied. "But if you're looking for Paul, then I'd say that online is a good place to start."

There was that dislike again, a dark fin of feeling that kept breaking the surface.

Liz summoned breath and asked, "Why do you say that? Why do you hate him so much?"

Tree slid back down the trunk, fire pole–style. "I don't hate Paul," he said. "I hate his type."

"What does that mean?"

Tree stared up at his dwelling as if there was no place he'd rather be right then. Then he looked back at her. "Your husband is a pretend radical. A mock maker of change who spends his time in books, not the environment he supposedly wants to impact. He does nothing of any substance. And any efforts he makes will amount to nothing."

Liz took a few steps back from the flood of vitriol. What a blow this man's presence on campus must have been. He saw through Paul in ways Liz herself didn't have the knowledge to.

Tree again began the ascent to his rooftop canopy. "Paul talks a good game," he said as he climbed. "And sometimes he doesn't even do that."

Suddenly, the forest floor felt as if it were giving way beneath her feet. Liz began to make her retreat, stumbling over broken twigs and leaf matter in her haste to depart. She hadn't been able to find Paul on that site, amongst all the clucking and the chatter. But there was a more obscure thread there, a place where people hardly spoke at all. And Liz could imagine her husband having found in it yet another place to reign.

CHAPTER THIRTY-EIGHT

The desire to call Jill was pure instinct—*You will not believe the character I just met*—and she speed-dialed as she drove. Jill spent enough time at home that the first number that came up was her landline, but she didn't answer.

Instead, the person who picked up responded to Liz's greeting in a quavering voice. "Are you a good friend of hers, dear?"

"Yes," Liz said with a frown, turning the steering wheel one-handed. "I am."

"Would you be able to come by? I'm here caring for Jillian's boy, and he's gotten himself a little upset."

Liz swung the wheel the other way and headed into town.

When Liz arrived, an older woman was standing in the doorway, twisting a dishcloth around her hands. The woman's hairstyle was a tight swirl of curls, unlikely to move, but her dress and stockings were rumpled, indicating the extent of her distress.

"I'm so sorry," the woman said. "I only asked how he was—"

Liz had called Jill's cell, but hadn't gotten ahold of her friend. "Do you know when Jill is coming home?"

"I tried calling her, but you know how the cell pockets are. She said something about meeting a new doctor. And she was going down-state for seeds."

Fall-planted wildflowers that needed a winter's dormancy to settle in. Jill had such high hopes for that meadow—if the yield could produce enough to supply florists, their revenue would treble—and yet it all seemed so silly and distant to Liz now.

A pretend radical, she heard Tree say. Liz was a pretend grower. Flowers. Frippery.

She became aware of a knocking sound upstairs. "Is Andy up there?"

The woman nodded, still wringing the towel.

Liz started up the steps. The sound grew louder as she went, headache-inducing by the time she was at the back of the house, where Andy's bedroom was. Liz found him sitting on the floor, a hockey puck in his hand, which he was rhythmically banging against the floor. The floorboards shook, and Andy's whole body moved as the recoil entered it, but he didn't stop banging, a vacant expression on his face.

Liz spoke from the doorway, gently, as you would to a cornered animal.

"Andy?" What to say? "I'm sorry you're upset."

He gazed at her blankly, still hitting the floor with the puck. Liz wanted to bring up her hands to block out the noise, but who knew what that would do to Andy?

What had the woman said to upset him? A greeting as banal as Liz's own.

"How are you," she said. "That can be a pretty dumb question. Hard to answer, too."

Andy continued to tap the heavy black disk of rubber, but he was pulling his punches now, not using as much of his immense strength. The floor was no longer vibrating.

Liz squatted down beside him.

"You're the lady who was here before," Andy said.

He had held on to the memory of her visit. That must be a good sign.

"I'm your mom's best friend," Liz said after a moment. "I've known you a long time."

Thud, thud, thud with the puck. The edge caught Andy's thumb, and he winced.

"That means I should remember you," he said.

Liz caught sight of his stricken thumb, bright red and even larger than usual, bulbous on the end where the puck had hit it. She wondered what Andy would allow her to do. A bandage, some ice? He was still beating the puck, oblivious to the way his thumb must be smarting. The rhythm was getting into Liz's head, making her flinch in preparation for every new strike.

"But I—" Andy finally ceased banging. "I don't. I just don't."

"I know," Liz said quietly. "It's all right."

"It is?"

Andy looked down at Liz from their shared position on the floor. He had an expression of such despair on his face that Liz had to steel herself against tears.

"And?" she said. The boy didn't respond, and she realized he didn't recognize the nickname. Liz reached up to his shoulder, a good six inches above hers. He watched as she did it, the puck motionless in his enormous hand. "I used to call you And."

A pause. "You did?"

Liz nodded. "Ever since you were a baby."

He closed his eyes. Liz could see his broad chest rising and falling with each breath.

"Can I have that?" she asked, reaching for the puck.

After a span of time, Andy handed it over. "You can keep it." He looked down, finally noticing his swollen thumb. "I don't think I'll need it again."

The sight of the old woman made Andy recoil, and take a huge, ungainly spin around on the floor. He lowered his face what seemed a great length to hide it against Liz's shoulder. The incongruity of the gesture, how young and vulnerable Andy seemed, made Liz decide to do what she'd done with her own kids during moments of trouble, the brief spurts of pain they had experienced until now. Immersion in dirt, being surrounded by live, growing things was the way Liz knew to bring a body back to life.

She located an ice pack for his thumb, and then she brought Andy home to Roots.

She set Andy to clearing the heirloom variety of cornstalks they had experimented with this season. The corn had a reputation for pest-resistance, and Paul predicted an effect of far-reaching importance on the entrenched corn lobby.

"Revolutions have been fought for less," he'd said.

Liz remembered regarding his words with something approaching awe. Paul said the world was changing, and she'd believed him. And then he destroyed her whole world.

Liz bore down on the soil, fistfuls crumbling away in her hands.

But Tree said that Paul had done nothing of real importance. Was her husband trying to remedy that somewhere now? Liz needed one last try with PEW. She glanced over at Andy, who seemed calm finally, clearing enormous armfuls of stalks as if they were blades of grass.

"Leave those two rows back there," she called. "We'll let them go brown for the Halloween decorators."

Andy took in her words, then gave a nod of assent. "They'll put bunches on their porches when the kids come to get candy."

Liz looked at him.

He yanked up another towering stand of stalks. Half the field had already been emptied.

Footsteps came from alongside the house, and Liz rose.

Jill rushed toward her, but swerved upon seeing Andy. She gathered her son into her arms, although it looked more as if she were swallowed up by him. When she spoke, her face was muffled against Andy's shirt. "Mrs. Williams told me. I'm so glad you could come. I can't imagine what might've happened."

"He's okay. We've been fine."

Jill looked at her, then up at her son. "But she said he became completely out of control—"

Liz caught Andy's eye over his mother's shoulder. "He's fine, Jill," she said, a bit sharply. "Aren't you, Andy?"

The boy gave a nod.

"Come on," Liz said. "Let's go inside and make dinner and then we can talk."

Liz described her arrival at the house, moving on to the connection Andy had made with her once Liz stopped taking huge steps around his memory loss, and just spoke normally.

And Jill listened, dismay, then surprise, and then even hope moving over her face like clouds across the sky.

"Maybe . . ." Liz turned from the pot of ravioli she was stirring on the stove. It was the first food she had made in days, and her stomach rumbled. "Maybe Andy doesn't need you to try so hard, Jill. The doctors, the alternative remedies. Maybe what he needs is for us all to stand back and get out of his way."

Jill looked down at the table, smudging a coffee ring with one finger.

A noise came from above.

Liz and Jill both looked up.

"Did you hear that?"

Jill stood. "I'll check."

There was another thump overhead, loud enough to make the ceiling shake.

The penetrating branch, the fake repairman. Liz's chest clamped, remembering.

"Call 911—" Liz began, but Jill shouted, "Andy?" and then both women ran for the stairs.

Liz got there first. Paul's study was intact. The noise had come from the opposite direction, over the kitchen.

Where Reid and Ally's bedrooms were.

CHAPTER THIRTY-NINE

Reid's room was empty, undisturbed. Liz couldn't stand to look at the ghostly neatness that had replaced its former shambles. Her son used to make snow angels on his bedsheets. He discarded pilfered items like a cracker-crumb trail. But she'd cleaned the room before they left for vacation. Now every toy sat on its shelf, and all the sports equipment was neatly stowed.

Liz pulled the door shut, then walked across the hall to Ally's room.

Andy was inside it. He had one of the dresser drawers open, pulled out so far it had overslid its casters. The drawer must've dropped, and Andy was in the process of putting it back. That was what accounted for the thud they'd heard.

"And?" A sour taste filled her mouth, not the residue of tomato sauce, but something else, something inedible. This boy she'd known since he was kicking inside her best friend's stomach had encroached upon her missing daughter's things. He was an intruder now and she wanted him gone. Liz forced her face to smooth out so that Andy wouldn't become alarmed. "Did you need something?"

He didn't respond.

Jill was there, pushing Liz aside. "Andy! What are you doing? Come downstairs with me."

Andy studied both of them with an expression that was sharper than usual.

Jill tugged at her son's thick arm, but she wasn't able to budge him. The pressure resulted in Andy shifting on his feet, which caused a swath of cloth to become visible behind him. It was hanging out of the drawer, one of Ally's leotards.

Liz felt her throat close. She had to cling to the side of the door for purchase. Jill didn't seem to notice, monitoring Andy's increasing agitation. The boy was shuffling from one large sneakered foot to another.

"I have to put back the drawer," he said. "It goes back in."

"I can do it," Liz said.

Neither of them heard her.

Jill was still pulling at her son's arm.

"I have to put back the drawer," Andy repeated.

He had lost the renewed cogence he'd come to.

"I can do it," Liz said again. Though how she would manage the task without touching Ally's leotard—feel the synthetic slick of its skin—she had no idea.

Andy leaned down, his strength great enough to reinsert the drawer single-handedly, since Jill still had hold of his other arm. But he was about to catch the leotard in its lip—

"I can do it!" Liz screamed, and both Jill and Andy swiveled.

Jill yanked Andy, and this time he stepped forward.

"Really," Liz said. She was crying, though she hardly registered it and they didn't seem to either. "Just take him, Jill. Just go."

Liz stumbled forward, snatching up the leotard and pressing it to her face like a caul. Her tears soaked the fabric, making it sheer, allowing a passing glimpse of Andy, whose face had folded in on itself in an expression of dreadful knowing. He was fully aware that he was the fiend Liz had just begged her friend to remove.

Why would Andy have been looking in Ally's room? Reid's, she could have understood; Andy might've wanted something to fool around with, a hockey puck or stick. But Ally wouldn't have had anything desirable, although it could be that logic was lost on Andy.

Liz laid the leotard down. She made sure the drawer rolled smoothly on its casters. Then she left Ally's room and went down the hall to Paul's study, where she turned on the computer.

Liz found her husband exactly where she had expected to after absorbing Tree's pronouncement. Tree had described Paul as a talker not a doer, and occasionally someone who didn't even say much, and the words had snagged a corner of her memory.

PEW had a thread that came and went, going all the way back to the origin of the site. It was there to lure certain members out periodically, people who read and kept up with threads, but didn't tend to contribute themselves.

The latest batch of posts was dated the night of the faculty dinner.

Liz could imagine what had created Tree's impression of Paul: the uncharacteristic speechlessness her husband would've exhibited in the face of a rival who'd attained far greater levels of accomplishment.

She clicked on LURKERS DE-LURK!

"Hello, Paul," Liz whispered.

And in the deep hush of the room, the Professor began to speak.

Liz saw Paul sitting at this screen; she felt the ropes of his dilemma, drawing and quartering him. These were the people whose preoccupations he had dismissed when Liz was juggling them, the day-to-day detritus of raising young children. Paul had held himself above it all during the years and months of threads Liz had scanned. Then, prompted by Tree's attack and a craving for new sources of adulation, Paul had quit lurking and waded in.

If only Liz had known to click on this thread. It contained relatively few posts and as such had passed unnoticed. But LURKERS DE-LURK! seemed to embody the real purpose of PEW, an acronym whose meaning someone called *The Town Crier* finally explained.

PEW stood for Parents at the End of the World.

THERE'S A LONG HISTORY, a woman who went by *Magpie* had written, OF PEW MEMBERS WHO REALIZE BAD TIMES ARE COMING AND WE'D BETTER DO SOMETHING ABOUT IT. WE'RE NOT JUST COMPLAINING ABOUT PLAYDATES. THE ONLY PROBLEM IS, WE CAN'T FIGURE OUT A SOLUTION.

Magpie, Liz thought. *The agitator bird, the one who incites movement.* She bowed her head to begin reading again.

OTHERS ON THE SITE THINK WE'RE TOO RADICAL. OUR THREADS NEVER GET MANY RESPONSES.

SO WE COME HERE. KIND OF A ROOM-WITHIN-A-ROOM.

WE'RE NOT ACTIVE ALL THE TIME. AND SOMETIMES WE DO JUST HANG OUT WITH THE REST.

BUT WHEN WE GET GOING STRONG, WE'RE BRAINSTORMING INSTEAD OF JUST COMPLAINING. IT'S NOT ABOUT WHETHER YOU CAN GET A FAST FOOD BURGER THAT ISN'T FACTORY-FARMED. IT'S WHETHER OUR CHILDREN ARE GOING TO BE EATING ANYTHING BESIDES WHAT THEY CAN FORAGE A DECADE FROM NOW.

THIS IS WHY NOBODY WANTS TO ANSWER OUR POSTS. THEY'RE SO HOPELESS.

AT LEAST WE FACE REALITY.

THERE'S JUST NOTHING TO DO ABOUT IT.

And then the Professor had waved a flag. Liz studied Paul's avatar: a bespectacled owl that looked more severe than avuncular.

I HAVE SOME IDEAS.

Liz sat forward in the desk chair, her eyes wide and unblinking. She tried jumping from post to post, scrolling for those written by the Professor, but they made no sense out of context. And since each entry had the potential to tell her where her children might be, she knew she'd better read closely. Liz followed the evolution of Paul's presence in PEW, witnessing the balm participation must have been to the ego Tree had bashed.

Someone had responded immediately, avidly, to Paul's first post.

TELL US! WELCOME, BY THE WAY. AND WHAT DO YOU MEAN?

WE DON'T HAVE TO BE PRISONERS TO THE FACTORY SYSTEM, Paul had typed.

GO ON, wrote someone named Processed whom Liz remembered from other threads.

MY FATHER'S RENTED OUT HIS LAND TO PERVADON FOR TWO DECADES. BUT HE ALSO EXPERIMENTS WITH VARIETALS THAT HAVEN'T BEEN GROWN IN A HUNDRED YEARS. FUNNY, HUH? BIGGEST AGRIBUSINESS IN THE COUNTRY DOESN'T REALIZE IT'S PAYING HIM TO FIGHT GMOs.

People typed in a train of emoticons to recognize the irony. Smiley faces, toothy mouths. Here was a whole new crowd of Adoring Girls, Jakes, and Lias, just waiting to be schooled. A chorus of questions asked Paul about food production in colder climates, whether Cuba surviving the embargo was merely a result of its long growing season, and if pest resistance could begin in the soil.

IT SURE CAN, Professor replied. YOU SHOULD SEE MY FATHER'S FARM.

Tears were rolling, silent and salty, into the corners of Liz's lips. She felt as if she'd found the seeds of her undoing, preserved like amber in distant cyberspace. They were here for the discovery, but unable to be impacted or changed.

THERE ARE MEASURES WE CAN TAKE, Paul had added. RIGHT HERE AT HOME.

LIKE WHAT?

SAYING NO TO CORN, EVEN IN ANIMAL FEED. MAKING OUR OWN DISH-WASHING DETERGENT. COMMERCIAL DISHWASHING AGENTS ARE RESPONSIBLE FOR TWELVE PERCENT OF THE POLLUTION THAT SHOWS UP IN AQUIFERS. OR HOW ABOUT ESCHEWING ANYTHING IN A CONTAINER SMALLER THAN DRUM-SIZED? BUY IN BULK. THAT MEANS NOT USING DRUGSTORE HYGIENE PRODUCTS OR MOST SUPERMARKET WARES.

Liz herself could've typed that list. But from the clamor of responses, she could see how welcome the ideas were, and how novel. She saw Paul come alive, his posts entered faster, fewer seconds between, his tone more and more commanding as he was asked to elaborate.

Magpie tried to wrap things up, the late hour marked by the time-stamp of her post.

WE SHOULD ALL CALL IT A NIGHT. THIS THREAD HAS BEEN A RALLYING CRY.

I KNOW, wrote someone with the handle *Unplugged*. IT MAKES ME FEEL LIKE WE SHOULD DO SOMETHING. LIKE WE COULD DO SOMETHING.

KEEP ASKING QUESTIONS LIKE THESE, Paul had counseled. DEMANDING ANSWERS. SMALL CHANGES ADD UP. IT DOESN'T TAKE A LOT. THINGS WILL START TO CHANGE.

I GUESS, Magpie typed. ISN'T THAT GANDHI? LIVE LOCALLY, ACT GLOBALLY?

IT'S THINK, NOT LIVE. AND YOU'VE GOT THE LOCALLY AND GLOBALLY REVERSED.

Magpie entered the emoticon with its tongue thrust out for reply.

GANDHI SAID BE THE CHANGE WE WANT TO SEE.

THAT'S WHAT I'M SUGGESTING, Paul wrote. You could hear sagacity even in the toneless quality of chat.

No, someone else typed impatiently, a few errant keys stroked. I DON'T WANT MY GARBAGE TO DWINDLE WHILE MY NEIGHBORS LUG THEIR OVERENGINEERED, FIFTY-FIVE GALLON RUBBERMAID TRASHCANS TO THE CURB EVERY WEEK. ANY CHANGE I MAKE IS LIKE TRYING TO SWIM UP A WATERFALL. I WANT A WORLD WHERE WE CAN START FRESH AND THE DAMAGE HASN'T ALREADY BEEN DONE.

A man who called himself *the Shoemaker* spoke up for the first time. De-lurking after the initial flurry of posts.

WELL? LET'S DO IT.

CHAPTER FORTY

Although everyone's enthusiasm appeared to be sparked, the Shoemaker was clearly the most serious. He asked questions about everything from fast-growing crops to natural medicine, soaking up the information like a root system took in water.

He also clearly had a deep regard for Paul. A long string of posts culminated in, YOU SEEM TO KNOW EVERYTHING, PROFESSOR. YOU JUST NEED A SHIP TO STEER. WHY HASN'T ANYONE EVER GIVEN YOU A SHIP?

There was a lag in the thread after that. Liz took in the silence, from Magpie and Unplugged and Processed and others, as if everyone were holding a collective breath.

LOTS OF SMART GUYS OUT THERE, Paul had at last replied.

SMART IS ONE THING, came the next post from the Shoemaker. I AGREE WITH YOU. GOOD MINDS ARE A DIME A DOZEN. BUT VISION? THAT'S ANOTHER.

Paul had logged off then. He hadn't entered another reply.

The next day, though, the conversation continued unabated, Magpie and Unplugged and Processed and the Shoemaker and others cross-posting, the virtual equivalent of everyone speaking at once.

HOW MANY WOULD WE NEED?

A FAIR NUMBER.

THERE ARE A LOT OF ROLES TO FILL.

LET'S MAKE A LIST.

I wouldn't know where to start.

You can't breathe the same air as the Professor and not know where to start.

As if summoned by the admiration, Paul appeared for the first time that day.

Too many is worse than not enough. The dangers of something like this collapsing have been proven time and time again.

The Shoemaker responded, each word precisely whittled to engage Paul, and puncture any resistance. How welcome his contribution must've been in the wake of Tree's assault.

Come on, Professor. We all know what you are capable of. Why are you reserving your power for this little box? Have you never wanted to do something big? Not just think about it, but actually do it?

Even as Liz grew chilled to the core, shivering and shaking in the desk chair while she watched the theft of her children approach, she also experienced a dawning sense of bafflement. How had the Shoemaker known so exactly what to say?

Liz clicked swiftly, entering another thread where she'd seen the Shoemaker's avatar. Its association was less transparent than Paul's: one of those elliptical faces from an old-time magic show or carnival.

There was a less frequent poster on this thread—young, from the sound of her comments—who was expecting a baby. She called herself *Mommie's Dearest*, an odd twist on handles used by people who identified themselves by their children's names. Mommie's Dearest got lots of support and interaction from the other moms on the site, but the Shoemaker also seemed especially focused on her, asking minute details and following up.

The Shoemaker knew when her backaches, which Mommie's Dearest described as bolting her to the bed, started to subside; the names she had considered for her baby; and that the baby's grandmother had found a good pediatrician, a good secondhand crib, a good brand of formula. The Shoemaker engaged in long strings of posts, listening to speculations about what life would be like once Mommie's Dearest became a mother herself, and adding a few conjectures of his own.

HOW WONDERFUL IT WOULD BE TO RAISE YOUR CHILD AWAY FROM THE SHACKLES OF THE WORLD. THE FREEDOM YOU'D HAVE TO DO WHAT YOU WANT WITH HER.

HOW DID YOU KNOW I WANTED A GIRL?

It was true. Liz scanned back, but nowhere could she find Mommie's Dearest indicating a preference for either gender. She had listed more girls' names than boys'. Had that been the giveaway?

I ONLY KNOW THAT YOU DESERVE A GIRL. AND SHE DESERVES YOU.

THANK YOU. THANK YOU FOR SAYING THAT.

There was a time lag before Mommie's Dearest posted again.

BUT FREEDOM IS NOT SOMETHING EITHER OF US ARE GOING TO HAVE.

The darkest of emoticons accompanied the statement, a tiny yellow circle with eyebrows drawn down, and features contorted with fury.

Liz couldn't tell from the threads who was imprisoning her—an abusive boyfriend was her guess—but that was the thing. Somehow, the Shoemaker honed in on the truth.

SOON YOU'LL BE A MOTHER YOURSELF AND ABLE TO WREST BACK ALL THE POWER YOURS HAS ALWAYS WIELDED.

Her mother, not a boyfriend, then.

There was a long gap between posts. Liz assumed the girl must've logged off. But then a final entry came, wistful in its brevity.

HOW?

After that, the posts tapered off. Whatever reply or conversation the girl's query had led to must have occurred via private messages or even offline. The thread went into another phase of dormancy, and whatever came next took place in the real world.

Where had they gone? Somewhere near Wedeskyull? That seemed likely since there was so much space here, and also because Paul was the de facto leader. But could it be Junction Bridge; was that why Paul had suggested a vacation there? Or someplace Liz had never even considered, pegged to where one of the PEW people might have some land? She scrolled backward, but it wasn't clear from the posts where anybody lived.

Liz stared at the yawning maw of the computer screen, its cursor one winking eye. Her actions too would have to take place in the real world. She could call Tim and ask if his inquiries about Crane's had amounted to anything, although she knew in a place deeper than reason—the mothering place—that the company was false.

Jill's voice: *You're just going to see if someone else has done the work for you?*

Liz needed to call her best friend. Apologize for how she'd treated Andy, and figure out a way to ask Jill if she knew what her son had been doing in Ally's room.

Talking to an ex-con sounded easier.

It was time to locate Paul's football coach.

Liz found the coach's full name, although the search didn't yield an address, since until recently the man had resided behind bars. Christopher Allgood had done a portion of his sentence at Sing Sing, then served out the rest at Wedeskyull's maximum-security facility.

A human-interest article in an online Wedeskyull weekly described the recently released inmate's desire to "find peace in a quiet mountain setting," which narrowed things down some. There was only one mountain people could live on in Wedeskyull, in either a handful of spread-out vacation homes or a colony of condos. The other mountains were too steep for anything besides sport, even if environmental regulations hadn't prohibited building on them.

Liz drove to the small grocery that serviced the skiers and climbers and asked the clerk if he knew a new resident named Christopher Allgood.

"I don't know that name," the clerk said, his face revealing the lie. Distaste, too: ex-convicts probably didn't do much to drive tourism. "But the Palmer place just got itself a year-long rental. Nick Palmer was real happy about that."

The clerk told Liz the address.

Back outside, she stood for a moment, staring at the mountain. Devoid of snow, the peak had the look of a shorn poodle. Next to the slopes stood tiny trees, closely clustered as quills. Liz wondered what was contained up there that couldn't be detected from this vantage point.

She got back into her car and reversed out of the lot.

Flares lit in her belly as she drove. At the end of a sparsely populated road, Liz turned into a steep driveway and got out, making sure
to set her emergency brake. The house was an imitation chalet:
brown wood, cutouts along the gabled roof. There were no late summer flowers, asters or hyssop, nor much of a lawn. This had been
somebody's winter getaway, plain and serviceable. Liz climbed three
steps to an unfurnished deck and knocked on the front door.

The man who opened it bore no resemblance to anyone who had
ever been involved in football. Prison must have shrunk Allgood. He
was small and slight, though he might've appeared taller if he hadn't
been so stooped. His hair was cropped short, and he wore stiff new
jeans and an equally rigid shirt.

The sunlight seemed to stun him. He blinked without saying hello.

"Mr. Allgood?"

"Yes?" The man looked over his shoulder. "Today isn't the tenth, is
it?" His gaze darted inside. "It's the ninth." He twisted back around.
"I don't have an appointment today."

"No," Liz began. "We don't have an appointment. I just wanted to
see if we could talk for a few minutes."

"Are you a reporter?"

"No," Liz said again. Although she seemed to be getting asked that
a lot.

The man straightened then, and Liz caught a glimpse of what
might have enabled him, decades ago, to lead a bunch of unruly, barely
formed men to victory.

"Who are you then?"

Liz told him her name.

"Daniels?" Allgood echoed.

Liz waited a second or two for the necessary calculation, then said,
"Paul is my husband."

There was a longer pause this time.

The man turned and Liz realized that she was being allowed in.

CHAPTER FORTY-ONE

The house had a great room on the first floor, with the bedrooms cantilevered on a loft above. As Liz entered, a medley of sounds hit her: the TV and radio playing, steady ticking from a clock on a wood-paneled wall, water plinking into a metal sink.

Allgood seemed impervious to the noise. He sat down in a battered seat.

After a moment, Liz dropped herself on a pilled seat. An awkward stalemate arose between them. It was hard to muster words amongst the clamor of reality-show screeches and synthesized music.

Liz raised her voice. "Would you mind if I turned that down?"

Allgood looked up. "What?"

"The television." Liz spoke louder. "The radio! Can I turn them down?"

"Oh." Allgood looked around, as if unsure where both items might be. He rose slowly and took a few steps until, with some fumbling of knobs, there was blessed silence.

Liz spoke again. "Paul was on your team?"

Allgood nodded, taking a seat in the same beat-up chair. "One game and I knew that boy was destined for great things."

"Paul was a great football player?" Liz asked, disbelieving.

Allgood shook his head, looking out into the room. "Nah. He was a mediocre quarterback. Not enough power in the throwing arm, so-

so accuracy. And he couldn't read his blindside for shit. But he knew the playbook by heart, managed the clock like Joe Montana, and everyone could see how he commanded a team. No matter what play Paul was calling, his men always wanted to follow."

Liz couldn't make out all the references, but that sounded more like it. She sat in the grimy chair as the coach seemed to reflect, cast back somewhere in time. Finally, she worked up the courage to bring the conversation around in a different direction. "And Michael Brady? Was he a great player?"

The question delivered an electric shock; Allgood's body jerked in the chair. "I should've kept them from driving. I was there that night at the bar. They would've listened to me."

Liz wondered if they would have. Paul didn't listen to anybody besides himself, and Allgood didn't seem the type to command unparalleled attention. But perhaps her husband had been different back then. Perhaps the coach was, too.

She recalled a detail that hadn't added up. "Paul was driving Michael's car."

The coach's eyes shuttered. "I asked him to," he said, hardly above a whisper.

Liz wasn't surprised by the content of the disclosure, although the fact that Allgood had made it was unexpected. Marjorie had said the coach felt responsible, and this explained why.

He went on, talking more to himself than to her. "Brady hurt his ankle at practice that afternoon. I didn't want him having to use the clutch." A pause. "My boys always hung out at Darts the night before a big game."

Liz knew the place; it was still a haven for underage drinking.

Allgood focused his gaze on some distant spot in the room. "Paul hadn't been drinking hard. I didn't realize one or two beers would affect him."

It was a tragic domino row of events, a succession of carelessness and bad decisions, any one of which might've been preventable. But taken all together, they resulted in an endless fall.

Liz leaned forward. "Mr. Allgood, I didn't come here to resurrect old pain."

He met her eyes for the first time, and though his gaze was rheumy, it gave a hint of former steel. "No? Why did you come then?"

Good question. Liz looked toward the galley kitchen.

"Some water . . ." she croaked.

Allgood didn't respond to the request.

Liz got up and found a glass in one of the cupboards. She filled it from the tap, drinking thirstily.

When she returned, Allgood was standing. He thrust his hands into the pockets of his jeans, shuffling back and forth across the space in front of his chair.

"My husband—" Liz drank again, draining the glass.

Allgood didn't appear to be listening. He was shifting from one foot to the other while staring at the clock.

"Mr. Allgood, Paul's taken our children. Kidnapped them. I think he has this idea that he's going to build a better world for them. But he didn't tell me—involve me even—and now they're gone and I can't—"

Allgood paused in his pacing. The look on his face made the water in her stomach slosh, a slow, seasick roll.

"No," he said. His eyes darted again to the clock. "No." He crossed the room bit by bit, stopping by a slit of sliding door.

The coach let out a bolt of laughter that made Liz flinch.

"I have to take a leak, Mrs. Daniels. I've had to relieve myself for the past half hour. But I haven't gone, and do you know why?"

Liz scrambled to come up with the answer he seemed to be demanding.

Allgood's gaze pinned hers. "See, I had a cellmate once and he didn't like the close proximity of prison life. He came up with a plan—a timetable, I guess you'd call it—for our shared usage."

Liz frowned, and Allgood barked another terrible, wheezy laugh.

"Now you're getting it, huh?" Croupy laughter again. "I learned to piss on somebody else's schedule. Eat that way, too. That's what my life has been like for the past twenty years—"

The minute hand on the clock sprang forward.

Allgood shoved his way into the bathroom. When he'd finished, he reemerged, speaking as if they'd never been interrupted.

"I can't have a normal conversation," he said. "Certainly not with a lady. If you say you're thirsty, I don't know what to do till it hits me ten minutes later. I've lost all that."

"I'm sorry," Liz began.

"But I deserve it," Allgood said. "I killed him."

The words struck the room bluntly.

"You thought it was the right thing to do," Liz replied. Why had she come here? What good was it going to do to rehash the long-ago event that had destroyed two lives, three, more if you included what Liz and Reid and Ally were experiencing now? The torrent of destruction seemed uncountable, unending. "I understand. Marjorie Brackman in Paul's department told me the condition Michael was in."

"You understand nothing," Allgood replied, each word a separate charge.

Liz recoiled.

The coach looked over his shoulder. "It's too damn quiet in here." He walked at his hesitant pace to the TV and radio, flicking both on. Music soared and outraged cries burst forth. "Another thing I'll never get back. Peace and quiet. Peace and quiet aren't peaceful to me anymore. They're scary as hell. It only got quiet when someone was just about to kill somebody."

His words called to mind her images of prison, its stale breath and closed-in spaces.

"This visit is over, Mrs. Daniels."

Liz didn't respond.

"No manners, remember? Another of the things I lost? So you can bet I'll ignore the social niceties. Get out of my house."

Liz turned around to face him, speaking deliberately. "What don't I understand?"

He answered in kind, stony and low. "I asked you to go. Now I'm telling you." When Liz didn't respond, he went on, his control draining. "Get out of my house!"

Liz tried to speak over the shrill rise of his voice. "Mr. Allgood—"

"It's my house! Mine! Get out!"

Each harsh cry struck her, like the caw of a bird. "Mr. Allgood,

please! My children are missing. If there's something I'm not understanding that could help—"

Something in the coach's face sheared off, like a glacier calving. He
swiveled, a pirouetting reminder of the football player he must once
have been himself, and even from behind, Liz could tell that he was
crying.

"I did what I thought was right. I gave all I could for that boy." His
shoulders shook, vibrating up and down like a jackhammer. "And I
served the time. It's enough already. Enough!"

The coach's tears—combined with regret in his voice for the
young life he'd snuffed out—accomplished what all his anger and bit-
terness couldn't do.

They forced Liz to leave.

THE BIRTH

Madeline knew she was in labor as soon as she woke up. In hindsight, she'd been experiencing contractions all night, waking to wriggle around on her side, even more unable to get comfortable than usual, faintly sickened by the water her mother brought in when she checked her at four-thirty in the morning.

At dawn Madeline threw up.

But she didn't say anything to her mother.

It wasn't that she thought she could keep this from her; she just wanted a little breathing room first.

There wasn't room for any breath.

Sweat poured down her back as if she were taking a shower. Madeline tried to climb back into bed, but she didn't make it.

She pitched forward, holding on to the side of the mattress as if it were a life raft.

Her mother appeared in the doorway, a tall and looming form.

"Oh, my gracious," she said. "It's time, isn't it?"

Cara was dressed for the day, makeup on—just enough to smooth out the worn edges, never to adorn—and hair combed.

"It's time," Cara said again. The alien tremor in her voice, striking enough that Madeline had heard it through the surf pounding in her ears, was gone. "We'll stay home for as long as possible. No reason to let those nurses have at you."

A pain took hold of Madeline's whole body and wrenched it. She sucked in a breath, then hurled herself onto the bed.

Her mother strode over. "I would've helped you." She drew the sheet up, frowning when Madeline kicked it back, emitting a guttural grunt.

"Nuh . . ." Madeline tried again. "N-nothing on me—"

Cara cut her off with a knife blade of words. "There's no cause to speak like that." She pulled the sheet up again, tucking it around Madeline's body.

"Nuh!" Madeline sounded like an animal. "N-no sheet!" She tried to curl, tried to straighten, anything to take away this pain, and a slimy gush of water spewed out, as if her body were unleashing a storm.

Cara mopped it up briskly, raising Madeline's bottom and sliding a towel underneath.

Madeline screamed.

"There, there," her mother said, the most calming phrase Madeline had ever heard her utter. "It won't be long now."

The hours, days, weeks—Madeline no longer had a concept of time—passed in a blur of agony. At one point, scuttling like some kind of bug, a stricken, lowly creature, she made it to her computer and hunched over the screen. Madeline didn't have time to scan the recent posts; another pain was building. They were sparse now anyway. Everything was ready.

She typed two words in a thread started weeks ago: ITS TIME

Her mother appeared behind her. "What are you doing up?"

Madeline wouldn't have thought she could move—she was being ringed around from behind by some enormous creature—but she jumped back from her mother.

"I've been timing your cries," Cara said matter-of-factly. "We'd better go."

Madeline managed to close the window on the computer screen just before she was taken up into King Kong's fist again and shaken back and forth.

The recovery room was bathed in late afternoon sunshine, honeyed hues of peach and amber. Madeline lay against more pillows than she could remember ever seeing in one place, her baby wrapped in a blanket like a shrimp.

A girl.

Madeline gazed down at the tiny face. She had never seen anything so sweet in her life as those slowly blinking eyes—her baby could blink!—and miniature rosebud mouth.

"Hello, Dorothea," Madeline murmured. It was a pleasing, old-fashioned name. Cara would approve. Her mother hadn't been allowed into the labor room—kept out by the doctor when Madeline uttered one long endless, "Noooooo!"—but she would be back any second. For now though Madeline intended to hold on to this precious time with her baby. "Hello."

"Hello," someone said from the entry to the room.

It wasn't her mother.

The woman was dressed in jeans, and a knapsack made a hump on her back. She wore the kind of boots Cara deemed ridiculous, designed for trailblazing and other sport. And she regarded Madeline with an expression that was shrewd and assessing and very, very kind.

"Hi, Mommie's Dearest," she said. "I'm Magpie."

The baby slept on. Magpie told Madeline to hurry. She had watched until the last nurse left Madeline's room after supervising a feeding, which would give them the longest stretch of time in terms of hospital procedure and the baby's own needs. But it wouldn't be much, Magpie said, laying the baby on the bed—*Don't worry, she can't go anywhere*—and helping Madeline into a shirt and a pair of maternity pants that bagged.

Magpie was all business, issuing instructions as she rolled the baby back and forth on the bed. Madeline was about to stop her—Dorothea's tiny arms were going to snap off—when she saw that the baby was dressed.

"You're going to be stopped," Magpie said. "They'll need to see that the baby's bracelet matches yours. Just show them your wrist, then say you want to step outside for some air. They shouldn't have a problem with that."

Had Magpie done this before? Not for the first time she wondered about the people who were going to save her and her baby. Did Magpie have a Cara in her life, too? Is that why Dr. Shelley had known where to send her?

Magpie laid the baby in Madeline's arms. "I'm in the north lot, right outside this wing. Wait for me by the doors. I'll be driving a blue Sentry."

It all went according to plan, as if the PEW participants were actually able to structure whole worlds, as their conversation topics made it sound.

Madeline gave the charge nurse the explanation about wanting some air, and was told it was wonderful that she was already up and about.

"Usually our moms are down for the count. How's your pain?"

Madeline was too adrenaline-charged to feel much of anything. Her life was about to begin, same as Dottie's had today.

She emerged from a pair of sliding glass doors into the gloaming twilight. The air was a cool bath on her face. She glanced down at Dottie, who was unaware of the enormous turn her life had just taken, sleeping placidly in Madeline's arms.

A Sentry pulled into the no-parking lane in front of the hospital.

Someone else came walking up from the lot.

Her mother. Carrying an enormous bouquet of balloons, and wearing an expression of total bewilderment.

Madeline's heart started gonging. She suddenly felt the effects of all she had been through today. Only Dottie kept her upright, the need to maintain her hold on this tiny life. A cramp—nothing like the ones that had delivered Dottie into the world, but still harsh and grasping—tightened her belly and Madeline sucked in a breath.

"Madeline?" her mother called. Cara was trying to close the gap between them, but the balloons blocked her sight for a moment. "What on earth are you doing?"

Madeline looked over her shoulder at the car that had come to convey her away. Which didn't turn out to be a very good idea because her mother noticed it, too.

Madeline stared down at the pink shell of cap upon Dottie's head.

There was a pink balloon in the bunch her mother carried so awkwardly. They looked as foreign in her hand as a strand of pearls on a hawk.

Magpie appeared beside Madeline.

"Is that your mother?" She spoke calmly, but the last word was uttered as if it tasted foul.

Cara's face changed. It wasn't confused anymore, but alarmed, with a trace of fury beneath. Her fist opened and the balloons escaped her grasp. They drifted upward, out of reach.

Madeline twisted around.

Magpie was holding out a knife, its blade wicked-looking, long, as she snatched quick peeks over her shoulder at the hospital.

"Get into the car," Magpie said, still in that level tone. "On my side. Don't let them see that you're taking the baby. Hold her in your lap for now. And hurry—they come out to check car seats."

Madeline only got half of what Magpie was saying, but she followed the instructions as best she could, thinking fast enough to leave the driver's-side door open while she got herself and the baby over the gear shift and wedged them both into the passenger seat.

Magpie was still aiming the knife at Cara, who had begun to stride forward anyway.

"Help!" Cara cried shrilly. "Help! Police! She's taking my daughter!"

A blue-suited security guard stepped through the hospital doors. "Ma'am," he called. "If you're leaving the hospital grounds, I have to check that your car seat is installed properly."

Madeline looked down at Dottie in her lap. It took her a moment to register the widening stain of blood on the upholstery. And then she became aware of the pain, as if she were the one being stabbed.

She looked through the window at the sky. The balloons were dots against the blue expanse. Soon it would be as if they'd never been there at all.

Magpie reached for the door handle at the same moment as Cara did. Madeline saw the blade of the knife whicker down. Cara leapt back faster than Madeline had ever seen her move. Then Magpie was in the car, slamming the door shut. The security guard jogged forward.

Cara intercepted him, gesticulating wildly, her mouth contorted.

Magpie gunned the gas and the car hurtled out of the lot.

CHAPTER FORTY-TWO

Liz dialed Tim as she drove home, leaving a message at the station, and getting voicemail on his cell. She spoke into the phone on her lap, looking up suddenly and wrenching the wheel when her car swerved toward a steep bank of coneflowers.

"Tim. It's Liz. I need your help looking into a crime that would've taken place more than twenty years ago. Manslaughter, I'm guessing, but I could be wrong. The victim was Michael Brady."

She pressed down on the gas, in a hurry to search online for back issues of the Albany *Times Union* and the *Wedeskyull Daily Record*.

The first thing she learned was that Allgood had been convicted of first degree murder. His lawyer argued that it was a mercy killing, and thus should be considered manslaughter, but there had been a couple of vigilante cases that year—in one, barely a month before, a domestic violence victim had shot her boyfriend sixteen times—so both the prosecutor and judge were taking a strong stance. Even given Allgood's lack of malicious intent, a sentence of twenty years was imposed.

Liz peered at the blur of skewed typesetting on the screen. A blog had also come up in her search, which included Allgood's case amongst other travesties of justice. Liz clicked on it, skimming the piece before scrolling to the comments.

No just outcome was possible in Christopher Allgood's trial, said one in a long string. *Because there was no crime except the caprice of life.*

Something in the voice contained a tinny echo, and Liz scrolled over it to read the user profile. The commenter called himself *Professor*. Too much of a coincidence; that had to be Paul. It was as if he had spoken from wherever he might be right now, arched a beckoning finger. The smugness with which he spoke about Coach Allgood's murder of Michael Brady. The comment read with the same detached tone Paul used to analyze the bloated uses of corn.

Liz was rigid with fatigue. This day had been abominably long. She wondered why Tim hadn't called back. Liz pressed a button on the keyboard and watched the screen fade to black. She trudged downstairs, blinking away afterimages of the powering-down computer. Liz curled herself into a shivering ball on the couch, pulled down an afghan, and prayed for sleep to take her.

A song was playing, lilting, light. Liz didn't want to open her eyes because that would force her to leave behind the place she had come to. Her children were there. She heard their voices, high and sweet. Behind her eyelids, the sun had risen and all was yellow, and bright.

And then she opened her eyes and it really was daytime. Somehow she'd slept a whole night away. And a song was indeed playing. It came from her phone.

Liz sat up stiffly on the couch. Her back felt like iron. She twisted and heard a series of small pops. The notion of standing up seemed too taxing, so she settled for leaning over and cocking her ear to hear where the chiming notes came from.

Her phone was buried somewhere in her bag. Liz pawed around amongst items for it—her wallet, a notepad, some kind of sticky toy. She slid her finger across the screen, the call about to go to voicemail, and didn't take notice of the number.

Tim. It had to be. Or maybe Jill.

"Hello?" Her voice was croaky. She coughed to try and clear it. "Hello?"

"Hi, Mommy!"

A thousand impulses crossed Liz's mind at once, like fissures across ice. Some practical, some far-fetched, out of movies or TV shows or the news. Identify the number, find a way to record the call, triangulate the signal. In the end she did none of those things, unwilling to move the phone so much as an inch away from her face in order to look at the screen. What if she accidentally hit the *Back* button and lost the call? Liz kept the device pressed snugly to her ear, just as she'd been wanting to hold her children for almost two long, lonely weeks. And she remembered to subdue her voice, make it sound normal.

"Ally," she murmured. "Hi, sweetie. Where are you?"

There was silence, and Liz thought she had lost her daughter, despite her warring switchboard of thoughts.

But then Ally spoke, her voice so piping and clear that Liz began to cry.

"On vacation," she said. "I thought you were going on vacation, too. I thought you were coming."

"I know, sweetie," Liz said, feeling her way. There were stones here, and if she tripped, she might never get this chance again. She stood up and began making her way toward the landline, still focused fiercely on Ally. "I'm just—trying to get there. Get back there. You mean that you're still on Grandpa's farm?"

Would Ally even know whom she meant by *Grandpa*? Liz supposed she'd have to, if they had spent this much time together. If Matthew had lied to her that baldly and brazenly. Like father, like son.

Liz ground her teeth, willing the right response to come. The pause went on longer this time, every second harrowing. But it gave Liz enough time to hit the *Talk* button on their landline and dial 911.

She set the cordless down on a table. Wedeskyull had gotten full-fledged emergency services last year when its longtime chief was forced to resign. Now 911 calls were no longer routed through to the station, but went to a service, and if the person who had placed the call didn't answer when the dispatcher picked up, then the police were obliged to send a car to check on the situation. That was about as far as Liz could envision. She had no idea what the cop who came would do; she only knew that she needed help.

The seconds spinning out pricked her consciousness and she spoke. "Ally? Are you there?" Too sharp. She had to mute her tone.

"Mommy?"

"Yes?" A quick hiss.

"Is Grandpa the one who has all the corn?"

"Yes," Liz said again. Thinking, *Goddamn you, Matthew* . . .

"Oh," Ally said. It was her decided voice, her now-I've-solved-it satisfaction. "We're not there. That was last vacation."

Liz frowned, unwilling to let confusion creep into her tone. She feared she might frighten Ally—alert her somehow that all wasn't right—and who knew what that could lead to? There were too many unknowns; Liz's brain scrambled with them. The fear that she might mess this up descended like a parachute.

When Ally next spoke, her voice was heavy, weighted down with sorrow. "That was the vacation I lost Iz-Biz."

Liz clutched at the words like a lifebuoy. Here at last, in a missing sea of tasks, was something she could do, could give to her daughter. "Oh, sweetie, no, you didn't lose her."

But Ally was so lost in her grieving that she didn't hear. "Daddy made us hurry to take a nap. It was so cold down there." A hitch in her voice. "And I don't even take naps anymore!"

As if that were the outrageous part.

Had they been in the bunker after all? Paul must have enforced a rest period after absconding with the children in the middle of the night. The thought was oddly reassuring.

"Ally, did you hear what I said?" Liz asked. "I found Izzy. You dropped her on the ground."

"I *did*?" It was the kind of screech only a child could make. "It was so dark out. I couldn't see anything. Iz-Biz must've been so scared!"

"She's not scared," Liz said fiercely. "I have her right here with me and I'm going to bring her to you."

Carried over the unseen cell signal, across an unknown number of miles, there came a weak, trembling sigh of relief. "Oh, Mommy. That's good. That will be good."

"Yes," Liz echoed. "That will be good."

Ally swerved back to her original train of thought. Liz had missed desperately the tilt-a-whirl pace of conversing with a six-year-old, but just now it was dizzying.

"Grandpa got so mad!"

"Grandpa got mad?" Liz asked. Too late she remembered that Ally hated this standard parental stall tactic. She'd either get angry, or turn it into a game, an endless succession of echoes they didn't have time for.

But Ally did neither. "Uh-huh. Yup."

"You mean at Daddy?" Liz said, her mind scurrying to keep up.

"No!" Half-delighted at her mom's mistakenness, half-veering toward impatience. "I don't know if it was Daddy. I think maybe Grandma."

"Why did Grandpa get mad at Grandma?" Liz asked. Too urgent; Ally would shy away.

A scenario born of vague, unformed images began to cloud her mind. Had Mary tried to intervene somehow, welcome Paul against her unforgiving husband's wishes?

"Mommy," Ally said, both chiding and annoyed. "I *said* I don't know."

Her daughter couldn't get upset now. Liz had to make use of this chance, squeeze every drop of potential and sustenance it had to offer. She changed course.

"Ally, sweetie, how's Reid?"

"He's good," Ally said, using her thoughtful tone. "He's not afraid of dead people anymore. And he hardly steals hardly at all. Well, excepting for this phone."

Good job, Reid, Liz thought with a trembling smile. She wanted to hold her sweet, sturdy son in her arms so badly that they shook.

"Sweetie?" she said at last. She should've done this first. But the sound of her daughter had been too precious to relinquish. "Let me talk to Daddy, okay?"

"Mommy?" Ally said.

"Yes, sweetie?"

"You sound funny."

"Oh," Liz said lightly. "That's just because I miss you, sweetie. I want to get to vacation right away."

"Yeah," Ally said contemplatively.

"Is Daddy there?"

"No."

"No?" Liz's voice rose and she fought to lower it. "Who is, then? Whose phone did Reid take?"

There was a pause. Liz waited as long as she could, then spoke Ally's name.

"Mommy?"

"Yes, Al?" she cried. Her daughter was slipping away, Liz could tell, and now there was no fighting the panic.

"I don't like him."

"Don't like who, Al?" Her mind spun, trying to keep up with her daughter's. "The person whose phone you're using?"

"What?" her daughter said.

Liz gathered breath. "I was just asking if you meant—"

"What?" Ally said again, only now her voice reached a scaling note. "No, don't!"

Liz realized her daughter was talking to somebody else.

"I said, don't do that! Mommy, help!"

There came another screech from her daughter, wordless, and utterly terrifying.

Liz felt everything inside her come to a halt: thoughts, heartbeat, blood flow. There was not one thing she could say or do to make whoever was threatening Ally stop, and helplessness ground her from the inside out.

She let out a shrill scream that joined Ally's.

The call dropped, or was ended.

All was silent in the wake of the cutoff cries.

Liz held the phone so tightly that its back panel popped out and skittered across the floor.

In the sucking vacuum of silence, two words flashed on the screen.

Signal lost.

CHAPTER FORTY-THREE

After the call ended, Liz became a wild animal trapped in a cage. She stalked back and forth across the length of the house—living room to front hall to parlor and back again—with no awareness of where she was. The urge to do something was so strong, it couldn't be contained, and yet it was utterly futile. There was nothing she could do. She couldn't reach Ally, make sure her daughter was safe. Couldn't learn who had caused her to let out such a high, awful scream, let alone get the person to stop. The flats of her hands hit a wall and Liz began to beat at it, rhythmically, furiously, as if she really were in a cage.

The phone's backing caught her eye and Liz dropped to the floor and crawled over to it. Her hands were lumpish, too swollen to reassemble the device. It wasn't necessary. She dragged a thumb across the screen and the call log dropped down. Besides a few missed calls from Jill, there was only one other number, with its caller listed as *Unknown*.

She stared at the command, whimpering, "Ally, Ally, Ally."

Then she touched the number on the screen.

What was happening to her daughter right now?

A mechanical voice intoned that the service provider was out of range.

Liz began digging her fingers into the floor, curls of wood coming up, and the only thing that stopped her was the sight of blood on the boards.

The front door opened in one swift move, and a gray-clad body entered the hall, its back to the wall, gun arm extended.

Liz glanced at the landline, still off its base and lying on an end table. She had been hearing a series of knocks, possibly shouted instructions as well, for she didn't know how long. She was sitting on the floor, legs splayed out, arms wasted, voice utterly gone.

Tim Lurcquer's eyes found hers amidst the wreckage of the room. Actually, there wasn't all that much wreckage, not that was apparent. One dashed cell phone panel. A section of floorboard ribboned. And yet Liz's whole world again lay in ruins.

Tim was beside her without seeming to have taken a step. He hadn't looked around or checked any of the other rooms. He leaned over, picking up both her bloodied hands in his, cradling them gently, like glass.

"Liz, good God, what happened?"

Seeping tears prevented Liz from seeing him.

Tim spoke into his radio. "Two-oh-three all clear, I need an EMT on-site."

Liz felt her useless fingers tremble in Tim's palms.

Tim said her name again.

She opened her mouth and he dropped to her side. But then her lips clamped shut.

"Liz, what happened? Tell me."

The words would poison her if she said them out loud.

He knelt, not letting go of her hands. "Liz, please, talk to me . . ."

It was the sight of naked fear in his eyes that got her. Tim didn't know what had happened. He thought it might be something even worse.

Burning embers seared her mouth, and tears dropped, scalding her cheeks. "Oh, Tim, Ally called. Ally called, and I think she's being hurt—and Tim, I don't know how to find her!"

An ambulance arrived, and the medic examined Liz's hands, removing shards of embedded wood, but deeming nothing broken. He used some kind of soothing ointment, broke ice packs over his knee and applied them, which provided relief Liz knew she didn't deserve.

Not when her children were out there, scared and alone.

At some point the ambulance left, but Tim remained behind. He asked her to tell him about the call again and she recounted it from the edge of a kitchen stool, willing herself not to slide or fall back, her legs odd- and crumbly-feeling.

Every word she had said and Ally had uttered in return was branded in her memory.

Tim took notes, but his hand slowed as the paucity of information became apparent. He asked her a few more questions, then shook his head.

Liz dropped her own in defeat.

"You must—"

"What?"

Tim shook his head again. "Sorry. It was stupid."

"What?" Liz said again.

Tim stared at his fists, balled on the counter. "I was going to say that you must hate him. You must just fucking hate him."

The statement was like a lightning rod for all her emotion; it was the best thing Tim could've done. Her response was cold and brittle enough to shatter.

"Oh, Tim," she whispered. "I hate Paul so much, I'm afraid that if I ever see him again, I'll kill him before I get any answers."

CHAPTER FORTY-FOUR

Tim knew a guy named Mackenzie who'd recently moved down-state. He was a bit of a character, according to Tim, but an ace when it came to technology, and he was doing a training course in cyber crimes. Mackenzie might be able to recover the number Ally had called from.

"But—I can't be without my phone now. What if Ally tries again?"

"You can port your number to another phone," Tim said, sealing Liz's cell away in a compartment on his belt. "Buy one of those pay-as-you-go jobs and use that."

After a moment, Liz nodded.

"Mackenzie's good, I promise," Tim said. "He used to be on medi-cation, and he was good then. But this holistic guy at the hospital weaned him off, and now he's pretty damn close to a genius."

How ironic, Liz thought, tears welling. Paul would approve.

"Liz," Tim said. "Listen to me."

His face swam as she looked at him.

"I don't have kids of my own, but I've dealt with plenty. And I can tell you that they scream for all sorts of reasons. Not only fear. They scream in outrage. In protest. They scream because their brother is taking something away from them."

Tim's face came into focus before her, then was replaced by an image of Reid and Ally fighting over a charm Reid had lifted from his sister's wrist.

"Ally may not exactly be having the time of her life right now, but she has access to a phone. She called you. She's all right."

It occurred to Liz that Ally had started out the call on a fairly normal note, wondering where her mom was. Something had happened—to outrage her, as Tim said—but Liz could've been imposing danger on a situation where there was none.

Something inside her started to calm, to settle.

She took a breath and asked, "Did you get my message?"

Tim nodded. "I remember that case. I was the same age as the guy who was murdered. But I didn't know Paul was driving."

"Back then there wasn't as much awareness about drunk driving, I guess," Liz said. "They didn't charge Paul."

"There was awareness," Tim said quietly. "But this was an accident. Paul might've been drinking, but his level was under the legal limit."

"You checked?"

Tim nodded.

Liz felt raw and exposed. There was information about her life, her husband, available for the taking. And she had never known.

"What do you know about the coach?" Liz asked. Briefly, she described her visit with him, leaving out the prison details Allgood had seen fit to share.

"Liz, I don't want to take away your options, but this one might be better left alone. The man was convicted of murder. And prison does strange things to people."

Remembering Allgood's demeanor, the way he'd broken down at the end, Liz had to concede the wisdom of Tim's words.

"Do you think you could go talk to him, then?" she asked.

Tim shook his head. "Not in any official capacity," he replied, and when Liz looked up, hope sparking, he added, "And I can't see what that would accomplish anyway." He paused. "Let's focus on this call from Ally. Try and make some headway there."

Suddenly Liz remembered. "Ally said she didn't like him."

"Any idea who she meant?"

Liz extended her hands helplessly. "They left the hotel with a man, according to the bellhop. Maybe that's who Ally meant. But there are other people with them, too."

"There are?"

Liz realized Tim had no idea what she'd learned about the site. She filled him in on what *PEW* stood for, and how the Lurkers thread had evolved into a conclave of its own.

Tim folded his arms across his chest. "So Ally and Reid are holed up with a bunch of mostly moms who believe in making things as pure and healthy as possible?"

Fifteen minutes ago, Liz would've said that she'd never smile again, but now she felt her lips quiver. "Tim."

His eyes held a shared flicker of amusement, and a fleeting image came to Liz: of their having met again for a completely different reason, in a world where there were such things as senses of humor and getting to know one another and a deepening connection.

Then Tim was back to business. "So we've got some kind of utopia thing going on. That's why they stole Paul's books."

The missing journals from the night the window had been smashed. Liz felt something crowd her throat. "I guess so. And maybe they needed something from the farm, too."

Who knew what kinds of people Paul had chosen to make his companions in this? Some of them seemed all right—mothers, as Tim suggested—but meeting people online was inherently risky. What were they doing out there, wherever they were? How were her children living?

"Ally didn't say anything to give you any sense where they might be?"

Liz stared at him, and Tim spoke with a note of explanation. "Sometimes if you ask a question twice, you get a different answer."

"I don't have a different answer," Liz said, her voice small. "I wish I did."

Briefly, Tim looked away. "Your two main options would appear to be somewhere around here—where Paul works and lives—and his hometown. Junction Bridge, right?"

Liz felt a perilous dip. Junction Bridge. It was the last place she wanted her children to be.

She addressed Tim with a quaver in her throat. "The phone Ally used was out of range when I called back."

Tim shrugged. "Doesn't mean anything. There are cell pockets all over Wedeskyull."

Liz seized on his words. "So you do think it might be someplace nearby?"

Tim hesitated. "Paul is the ringleader, and this is his territory. But when it comes to a search, to any kind of investigation, you don't want to cut off possibilities prematurely." He leaned closer, gentling his tone. "Look, you've had the strange incidents here at the house. The mother and her child. The fake glass worker." He paused. "That could suggest proximity."

Gooseflesh rippled over her, triggered by Tim's reminder. Voices from PEW were loud and livid in her ears. One voice in particular. Liz ran for the stairs.

Tim joined her as the site loaded, and Liz began to scroll through threads where the Shoemaker had weighed in.

She looked up from the machine. "This might sound like a leap."

Tim folded his arms. "I'm all about leaps."

Liz nodded. "Okay. I think this man—his online identity is the Shoemaker—is the same one who came here. There's something about his voice. It's very precise. And he seemed to sense things about me, just like he figures stuff out about people on the site."

Tim peered down at the screen. "What the hell is a shoemaker?"

"Somebody who makes shoes?"

"Other than that," he said, suppressing a grin.

Liz surprised herself with another small smile back. "I have no idea."

"Let me give this to Mackenzie, too. See if he discovers anything. Can you get me the link and Paul's password?"

Liz opened a different window and entered the information, clicking Send and speaking with a bitter clip to her tone. "This email will come from Paul. If he's checking his account, wherever he is, he'll know I'm getting close."

THE SNATCHING

"I don't want to go to school," Cody whimpered.

"Oh, Bun," Abby said sleepily. She was staggering between the coffeepot on the counter and the cereal box in the cupboard. One kind of cereal. Bill used to have her buy ten.

The scarcity wasn't only a function of Abby's reduced standard of living, it was also a feeling of kinship with the people who would soon be housing Cody and herself. Americans were used to staggering numbers of things, Abby included, of course. But when you had to start from scratch as she would soon be doing, growing, harvesting, and ultimately contending with how everything broke down, then one variety was enough. Of cereal and most everything else.

Whether they ate French toast or cereal, however, the morning routine was turning out to be surprisingly hard on both her and Cody. The earliness of the hour, the endless array of tasks it took to get one little boy off to school. Wake him up, impart some form of nourishment, make sure an adequate lunch was packed. Check and see if a permission slip, form, or piece of homework was missing while deciding on an outfit, tracking down the inevitable wayward sock/jacket/shoe, all before getting to the bottom of the hill in time for the bus to come around the corner. By the time Abby had squired Cody up those three ridged steps, she felt as if she had lived four lifetimes.

And now this.

Complaints about the point of the whole enterprise.

The complaints seemed to be increasing in volume and duration. By the end of the week, Abby had a feeling she'd be limp, sweating with her attempts at persuasion.

Unless they were gone by then. Please, let them be gone by then.

The nail-gun precision of Bill's routine would've prevented any such arguments. But then, the nail-gun precision had also left them both punctured and bleeding.

"Mama?" Cody was shaking more flakes into his bowl.

"Yes, Bun?"

"I'm supposed to get dressed now."

Abby looked at the clock on the thirty-dollar microwave. Cody was right.

Wicket Road was mean and curving, and Earl had always hated it. They included it on his route because he was the most experienced driver in the fleet—a nice way of saying he was the *oldest* driver in the fleet—and so they figured he could handle it. And he could. But that didn't mean he liked it. It was September now and frost laced the shoulders most mornings. Earl kept to the middle, which meant that whenever a car appeared he had to edge over onto one of the sharp bends. He liked to be courteous to other vehicles; besides, he'd never get into a game of chicken with kids on board. Earl used to feel completely in command of his ride, keeping it steady at the steepest juncture of a switchback like another man held the reins on a stallion. But that feeling had been receding on him. Now Earl was weightily aware of what he held in check. An eleven-ton vehicle that could go hurtling down the mountain as easily as a leaf blew away in the wind.

He wasn't sleeping well these days. Woke up sweaty and gasping, the missus stirring beside him. He had to make water, but he couldn't make water, and it kept him awake all night after that. He and the missus were both tired out. For the first time, Earl began to consider retirement. He'd always said he would drive his route one day, die the next. But he didn't have a good feeling about this year. He started bargaining with something he had never believed in,

Let us make it through this year. Me and the kids. And then I'll let one of the young bucks take over my route, and the hellish Wicket Road.

He didn't want to let the missus see him uneasy so he stopped going home between runs. The middle of the day used to be the best part of his job, that and getting to know the children. When they were young, kids themselves really, he and the missus would make love right in the afternoon. And even once they were older, and neither of them had the appetite anymore, the core of Earl's day gave them a chance to talk, catch up before the exhaustion of the evening was upon them.

"Refill, Earl?"

The waitress behind the flecked countertop paused by his cup.

Earl brought a napkin to his mouth. "No, thanks, Audrey. Time for me to be going."

Audrey looked at the round clock on the wall. "School day over already?"

"Seems it gets earlier every year, don't it?"

"I'll say. If my Petey had been let out now when he was school age, I wouldn't have earned enough to feed him."

Earl made sure to leave a generous tip by his plate. He went to the lot behind the Crescent Diner and started up his bus.

The bus was loaded; they were on their way. Behind Earl's seat, the noise was reaching headache level. Afternoons were loud, mornings quiet, the kids disbelieving that another day had come around.

"Hey, hold it down back there, okay?" Earl called out good-naturedly.

No one answered, of course.

Earl thought to ask the kids sometimes, *How do you think this bus gets you where you need to go?* Most of them wouldn't have a reply. But that was his job. To get them to school and back home so seamlessly they didn't even have to think about it.

He didn't mind the volume actually. He tried to do his part in keeping everyone to the code of conduct the board had set, but in truth, the noise faded into the background for him. Engaged in the act of driving, Earl's doubts tended to ebb away, drowned out by the engine and the laughter. The children's shouts and cries told him that life couldn't be the dread, lonely battle he had started to picture, not if the kids were this happy and unseeing.

Although maybe they were happy *because* they were unseeing. That hadn't occurred to him before, and it didn't help his mood. For all of his adult life, Earl had been the unseen, unheard companion to children, most of them now grown and in the muddy midpoints of their lives. Where did that leave him?

He made the turn onto Wicket Road.

A kid hurled a balled-up jacket; Earl caught sight of it in the mirror.

"Uh-uh," he called out as the owner of the jacket started to stand up. "Sit. You can pick that up when you get off the bus."

The kid obeyed.

The switchbacks were upon him now, but a car was coming around the bend. Earl pulled over to the side of the road. At least the scum of frost had melted under the midday sun. Shoulder didn't feel as slick as it had this morning. Earl waited for the car to pass.

But the car didn't pass. It stopped.

It was a little green sports car, or what passed for a sports car these days. Nothing muscley or strong.

A man got out, approaching the bus.

He didn't walk up to Earl's window, but headed over to the other side, where the door was. Earl frowned. He stood and took a look down the aisle. The kids hadn't noticed anything amiss and were making use of the pause to shimmy up as high as their loose seatbelts—really only a nod to buckling—would allow. Taking quick, furtive peeks behind them, trading punches with their friends.

The man stood before the accordion door, separated only by a barrier of glass. Earl peered through his windshield and saw that the sports car blocked the bus's access to the road.

Some instinct made him lock the door. He couldn't recall ever doing that before in the course of his career. He hadn't even been sure the mechanism would operate, and he wondered how it would hold if put to any sort of test.

"Help you?" he called out.

"Can you open up?" the man said.

"Sorry," Earl replied. "Short of time. Got a busload of kids to get home."

"I know that." The man raised his voice. "This won't take too long."

Now the kids were starting to become aware, not fooling around as much and craning their heads to see what might be going on in front.

"Why don't you tell me what you need?" Earl chose the word carefully. *Need*, not *want*. Make this man think Earl was taking him seriously.

"I'll be happy to," the man said. "I'd just rather do it face-to-face."

"I'm sorry," Earl said after a moment. "I can't do that."

The man squinted at him, but sunlight glinted off the glass, blocking sight of his features. Then he stepped out of the glare, and Earl saw his eyes.

"Can I ask you to move your car?" Earl said, hoping the quaver in his voice couldn't be heard. Good God, he really was an old man.

"I'm sorry," the man said. "I can't do that."

Earl caught the eerie echo of his own words. It seemed to escalate things somehow, confirm that this wasn't just a slightly out-of-the-ordinary encounter. It held the potential for something bad, which Earl could feel swinging slowly, like the heavy bag at the gym.

Without revealing what he was doing, Earl put his hand beneath the dash and reached for his radio. Also not something he'd ever had cause to do in his thirty-plus-year career.

"This is Earl," he said, low, when it crackled to life. "I got a situation here on Wicket Road."

A spurt of static, then: "What kind of situation, four-twenty-oh?"

"Don't know for sure. Vehicle blocking my path. Manned vehicle. The driver won't move."

"Can you get out and direct him to leave?"

Earl hesitated. "Don't know that I want to do that."

The man was trying to peer inside the bus, but the descending sun blocked his vision. He seemed to catch sight of Earl, though, or else just piece together what Earl must be doing, because he began pounding on the door with his fist. The bus shook.

In the rear, one of the children screamed, while others started to laugh. Some began banging on their own windows.

Earl turned in their direction.

"Quiet," he commanded. "Settle down. Let me take care of this."

The children were still straining to see, but they quit making any noise.

Outside the doors, the man took out a handgun.

Earl registered the sight with a single jolt of fear, then weary resignation.

So this is what it's come to, he said to the being he'd never believed in. Yep. Something bad was coming down the pike. He'd known it for a while now, hadn't he?

"Four-twenty-oh, are you clear?" whoever was on call at the bus yard asked.

"Negative," Earl said. "Not clear. This is an emergency situation. Repeat. Emergency. Man with a gun trying to board. Send the police." He spoke hushed and fast so as not to alert the children, who at least for now hadn't yet seen the gun.

Earl clicked off the radio. He didn't want it putting out blurps of static or demands for information. There was nothing anyone at radio's distance could do for them now.

"I want my son," the man was saying. "If you send him out, nobody gets hurt. If you don't, then I kill people, one by one, till I get my son." A pause. "You'll be last."

He meant Cody, the new kindergartener. The rhythm of the school year—Monday, Tuesday, Wednesday, Thursday, Friday in succession—had already begun lulling Earl into a state of complacency. Dispatch had told him about the little boy's situation, but he'd just about forgotten.

Earl drummed his fingers on the warm dash. This was the oldest member of the fleet—just like him—and her dashboard was cracked and worn. *Oh, Nellie,* he thought, *let's get out of this, and then we'll retire together. One last ride, girl.*

He glanced at the road, wondering what eleven tons of metal would do to that little sports car, presuming he could keep the man from getting off a lucky shot. An unlucky one.

The children all seemed possessed by the same collective impulse at once. The ones on the left side unlashed themselves and scrambled over to the side where the man was standing.

They saw the gun, and their voices rose in a volley of screams.

Earl strode to the middle of the aisle and shouted to be heard over the screams. "Quiet! It's going to be all right!"

Almost as one, the kids looked at him.

"But I need you to buckle into your seats—those over there, on the left. Crowd in three, four apiece if you have to. No one stays on this side."

The side where the man was. He could walk around, of course, but Earl intended to give him a reason not to. Safer would've been to have the kids lie down under the seats, but not if Earl was able to drive off. Then the steep pitch of Wicket Road would send them all hurtling to the back of the bus in one broken crush.

"And lash 'em tight, not like you usually do," Earl commanded. "You got that?"

All of the kids nodded except for Cody.

"You gotta stay quiet. Think you can manage that? If you can, then I promise you, we're gonna be just fine."

The kids began cinching in their belts, older ones helping younger.

"One more thing," Earl said.

Everyone looked up.

"At least one of you has a cellular phone. I know you do."

No phones at school was a rule, but the kids had been pushing the policy, especially over the last year or so.

"I do, sir." An eighth-grade boy began digging around in his knapsack.

"Good boy," Earl said. "If you can get a signal, call 911. Tell them we're on Wicket Road. And make sure whoever you get stays on the line till we see the first police car drive up."

He offered his flock a smile, and one by one, they smiled back.

Except for Cody. The boy was hunched over, small shoulders showing that he was crying without looking to stop.

"Somebody share his seat," Earl said roughly. If he started trying to comfort the boy himself, he wouldn't be able to leave him. And he had to get up to the front of the bus. "Tell him it's okay, and his dad's gonna be just fine, too."

Earl was going to have to steer the bus over the obstacle in its way. It would mean entering the switchback at a bad angle, but Nellie could handle that. He looked out at the engine, thrumming under the hood all this time. His girl. After the missus, this bus had been the biggest constant in his life.

Earl sat down, shifting into gear while trying to calculate the physics, figure out how he could get up the most speed.

A sharp crack split the air. The man was outside the doors, so close that for a hallucinatory moment it seemed to Earl he had made it inside.

Earl's heart clutched in his chest, hurting bad enough that he began to beg that being. *Please don't take me yet. I've got these kids to protect.*

"That shot didn't hit anyone," the man yelled. "But the next one will. Give me my kid, or you can explain to someone else's father why you let me kill him."

A quaking cry came from the rear. "I'll guh-go with you, Daddy!"

"Yes, that's right, son. Everyone's happier when they do what they're told."

"No!" Earl said. He looked around so fast that he saw pinprick dots. He could barely make out Brian Rudolph sitting beside Cody. "Rudolph, you don't let him up, you hear?"

The children had gone quiet, unresponsive; their eyes were glazed and staring.

The man fired twice and the bus gave a groan, sinking down heavily on one side. He had shot out her tires. *Oh, Nel, I'm sorry.*

But another thought came hard on the heels of that one.

He doesn't want to do what he says he's going to do. I'll bet he's never killed anyone.

Earl stood up. "I'll come out. Okay? We'll talk, man to man. Figure this thing out."

He looked back at the children. Now was the time to get them under the seats.

None of them looked capable of moving.

And Earl guessed this man didn't mean to give them much of a chance for maneuvering.

"I'm going to unlock the door," Earl said. "But only if you move twenty feet back—"

"You old fuck. Nobody tells me what to do—"

"I said, get back!" Earl roared. "Because the next thing I'm going to do is get every single one of these kids to lie down. You'll have to shoot your way through me to try and find your son. That's if you can make it onto this bus. And the police are already on their way." *Dear God, let the police be on their way.*

For the first time, the man looked uncertain. Then he took a few steps backward, gun thrust out to the side.

"That's right. Keep going," Earl said.

He looked up and down the road. Empty.

He twisted the key in the ignition, feeling the engine die with a shudder. Wouldn't do to leave the kids on the bus, engine running, even crippled as she was.

Earl heaved back on the arm that opened the accordion door. He climbed down the steps, hiding the pain in his knees caused by the descent.

The man rushed him.

Earl surged forward, trying to drive the man as far away from the bus as possible. Pushing him backward like a tackle, every foot, every inch a precious bit of space away from the children.

The two of them went down in a ditch.

The gun felt fiery against Earl's neck, heated from the man's grasp.

Was that the hum of an engine?

And a silvery piping note. It sounded like a whistle.

Or was it sirens at long last?

Earl smelled exhaust that wasn't diesel.

They were going to be okay. All of them. He and the missus, too. Once he got out of this, Earl intended to share the thoughts he'd been having lately, about the end, how fast it came upon you. The two of them would face it together.

They still had time.

The man fired.

Earl felt resounding pressure between them, then the weight on top of him was gone. Borne away or lifted or maybe left of its own accord, for he heard the slapping of feet.

"Daddy!" Cody cried from the back of the bus. "Where are you going?"

There came the sound of more beating feet, and then a roar, not of gunfire, or from an engine, but a human one.

"Stop and throw down your weapon! Now!"

"—went into those woods over there! Draw your weapon, Officer, and proceed—"

"Yessir, Chief—"

"Landry! Accompany him!"

There were too many voices for Earl to make sense of.

So many wonderful voices.

"Sir, are you all right?" He felt the press of two fingers against his neck. Then everything ramped up in urgency again. "Medic! I need a medic over here! *Now!*"

"Bus is clear, Chief—"

"What's your name, sir?" said the voice beside him, a whole hand pressing down on him now. Hard. Too hard. It hurt.

"Don't worry if you can't tell me," the voice went on easily. "You can just call me Tim. Can you hear me, sir?"

Earl thought he could.

"I want you to listen real close, because I've got something to tell you. You listening? Here's the thing. I'm the Chief of Police and I have never lost a man. I don't intend to lose one now. Sir, I hope you won't mind my saying, but you accomplished a goddamn miracle here today, not a single child hurt. I want you to hang on for me, sir, hang on, can you do that—"

"Chief! Chief, stop. Move aside. It's okay. We'll take him."

Earl stared up at the sky. *Thank you,* he mouthed to the being.

CHAPTER FORTY-FIVE

After Tim left, Liz sat back down at Paul's desk, suddenly pan-
icked. She'd experienced a certain degree of satisfaction at the
idea of Paul sensing her at his heels, but what if he actually were
checking email, and saw that she had learned about PEW? Might he
leave the place where he had gone, take Reid and Ally even farther
away? Liz forced a breath down. Wherever he was, Paul must be
deeply entrenched, and Liz had the feeling that finding another such
place wouldn't be easy. Still, she went to her husband's *Sent* items,
and deleted the email to Tim.

The tab for PEW blinked at her, a jittery taunt. This group held the
answers Liz was searching for, at least the live version of them did,
but all she had access to were static statements and pixelated images.
These people had her children, and Liz hated and envied them with a
fearsome fury. Staring at the screen, she began Googling *shoemaker*,
rage in every strike of the key.

Given the nature of PEW, Liz's guess had been that the online
identity was someone who cobbled things together. But cobblers repaired shoes, they didn't make them. She continued scanning pages,
coming to more and more far-fetched links. She stumbled across an
announcement for a school play, and wondered if the town where the
play had been performed might proffer some information as to the

Shoemaker's identity. It was in Iowa. There was a link to an out-of-print title, a true crime paperback on a used book site, which Liz clicked on. She'd just begun skimming it when a new email came in.

It was from Tim. It contained ten numbers, and a message.

Mackenzie traced the phone that Ally used. Don't use a landline—they might not pick up if the number is identified. Call from the pay-as-you-go.

Liz hadn't had the chance to buy a temporary cell yet, and Wedeskyull had blocked the encroachment of most chain stores. She was going to have to drive all the way out to the Northway. Liz printed out Tim's email, then raced downstairs and wrenched open the front door.

She covered the distance to Verizon, unable to recall a single length of road she had traveled, or any turn she'd made. Inside the brightly lit store, she ran for the counter. An array of devices was laid out in glass cases like pinned bugs.

"I need something I can use right away," Liz told the guy behind the counter. "Do you have anything like that?"

"Sure." The guy nodded. "Did you want a disposable? Or something you can renew—"

"I want any phone you have that will make a phone call!" Liz cried.

The boy took a step back. "Yeah. Sure. Take it easy, lady."

He pulled out a drawer beneath the display case and removed a box. "This one's the most basic model we've got. $29.99 plus tax."

"Fine," Liz said, desperation ragged in her voice.

Starting to hold the box out to her, the boy glanced up. Then he removed the device from its packaging, and keyed in a few numbers himself.

Liz put two twenties down, all the money she had in her wallet. She snatched the phone out of the guy's hand, clawing Tim's email out of her purse. She walked out, seeing nothing besides the keypad.

"Ma'am! Don't you want your change?"

Liz banged open the door, entering the number Tim had sent.

The call went through, the signal strong in this spot.

Still, each ring was harder and harder for Liz to make out. Her ears were filled with the tinny notes. She pressed the phone so close to the side of her head that she felt the imprint of each key.

The generic voicemail prompt took a moment to register.

"No," Liz said to no one. "Ally?" She spoke into the phone. "Are you there, Al?"

She stumbled backward to her car, hardly aware that she was climbing inside. She ended the call and tried again, comparing each digit to the ones in Tim's email before pressing Send.

Nobody is available right now.

Robotic, uncaring.

Please leave your message after the beep.

"Hello," Liz whispered into the phone. She coughed to clear her throat. "If somebody gets this, please call me. Please call me back at this number." She quickly scanned the card that had come with the phone and read off the ten digits. "Or else this one." She recited her real cell number in a voice as machine-like as the voicemail prompt. Tim would see if someone called on it. Liz added the only other thing she could think of. "Please."

Then she sat in the lot, blind with disappointment, making no move to start her car.

The phone lay there blackly, taunting Liz with its refusal to ring. She idly pressed keys before registering the sequence she'd dialed: her own childhood phone number. Her parents hadn't been in touch in the last several days; it wasn't yet time for their biweekly check-in. Thinking of her mother—as good as a calendar—Liz hit the button to end the call before anyone had a chance to pick up.

No car had driven by in a while. Liz was all alone out here. She re-entered the river of road, straddling lanes as her car surged forward.

Only when she crossed Lee Bridge with its arched metal hump-back did she realize how close she was to the center of town. She had never apologized to Jill for how angry she'd gotten at Andy. Liz wondered if she could do it now, weighted down with loss as she was.

At least Jill had her son.

When the phone rang, she nearly sobbed with relief. "Ally?" she said into it, swerving wildly onto a side street. "Hello? Hello?"

"Elizabeth? Did you call from this number?"

Liz's shoulders settled. She eased the car out of the way in case anyone else should come along, and shifted into Park.

"Are you there? Are you all right?"

"Yes, Mom," Liz said into the phone. "I'm here."

"Oh good." Her mother's voice didn't usually contain much emotion, but it had risen for a moment. "How are you, dear?"

Well, my children are still missing, Liz thought. She had to pause a moment before speaking, and when she did, she ignored her mother's query. "Mom? What would you have done if Dad—"

There was silence on the other end, a caving vacuum that Liz knew wasn't related to the weak signal.

"—if Dad had done something like what Paul is doing to me?"

"Why, what a strange question to ask, Elizabeth."

"Yes," Liz said simply. "I suppose it is."

The silence lasted longer this time.

"I imagine a lot of women would've gone to a judge," her mother said at last. "It was the era of divorce back then; everyone was doing it." Her voice struck a derisive note. "Even here. Those things used to happen only in big cities."

"Right," Liz said, wondering why she'd bothered. Divorce wasn't on the table right now; it was practically a given. At issue was only how to find her children.

"But I wouldn't have," her mother said.

It took Liz a second to register that she'd spoken.

"I was raised to believe that the man made the decisions, and that he knew what was best for his family. It's old-fashioned, I suppose."

Liz bit back the rejoinder that leapt to her lips. *You think?*

"How I would've missed you, Lizzie," her mother burst out.

For the past thirty years or so, only Jill had used that name. Coming from her mother, it triggered a childish rush of tears.

"I can't imagine what you're going through." A gap before the next words came. "But I don't think it would've occurred to me to fight. Oh, child, if Daddy had decided to do something like this, I don't know that I ever would've seen you again."

There was another pause as Liz took that in, and then her mother spoke again. "You know how word gets around in this town. Do you remember Mrs. Watters, from church? Marjorie Brackman is a good friend of hers." Her mother took in an audible breath. "Oh, honey, I never would've had the strength you're showing right now."

She was crying, and Liz spoke through tears of her own. "Thank you, Mom."

CHAPTER FORTY-SIX

Jill didn't answer Liz's cursory knock when she got there, but neither of them stood on ceremony at each other's houses. Liz nudged the door open, walked inside, and collapsed on the couch.

Just as fast, she was upright again.

Whimpers were coming from the second floor. Liz followed the sound, the strangled cries growing louder.

"Stay away!" Jill cried out hoarsely.

"Jill? It's me! What's wrong?" Liz ran up the flight of steps.

Jill was crouched in the hallway, arms wrapped around Andy's enormous rocking form.

"Jill?"

"I said, stay away!"

Andy's big body was folded in on itself, his elbow twitching as if he were shooting infinite passes.

"What's wrong? What's happening?"

Andy started to buck in his mother's hold, craning to look up at Liz.

Jill fought to hold on while waving Liz away. "It's okay! He'll be okay! Some of his memory is coming back, that's all. The doctor said it might happen this way, in bits and chunks."

"But—" Liz stopped. "That's good, isn't it? If his memory is returning?"

"It's scary for him," Jill said, and indeed Andy was mewling again, making tiny sounds more suited to a newborn creature than a man-sized boy. "Go downstairs. Please, Liz."

Liz turned to go. It was hard to see—no lights had been turned on and full dark had wrapped itself around the house—so she had to pick her way, taking care.

"Aunt Liz?"

Liz stopped. She hadn't heard those words in so many months. After *Mommy*, they were the words she'd been most longing to hear.

"Shhh, Andy," Jill said, smoothing her son's hair. "Go on, Liz. I'll be right down."

"Where are your kids, Aunt Liz?" Andy let out another tortured mew.

Liz had to turn away, lest Andy see her reaction, and become even more distraught. She headed down the hall toward the steps, hand extended to reach for the railing. She would let Jill remain behind, try and keep her son from tripping and falling into the holes in his memory.

"Are they in the woods?"

Liz came to an abrupt halt at the top of the stairs. Her foot hovered in the air over the first step, and she had to cling to the banister to keep from falling down the whole flight.

"Did he take them into the woods? Are they with ... are they with—" Andy let out a bellow so deep that the walls shook. "Are they—argh!" he cried, tearing at a clump of his hair. And then the words emerged like a burning coal from his raw, red throat. "Are they with Paul?"

Liz's ankle had turned when she'd almost fallen. It throbbed as she made her way back to Jill and Andy, walking through darkness as if in a dream.

"How do you know that, And?" she asked softly. "What do you mean about the woods?"

He stared up at her through smeared eyes.

Jill continued to grasp his shoulder, though her hold on him had loosened.

"I was—I was at your house," Andy said.

All other sources of sound had vanished. There was no rush of water through the pipes, no refrigerator humming, nor leaves rustling outside.

"You—you and my mom were outside. In the—in the—" His voice began to pitch again.

"Garden," Liz said, hushed.

"That's right!" Andy said, his relief so great it made his eyes stream. "In the garden! You both like to garden!"

"Yes," Liz said quietly. "We do."

"Liz—" Jill said.

"Shhh," Liz hissed at her.

"Paul—is that your husband, Aunt Liz?"

"Yes," Liz said again, still low. "It is."

"He told them something. I can't remember exactly what."

"That's okay," Liz said. "Just tell me what you do remember."

"Something about getting ready to go on a long walk. Through the woods."

"The woods," Liz echoed. "Did he say which woods? Are they nearby?"

Andy shook his head back and forth. "I told my mom a long time ago." A pause. "I think it was a long time ago. She asked me the same thing, but I couldn't remember." He looked up. "I don't remember any more than that, Aunt Liz! I'm sorry!"

Liz hardly heard his last desperate bleat. "Did you say you told . . . your mom?"

Her gaze dropped to Jill. She was shifting on the floor, away from Andy as if not even conscious of the movement. Her gaze wouldn't meet Liz's.

"You knew this?" Liz asked.

Silence.

"You knew?" Liz cried.

Jill lifted her head, chin thrust out. "Knew what, Liz? That Paul once said something about some woods? We're in the Adirondack Park, dammit. We're all about woods up here."

It was like being plunged into a cold sea. Every part of Liz stopped functioning and she was left gasping for breath. Her throat worked soundlessly for a second until finally she burst out, *"Anything!* Any . . . tiny . . . bit of *any*thing—I've been dying for! You know that, Jill! You have to know that!"

Her friend let out a sob. "I didn't think it had any meaning! Lots of things come back to him and are discarded. I had no idea this was any more real than—"

Liz began to back away, feeling a pulse each time her ankle came down.

"Lizzie!" Jill screamed. "He got so upset! Every time Andy started talking about this. I couldn't let him get upset! You know what the doctor said. It was the worst thing we could do, to let him get . . ."

Liz held on to the banister as if it were a lifeline, belaying down the stairs to spare her wounded ankle, and hobbling out of the house at a run. The last thing she heard was Andy's voice rising again— something about was Aunt Liz feeling sad—and Jill shouting at him to be quiet, to just please, please shut up.

CHAPTER FORTY-SEVEN

Liz knew something was wrong the instant she got out of the car. She stood motionless in the curved sickle of her driveway, and took a craning look around.

The house stood in shadows, its front porch a sagging sweep. The woods grasped in their usual way, branches reaching toward the property.

Maybe it was just the aftermath of betrayal, tipping her whole world a few degrees. Jill had known her, stood by her, supported her ever since they were in kindergarten. How could her best friend have abandoned her during the hardest time of her life? Andy's words may not have meant much, but they were better than nothing, and they indicated that Paul had been preparing the children.

Smoldering fury filled her, directed at her husband, but also at Jill. Liz reached a hand out to the car to steady herself. A grim vision returned to her: Andy's trembling body, his precarious mental state.

Jill had simply prioritized her child. Would Liz herself have done any different?

She took another glance around. What felt so wrong?

The tops of the tallest plants—the hollyhocks and cornstalks she'd had Andy leave behind—weren't standing at attention. This time of year, tips and fronds could always be seen from this vantage point.

Liz headed in the direction of Roots, taking out the new phone to call Tim.

She limped a little, going downhill past the looming outline of the house, then kept to the perimeter of woods. The wreckage appeared before her and she came to a shuddering halt.

It was possible that nobody else would've registered this, certainly not in the dark. But as if she herself had been bodily violated, Liz felt the full extent of the disruption, the terrible tearing hands.

Bush beans and Armado cauliflower, carrots, broccoli, and four varieties of onion, all the crops planted to winter over, had been scooped out of the ground. Cuts had been made in the earth with a trowel or spade, far deeper than was required to lift the tender young roots. The field of holes looked like empty eye sockets, blank and staring.

For Liz it was like botched surgery, an amputation or incision performed by somebody who didn't know how to wield a knife. Whoever had done this hadn't taken care as he walked, so anything left behind had been trampled. Blooms were broken at the stem, seedlings destroyed before they'd had a chance to grow. Sunflowers were bowed by someone's brushing body, the leaves on succulents had been crushed into an oozing mess.

Terror hit Liz like a train. The Shoemaker had come back.

All was empty and deserted now. If he had been here, he was gone.

Liz checked the house, but as expected, it was undisturbed.

A moon had risen, casting a ghostly, lonely light. Only Roots had been laid to waste, its bounty needed wherever Paul was.

Liz walked toward the thin woods on their property. They were incapable of hiding anyone, of being the location Andy had spoken about. She howled a great, billowing cry of grief.

"Where are you? You bastard, you want my plants, you want my children, then take them when I'm here, confront me to my face!"

She didn't know whom she was speaking to: Paul, or the Shoemaker, or both.

From behind her came the beat of footsteps, and she remembered calling Tim. She spun, feeling her ankle twinge, then stopped short at the sight of his face.

Tim's expression was so fierce that at first it seemed he had to know what had happened—was reading the soil as Liz did with her fingers and her soul. But then she realized that something else was driving him, that Tim had troubles all his own.

He strode toward her and she met him at the same speed, her ankle forgotten. He clutched her wrists, and bound, she reached to stroke the sorrow on his face.

She hadn't realized how dirty she'd gotten, touching crevices and gaping wounds in the garden, until she took in the sight of Tim's dirt-streaked face. She tasted salt and earth when he bent down, opening her mouth with his.

Liz let out a moan of loss and hunger.

Tim lifted her into his arms, moving back with her across the ground. He parted the leaves on a tree, setting her down on one thick branch. She felt the scrape of bark against her thighs, then the rasp of Tim's hands. His form was so solid and reassuring, like a part of the tree itself. She rocked against him, off balance on her perch.

Tim kept her from falling. They clung to each other before Tim pushed himself away, the effort captured in his averted eyes, veins standing out like reeds in his throat. But Liz's hands sought him, and he finally let out a grunt of surrender. And as he made himself part of her, they both cried out, their sound soaring up to the sky. Tim touched her as they moved and moved together, taking each inch of her cold, dead flesh and bringing it achingly back to life.

"I'm sorry," he said when it was over.

Liz raised her face to his. "You are?"

"No."

She let out a bitter laugh. "Why should you be? You're not the one who just cheated on her husband while her children are missing."

"I don't know that you can call it cheating when your husband's the one who kidnapped those children."

"Ah," she said, looking off into the night. "So it is a kidnapping."

Tim was reaching for his holster on the ground. "In all but the legal sense, yes."

Silence descended.

Tim handed Liz her phone, and she pocketed it as she readjusted her clothes.

"Should we—" Liz began.

"You should know that—"

They both broke off, shaking their heads.

"Could we not?" Liz said after a moment. "For a little while?"

"Sure." Tim held her gaze. "Of course."

Liz looked away.

"You called me," Tim said. "After you tried that number Mackenzie dug up, right?"

Liz couldn't imagine recounting the disappointment she'd lived through, nor sharing the information—in all its dread incompleteness—that Andy had offered. Never mind the awful crippling of her garden. A weary wave broke over her.

Tim was watching. "Mackenzie will try to get info on the owner. Kind of like a reverse phone book. But that can take a while. I was hoping you might get lucky and someone would pick up."

The possibility hurt to consider.

"When you got here," Liz said. "You looked so upset. Broken almost."

Tim squeezed his hand into a fist, and aimed his gaze away. "There was an incident today. An attack on a school bus on Wicket Road."

Liz looked sharply at him, peering into the darkness.

"All the children are okay, thank God. But the perp—the man who did it—fled into the woods. Took us four hours to find him. And the bus driver is hanging on by a thread."

Liz hadn't taken in any of that. Woods. Wicket Road.

It was the site of Paul's long ago accident. The connection she'd been looking for.

"Tim," she said.

He'd been scrubbing tiredly at his face. Now he lowered his hand to look at her.

"I know where Paul has them."

THE MURDER

Madeline had never felt so free in her life as she did trapped in a hot field of grasses, sweat pouring off her skin, machete in her hand.

Their first big task was to clear any unwooded areas for planting. Madeline had already completed one section, and today one of the ladies—Magpie or Katrina—was going to transplant the seedlings Kurt Pierson had brought back last night. But they would need more acreage if they intended to sustain themselves by next year.

The season was about to come to a cold, screeching halt, so this year they would subsist mostly on stores people had brought in. Sacks of flour and bulk grains for bread and a thin, nourishing gruel Madeline had already sampled. It wasn't bad. Tasteless, but not bad.

A flock of hens pecked and worried by the barn, its rooster strutting around, which would ensure a supply of eggs. There was even a grove of old apple trees, bearing small, hard fruit, which Katrina had been laboring over.

Madeline worried about milk for the children. She was nursing Dottie, so no need for concern there, but what about the older ones? Maybe one day there would be a cow.

A platoon of beehives was housed in square vats. Katrina had given Madeline a chunk of comb to lick, but Magpie—whose real name was Terry—had come up and steered her away, warning her not to let a single droplet fall anywhere near Dottie's mouth, or touch Madeline's bare breast.

"It could kill her, do you understand?" Terry said, making honey sound as dangerous as a gun. Then she went into this long, drawn-out explanation, botulism that somehow didn't bother adults but was terrible for babies.

After that, Madeline didn't go near the apiary—Katrina's name for it—again.

It had been impressed upon her how much space she had to cover by the first hard frost. And even though it seemed as if the blue skies and warm sun would never abate, Madeline knew winter was coming. So she pushed herself through the sharp stalks of grasses at a pace that left her panting, and wrenched her deep inside, where until recently Dottie had lived.

Each blade of grass was covered with rows of tiny teeth, sticky, nibbling things that clung to Madeline and slowed her down. But even though the task was arduous, hot, and occasionally treacherous—she'd nicked herself with the tip of the machete twice yesterday, the wounds requiring treatment with calendula and wormwood—Madeline loved it. She loved feeling essential to the whole operation. And she loved being in this enormous expanse of open space, and blissfully, utterly alone.

She swung the machete, lashing at a swath of stems, then swiveling to get out of the way of the blade. Madeline wiped her face clear of perspiration. The intense effort was good for her; it would restore her body to what it had been before she'd gotten pregnant. She stepped over the pile of grasses she'd just struck down. These would be separated and dried, woven into baskets eventually, but that was someone else's job.

She felt a rush of heat in her breasts, and glanced at the sky overhead. Madeline wasn't good at telling time this way yet, but it looked to be around noon. Dottie must be getting hungry. For the past week or so, the baby had stayed with Terry while Madeline worked. The first time Terry had proposed this solution, Madeline had recoiled, saying that she could take care of her baby herself. Her plan was to lie Dottie on a blanket a safe distance away, tend to her in the green and fragrant grasses.

But Terry had pointed out all that was wrong with that idea—the baby would get too much sun; Madeline was going to cover enough ground that she wouldn't be able to keep a close eye—and she had admitted defeat. Besides, Madeline saw the expert care and attention Terry bestowed, and was glad for Dottie's sake.

Terry changed Dottie's cloth diapers, swaddling her in blankets made of organic cotton, which had belonged to Terry's children when they were babies. Terry said that her favorite time of all was when her children were first born. They give you trouble after that, Terry had explained, although Madeline looked forward to the ways Dottie might get into mischief, developing a personality of her own.

Her infancy was certainly turning out to be blissful. Terry gave her baths with some kind of apricot oil that smelled like heaven. She was insistent that breast milk was all Dottie take, which was fine since there was no formula here anyway. When Madeline pumped, it had to go into a glass bottle, though. Madeline couldn't imagine what was wrong with plastic. She worried about glass breaking in Dottie's tender bud of a mouth.

Terry had started taking over during the nighttime too, so that Madeline could rest up for the hard work of clearing fields. But Madeline was permitted to do one feeding each day by herself, and she looked forward to it with a hunger as great as Dottie's. It was time now; she could tell by the surging in her breasts.

Madeline washed up first by the creek. Terry insisted that all the dust from the field had to be gone before Madeline touched Dottie, otherwise the baby would have to skip nursing and be given an extra bottle. It had already happened once. Terry assured Madeline that she knew microbes and bacteria were key to immune system development, so it wasn't the dirt, but the spores and bits of chaff that might trigger allergies if inhaled at too young an age.

Madeline splashed and scrubbed ferociously, turning her skin raw, letting her long, wet hair slap her back, no danger of missing this one precious encounter.

Dottie was lying on a blanket in the shade by the barn, just beginning to stir and whimper. Terry knelt beside her, singing softly into her ear. When Madeline whispered her baby's name, Terry looked up. "I was just beginning to wonder if I should fetch a bottle."

"I'm here," Madeline said, reaching down shyly for Dottie. She still felt awkward, ungraceful compared to Terry, when she picked her baby up. "I'll be down by the creek."

"Not too close to the falls. The men are working there today."

"Of course not," Madeline said, shushing Dottie and turning away before Terry could remark that she might be able to calm the baby better.

Madeline never went near the falls. There was a willow tree upstream a ways, whose boughs overhung the creek, offering a broad base on which she liked to sit. You had to ascend a sloping hill to get there, but at least the rush of the falls was muted at that distance. Madeline found the falls a little scary, though she wouldn't have liked to admit it. Everyone else was so brave here. But the roar of the waterfall was deafening and she'd seen a huge boulder taken up and sent hurtling down to the pool below as if it were a pebble. One day, the falls would provide the power for this place, but right now they seemed more menace than anything else.

The water at this lazy portion of the creek moved in slow whorls, however. Terry had instructed Madeline to remove the baby's diaper when she switched sides in the hopes that Dottie would pee or poop. It was supposed to help with potty training later. Madeline thought she must look a little nuts, holding an infant at arm's length, her naked bottom dangling. She did it over the creek just in case anything ever did come out, but so far nothing had.

Madeline looked down at Dottie, fingering a lock of her hair. It was growing in nicely, thick, with a shine to it. Terry had put avocado in Dottie's hair a few times, till Katrina got angry and said that any food should go toward eating. They'd run out of avocados a few days after that anyway, and Madeline guessed she might never see one again.

"Okay, Dottie," Madeline murmured. "Guess you don't have to go right now. Are you still hungry?" Dottie latched on with such ferocity that Madeline felt a tug in her groin. "Whoa," she said softly. "I should say you are."

"Madeline Powers Jennings."

It was as if two planets had collided. Madeline felt rocked by their force. She looked down to make sure Dottie still lay in her arms because for a moment she believed that everything, her baby, the last week, even herself might be gone. Dottie was still nursing hungrily, unperturbed by the fact that the two of them were about to lose everything.

"Did you think I wouldn't find you?" Cara Jennings said.

"How did you?" asked Madeline in a small voice.

Her mother shook her head impatiently. "I followed you to the end of the road that first day. Then I lost you for a while, but I found a way in eventually." There was a triumphant note in her voice before Cara returned to her usual tone of displeasure. "The police wouldn't help me at all. Something about you being of age." She brushed dirt briskly off her hands. "Anyway, the only important question now is, what are you doing here?"

Madeline shook her head soundlessly.

"I'm assuming that you're experiencing something called postpartum psychosis," her mother continued. "I never would've believed such a thing existed—so much women's foolishness to get out of caring for their children—but there's no other explanation for your behavior. Standing there in the river, half nude!"

Madeline stared down at the creek. The amber water flowed by like syrup. It would gather force later on. Madeline wondered what would happen if she jumped in with Dottie.

"I'm happy here," she said hopelessly.

It wasn't clear whether her mother heard that or not.

"Come on," she said. "Get out of there and give me the baby. We'll be home before you know it. Just half a day's drive. How you met up with these lunatics, I'll never know." She bent down toward Madeline, tsking her tongue and reaching for Dottie.

Madeline stood amongst the tangle of willow roots. She began to climb awkwardly up the bank.

Her mother leaned forward.

Dottie shrieked, either in alarm at being taken or anger at losing the breast. Her cries increased in volume, spiraling out into the still air.

Then two bodies appeared over the rise.

"Get the infant," Kurt Pierson commanded.

He was a good-looking man, tall and strong, with a sweep of dark, glossy hair that almost made you need to touch it. Madeline could've stared into his jeweled eyes forever. She had developed a schoolgirl's crush on him the first few days they were here, before acknowledging that Kurt was far too smart for her. Still, second only to spending time with Dottie, the thing Madeline loved most about life here was getting to talk to Kurt. He listened as if what she had to say truly mattered. He seemed to believe that she might really contribute something.

Madeline was relieved to see him now. Kurt would come up with the right way to deal with her mother, but just as important, he would listen to the background Madeline had to provide. Her relationship with Cara was unusually close; Madeline was aware of that.

Kurt's shirtsleeves were rolled up above his elbow, exposing muscled forearms, and his pants legs were damp. He'd been working at the falls, Madeline recalled.

Terry was there, too, lifting Dottie out of Madeline's trembling arms. There wasn't so much as a jog as the baby passed between bodies, so smoothly did Terry orchestrate it. Dottie started to calm as soon as she'd been lifted, and quiet filled the air. For a moment the only sound was the constant sigh of the brook.

"Go," Kurt commanded, and Terry departed over the hill.

Cara Jennings was looking from Kurt to Madeline again.

Madeline felt frightened for no real reason. She wanted Dottie. She sneaked a look at Terry, taking her leave across the fields, only the regal straight of her back now visible.

"Who is this, Madeline?" Kurt asked.

"Who am *I*?" Cara Jennings retorted. "I should be asking you that question. Who are you, and why have you taken my daughter?"

Kurt took a step closer to Cara. "I ask the questions."

Cara Jennings was uncharacteristically speechless. Madeline felt a lick of relief. Maybe this would still turn out all right. Maybe she could stay.

But then her mother opened her mouth. "Let's go, Mad—"

Kurt raised his voice and spoke over her. "The first one was a gimme. A test. I know perfectly well who you are."

Both Madeline and Cara frowned.

Kurt took another step forward. "I know a lot about you, in fact."

His voice was mesmerizing, hypnotic. Madeline felt lulled, becoming calmer yet when even her mother went quiet.

"I know that you've cowed your daughter all these years, bending her to your will. I even know how you've done it, undermining her faith in herself to such an extent that she felt lucky to have you." Kurt paused momentarily to seek out Madeline's gaze. "Much as our own Magpie is doing to you again right now."

Madeline's vision blurred, distorting the sight of Kurt.

"The only thing I don't know is whether you've told anyone else we are here," Kurt said to Cara, taking another step.

She looked at him.

"And your eyes and that flinch just told me the answer to that."

Cara Jennings narrowed her gaze, but it was too late.

"Good." Kurt gave a ringing clap of his hands. Then he bent down and drew up his pant leg. He took a gun, blue steel and thick-barreled, from a contraption on his ankle.

The next seconds passed in a watery rush.

Kurt lifted the gun.

He was close enough to Cara Jennings that they appeared to be dancing.

Kurt fired, the blast momentarily drowning out the noise of the falls far away.

An enormous rose exploded on Cara's chest, red and bursting with blooms. Cara fell backward to the ground, still wearing that habitual expression of thin-eyed distrust.

"No!" Madeline wailed. "Mommy!" She ran to her mother's fallen form, cradling her as if she were holding Dottie. "No," she said again. "Mommy, come back. *Mommy!* I love you, Mommy, I—"

A shadow descended, blocking out the warmth of the sun. Madeline felt the snub snout of the gun nosing the flesh by her ear.

"Madeline," Kurt said.

Madeline had the urge to retreat, try and scoot back, but she couldn't leave her mother.

"I did not expect a formal *thank you* for freeing you from that bitch. But if you don't stop whining over her body, I'll kill you, and that infant of yours, too."

CHAPTER FORTY-EIGHT

Liz had remembered as soon as Tim said the words. Wicket Road was the twisted, winding site of Paul's accident. A mean road, Marjorie had called it. A connection between Paul and Michael Brady had allowed Liz to find her husband in cyberspace. It might just work in real life, too.

Andy had said they were in the woods.

She told Tim all of this as he was preparing to leave. The prospect of the endless hours standing between her and her children was unbearable, but Liz knew that exploring wilderness at this hour would be impossible.

Suddenly Tim's radio crackled; then there was a bang on the front door.

Liz opened up, but the policeman who stood there spoke to Tim.

"Chief, the old guy just woke up at the hospital."

How had he known Tim was here?

Tim's face went ruddy. He didn't look at Liz as he headed out with the other cop.

But in the doorway, he paused.

"All right," he told her. "We'll leave at first light tomorrow."

He picked her up in his official vehicle when dawn was just cracking open the sky. Liz was dressed and sitting on the couch, jacket buttoned up against the early morning chill. She and Tim didn't talk as they walked out to his police SUV and got inside. Second-growth forest streaked by outside the windows as they drove. You couldn't go anywhere in Wedeskyull without seeing trees, only now they weren't parsing themselves into identifiable bark and foliage as they usually did for Liz. Instead they'd become sites of concealment.

"I pulled the accident report," Tim said. He withdrew a tablet from the console, calling up a screen as he kept one eye on the road. "Look at this."

Liz tilted the device. It showed an aerial view of a section of road with a downed tree lying across it, and a totaled car whose windshield had been punctured by the trunk. Imagining the physical devastation that would've occurred to the person sitting where the tree had come through made her stomach lift with a woozy pang.

Tim entered the location into his GPS and made the next indicated turn.

What Marjorie had meant about the road became clear as soon as Tim and Liz were on it. This was a remote mountain pass, twisting back and forth upon itself in a series of turns that were difficult even for the SUV to take. In the dark, with the buzz of a drink or two in you, flying off into oblivion on the other side of the mountain would be entirely too easy. But that wasn't it, or not all of it anyway. The trees grew so thickly that they seemed to be snaring the SUV as it tried to pass through. Dense September foliage smothered both sides and a canopy loomed above, blotting out the sun. Wicket Road looked like a leafy, green trap.

Tim pulled the car up onto a hummock of earth—the road too narrow for a shoulder—and turned off the engine.

"Is this where the school bus incident took place?" Liz asked.

"No. That was a ways farther up." Tim paused. "This was the site of the accident. I figure it's the best starting point we have. There are a lot of acres out here."

Liz looked right and left of the road, all the potential ground.

"The school bus driver?" she asked. "Will he be—"

Tim nodded. "Looks like he's going to pull through."

His face didn't appear any more relaxed or at peace, though.

"I took his statement last night," Tim went on. "Seems the guy who attacked the bus was trying to kidnap his son."

Liz felt everything inside her go cold. Her jacket was too thin a barrier to protect against the chill evaporation of early morning dew from all these endless leaves.

"That's part of why I'm here," Tim said. "On the strength of a—we gotta admit—far-fetched hunch."

Liz looked at him.

"A second father from the same town kidnapping his child in the space of a month?" Tim shook his head. "Coincidences."

Tall trees stood like soldiers on both sides of the road, and with no reason to choose one direction over the other, Liz simply followed when Tim turned right.

"Paul's right-hand dominant, correct?" he asked, holding a branch back for her as they entered the forest. "Most people go with that."

"What are we looking for?" Liz said, grateful when Tim didn't remind her that this was her idea.

"Any indication of disturbance," Tim replied. "We're not on a hiking trail—I doubt anyone's passed this way in months. So look for broken branches, crushed plants. Could be from an animal, but you never know. We might get lucky."

Something inside her flagged. It would be like stumbling on a bread crumb at the beach.

"You know how things grow," Tim went on. "Look for signs that they've been interfered with."

Liz felt a gust of confidence at his words. "Okay," she said. "I'll look at eye-level. How about you take the ground?"

Tim nodded approvingly, and tramped ahead.

But after a half hour of walking, the task felt hopeless. For one thing, they were introducing disruption themselves, try as they might to walk stealthily. And thirty minutes of blind focus on flora meant that it became hard to distinguish detail of any sort. There was an infinite banner of leaves. If Liz had been expecting to come upon some utopian installment—outbuildings, a water wheel in a babbling brook—she wasn't going to find it here. These endless, unbroken woods didn't look as if they housed any being more sentient than a bear or a coyote.

"Tim," she said, and he stopped.

Futility was mirrored in his eyes and Liz turned away from the cool, blank sight.

He walked over to her. "Why don't we try the woods on the other side of the road?"

She looked up at him. "Really?"

He nodded. "And you know what—that aerial shot gave me an idea. I know a guy with a helicopter. He uses it for crop-dusting and an air taxi business. I can't justify a SAR, but I can ask this guy to go up as a favor, circle around."

Liz clamped down on a dizzy spasm of hope. It would amount to the same thing as a search and rescue, just an unofficial one. "You can?"

"If I can get a signal, I'll put a call in as soon as we get back to the road."

The walk out took half as long as the way in. Tim removed his radio when they were still a ways from the car, starting a small trickle of anticipation in Liz. He had to walk to get a connection, and Liz listened to the distant, staticky exchange, her hands clenched. Tim was asking someone at the station to place a call for him. Liz set off into the expanse of woodland on the other side of the road, reassured by the thud of Tim's boots on the packed soil behind her, and the thought of how glorious helicopter blades would sound biting into the air.

"Come here," Tim said, after they'd been walking for another hour or so. He was crouching down, studying the ground, hands extended to avoid touching anything. He looked up at the sky, getting his bearings. "This is where I'll tell my guy to start looking."

Liz took the uneven ground at as fast a pace as she dared, rocks and bleached bones of branches tilting her off course. She skidded to a halt as Tim raised a warning hand.

A few minutes before she'd been falling behind, tired from beating back leaves in this near-impenetrable section of woods, spent from disappointment. But hope never really dies; it just goes dormant. As soon as Tim indicated this patch, seedlings began to send up shoots inside Liz again, and her feet felt airborne.

She instantly saw what he had. The earth here was different from the area through which they'd passed. It looked bare, almost brushed clean, and the undergrowth had all been cleared.

The ground felt as if it might be moving, quick and alive.

By mutual, unspoken agreement, they both went still, barely even breathing. Liz was suddenly aware that they were probably being observed.

Hairs pricked on the backs of her arms. She and Tim were encroachers, their presence unwelcome. At the same time, her children could be nearby, and so everything inside Liz was at war, fighting to look around while trying not to do anything that might prompt notice.

She strained at the soundless air, listening for a faint call, or regular beat of footsteps, any sound of human occupancy. Tim had his hand on his radio, but for the moment he merely turned his head, left with a pause to look, right with another pause, and finally straight ahead, before repeating the whole sequence.

Liz hardly dared to move. For the first time, the particulars—what could come *after* she found Reid and Ally—began to occur to her. Locating them might turn out to be the easy part. She hadn't thought about what would happen when she tried to take them away from Paul, or anyone else out here.

The Shoemaker.

She heard an echo of his hypnotic, melodic voice, felt that single pressing finger on the cut on her arm, and something inside her shriveled. A bristly branch of fir caught her shoulder and she jumped.

Tim held out a steadying hand.

He stepped over to her with care, taking care not to disturb the bare ground. He lowered his head and spoke into her ear. "This is what I say we should do . . ."

Liz felt a surge of desire for her children, a tug in her belly so strong that it hurt. She straightened so as to attend to Tim's instructions, and that was when she saw.

She cried out.

Tim aimed a warning look in her direction, instructing her to be quiet.

Disappointment sent her to her knees.

Tim's face changed, and he dropped down. "What is it?" he whispered. "What's wrong?"

Liz stayed there on the ground, cold leaching into her jeans. She spoke at normal volume, puncturing the stillness. But her voice was dull and toneless.

"Those are Maker firs."

Tim followed her gaze.

They were a rapacious, virulent species of tree, particularly dense and arched at the canopy, with no twigs or foliage descending the trunk. In effect, the Maker killed itself off the closer it got to its own roots.

"They're the most acidic tree you can find," Liz went on. "Nothing will grow beneath them."

Tim looked down at the ground again.

"This area hasn't been cleared," Liz said. "In fact, for that grove of Makers to grow so thick, I would say nobody's been here in years."

CHAPTER FORTY-NINE

Liz sat on the couch with night descending. She held a throw cushion tightly between her hands, compressing the stuffing.

She'd been wrong. Stupidly, idiotically wrong to think she could outsmart Paul, the Shoemaker, and the whole Adirondack wilderness, which might or might not contain her children. They could be in any of six million acres within the blue line of the Adirondack Park. Or anywhere with woods.

She was never going to see Reid and Ally again.

A sob rose in her throat and she pulled the cushion to her face and bit down.

For the thousandth time that evening, she checked both her recently returned cell and the new disposable for incoming calls, before dialing the number Ally had called from. Liz had memorized it, but the disappointment that blanketed her each time the anonymous voicemail came on made her check and recheck Tim's email, praying she'd gotten just one digit wrong.

The only person she could imagine talking to now was Jill. She didn't care what her best friend had done anymore. Perhaps Jill had willfully not questioned Andy, but if so, it had only been to avoid upsetting him in his tenuous state. And maybe Jill truly hadn't grasped the potential import of her son's words. It didn't matter. Especially since in actuality, those words hadn't turned out to help at all. Liz's fingers probed blindly for one of the phones. The devices skittered around on the sofa like live things.

Outside, a car door slammed.

Liz put down the sodden lump of cushion. She twisted to kneel on the couch, lifting the curtain from the window.

A pickup truck sat in her driveway. And the person getting out of it was the last one Liz expected to see. Not the phantom driver of that first pickup they'd encountered, streaking by at the terrible start to what had been deemed a vacation. The enraged face of that man flew into Liz's mind as she watched this alien truck in her drive.

But it wasn't him, nor was it Matthew, striding up the walkway in his stiff-legged gait.

It was Mary.

Her mother-in-law went around to the other side of the truck. The passenger door had been unlatched. Mary reached inside, then closed the door with effort, starting a bit at the thud. She was holding a shopping bag, which looked heavy from the way it pulled at her grip.

Liz got up and opened the front door. Mary climbed the porch steps one at a time, bringing both feet to rest before she attempted the next, and clinging to the railing for support.

"Elizabeth," she said, not quite meeting Liz's gaze. "May I come in?"

Liz stepped aside. "What are you doing here?" *Asinine*, she heard Jill say. She wondered what question Jill would've come up with to ask.

But Mary's reply caused tears to strike. "I suppose I came because I'm a mother, too."

Liz turned, going back into the house. "A mother who chooses to have almost no contact with her child. While I had no control over losing mine."

Was that true? Or had Liz played a role in what Paul had done by allowing him to be what he'd become?

Mary's hand wafted down, coming to a rest on Liz's arm. "I didn't have a whole lot to do with losing mine either."

Liz jerked free. "I suppose you're right. It was Matthew who called a stupid, tragic accident unforgivable. Saw fit to disavow your son over it." Mary began to reply, but Liz spoke over her, surprising herself with her shaking rage. "Paul hadn't even drunk that much. I saw the road they were on. Anybody could've crashed their car."

"Matthew didn't reject Paul because of the accident," Mary said.

The pale timbre of her tone was hard to make out. Liz wasn't sure she had heard correctly. She blinked, trying to bring her mother-in-law's face into focus.

Mary set the bag she was holding down in the entryway. "I've always believed that the past belongs where time has taken it," she said, so low she was almost whispering.

Liz leaned forward and took Mary's wrists in her hands, surprised to find them strong as stalks. "Mary. This isn't the past anymore. Please tell me why Matthew disowned Paul."

Mary looked over her shoulder, the movement rendering her unsteady. She walked to the couch and sank down.

Liz followed but remained standing, looming over her mother-in-law's bent back.

"That road is a monster," Mary burst out. It was an utterly spontaneous eruption of words, spoken with uncharacteristic fervor. "We drove there after the accident, too. And Paul was so very young." Mary raised a hand to her face, wearing lines and divots in it that hadn't been there a moment before. "They were both so god-awful young."

Tears seeped from Liz's eyes; then she felt a charge of fury. Not at Mary, but at herself. What was she doing, standing around weeping instead of ferreting out the reason Mary had come? "What made Matthew turn his back on Paul?"

Mary looked up at her through cloudy eyes. "He called him a dirty, stinking coward."

The brutality of the statement winded Liz like a fall, or a punch. What a hard, unyielding man Matthew was. And also, how similar were father and son. Only the nature of their denunciation differed.

"Oh yes," Mary said, an odd note of merriment in her voice. "That's what he said. Can you imagine saying that to your own flesh and blood?"

"Well," Liz said. She turned and walked toward the door. "I suppose now I understand how Paul could do something as cruel and drastic as this."

Mary bowed her head.

"I still don't understand why you came," Liz said, looking back. "Just to tell me how much Matthew hates his son? How helpless you were to do anything about it?"

"No," Mary murmured. "That isn't it."

Liz's hand stilled on the knob.

Mary got up and crossed to Liz at a halting pace. In the entryway, she lifted the shopping bag. Her fist gave a palsied shake.

Liz frowned, but a pulse of faint hope was starting to tick inside her.

"I thought we should both see what's inside this."

When her mother-in-law didn't seem inclined to go on, Liz parted the folds of the bag and peered into the gaping space.

It held the missing lockbox.

THE DINNER HOUR

Abby was preparing dinner with the other women when they heard it. The blast split the deep quiet around them, inciting a cacophony of bird cries, followed by a high, tailing-off whistle. All three of them looked up at once, but Abby was the first to run for the barn door and heave it open.

"Cody!" she called, a note of alarm in her voice. "Children!"

"Yeah?" Tom shouted back. "Whaddaya want?"

His voice held a faint underlay of menace, but that seemed to be normal for Tom. The boy sounded casual. Nothing wrong.

Abby threaded her way through the trees, coming out behind the barn.

The children were at work netting a berry patch so that it wouldn't be picked clean before the fruit could ripen next season. Tom, the oldest, was driving stakes into the ground, letting out a karate-like *"Hi-ya"* as each one spiked the earth. Reid and his sister Ally cut lengths of net. Even Cody had been given a job. Abby felt a flush of delight as she watched her little boy solemnly hold a piece of netting so that Ally could affix it to the stake.

"Good job, Cody," Abby heard Ally say.

Ally appeared to be a natural teacher, especially if the lesson had anything to do with plants. The way the kids were getting along promised to be a surprise bonus of this whole venture. Older ones teaching younger, younger reminding older of a sort of wide-eyed state of innocent delight. Cody, who was destined to remain an only child, seemed to take particular pleasure in the group he had joined. Abby felt more relaxed than she had in months, although she intended to keep a watchful eye, especially where Tom was concerned. He was a big kid, rough, but neither of those things were what concerned her. No, it was that Abby sensed a cold sheen beneath Tom's loudmouth ways, as if his insides were made of chrome or tin instead of blood and pulpy organs. And the other moms seemed to be similarly wary, although they hadn't talked about it yet.

In some ways, the reality of this place was turning out to be better than Abby had anticipated, the kids being the most shining example of this. But there were downsides she hadn't imagined too, and Abby had wondered once or twice what she'd gotten herself and Cody into. This wasn't some well-planned utopian compound; instead, it was a motley group of people who seemed to be figuring things out as they went along. She and Cody had only been here two days, and she could already tell how many holes there were, gaps that would have to be filled in, with winter fast approaching.

But what choice had she had but to come?

Abby had hoped that Sue, who had put Abby in touch with the women from the chat room, would also join them. Abby and Sue had met in a moms' group four years ago. But Sue had never given any thought to meeting her cyber friends in person, let alone following where they led. That was an avenue she'd thought of for Abby, Sue explained, when Bill caused the situation to become so desperate.

Sue assumed that once Bill was arrested, Abby would decide against leaving. But the opposite was true. Bill's assault on the driver—the fact that he'd been willing to hold a bus full of children at gunpoint—only convinced Abby that her ex-husband was capable of the worst. Bill would hire the top criminal lawyer in the country and be out on bail within a week.

Abby took one more look at the brood of kids.

Tom and Reid were pretend sword fighting with the stakes, and Ally was feeding Cody a berry that somehow hadn't gotten consumed by birds or bears. For a moment, Abby thought about stepping in;

Tom's thrusts looked especially vicious. But Reid seemed to be holding his own, and after all, Abby wasn't either boy's mother. It took a village, but her role as villager hadn't been fully determined yet.

She couldn't help wondering about the two missing moms. Kurt's wife had clearly died: he'd hinted at a grief too deep to share, and Abby held out hope that she could coax him to a greater level of intimacy. It wasn't Kurt's looks that drew her, although that dark hair did appear thick enough to lose your fingers in. Abby hadn't expected this—a utopian singles meet-up—especially not so soon after leaving Bill. But she and Kurt had a connection she'd never experienced with anyone else. In a few scant days, he'd learned things about her that even Bill hadn't figured out.

The story with Paul was more opaque. Aside from a clipped revelation that his wife would never support what they were doing, Paul hadn't mentioned Reid and Ally's mother, although the kids talked about her a lot.

Abby switched her attention back to Cody, whose mouth was bright with berry juice. In addition to being a natural-born teacher, Ally clearly had a gift with flora. She would know what was safe to let Cody eat, and what wasn't. No need for Abby's supervision.

Abby turned and walked back to the front of the barn so she could pick up where she had left off, stacking sandwiches on a platter. Peanut butter tonight. Again. They had sixty cartons, each containing twelve jars of all-natural peanut butter, which must have been a real drag to lug in.

The food was the not-surprising part of this place. In fact, it was about what you'd expect in terms of bare-bones monotony when trying to feed a bevy of people with no new supplies arriving. It was supposed to get better. Paul had promised it would. Plus, there were a few slightly more exciting wares, canned goods, home-jarred fruits and veggies, boxes of jerky, which the women had told her were to be saved for the real depths of winter. For now there were still wild onions to forage, mushrooms, greens, and flowers, which Abby figured even the children would come to regard as treats.

The night she and Cody finally got to leave, Abby had run around the condo, grabbing the scant supplies she had off cupboard shelves and shoving them into bags. Terry had stockpiled these things as a just-in-case for winter, but she wouldn't let Abby serve them to the children.

"But granola bars are healthy," Abby had protested.

Terry had reached for the box, pointing out three sources of sugar in the ingredients, not to mention the soy.

"Soy's bad for you?" Abby had asked skeptically. "It's in tofu!"

"Tofu's quite possibly the single worst thing you could put in your body," Terry had replied calmly. "You may as well eat a McDonald's hamburger."

Abby's thoughts flew to the Happy Meal Cody had gobbled down the night before.

"Tofu was never meant to be a food," Terry went on.

Abby had begun to talk about Chinese and Japanese people, soy sauce, but Terry seemed to anticipate her line of argument. "Asians eat small amounts of fermented soy," she'd said. "In their native countries, Asian people would never eat tofu. It's an American abomination because soybeans are a cheap and hearty crop."

Despite their slight level of nuttiness, Abby already liked Terry and Katrina. Terry was a devoted caretaker of the infant another woman had arrived with, the baby now sleeping now in a sunny patch of barn, dust motes twirling in a shaft above her curlicue of a body. And Katrina had her own baby strapped to her chest, although Abby had yet to see it.

"What do you think that noise was?" Abby asked, taking two sandwiches out of Terry's full hands and adding them to the stack on the platter.

"It was awfully loud," Katrina said, adjusting the bundle on her chest. "Almost sounded like a—"

"They're working down at the falls," Terry interrupted. "They might've had to set off an explosive."

"An *explosive*?" Abby said.

Terry shrugged. "Do you know anything about building a hydro-powered energy source?"

"I do," Katrina said. "And I can tell you that either it isn't possible for two men to do at that scale, or else what is possible wouldn't require any explosives." She paused to touch her baby tenderly. "Plus, Paul would be working with the environment, not exploiting it."

Katrina was one of those women who seemed like she could do everything. Today she had boiled down some thimbleberries she'd harvested—a variety that apparently tended to be left after the animals had eaten everything else—and made jam. She was spreading the mixture on the sandwiches now, reaching underneath her sling every now and then to make sure her baby was latched on.

A noise came from behind the sling; it almost sounded like *mama*. Abby recalled Cody's earliest days with an inner smile. How lucky Katrina was to have the first word, maybe even the first smile, all of that still ahead of her.

Platter filled, Terry lofted it and brought it over to the table. There was a dilapidated farmhouse on this piece of land, structurally sound but in need of repair, and several salvaged pieces had been moved to the barn. Paul and Kurt had sanded down a door for a table and laid it over two barrels. Another barrel was being turned into a rainwater catchment system. For now they were purifying water from the creek, but the iodine tablets made it taste terrible.

Katrina reached down absently and plugged the baby's mouth again. She had made burdock tea and she poured some now for Abby and Terry, as nimbly as if she didn't have ten extra pounds stuck to her chest.

"Maybe there's a thunderstorm building," Katrina suggested, handing around the mugs.

Abby glanced toward the barn door, which had been left partway open. "Looks pretty nice out."

"It's always nice here," Terry said. "Until it's not."

"That's true," Katrina said. "Which reminds me. How are they doing with the woodstove?" She gestured to the place in the barn where it was supposed to be installed. Heating this vast space—used for tasks ranging from food preparation to furniture assembly—was priority number one. After that, the decrepit farmhouse would be tackled. "I was freezing this morning, and so was Carthage." She reached down and touched the baby.

"It'll warm up again before real cold sets in," Terry said decisively.

"They have a little time. Power is more important. They'll need it for tools before any building can begin."

Abby sipped her tea. "We should probably call the children in. They must be starving."

"I'll do it," Terry said. "I have to get Dorothy's bottle ready anyway."

"Isn't her name Dorothea?" Abby asked.

Terry glanced at her. "I always shrink at difficult names for kids. Gives them such a trip in life. No offense, Katrina."

Katrina sat back easily against the rough barn boards. She stroked the lump under the sling. "None taken. Carthage is a family name. And it lets us escape the whole gender imposition thing."

Terry headed for a cooler that was stored in a root cellar on the other side of the barn. "Anyway, Dorothy seems a better choice to me. Let's just call her that."

Katrina rose, and as she did the baby on her chest slid out of the sling. Abby let out a yelp, trying to dive for it, until the sight before her resolved.

The baby wasn't falling out of the sling; he—or it could've been a *she* with that gossamer froth of hair—was climbing out. Extricating him- or herself from the wrap of cloth before standing up on the floor. This wasn't any baby, or even a toddler; instead, it was a good-sized preschooler.

Katrina hoisted the child into her arms as she sent Abby a calm, tolerant look. "Children are forced into independence so early in our culture." She glanced down tenderly. Now that it wasn't curled beneath the sling like a larva, the child actually overlapped a large portion of Katrina's body. "These years we've had to breastfeed have been so special, especially once Carthage could really communicate."

Abby was trying to come up with a reply when the door to the barn slid back with a solid *thud* and sunlight filled the new space, only to be blocked by a body.

Kurt had come back. He looked a mess, soaked and muddy.

"The children should be fed now and put to bed in here," he said.

Kurt gestured to a neat row of sleeping bags, rolled like slugs on the far side of the barn. They had spent several hours cleaning the bedrooms and living room of the farmhouse, making them habitable for sleeping. But there seemed to be an unspoken desire to stay together, sharing their warmth in one communal sleeping space in the barn. Blankets were laid out on the floor, touching one another in a connected mesh. The children also enjoyed camping out under the stars.

As if reading her thoughts, Kurt went on in his mild tone. "No campouts tonight. In fact, don't let the children out for any reason. No one can be on the grounds. Is that understood?"

Abby watched Terry and Katrina nod in unison.

"Paul is finishing up by the pond," Kurt went on. "Don't wait for him."

Carthage started circling in Kurt's direction, but something made him suddenly swerve off course. Not *him*. Carthage had to be a she. She began to whimper, clambering up Katrina's body like a ladder.

Kurt was studying them. "You keep that child close to you, don't you?"

Katrina inclined her head in a shy nod. The brusque, confident woman was gone. She looked younger, smaller even, eager to please.

"Give it an identity of its own," Kurt said. "And if you ever put it in that contraption again, I will cut it off your body, along with your breast. Is that also understood?"

Katrina's face went a sickly white.

"Good," Kurt said. "I'll send the children in now. And ladies . . . ?"

They all looked up at once.

"This door will be locked from the outside."

CHAPTER FIFTY

Liz bolted for the stairs with the bag, her mother-in-law's voice a distant, seashell rush.

"It doesn't have a key," Mary said. "Perhaps we can pick the lock—"

"I've got it," Liz shouted over her shoulder.

She snatched up the key from a little dish on her bedside table. A place for special things, mementoes. The key had felt like a last tangible link to Paul, and thus to her children, though she'd lost hope of ever using it.

Liz inserted the key into the slit in the box, gave a twist, and lifted the lid.

Crushed inside, barely able to fit, was a pillow.

Liz lifted it out, not with an air of wonder or closure—*Ah, so that was it all along*—but instead cloaked by pure bafflement. Only what had she expected? A treasure map to Paul and the Shoemaker's lair with an *X* marking the spot? Maybe not that, but bedclothes certainly would've been even lower on the list.

The pillow was thin and flat, not only from being crammed into a box, but also because it was made of cheap foam with little loft. The pillowcase was polyester in an ugly calamine pink.

Liz suddenly released the fabric as if it were burning.

She began to back away, staring at the pillow as if it had the potential to harm her.

As if it had the potential to kill.

She walked to the bedroom door on numb feet, the vile artifact held out in front of her. In the hall, she met the sloped form of her mother-in-law. Liz came to a sudden stop.

On Mary's face was the expression of understanding that had been missing from her own.

Liz thrust out the pillow, and her mother-in-law reared back as if a pistol had been shoved into her face.

Or a different sort of murder weapon.

Marjorie had told Liz how it had happened, that Michael Brady had been smothered to death in the hospital the night before he was supposed to be moved to rehab. He was going to live out the rest of his days ensnared by tubes and machines.

This was the pillow Coach Allgood had used to put Michael out of his misery.

The cloth sheath was hospital pink, and now that Liz had put the pieces together, it was clear that this pillow had never graced someone's bedroom, or any place a person would sleep voluntarily. It was another macabre piece of Paul's memorial, a form of tribute that couldn't be left outside in the elements.

"How did you get this lockbox?" Liz asked. "Did you know what was inside?"

Mary fought to straighten. "Paul gave the box to me all those years ago. He asked me to hold on to it for him." A pause. "But no. I never tried to open it." A longer break before she spoke again. "I suppose Paul knew that I wouldn't."

"Why did Paul have the pillow Allgood used to kill Michael Brady?"

Mary's gaze snagged hers. "Coach Allgood didn't use that pillow."

The floor seemed to pitch and slant beneath Liz's feet, tilting like the deck on a ship. "He didn't?"

Mary shook her head, a slow, jerky back and forth.

"What did he use, then?" Liz asked. "And why did Paul have this?"

It took a moment for Liz to recognize the look on Mary's face. It was the expression someone wore just before they were about to be sick. "Paul had that pillow," Mary said, pausing as if to swallow something back, "because Mr. Allgood didn't kill poor Michael."

Rocking underfoot again.

Liz looked at Mary, though she suddenly sensed that she might not want to.

"Paul did," she said.

Mary's whole body sagged as if the disclosure had scooped her out inside. She steadied herself against the door frame. "I'm sorry," she said in her whispery, spider-thread voice. "I shouldn't have—I never should have told you that." Mary pressed a hand to her lips, too late to hold any words in. "If I had known what was in the lockbox, I wouldn't have come."

She turned and began making her way downstairs.

Liz was trying to take in the loss of the level ground she had only just staked out when she realized that Mary's rare emergence was about to come to an end. Her mother-in-law would scuttle back into her home and never be seen again. Liz began running, following Mary's route.

Mary got to the driveway just as Liz reached the front hall.

Through the window Liz saw her mother-in-law place one foot on the ridged step of the pickup truck before summoning the strength to hoist herself inside.

Liz yanked the door open.

Mary sat down in the truck, staring out into the night without seeming to see anything. The engine started with a choke.

"Mary!" Liz cried. "Wait!"

Tires ground up the gravel as her mother-in-law began to navigate the curving drive in reverse. Liz took the porch steps as one, then raced after the truck. She reached the hood and thumped on it. Mary braked, startled. She rolled down the window.

Liz looked into the cab of the truck.

"Elizabeth," Mary said quietly. "No more, please. That secret wasn't mine to reveal." She clamped both hands around the steering wheel. "And I can't see that it helps you anyway. I should've checked the box myself before coming."

Liz thrust her hand into the truck. She wanted to stop Mary from sealing herself up inside. Or maybe she just wanted to make contact.

The truck's motor died. Liz couldn't tell whether Mary had turned it off, or whether the engine had simply given up. Either way, her mother-in-law started to speak in a river rush.

"Coach Allgood arrived at the hospital right after Paul did it," Mary said. "Folks were keeping a round-the-clock vigil, and the coach's shift followed Paul's."

Liz stared up at the moonless sky, hoping the dark would mask her tears.

"Mr. Allgood stepped in," Mary continued, her own cheeks glistening. "What a good man. He sent Paul away like he'd never been there at all. I suspect he must've felt he was responsible."

"Yes," Liz whispered. "He did."

A current of air moved across the night.

"Matthew said that the coach wasn't, though," Mary said, a hiss to her whisper. "He told Paul that he should be held accountable for his actions, both accidental and deliberate. But Mr. Allgood believed that Paul was going to accomplish great things, and that his freedom needed to be preserved."

Liz swiped angrily at her eyes. Had Matthew been a father whom Paul counted on for counsel, perhaps Paul would've heeded his advice to confess. The coach wouldn't have had to give up his life for a crime he didn't commit, and Paul wouldn't have gotten away with murder, which ensured that he'd never truly be free again.

Mary shifted on the plank of seat, and when she spoke there was a deep thrum to her voice. "I vowed to protect the coach's sacrifice. No one would ever learn the truth. Until tonight, neither Matthew nor I have ever mentioned the accident, or what followed."

It was like watching a rind peel away, revealing the full flesh and color of the fruit beneath. Suddenly Liz heard Mary telling Matthew to let Liz into the farmhouse, informing him that Liz would have to spend the night. It was Mary who had accepted the invitation to their wedding, and Mary who structured the visits, rare as they were, with Ally and Reid.

Mary who had driven here tonight.

Whose hunched back hid iron.

What had Mary done when her son finally made his way back home?

"Paul came back," Liz said, the words breathy in the dark. "To the farmhouse. He wanted the lockbox."

There was no statute of limitations on murder. Liz could imagine why Paul had been unable to part with, rid himself of, or destroy this last link to the tragedy that had befallen his best friend. But it was a crucial piece of evidence, and with the coach just released from prison, Paul must've been afraid to leave it guarded by only his mother and his merciless father, while he disappeared with the children.

Mary studied her. "He came back. But not for the lockbox. And he didn't get into the house. Matthew wouldn't let him inside."

Liz placed her hand on the ledge beneath the driver's side window. "What happened?"

Mary's lips compressed. "Matthew would've broken Paul's fingers if I hadn't held him back. They scuffled by the entry." She looked away momentarily. "Fought really. At one point, Paul threw a punch. Or maybe he was just trying to put his hand out, to use his fist as a wedge so Matthew couldn't close the door. That was the damage you noticed."

Tiny bits of rubber rimming flaked off beneath Liz's fingers.

"I stepped in between and led everyone up to the bunker. I took them some sandwiches later," Mary added.

While Liz had been delirious with fear, imagining her children kidnapped, or worse.

"Even that horrid man," Mary said. "I don't care how handsome he is, or that the children hung on his every word. He's rotten to the core, and more the worse for my son that he couldn't see it."

The Shoemaker. Liz felt a cold bath of air all around her.

Mary twisted the ignition key, and the truck started to rattle.

"So why did Paul go to the farm?" Liz asked, her voice rising. "If it wasn't for the lockbox, did he want something else? Something he needs out there, wherever he is?"

Mary took one last look through the lowered window. "Oh, Elizabeth, how I hope you get the chance to give Paul what Matthew wouldn't."

Liz felt her brows draw down.

"And I hope you get the chance to hold your beautiful children again."

The pressure in Liz's face was crushing.

Mary reached out and laid her hand on Liz's cheek. The touch was gentle, but Liz felt a strength she hadn't noticed before in Mary's fingers.

Her mother-in-law shifted into Drive and the truck lurched forward. Mary's final words carried through the night. "Paul came back to the farm that night to ask his father for forgiveness."

CHAPTER FIFTY-ONE

L iz couldn't believe the moon was still absent, concealed by shred-
ded clouds, not even stars visible to offer pinpricks of light.

She could see so much better now.

Matthew's note. Allgood's thrumming rage. Even Ally's statement about Grandpa getting mad, which in retrospect hinted at
Mary's ability to drive things.

Motivations appeared as if they'd been written in ink.

Her husband had always displayed a tendency to play God, believing he could change the whole world. Paul had caused a fate worse
than death for his best friend. And in response, he acted to make fate
behave differently, using his own hands to free Michael Brady from
the prison of his body.

Liz walked back inside, weighty with exhaustion, and wondering
what to do with her newfound knowledge. She trudged upstairs and
undressed. The distance across the bedroom felt like it encompassed
hectares of space. Liz less lay down than fell on the bed, emitting a
relieved breath as the mattress rose to greet her.

It was funny. Just before in the driveway, Liz had been noting her
newly acquired ability to see, an antenna, hair-fine and acute. But
maybe she wasn't as alert as all that. Either the distraction of the
night's events, or the profundity of the dark outside, had kept her
from realizing until now that she wasn't alone in the room.

There was nowhere to go.

If she stood up or even extended her arms, she might hit the person whose breaths were rising and falling somewhere in this room, like the surface of the sea.

The crazy thought came to her that it could be Paul. Returned for the pillow, come back to keep her from sharing what she knew.

But of course it was the Shoemaker, who had been here illicitly at least twice before. The knowledge settled as heavy as sand in her limbs, keeping her pinned to the mattress, teasing her with the temptation of hiding her head beneath the pillow like any terrified child.

She had a sense memory of the Shoemaker's finger on her cut, the small pain he had caused her. How much worse would he do once their costumes were off, no pretense made of civility or reason?

She wanted to say that she knew he was here, but it would be insanity to call out. She retained enough of a hold—on something—to understand that if the Shoemaker didn't realize she was aware of his presence, then there might still be a chance.

If she stayed still, would he leave? Or wait?

The passivity of the plan assailed her. This wasn't who she was, not anymore.

It occurred to her to call Tim. Or 911. But once she made that call, she wouldn't have the marginal advantage of silence, invisibility.

A small sigh escaped her.

Or had that sound been made by someone else?

The blast hit her eyes, a stinging spray. It called to mind a forest in flames. Liz envisioned leaping sparks, and then she could see no more. Something had engulfed her whole head, fiery and searing, rendering her blind. She couldn't make out even darkness. Liz sat up in the bed, twisting and turning and tearing at her eyes. Her screams of agony filled the room before a voice severed them.

"Shut your mouth if you want to live," it said.

Liz's fingers dug into the sheets. She felt the fabric fray beneath them. It didn't matter if the Shoemaker left her alive or not. She wasn't going to survive. Nobody could live through such pain.

"Please," she whimpered. "Do something—"

She took her hands from her eyes, and the onslaught of air ignited another blowtorch of agony. Liz fell back, howling, before remembering the command to be quiet.

The silence that followed was worse than any inklings she'd gotten of the Shoemaker's presence. Where was he in the room right now? What was he going to do to her? Through a mummy wrap of pain, Liz made out the sound of footsteps. They stopped inches from where she lay.

That cool, distant voice. "You are to stop."

Liz opened her mouth, causing a level of pain that surpassed anything she'd experienced. The motion required to form words creased the skin around her eyes, and whatever they had been scorched with began working its way deeper into the orbs. Why weren't tears providing any relief? Could she not cry? Panic seized her whole body at the thought of Michael Brady, who had lost his ability to cry along with everything else.

The intruder leaned over her and said, "If you don't stop, I'll do something that will make you long for the level of pain you're feeling right now."

His breath felt like a blade in her eyes. Liz fought to make sense of his words.

Stop what? Looking for them? Had she been close when she and Tim had gone out to Wicket Road?

The answer was right here in this room. A bolt of fury seized her and she tried to rise. "I know you," she spat out. "Tell me where they are, Shoemaker!"

It took a while for the fact of her aloneness to descend, along with the understanding that if he had been there to hear, the Shoemaker might very well have killed her.

Pain had become a constant, livid presence.

She dropped back on the bed. Minutes passed, hours, years, before she was finally able to sit up.

Liz used her hands to register obstacles before her as she made her way to the bathroom by memory. There, she flooded her face with water, the relief of it indescribable upon her ruined eyes. After a long time, she was able to see well enough to find her phone. She dialed 911, still mostly blind, fingers figuring out the right keys to press. She asked dispatch for an ambulance. And then she broke into a sob and also asked for Tim.

CHAPTER FIFTY-TWO

Liz didn't register much of the ambulance ride, nor her arrival at the hospital, or treatment there. An IV was inserted, and her eyes were flushed with some blissfully cool, unctuous fluid. Her head was wrapped in soft gauze, the fluorescents in the room kept low. She heard murmurs that the initial application of liquid had prevented any real damage; she'd done the right thing back home. Then a door banged open and painful light spilled across the room. Liz tried to sit up, but gentle hands eased her back down. It didn't matter whether she could see or not. She knew who had arrived, and she stretched out her arms.

The mattress bowed as Tim leaned over the bed and gathered her to him.

"Hello, Chief," someone said, a smile in the voice.

Liz could imagine the looks being exchanged, but she didn't care. Tim's arms around her felt like ramparts; his uniform smelled of pine and detergent and faintly of closed-in spaces.

Voices faded out, speaking at a distance.

"We've given her something," a woman said.

"It'll take her through?" That was Tim.

"At least till three a.m.," the woman responded. "She won't be awake for much longer now." Then she spoke to Liz. "Can you tell us where your pain is on a scale of one to ten?"

"I'm all right," Liz said softly. "It's better."

"Rest," an unfamiliar male voice ordered.

Liz sensed a retreat from the room.

Tim returned to hold her, taking care not to touch any part of her face. "Jesus, Liz. I'm so sorry I wasn't—"

"You have . . . nothing to be sorry for."

Tim let go of her and she could hear him pacing around the room, anger apparent in his strides. Then he was back, conducting heat between them. She found his face with her fingers and felt the rasp of his beard.

"Shh," she said, trying to still his roving hands.

"The goddamned school bus attacker is on suicide watch at the jail. We don't have enough men to monitor him and I've been taking shifts."

The drugs were a tide inside her now, rising up to take her away. "S'okay," she said, slurry. "You wouldn't have been at my house. Anyway."

"Landry read me your statement."

There was a gauzy world before her, beckoning her to lie down. She was already lying down. "Tim," she said woozily.

"I'm here." He gripped her hand. "So our guy is escalating. You're positive it was him."

"I'm sure." Words slipped from her mouth. "That voice. I could never forget that . . ." Another loose stream of words, slippery as lozenges. "He's washing me. *Watching* me."

"The Shoemaker," Tim said.

It was the last thing she heard that night.

Liz couldn't tell through the gauze, but she had the sense that it was the middle of the night, or later even. Dawn. She'd slept all the way through.

She was also pretty sure she was alone.

On the bedside table, which swung on an arm to hold trays or meds, her cell phone was thrumming and turning.

That was what had awakened her.

Tim, she realized. He'd had to go—she had a faint memory of a prisoner who needed guarding—and was probably calling to check on her. It occurred to her that Tim would think to call the charge nurse so as to avoid disturbing her, but by then she was patting around for her cell by feel, finding the Send button with her finger.

"Hello?"

The voice on the other end arrowed straight into her heart.

"Mom."

It was Reid.

He spoke in a low, hushed tone that nearly broke Liz apart. Her son sounded so much older now. Not weeks older than when he had been taken. But months. Or years.

"Oh my God, Reid, thank God you called."

"It's hard to get a signal here," he said, still low. "I had to walk and walk."

"I'm so—glad you did," Liz said. Then she wondered whether she should be. Could walking away get Reid in trouble? He'd had to steal this phone; Ally had told her that. "You're all right? And Ally? She is?"

The drugs they'd given her were wearing off, but Liz was still having trouble piecing words together. She wondered whether Reid could tell anything was wrong.

Her son hadn't answered.

"Reid!" Liz lowered her voice so as to keep from alerting the nurse, not to mention anyone who might be close to Reid right now. The Shoemaker. Liz swallowed back a cry. If the Shoemaker was there after just being at her house, then they were nearby. Liz simply had to get Reid to tell her where.

"Mom?"

"Reid, yes, are you and Ally okay?"

There was a silence so lasting that Liz's heart clenched. She had been mentally practicing for this ever since Ally had called, praying for a second opportunity. This time she wasn't going to take the same pains at deception as she had with Ally. They hadn't helped, and anyway Reid was older, more aware. But now Liz feared she had squandered her chance. The call was lost—signal spotty wherever they were—and she would never be able to talk straight, or pry out anything that Reid might know.

"Mom, something really bad happened."

Relief crushed her before the meaning of his words hit.

"Oh baby, oh Reid, what do you mean? Are you—you're not hurt, are you?"

The gauze wrappings felt like constrictors around her eyes. A memory of the pain she'd experienced—its lethal, searing hold— returned and Liz bit down on a scream, imagining Reid or Ally feeling anything like that.

"Mrs. Daniels?" A nurse opened the door a crack, peering into the room.

Liz waved her wildly away.

The nurse frowned. "You can't have cell phones on in—"

"I have to take this call," Liz hissed. "Get out of here—or I'll call the police."

Maybe it was seeing her with Tim last night. She heard the nurse retreat from the room.

Her son was still speaking in that ageless tone. "I'm okay. So's Ally. But this lady—this lady got hurt pretty bad. Mommy, I think she got all the way hurt."

It was one of Reid's euphemisms, a term they'd come up with to cope with his fear of death. And in the rescinding of that strange, unnaturally mature voice, Liz found her son again, and a sob rolled up.

"Reid, is anyone else with you now? Daddy? Or . . . another man?"

"No," her son said. "I'm all alone."

Such emptiness, so much sorrow in her boy's voice. Liz's chest cracked; she felt something inside her let go. Behind the gauze, her vision darkened further, and she lay back on the bed.

"Reid," she whispered. "I'm going to take care of this, do you hear me? Reid? Only I have to know where you are. Where are you, Reid? Can you tell me?"

"In the woods somewhere." A pause. "There's a falling-down house. And a barn."

She clutched at the details, although she couldn't see how they helped her.

"So it's a farm?" she asked. "How did you get there? Did you drive?"

"We walked."

Faint hope lit. They were getting somewhere, at least eliminating options.

"Walked. Okay. From where? From our house? Were you on a kind of twisty road?"

"I don't know, Mom! I don't think so. I've never seen this place before. I've never seen any of these places!"

Frustration, desperation hard on the heels of the hope. "Okay, Reid, calm down. Can you tell me anything at all? That you might remember seeing?"

"Just a lot of trees! Tons and tons of them. There wasn't even a path, just brush and stuff. We had to bushwhack. Only, wait, first there were some gravestones."

Her son spoke the word with ease. As frantic as she felt, Liz's heart lifted at Reid's obvious growth, the erosion of his childhood phobia despite the indescribable circumstances that had befallen him. And then her heart lifted even higher, soaring as if it might leave her body, because Reid had told her where they were.

Someone else spoke then. The flat, deceptively mild tone belonged to the Shoemaker. "Reid. Give me that," he said.

Coldness clasped Liz. The phone shook in her suddenly quaking hand.

"Give you what?" Reid said.

It took Liz a moment to parse what must have happened. Reid had made the phone disappear without ending the call.

The Shoemaker spoke again, sliding Reid's confidence out from under him, displaying his weakness like a specimen in a dish. "You want to be the doer, don't you, Reid? The fixer, the taker. Those fingers of yours. It's too bad you're so scared. Fear will keep you from being all you're meant to be." A pause. "Now show me where you put that phone. Reid. *Show me where you put it.*"

"No!" Reid's voice rose, high and frightened. "Go away! Get away from me!"

"I don't think so," the Shoemaker said. "You see, I knew where you had the phone all along."

And the connection was cut.

CHAPTER FIFTY-THREE

Terror encased Liz like cement.

She had to get there. And get the children out.

At least now she knew where to go.

Liz had been right when she'd made the connection to Michael Brady; she had simply chosen the wrong woods. Paul and the children weren't in the ones off Wicket Road, where the accident had taken place. Instead, they were in the impenetrable forest that barricaded Michael Brady's memorial site.

Gravestones, Reid had said with casual aplomb, having no idea what he was giving her.

Liz should've figured it out back when Ally had called. Hadn't her daughter said that Reid wasn't scared of dead people anymore? A cemetery was one thing that could've led Ally to that conclusion.

She reached up, and despite her crest of panic, unwrapped the bindings with care. She couldn't do anything if she were crazed with pain, or worse, drugged again.

Even the muted light bit her eyes as she raised gluey lids. She shut them instantly, then tried again, keeping them open for a longer spell this time, until convinced that she could see well enough to look down at her phone.

She tried Reid back with trembling fingers, but got the anonymous voicemail she'd expected. She phoned Tim after that. He had a friend with a helicopter; they could search from above. But Tim didn't pick up his cell and there was no answer at the barracks. Liz left her message with a feeling of despair.

She dialed the emergency line then, about to press the final digit, when something made her finger falter. How long would it take if this became official? To get a helicopter off the ground, maybe call in SWAT from downstate since the potential for a hostage situation was clear even to Liz, making her sore eyes fill, inflaming them all over again.

Whatever time it took, she didn't have. She would lose all control once she reached Tim. And the Shoemaker had Reid in his grip.

Liz patted her eyes dry with a piece of gauze before hitting the Call button by her bed.

The nurse returned. "Mrs. Daniels! Is everything all right?"

Asinine thing to ask, Liz heard Jill say. *I just threw you out of my room and now I'm about to walk out of here. Of course everything isn't all right.*

"Do you know when Tim—when the chief left here last night?" she said.

The nurse nodded. "There was an emergency. It's been on TV. A suicide at the jail."

That explained the silence at the barracks.

But maybe it was a blessing in disguise.

Even if the police did eventually rally forces to go in—with a helicopter yet—their proceedings would be loud and unmistakable. What would the Shoemaker do if he knew he was being hunted? Even a skilled and expert search might be sensed by him; he had such uncanny awareness. Whereas now he had no idea that Liz knew where they were. She could go there undetected. And get out with her children the same way.

"Thank you," she said.

The nurse nodded again. "The doctor will be in during morning rounds. Given your progress, perhaps we can release you this afternoon."

As soon as the nurse was gone, Liz shimmied out of her gown. She found her clothes, then got dressed beneath the thin sheet, wriggling to hide her maneuvers just in case anyone walked by. She couldn't see as clearly as she would've liked—her eyes still felt rheumy and had a tendency to run—but at least all motion didn't send vibrations of torture up her face. She slipped into her shoes and shuffled over to the door. It took a few minutes for another patient's call light to flash, causing the nurse to leave her station. Once she did, Liz eased through the doorway and down the hall to the stair, stepping lightly, fast.

On her way out, she ducked beneath the closed gift shop's ribbed overhead door, which hadn't been lowered all the way, in order to grab a pair of sunglasses. Perhaps Reid didn't have it so wrong with this theft thing after all.

Liz used the last charge in her cell to call Wedeskyull's only cab.

At home, Liz changed into hiking boots and clothing suitable for walking: waterproof pants and a T-shirt. Then she loaded a knapsack with other items: a change of clothes, a rain cloak since the sky was overcast, some food, and a water bottle. Glancing at the contents of the cupboard, it occurred to her that the kids might need sustenance, too. Who knew what they'd been surviving on these last weeks? The prospect of feeding her children bathed her heart in such warmth that Liz stole a few minutes to slap together sandwiches, then added cookies and every treat she'd ever sneaked into the pantry under Paul's watchful gaze. She went upstairs for the children's raincoats as well. At the last second, she added Izzy to the now-bulging knapsack.

She had promised Ally.

A sob rode up her throat, and Liz swallowed it back.

Two poles warred inside her, one that cautioned forethought and judiciousness, another that infused every cell in her body with urgency. Liz had to fight the second. Panic in the wilderness could get you killed, especially a wilderness as dense and impenetrable as this promised to be. If Liz fell down—likely, given her depleted state—and got hurt, then the chance of anyone stumbling upon her was almost nil. She took the precaution of leaving another message at the barracks, then texted Tim information about her route. But a recollection of the depth of those woods overshadowed everything as she typed. If Liz migrated even a quarter of a mile from her intended direction, she might get lost and be impossible to find.

She quelled another surge of franticness, picked up the knapsack, and walked out to her car.

CHAPTER FIFTY-FOUR

The dim sky cast no light over the circle of green, rendering it dull and gray. Without Paul here to keep this area trimmed, the blades had grown scraggly. Soon the circle would be taken over by encroaching meadow, Michael Brady's tribute swallowed up.

Liz entered the cemetery, pausing for a moment by the graves Reid had seen. She crouched down, fingering the deep trenches of the letters, then gazed upward. The sky looked ready to release, spatter everything below with its contents.

It would be drier in the woods than out here once it rained.

Liz stood up and went silently on, knapsack swinging against her back.

No sound issued forth as she approached the forest, not even the whisper of leaves. The air was still, heavy with impending downpour. She smelled the coppery tang of ozone.

Liz pressed herself through a latticework of branches, visoring her forehead with her hand. She took the sunglasses out and settled them on her face, even though they stole the scant light. The thought of a twig getting anywhere close to her eyes made her knees weaken.

These trees were like fangs, so closely packed you could barely make your way between them. Liz had to shoulder her body from trunk to trunk, only the knapsack preventing her jacket from getting torn. Within minutes, she was breathing hard from exertion. At least the glasses shielded her sore eyes from a kaleidoscope of fall color overhead, and the toneless sky helped keep the light low, too. Still, Liz had to stop often to wipe away tears. When she looked down to check her compass, she let her eyes flutter shut for a few seconds until she could see clearly again.

It was chilly in this sunless throat, but Liz had gotten warm from her efforts. She edged forward, selecting one tree to go for before considering the next to try and breach. The slow pace helped ensure that she kept the memorial site directly behind her. She had to hope that Paul and the others hadn't turned far left or right of it. It was impossible to tell whether people had come this way recently; the forest was so dense it immediately consumed any hints of trespass. But Liz had grown up in the wilds of the Adirondacks, and knew different methods of orientation: sun, compass, the way the moss grew on trees. It seemed likely she was heading as they had, if only because other routes looked to be even less passable.

This wasn't territory that encouraged recreation. There were no paint splotches on tree trunks to guide hikers, nor a single check-in station or hut. There weren't even the spent shell casings or stray piece of litter that would've marked a hunter's passing. There was big game to feast on in this wilderness—deer, moose, bears—but no one had come to stalk it.

Despite the way they rebuffed passage, these woods didn't feel ominous. They were thick and full with a lusciousness to them, wet even though the sky hadn't yet spilled over. Water seeped from the ground, beading in the silvery air. The remaining green leaves looked juicy this late in the season, while others had burst into fireworks of red and orange. The trees teemed with occupants: small, skittering chipmunks, screeching birds. The earthen layer at Liz's feet provided lush nourishment; velvet crumble raged with tiny insects.

The rational part of Liz knew that such density of life had no bearing on whether she would find the hidden huddle of existence she was searching for. But it felt like there was a link. A group of people had come here to feed off this land, and each sign of how much would be theirs for the taking caused hope to flare.

She used her arms to push past twiggy encumbrances, hearing

wood snap in her wake, but intent only on moving forward. There was nothing ahead of her or behind except for more trees. Liz felt as if she were swimming in a sharp sea. Her arms grew sore from holding them up, but if she had lowered one, her face would've been instantly scored.

She began to wonder if she would be forced to turn back. She wasn't equipped to stay out overnight if the weather did its worst. The canopy was so thick that you couldn't see clouds to gauge when they might rupture, but a storm was definitely coming. Distant thunder rumbled, like an animal gearing up to attack, and Liz could feel an electric crackle in the air as surely as if she'd brushed against an outlet.

And then she wondered if that sense of electricity was due to something besides lightning. Some ways ahead, not close enough to run for, especially since running was an impossibility in the depths of these woods, she saw flickers of light.

They could be actual lights—lanterns or a torch against the gloom—or they could merely be clear patches through the trees. Either way, they represented something different from the identical vista she had been seeing for what felt like years. Liz continued moving from tree to tree, taking care to muffle any sounds, waiting for the ordinary camouflage of rodents or deer to hide the crackle of leaves and breaking branches for which she was responsible. The imposed pace was an ordeal. She felt a constant temptation to barrel forward, screaming out Reid and Ally's names.

And then, as if they'd been conjured up by desperate desire, she saw them.

Liz skidded to a halt, planting her feet in a feathery well of ferns.

No, it wasn't them. The figure was much too small to be Reid or even Ally. But Liz was sure she had seen something human, moving with purpose and precision, not just one of the lumbering animals contained by these woods.

Two somethings actually.

Liz's eyes ached. They felt as if they were bulging, swelling in their sockets. She leaned against a tree trunk, covering her face with her hand even though she wanted nothing more in this moment than to see. But she knew she was straining, pushing the limits of tender, barely recovered tissue. If she didn't rest her eyes, they might fail her altogether. And the thought of being blind out here sent a spear of terror into her very core.

She opened one eye, releasing a stream of cleansing tears. Liz cracked the other eye, likewise overflowing, and mopped at her face. Then, praying that too much time hadn't passed, that she hadn't missed whatever sight had been before her, Liz squinted into the tunnel of trees.

Nothing.

No flitter of movement, candle-quick and darting.

All was still, weighted down by the impending storm.

Liz dropped her head and trudged forward, though she feared that this walk was hopeless, and that if she didn't turn back now, it might be too late.

She stopped so short, she nearly fell forward. One hand shot out, scraping rough bark, and she braced herself against a tree.

Right there—that was a moving body behind the branches up ahead.

Liz's fists were clenched with hope and fear; her fingernails pierced her palms. The screen of leaves was maddening, making whoever was out there disappear and reappear in an endless succession of illusion. She blinked her runny eyes and tried to focus. If this was an adult— the Shoemaker for all she knew—then calling out would be the worst thing she could possibly do.

There was a growl of thunder overhead, and Liz used the noise to disguise her creep forward, abandoning the shelter of trees. She was visible now; the forest had thinned out. A wind came up, rattling the timbers with a dry, husky sound. And when the leaping form finally resolved itself, Liz froze, not because she could be seen, but because she knew who that was, appearing in intermittent glimpses betwixt and between the blowing foliage ahead.

The crying boy who had fled her house with his mother just a week or so before. Liz suddenly remembered his name and whispered, "Cody!"

CHAPTER FIFTY-FIVE

A finger of green light, alien, glowing, signaled the gathering storm. In a few minutes the sky was going to crack open, and everything would get much harder.

"Cody!" Liz called again, trying to be heard.

But the boy didn't hear her over the wind and batting branches.

Another voice cried out, louder than Liz's. "Cody! Where'd you go? Where are you, Cody?"

Liz knew the voice like she knew her own skin.

It was Ally's.

Liz lifted her head and bellowed in a way she didn't recognize. It was a cry born of sheer instinct coupled with the knowledge that she had to keep quiet. A dirge from a tribal instrument, low and deep and long. Both muted and urgent as she drew closer. Liz's lungs went slack before the first syllable had come to an end, and she had to gather breath and try again.

"Alllll-yyyyyyy!"

The little girl turned. She realized in the same splinter of time, not an instant taken for processing or reflection. "Mommy, Mommy, Mommy!"

And they ran.

Liz felt the skitter of twigs by her eyes, but she didn't blink, or even avert her head, so intent was she on keeping her daughter in her sights. Ally leapt over branches and cavities in the ground, her feet flying above the earth without seeming to touch it. Liz dropped without intending to, her body knowing better than her mind how to make sure they met, chest to chest, Ally's head cupped in the crevice under Liz's chin so that their bodies formed a single heart. Liz rocked back under the force of their collision, arms wrapping around her daughter's slight form, as she laughed and sobbed out Ally's name.

"Mommy," Ally said. "Mommy, you came. You came on vacation."

Somberness dabbed her face for a moment, but for Liz laughter overtook tears, until finally she became aware of the sensation, the feel of her daughter in her arms.

"Ally, sweetie, you're wet. Why are you all wet?"

Imagining terrible possibilities out here, swimming trials, kids kept cold and damp, or even water torture at the Shoemaker's hands—

It was Ally whose laughter rose then, tinkling like seashells as she said, "Well, it *is* raining, Mommy. I guess I'm wet because it's raining so hard."

And Liz looked up and saw that the sky had finally split apart, unleashing the soaked contents of its clouds, and that her face and head and body too were slick with rain and she hadn't even known it.

Liz unzipped her pack, and got out the raincoats. In addition to the rain, Liz had also missed the presence of Cody, who had trailed Ally to the reunion and was standing, thumb in mouth, drops trickling down his face.

The canopy had prevented them from getting too badly wet. Liz brushed water off both children's clothes, then buttoned them up and secured their hoods. The routine maneuvers of care kept her from having to think about what came next.

Liz had to find Reid, but after that she had no idea. The existence of other children wasn't something she'd worked out.

Spotting another item in the sack, Liz beckoned Ally closer. She pointed to Izzy's yarn head, then looked up to drink in Ally's joy.

Ally snatched out the doll and cradled her to her chest, swaying back and forth, and murmuring words too hushed to hear.

Liz couldn't help but smile. "Okay, enough. You don't want Izzy to get wet."

Reluctantly, the little girl relinquished her doll.

"Cody?" Liz asked, once Izzy was sequestered again. "Where's your mom?"

Cody and Ally exchanged looks.

"Al?"

Ally hadn't let go of Liz's hand; now she dropped it reluctantly and turned to Cody. "It's okay, Cody. This is *my* mom."

"I don't know," Cody said, a tremor beneath the words. "She asked Ally to watch me."

Despite everything, Liz registered the pride that raised Ally's shoulders and leveled out her small chest, and she experienced a flush of motherly delight. Then she wondered what could've happened to make a woman entrust her child to a six-year-old.

"Okay," Liz said as if that were a perfectly natural state of affairs.

The children linked hands.

Continuing in a casual vein Liz added, "I think I'm going to walk both of you out. We'll meet your mom a little later, Cody, okay?"

Cody gave a single nod.

"But first we have to find Reid," Liz said, still briskly. If she acted as if all of this were completely reasonable, no problem at all, then perhaps things would fall into place. "Do you know where he is right now, Al?"

The scope of this place wasn't immediately apparent, but there was emptiness beyond the final rim of trees, and Liz sensed that it might be massive.

"Just Reid?"

"What, sweetie?"

"If we're going," Ally explained, and Liz nodded encouragingly. Her daughter seemed to be accepting the premise unquestioned, which was good. It had occurred to Liz that there might be protest. "Is it just me and Cody and Reid? Or the others, too?"

"The others," Liz echoed. How to keep her daughter from knowing that Liz didn't particularly care what the adults did? They had come here of their own accord; they could leave the same way. Getting the children out was key. "Sweetie, I think we'll let the grown-ups kind of come a little later. You know? I'm sure it won't be long." Though of course that was the last thing she was sure of. Especially in the case of Paul and his demon partner.

Ally was shaking her head impatiently. "I don't mean the moms or dads. I mean the rest of the kids."

CHAPTER FIFTY-SIX

Rain tatted overhead, lone droplets penetrating the roof of leaves. One swelled on Liz's cheek as she turned her face toward Ally's.

"There are—more children? You mean besides Reid?"

Ally nodded decisively. "There's Reid, and Tom, and that weird little girl, I can't remember her name—"

"Carthage," Cody said with perfect enunciation.

"Don't call someone weird," Liz said automatically.

She lifted her head to the elephant belly sky. How to find three other kids? The rain would both hide and hinder Liz. Ally and this little boy were too young to move fast, they would slow her down. But they also knew things; they could tell Liz where to go. Would she be putting them in danger if she asked for their help? Liz could put herself at risk to find Reid, but she wasn't willing to endanger Ally or Cody. If the Shoemaker came, would they be safer back here in the forest, concealed behind a tree? Or staying at Liz's side?

It didn't matter. Liz couldn't imagine leaving Ally ever again. Whatever they faced, Liz would simply have to protect both children from it.

But as she lifted her hands to her eyes, their soreness eased by the moisture in the air, she knew there was little she could do if the Shoemaker set his sights on her again.

Liz stayed crouched on the wet ground for a period of time she couldn't pinpoint. Time was like blood in these woods, endlessly replenishing itself, but she sensed she was squandering a resource they might need.

"Okay," she said at last.

Both kids had stood in place without making a sound. They were patient and compliant children, and Liz couldn't imagine anyone better to aid her in this recovery mission, yet she still feared for their chances.

"You said you thought they'd be inside the barn?" she asked.

Cody nodded solemnly. "Because of the raining."

"Nah," Ally said, sounding so like her brother that Liz's heart gave another dip. "They'll be outside."

Having Ally here beside her was a miracle, but Liz also needed her son. *Please don't let me be asking too much. Please let us succeed.*

"They don't care about getting wet," Ally went on. "I bet they're still taking down that laurel and the catberry in the barnyard."

Was that what the children were doing here at this enclave? Clearing brush? Liz allowed herself some small measure of relief.

"Okay," she said again. "Then lead me to the barn." Constructing an approach, she added, "We're going to make it like a game."

"Like Hide-and-Seek?" asked Cody.

"Exactly," Liz said. "And Follow the Leader. Kind of a mash-up."

The kids smiled when she did.

"And then we'll surprise Reid and the others and we'll—"

Which was when Liz's plan petered out. They would have to play it by ear. With any luck, those kids would be as unsupervised as Ally and Cody had been, and Liz could beckon them away, Pied Piper–style. All the treats in her pack would be put to good use.

Ally and Cody were nodding.

Then Ally said, "Why don't they just meet us here?"

"Well, that would be hard, sweetie," Liz replied. "I don't want to shout too loudly. And they might not hear us over the rain anyway."

"I know *that*," Ally said. "But we could call them."

"Call them?" Liz said. "How?" A thought lit. "Does the cell phone work over here? Do you have it, Al?"

"Not with a *phone*," Ally said, delighted by her mother's error. She turned to Cody.

The little boy began fumbling beneath the collar of his shirt, but the raincoat made his fingers trip. Soundlessly, wordlessly, Liz bent down and unzipped it for him.

The boy drew out a whistle on a string.

"We have a system," Ally said. "Of signals. Reid invented it and Tom makes us practice them. *All* the time. He forces us to."

"Signals?" Liz echoed, gazing down at the tiny silver whistle.

Both kids nodded fervently, faces lit up despite the grayness all around.

"Like . . . like—" Cody said.

"Time to eat," Ally put in.

"Or . . . or *a grown-up is coming,*" Cody said, finally getting the words out and beaming at Ally.

"Or," Ally said, ignoring the little boy to gaze up at Liz. *"Come right now."*

Liz stared at her. "And the grown-ups? They don't understand these signals?"

Ally laughed, spark-fast. "No way. They think we're just playing."

Liz reached down and took each child's hand in one of her own and began to walk them toward the edge of the woods where she had first spotted Ally.

"Well," she said, "I'd say that you both had a very good idea. Why don't you try the signal, Cody? The one that tells them to come?"

Cody nodded obediently. He pulled the whistle out of his shirt again, and put its miniature slot to his lips.

"You can do it," Ally told him. "Remember? Three short, three longs. That was for an emergency."

Three shrill notes cut through the air, then three longer ones sounded.

"Do it again," Ally suggested.

Cody did, his eyes on Ally.

The notes rang out, distinct and true.

Nothing. Only the soughing of the rain.

"Again," Ally urged.

"I'm all out of breath," Cody complained.

"Want me to try?" asked Ally.

Liz too was reaching out her hand.

But Cody opened his mouth again.

He was about to blow when out of the ghostly gales of rain, visible in parts, first feet, then legs, then torsos, three children appeared from different directions, covering the distance to where Liz and Ally and Cody stood.

CHAPTER FIFTY-SEVEN

Two of them resolved into clarity first and Liz was left scanning the mist for her son, her gaze flitting back and forth, raindrops obscuring her vision.

She heard Reid's voice before she saw him.

"You came."

It was dull and angry, though recognizable; the voice of the boy on the phone last night, rather than the nimble-fingered son who had been taken out of the hotel.

Still blind, Liz walked forward, arms reaching toward the sound of that voice until she met the block of Reid's chest, felt his wet face, a little higher now than before their so-called vacation, and spoke into the top of his head. "Yes, Reid. I did. I'm here. I came."

Her boy, who seemed older, who had grown in just these three weeks, began to cry.

There was a snorting noise from behind.

"Did you call us out for this happy family reunion?" a boy asked. "Because I'm not a part of it. So I'm leaving."

"No, wait!" Liz said.

She reached down, wiping Reid's face before tackling her own. She took in the sight of the other two children. The one who had spoken was oldest; he had a good half a head on Reid, and a burgeoning sturdiness in his legs and arms, while the other was that boy's polar opposite, a tiny sprite of three or four, with a froth of strawberry curls.

The big boy half turned, regarding her with a look of scorn.

And Liz knew whom he must belong to, and she also knew what she could say.

Two can play the mentalist game, Shoemaker.

"Sure you don't want to go with us?" Liz asked lightly. "Get out of here? Away from your dad?"

"We're leaving?" Reid said.

The other boy maintained his contemptuous expression.

Liz ignored it as she began digging in her pack. "Here. I thought you guys might be a little hungry."

The kids descended on the goods—fruit and nut bars, thumbprint cookies, knock-off M&Ms in diluted colors—as if they'd been stranded on a desert island.

"A *little* hungry!" Reid cried. "We're a lot!"

"Hey, Mommy, can we really eat all this?" said Ally.

"Can I have some?" asked the blond kid.

"Me too, me too!" said Cody.

The big boy stood there, watching the children scrabble around as if they had just knocked down a piñata. After a moment, he thrust out his hand.

"Hey," he said. "Leave some a that for me."

Liz told them her plan, and the children nodded chocolate-smeared faces and murmured assent with crumbs in their mouths. Not a single protest. Maybe the treats had reminded them of all they were missing. Or maybe they were just in a sugar coma, insensate, content.

"My mom already said we're leaving," Cody announced. "She just needs to do a little thinking first so the man doesn't find out. And we can't go in the rain."

The big boy—Reid had called him Tom when they jostled over the sweets—lifted his head when he heard that.

The children cast their eyes up to the sky, worriedly for the most part, although Tom wore a licking-his-chops expression, as if the coming implosion excited him.

Liz was worried herself. Thunder was harmless, getting wet only a little less so. But she had just seen a prong of lightning arc above the canopy. And lightning could fell a tree so fast in these woods, none of them would be able to get out of its way.

Cody's mom's hesitation made sense, but Liz knew the Shoemaker in ways the moms who had chosen to live with him clearly didn't. And the Shoemaker was worse than any storm.

"We'll meet up with your mom—with all your moms—once we get out. I have a friend who will come in and search for them here."

"My mom's not here," Tom said scornfully. "You think she's a nut-case loser, too?"

Liz had indeed been wondering who might have chosen not just to come with the Shoemaker, but to have a child with him.

She wiped her wet hands off as best she could and began to load up the remaining food. "Well, that's good," she said. "Then we can call the non-nutcase-loser from a real phone."

Tom looked at her, his expression flickering for a second. "Cool."

Liz gave Reid her raincoat, deciding that its draping folds would slow the little blond one down too much. Then she decided on an order in which they would walk, big sandwiching little, and indicated their direction. They would take the same way out she had followed in. There was something of a trail now; it would be a little easier to navigate.

"We can't go that way," Tom said.

Liz braced her hips with her hands and bit back a breath. "Why not?" Sweet, compliant, she'd thought about the other kids. But this one was trouble.

"Because we're going to be missed," Tom said, a *duh* in his tone. "They'll see our tracks and follow them." He paused until Liz looked at him. "My father will follow them."

Liz quelled a rising panic. Minutes had been devoted to mere treats. The Shoemaker may have already detected their perfidy. He might be stalking them now, unseen and unheard.

Cody began to approach Ally, moving amongst the twigs and brush on the ground. A stick snagged his leg and he tripped, crying out. The crack of the branch disturbed the whole woods, louder than all their voices combined, violent where the whistle had been playful.

Liz gathered the boy up, shushing him, looking around. Then she turned back to Tom. "Do you know another way out?"

For the first time, Tom looked doubting. "The only place I can imagine them not thinking we'd go ... it has a path if we can get across ..."

Reid picked up where Tom had left off. "The falls."

THE SHOEMAKER

Kurt had to deal with the body.

Yesterday had been spent finishing up a few essential tasks, as well as restoring Madeline's mood, making her understand why her mother had to be dealt with as she was. That hadn't been easy, but Madeline's girlish adulation had helped.

Kurt had succeeded in keeping the others close to the barn—he'd always had a hold on people, commanding them to his will without their even knowing they were being commanded—but children were an unknown quantity, as Kurt had learned from Tom. For the time being the horde seemed content, hacking at brush that blocked the entrance to an old haymow, but that job was nearly complete. And there was work to be done elsewhere on the grounds.

Kurt's misadventure with Madeline's mother was not why Paul had a composting method that would get them out of this predicament. It was just opportune that he did. What was less ideal was that in order for Kurt to make use of it, Paul would have to know what he had done.

Kurt wasn't worried about anyone coming to look for the dead woman. He could read her story as if it were one of the true crime books he used to love poring over. He'd always had that ability, and it hadn't failed him, even with things unraveling here in much the same way that they had when he ventured off to college.

But they hadn't spun out completely here—at least not yet—and this woman's death wouldn't be the cause of their doing so. Madeline was the sole person on the planet the woman had been able to convince of her importance. No one would search for her, not hours away from where she lived, in what was a nearly undiscoverable location. The woman wouldn't be missed by anyone that much.

Kurt hated the distant, knowing look in her eyes. As if she could read him as he did her. He leaned down, thinking to press her eyelids shut, but the idea of touching her with his hands was repellant. That cupped shell of skull would burst so satisfyingly, like the hull of a coconut, if he kicked it. Kurt forced himself to turn away. He had more important things to do.

Paul was pulling reeds from the pond, shirtsleeves pushed up for the messy task. He'd been at this since they arrived, asserting repeatedly that the pond was going to be key to their processing system. The reeds he was pulling out would also make excellent watertight containers; Paul laid each one down as carefully as a tube of glass.

"Ahoy, the pond!" Kurt called out, in the joking way he knew to adopt with Paul.

Paul looked up, screening his brow with a muck-streaked arm. "Hello, the meadow!" he shouted back. "Hey, does the meadow want to get down to the pond and help?"

Kurt put on a good-natured smile, parting tall grasses and descending the bank. When he arrived, he didn't enter the water, and he made sure his face turned serious.

"Paul, we have a bit of a situation."

Paul blocked the bright light with his forearm again. In a little while, he wouldn't have to. The sun was disappearing fast, covered over by scudding clouds.

"The children all right?"

"Sure, sure." Kurt nodded. "That isn't it."

Paul turned back to the diminishing stand of reeds, clearly itching to return to his task. "What is it, then?"

"This might be best as a visual," Kurt said. Water was lapping at his boots and he stepped back with a feeling of distaste. How would this slimy pool ever be put to use?

"Kurt . . ." Paul said. "I've got a lot to do here. As you can see."

The eruption was close to the surface; Kurt felt every part of his body fill with heat. But he managed to speak with the jovial demeanor Paul had come to expect from him. Kurt played the willing assistant so that Paul could believe he was in charge.

"I do see," he said. "And don't think I don't appreciate you getting your hands dirty. But Paul—we have a different kind of dirty work to do right now."

That was all the preparation he would give, the only hint he'd provide.

Paul finally turned away from the pond, a faint frown appearing between his brows. "And it's a visual, you said?"

Kurt nodded, glad to be leaving this slop bucket, even if the job ahead would be equally nasty. He waited until Paul had climbed out before indicating their direction.

The hardest part would be when Paul saw, and Kurt had already determined that warning him in advance would only make things worse. Best to be brisk about this relatively trivial blip on the radar of their creation. He had also concocted a story to engage Paul in the righteousness of this act. As the best stories did, this one contained an element of truth.

Paul flung droplets from his hair, wagging his head as they trudged uphill. He wiped a hand across his face, licked off damp lips.

"Don't you ever worry that what's in the pond shouldn't be ingested?" asked Kurt.

"Well, it's not like I'm drinking it by the jugful," Paul responded, and Kurt contributed a chuckle.

"By the creek?" Paul asked, scouting with his eyes as they walked.

"You got it. That big tree over there."

"The willow," said Paul.

Again, pressure rose inside Kurt. The idea that this rinkydink college teacher—this nothing of a man—thought he could inform Kurt of anything made him want to take Paul's windpipe and crush it. But Kurt suppressed the urge, speaking merrily, "That what it is?"

Paul gave a nod. "See those drooping boughs? That's why they say it weeps."

"Learn something new every day," Kurt said.

"Especially in this place," Paul responded, and turned to clap Kurt on the shoulder.

Kurt hid his instinctual wince, offering a nod for cover. "You got that right, too."

Paul slowed his pace. "Kurt?"

Kurt was distracted; it took him a second to work up a grin.

"Have I thanked you?" Paul said. "For making me—not making me, that's not the right word—"

Oh yes, it is, thought Kurt.

"—for giving me the support that enabled me finally to act?"

Kurt slowed down, too. "No thanks needed, buddy."

"No, but—" Paul broke off. "I *want* to thank you. I know some would criticize what we're doing out here, at least the way we did it. But I needed to make a better life for my children. For myself. And if we hadn't met . . . Well, I might've stayed where I was, fat and cushy, and never realizing my . . ."

Kurt knew Paul wasn't going to fill in the word, but he waited the required beat. "Destiny?" he offered after the pause had gone on for the right length of time.

Paul gazed up at the sky as if he owned it. Pressure boiled again inside Kurt but he managed to regard the scene neutrally.

"Yeah," Paul said at last. "That's right. My destiny."

"Well," Kurt said as they resumed walking, "I'm glad. But I still say no thanks are needed."

Paul would get the chance to repay him momentarily.

They had arrived at the place where Madeline had been suckling her mutt, and Paul registered what lay there before the truth slightly penetrated his consciousness.

Kurt could read the reaction in his shoulders.

He allowed for the inevitable denial. A snake's tongue of lightning forked across the sky, diverting Paul's attention, and Kurt waited that out as well. When Paul again lowered his eyes, one of two things was going to happen. Either Paul would drop to his knees and feel for a pulse, having no idea that this woman was almost twenty hours dead, or else he would ask Kurt how he had found her. What Paul wouldn't do was put two and two together. Most men couldn't stomach the idea of standing next to a murderer.

Kurt had killed somebody once before. Another nobody, a classmate who thought he would match wits with Kurt for an assistantship. Their rivalry had gotten out of hand; Kurt would've been the first to admit that. He hadn't meant his kick to land in the boy's solar plexus when they finally came to blows. It had been an accident, but Kurt had still served time and, of course, was forced to leave school.

It had been for the best, though. A wrong turn that wound up being right.

Everyone maintained they were innocent when they were inside, but for Kurt's celly it had actually been true. And the guy for whom he was taking the ride had intrigued Kurt. He learned more about Paul Daniels in the time he slept beneath Allgood's bunk than Allgood would ever know he'd given up. Once free, Kurt made it his calling to locate the man who had never paid for his crime. Paul hadn't spent one day in prison for murder, while Kurt had lost four years of his life to a brawl.

Kurt lived a regular life after getting out—got married, sired a child—but he spent his leisure time tracking Paul down, then identifying the chat room Paul stared at every night.

Kurt wanted to leave his icicle of a wife, and the chat room revealed that Paul was uniquely positioned to enable a disappearance. To a place where neither money nor resources were needed, and where Kurt and his boy would leave no tracks. The menial work of creating such a spread would've been beneath Kurt, but Paul had accomplished a great deal in a short period of time. With Kurt watching him every step of the way.

He looked at Paul now.

"Kurt . . ." Paul let out a breath. "You just found her here?"

Kurt had considered this as a way out, but ultimately rejected the I-can't-imagine-where-that-body-came-from ruse. He would've had to kill Madeline to make it work, and even if there'd been enough time, he rather enjoyed Madeline. More than that blabbermouth Abby. Abby reminded Kurt of one of those dogs who tagged along at your knees, tongue lolling out.

While Terry knew how to keep quiet. If Kurt indulged the woman in her quest to take ownership of Madeline's infant, she would avert her eyes from just about anything.

Which left Paul.

Kurt knew he could maintain a better hold on Paul if the man continued to see him as up-front, genial Kurt Pierson, nary a false word, certainly not a lie between them.

He spoke with weighty seriousness. "This is Madeline's mother."

Paul took a staggering step back from the body. "What the hell are you—her mother came *here*?"

Kurt decided to ignore the discourtesy. Paul was in shock. It was making him stupid in multiple ways. He nodded once heavily. "She did. And not only did she try to get Madeline to leave, she physically threatened her. Assaulted her really. I was forced to step in."

"Step in," Paul echoed. "Are you telling me that—you killed her, Kurt?"

Kurt had trouble not laughing. Laughter would've ruined all the work he had already put in. "I didn't have a choice," he said gravely. "It was her or Madeline."

A man like Paul would not look too closely at the body. If he did, then the mode of death would've argued against Kurt's explanation, or at least put holes in it.

One hole anyway. Again, Kurt had to suppress a smile.

The hardest part was still ahead, and after a moment, Paul set it on its course.

"All right," he said. "Okay. If you offer that explanation to the authorities, it will clearly be a case of defense. Not self-defense, but still, you did the right thing . . ."

Kurt let him go on a little while longer.

" . . . it's not great that people will find out where we are—I can't even imagine the battles we'll face—but it's not like there's much of a choice . . ."

Much, Kurt heard with some relief.

"There is a choice," Kurt said, and he took the measure of Paul's response.

"What?" Paul asked raggedly. "What else can we do?"

"What else can we do?" Kurt repeated. "Besides reveal the empire you are building? Lose it, surely? This place of salvation in a world hurtling toward destruction? What else can we do besides sacrifice our children to that?"

Tears were rolling down Paul's face. "Yes," he said. "What else?"

"Why, you know the answer better than I, Paul," said Kurt, masking distaste at the statement. "It's perhaps your biggest accomplishment so far," he added. "You were just describing it to me. How most compost entails a great deal of wasted product. But not your kind. Your system, you said, produces such heat that meat, bones, whole cattle break down within months." He paused to look at Paul. "Even big bodies are consumed."

Kurt could see the barrier between lawful society and the one they were creating crack in Paul's mind. And he could also detect a shade of appreciation for the fail-safe solution Kurt had come up with.

"Nothing we do now will bring this wretched woman back," Kurt said.

And then, with Paul preparing to mount his final objection, Kurt gathered together the words he knew would break him.

Kurt had aped frustration when they had to spend a few extra hours in the pissant town of Junction Bridge before coming here. An item had been forgotten at the hotel, and Paul decided to make a quick trip back, while Kurt and the children got some sleep.

But Kurt hadn't gotten any sleep.

Instead, he explored the grounds around the farm, keen and observing, the whole time Paul was gone. Keeping himself concealed, Kurt had peered into the windows of the house over which Matthew Daniels lorded. Matthew didn't know he was being watched while he knocked back a slug of whiskey, then another and one more. Nor did he realize it as he lay down, fully clothed on his bed, massaging a sore hand. Kurt crouched on a slope of roof, so close that he could've caressed the man as Matthew drifted down into an uneasy sleep.

Matthew had shut the door on his son, and in his dismissal resided all the information Kurt needed. But Kurt couldn't resist adding a few morsels. While Mary Daniels fussed around the three children, descending with blankets and sustenance and murmured reassurances, Kurt had quietly given in to the lure of the hidden.

"You're going to indulge a six-year-old's tantrum?" Kurt had asked when Paul first explained the change in plans, saying that his younger brat had forgotten some toy. Then, when Paul overrode Kurt's objection, Paul would feel as if he'd won a small skirmish, that he was in charge.

But in reality, Kurt couldn't have set things up better if he had tried. The chance to scrutinize how broken Matthew was following the ejection of his son, and to view Mary, whose stooped posture and whispered declarations controlled far more than they appeared to, gave Kurt the means to control any number of situations that might come up out here.

Like this one.

Paul wiped his face, resolve squaring his shoulders. "This isn't right, Kurt. We need to go to the authorities and—"

Kurt cut him off. "It's terrible how hard and hateful some parents can be, isn't it?"

Paul's hand stilled.

"Unforgiving," Kurt added. "If this woman had lived, she would have driven all life, all initiative out of Madeline. How lucky we have the girl here with us. How lucky that you, Paul, can help her live the life she was meant to."

They carried the body between them, shuffling awkwardly up the bank, Kurt facing forward, Paul turned away. Paul hefted his part of the load as they covered the acres to a scooped-out section of ground, but transferred it to Kurt when they arrived.

A thunderbolt shook the air, and Kurt staggered under the weight of the body.

Paul was digging out a scum of leaves and moldering brown, exposing an underbelly that was indeed steaming hot. He came back and picked up the legs.

"On my three," Paul muttered.

A similar storm swirled inside Kurt. *This is my body*, he thought. *My killing, my plan, my disposal, and you are no more than a tool.*

But Kurt could disguise himself as others could never be disguised, and he swung in affable concert with Paul's command. One and two and—

Another clap of thunder came, and Kurt lost his grip on the woman's rigid shoulders. Something was wrong out there.

"Three!" Paul shouted.

The body flew into the air, but nowhere near as far as it would've gone if they both had thrown with full force.

Madeline's mother landed in an undignified tumble, facedown, at the edge of the pit.

There was a snuffling sound from behind. An animal drawn to the kill, too hungry or curious to be wary. Kurt understood its nature, the impossibility of applying caution when there was something to be gleaned.

He turned around slowly. "Paul."

Paul saw, too. They both began to back away.

Suddenly, the coyote went loping off in the other direction.

Kurt lifted his head, scenting something from the same deep, instinctive place that had driven the coyote.

The children were out of the barn.

CHAPTER FIFTY-EIGHT

They kept to the perimeter of trees for as long as possible before breaking out into open space. There the rain fell down in long arrows. They had no protection and were instantly soaked. The children seemed to know enough not to screech or yelp, but their discomfort was clear. At first they tried to wring out their sodden clothes, wipe off their faces, but when neither did any good they gave up, trudging along, each covered by a dripping veil.

The meadow was enormous and otherwise untrammeled. Indian and switchgrasses stood tall, only their tips bowed by the weight of the rain. Liz had never felt more vulnerable, like a game piece on a board. She kept the children huddled close. Spread out, they made a whole host of pinpricks, any one of which might be spotted.

Although together they were one big moving target.

No one knew they were here. They couldn't. The Shoemaker would've had no reason not to have descended upon them by now, and even he couldn't be so noiseless, unapparent. The only sound was a faint hum of bees; there must be an apiary somewhere.

They had honey.

For the first time, Liz's gaze roved, trying to take in the place to which her children had been brought. She blotted her face with a drenched corner of shirt, but couldn't make out anything that justified Paul's treachery. Justified her pain.

Their small group trudged along, wicking moisture from the field.

She was aware, as she checked on the children, of a feeling she hadn't experienced since Reid and Ally were younger and she'd hosted playdates. You looked after each child equally, of course, but there was inevitably a deep vein of preference for your own. So you compensated. You called your own kid's splinter a trifle, but doctored the guest's as if it required the greatest mercy and care. You suppressed a pang of frustration when yours wanted yet another snack, but jumped to appease the other one's hunger. Reid and Ally had been snatched from Liz, however. Stolen. She couldn't take their childish selves for granted; having them back was a gift more precious than life. She gripped a damp hand in each of hers, keeping contact with the others with her hips or elbows instead. When she scouted, counting the brood over and over again, her gaze sought out Reid and Ally before landing on the other three.

She recalled the fight she'd had with her best friend, how Jill had ignored Andy's stabs at revelation about Paul. Jill too had gotten her child back from the brink.

Oh, Jill. I hope I get a chance to tell you I understand.

They walked on, Liz at a painful precipice of alertness, squinting through the rain for any hint of human invasion. Her clothes stuck to her like wet paint, but the downpour finally seemed to be easing up, and it had accomplished one merciful thing. Liz's eyes hardly pained her at all anymore. Her vision had been reborn, washed clean.

A glint of color flashed to the left. Not sunflowers or devil's cone or Indian paintbrush, the coppery, yellow tones of almost autumn. This was synthetic, a bright teal piece of clothing.

Liz pulled back on Reid and Ally's hands, and they reined in the rest.

Her gaze flew up to the clouds, slowly spreading themselves out against the sky. The woods were a half mile away. There was no place to hide except amongst these tickling grasses. She was just about to direct each child to lie down, hoping that the motion when they dropped wouldn't give them away, when it occurred to her that whatever had summoned her attention wasn't moving itself.

It was an unnatural color, and also unnaturally still.

Liz herded the group a little closer, an uneven amoeba of bodies. And then she was pulling them back.

"Children, don't look!"

An idiotic command—its only consequence to make everyone do the exact opposite—but shock had stolen any knowledge of childhood psychology away.

There was an enormous pit dug out of the pastureland here. And by its edge, a coyote's head was moving up and down. It looked like a piston, so regularly did the beast pull and chew and swallow. Liz would've assumed it was eating a deer or even a bear, the fruits of a kill, except she'd seen that spark of color.

"Children, *hurry up!*"

They heard the fierceness in her voice, and even Tom listened, backing away from the depression in the ground.

The coyote lifted its slowly bobbing head.

It had scented them, but it must've been satiated, for it turned and loped off into the woods. Coyotes were pack animals and this one was probably summoning its compatriots to the feast. Liz prayed the children hadn't seen what it was devouring.

Lying half-buried by a silt that Liz recognized as Paul's own composition, uniquely adept at breaking down organic matter, was the body of a woman.

CHAPTER FIFTY-NINE

The whole time they'd been walking, Tom had kept moving away from the group. Now she was glad for that. Of all the children, he would be the one with the most ability to understand what they'd seen.

Also, she suspected it was Tom's father who was responsible.

They had to leave this place. Now. Whatever was happening here was far worse than Liz had feared.

"Tom!" Liz called out with quiet urgency. "How close are we? Where are these falls?"

He either didn't hear her, or didn't choose to respond.

It didn't matter. A few minutes later, the drone of bees was replaced by a far louder roar, and vapor joined the remaining rain in the air.

They had arrived.

Liz walked to the bank and stared down, the backs of her thighs immediately weakening. A forked tongue of waterfall flicked over the mountainside. Liz had trouble hearing anything, and she could feel a misty spittle on her skin. She started to shiver.

The children were also shivering, huddled together in an attempt to conserve heat.

She had to get them out of here.

"Tom." Liz turned to the boy with a slowly rising feeling of horror.

Had he deliberately entrapped them? Led them to a dead end? There was no way they could cross beneath that pounding water. "You said something about a way out?"

He nodded, gesturing. If he was a liar, he was an awfully good one. Then again, he'd learned from the best.

"See that pool over there? We have to climb down to it. It's easier to cross. And there'll be a path on the other side."

Liz peered over again. Downstream, the water did calm. If they could get there, it might be possible to traverse—even for non-swimmers, as the youngest were likely to be. Tom and Reid could wait with Ally on the opposite side while Liz helped the smaller ones across—

"Liz."

It wasn't that it had been so long she had forgotten the sound of his voice. It was that whole worlds had been rounded since then, entire lives changed, and at first she didn't recognize what had once been the most familiar of sounds. For a moment, Liz thought that Tom must have learned her name. But he wouldn't be talking to her in such a low, resigned tone. A voice that held the weight of those worlds.

She looked up and saw Paul.

"Reid, Ally," Liz whispered. "Children. Go wait for me away from the edge."

Peripherally, she caught a glimpse of Tom at the head of a straggly line. He did seem to know this creek, and when he turned his back on the others, he appeared to be headed for a safe spot, where the force of the falls was damped and the bank sloped at a less steep angle.

Paul looked down at her, and despite everything, Liz still felt the force of that gaze.

"You could stay," he said, a bright, shallow note over the deeper thrum of sorrow.

Liz let out a laugh.

"You never really believed in me, did you, Liz?"

Liz laughed again, incredulous. "Is that what this is about? My not believing in the great Paul Daniels?"

He looked as much surprised as distressed by her tone.

"What was there for me to believe in?" Liz continued. "You think you're a leader, a ruler of men? Of our marriage?" *I suppose it was old-fashioned,* Liz heard her mother say.

Paul was regrouping, his gaze hard again now.

Liz saw the return of that forcefulness, and fought it with everything she had. "You're a coward who slunk away in the middle of the night!"

"Only because you undermined me at every turn."

"So you just cut me out? Rather than stay and have a real battle?" A wind kicked up, sending a blast of spray over her face, and Liz spat disgustedly. "Why did you come back to the hotel anyway? You didn't have to lie down beside me, wait until morning, make me think the children—" She broke off with a sob, but gathered herself before Paul could speak. "—the children had been kidnapped. Why didn't you just take them and go?"

Paul looked at her and for a moment he was her husband again, the man she'd married and had children with, performed the countless tasks, both shared and disputed, involved in creating two human beings out of nothing but the strength of love.

"Ally wanted Izzy," he said simply. "She threw a fit when she woke up and realized we forgot her. I had to come back from the farm, and when I did, you started to wake up."

Coldness descended along with another great wave of wake from the falls. Liz stared at her husband. A doll. He'd forgotten a doll. And then he'd gone and let Ally lose her anyway.

"You bastard," she said. "You stole my children. You want me to stay? You're lucky I don't kill you instead."

"I wouldn't call it lucky." The Shoemaker's bodiless voice rose from a cavity by the creek. Parted by the wind, a veil of mist revealed him. "For you would probably fail if you tried. Whereas I will not."

The Shoemaker lifted a thick-barreled gun.

CHAPTER SIXTY

Liz took in the strange triangle the three of them formed before recognizing that the gun was pointed not at Paul but at her. Sorrow assailed her with the strength of the falls.

Reid. Ally. I've only just gotten you back.

Then another thought hit—her children were going to be left here with this monster—and she let out a cascading cry.

A *snick* came from the Shoemaker's gun when he pulled something back, obliterating all other sound. It could be heard over the spiraling screech of a bird, over the great thrust of the water.

Paul strode forward, thrusting out his arm. "No, Kurt," he said in his forceful way. "Not again. There must be a better way."

An eerie clarity overtook things. Paul was referring to the woman whose corpse she and the children had stumbled upon. Liz was just another potential victim here, not Paul's wife, or the mother of his children.

"I was hoping you wouldn't say that, Paul," the Shoemaker said.

He didn't take his eyes or the gun off Liz as he spoke. The tone he used was all but unrecognizable, jovial and light.

"Clearly this woman doesn't believe in what we stand for," the Shoemaker continued. "She will undermine us at every turn."

Crossing the distance between himself and the Shoemaker, Paul paused.

A glint lit the Shoemaker's eyes.

Half-forged plans whirled in Liz's head. Make a run for the children, herd them toward the woods, where they could all disperse, hide amongst the trees. But she could never outpace the Shoemaker. And she'd be setting him loose on the kids.

Horror constricted her throat and she turned to face the man she'd married.

The Shoemaker was also rounding on Paul. "She will ruin us," he said, and now his voice was familiar, portentous and deadly.

"It doesn't matter," Paul said brokenly, as if he were giving up the whole world. "We've already lost what we came for. Surely you can see that." He began covering the remaining ground to the Shoemaker, his hand fisted with purpose.

"Come on, Paul," the Shoemaker said in a silken tone. "I'm not the only one who knows about murder here."

Shock purpled Paul's face. "What are you talking—" He broke off, then began again: "How did you—"

"Let me do this, Paul. And then we'll pick up where we left off."

Paul halted. "You're . . . crazy. You can't kill my wife."

A weary resignation took hold of the Shoemaker's features. "Yes, I can," he said, turning the gun on Paul. "But I see that I'll have to kill you first."

He fired.

CHAPTER SIXTY-ONE

The bullet caught Paul in the chest and he went down. First onto his knees, hands clasped as if in prayer before the great chasm on his body. He looked up at the sky, and the ground absorbed the flow of his blood, dirt staining red until finally Paul fell.

Her husband had been trying to prevent Liz from this slaughter. It had taken him a while—and of course he had put her, put them all in this mad situation in the first place—but still Liz looked on his fallen body and a wrenching sadness gripped her. For it to end this way, Paul splayed out amongst his ruined dreams. She let out a sob that turned into a heave.

"Even with our limited time, I probably could have appealed to your husband's misplaced sense of lordship," said the Shoemaker. "Women are always dispensable." His gaze shifted. "I might even have been able to get Paul to fire the killing shot. But it would've been a reach, I grant you, given the way he was going." The Shoemaker stared off distantly at the falling cloak of water. "I've learned enough to take over here. And I certainly won't miss Paul's presumption." He refocused on Liz with rage. "I doubt anyone will miss you much either."

He was twisting and turning things on her again, using words to make her dart. Liz drew in a breath. She had to concentrate. Getting the children away was the only thing that mattered.

The Shoemaker turned the single blind eye of the gun on her.

Liz spun and cried out. "Tom!" He was the oldest, the one who stood the best chance in those woods. "Take them! Run!"

The Shoemaker whipped around too, his body that of a snake. "Where is my son?"

Liz turned to look, but the children were out of sight. Relieved breath escaped her.

The Shoemaker was stalking toward the gentler stretch of creek.

"I have him!" Liz shouted. "Tom would've gone with anyone to get away from you!"

She checked once more for the children, and saw them then, distant flickers in the trees.

They were fleeing.

All except Reid.

The Shoemaker wheeled around, firing hand extended.

Liz shrieked. "No! No!" Words meant for Reid. "Get away! I mean it, now! Get away!"

But her son kept coming, gaze aimed down at the Shoemaker's hand.

The one that held the gun.

The Shoemaker's gator gaze slid past Reid and came to a rest on her. "You don't think I'm coming back because of your puny attempts at a lure, do you?" Contempt curled his lips. "I already know my son hates me. I also know that hate can be more of a bond than love."

Reid stopped a few feet away from them both.

Liz lashed at any attempt at distraction. "Hate is as good as love," she mimicked. "Guess we all rationalize. Just like the real Shoemaker did."

The Shoemaker loomed over her, cold breath chilling her neck. "What did you say?"

Liz fought to remember what she'd read in her search. She couldn't tell where the gun was anymore, although right now the Shoemaker looked able to kill with the sheer force of fury in his eyes.

But at least he wasn't paying attention to Reid, who was still approaching. Reid's eyes were big and wide and scared, fixated on the gun.

"He was a sad little man who was so afraid of women, he had his son kill for him." Liz let out a laugh that burned. "I don't think Tom wants the job."

The Shoemaker buried the gun in her side.

Reid's arm flicked out, fast as the tongue on a snake.

Liz let out a shriek that slashed the air, a stream of senseless words curdled with tears of terror. "Reid! Stop! No! Reid! Go!" She fought to see what her son was doing—tried to follow the motion of his fingers—but they moved so quickly, so adroitly that she lost sight.

The Shoemaker hurled Reid away with a flick of his arm.

Liz watched her son's body tumble with a sob of relief that nearly knocked the wind out of her. Reid landed on the ground, one hand folded as if he'd injured it in his fall.

Liz heard the click as the Shoemaker fired his gun, then felt a gust as it discharged against her body.

CHAPTER SIXTY-TWO

I t seemed to take forever for them both to realize that Liz was still standing. She and the Shoemaker were upright, so close they could've embraced.

From his prone position on the dirt, Reid lifted his fist, an incongruous gesture of triumph. He opened his fingers and the bullets he'd removed clinked onto the earth.

The Shoemaker let out a roar of rage. He reared up against Liz, pushing her on the storm-slicked bank, toward the falls. The ground was as slippery as sealskin; she couldn't stop herself.

She clutched at the Shoemaker's hair, his clothes.

He slammed a fist into her head. For a second, the sun came out in all its blazing glory. Liz's eyes were bathed in shafts of light; shutting them, she staggered.

If the Shoemaker had hit her with his right hand—if he hadn't been holding on to the gun—then the blow would have probably killed her. As it was, she was summoned back to life only by the sound of a voice.

"Children!" it trilled. "You know you're not supposed to play here!"

Liz tried to identify the source of the sound, looking around with uneasy hope. Her vision was gauzy from being struck, but the children appeared to be staying away from the carnage, and the battle playing out. The Shoemaker maintained total focus, using the diversion to unhinge Liz's hold on his flesh.

In hazy relief, the figure of a young woman appeared. She was older than the others, but not by much, still almost a child herself. She cradled an infant in one arm.

The Shoemaker pushed Liz backward along the slick run of soil.

"He's guilty of murder, you know!" the girl called out. "Kurt Pierson can be charged with the death of my mother." Her voice hit a high, bright note of madness.

"I should've killed you yesterday," the Shoemaker said without turning. He gave Liz a shove.

She would never overpower him. Not in muscle nor in wits.

A gong beat Liz's skull. The falls were so near that they deafened her. She tasted the water's breath on her tongue.

The Shoemaker seized her expression and she watched his triumph rise.

"You can't fight," he said. "Not even for your own children."

Their eyes met as he pulled her toward the lip of the falls.

The Shoemaker dipped his face so close that the pores on his skin looked like wells, and he whispered in her ear. "I'm going to kill them as soon as you are gone."

They were at the edge of the falls now. Water boiled at the base.

The Shoemaker's boots skidded; the earth was as slippery as fish scales. Liz's feet got tangled up in something, and she flailed for purchase. She gasped, looking down.

Woodbine.

A dense mat of it growing all over the bank.

Mist showered them, lifted by a great gust of wind. The Shoemaker was going to push her again, and when he did, he'd be leaning forward, off-balance.

Liz waited for the thrust of his arms and she grabbed them.

They both went over the side.

Liz's fingers raked a trail going down as she scrabbled for the woodbine. She seized two meaty handfuls and held on with all her might.

The tiny suckers on the vine gripped back.

An unholy scream echoed above the thunderous water.

The Shoemaker's body plummeted, twisting and turning like a twig before disappearing entirely, caught up by the suctioning river.

Liz hung there, wrist-deep in greenery.

But she couldn't pull herself up. She would never have the strength.

She twisted around to look, knowing she was about to fall.

A hand reached over the side. It grasped Liz by the elbow.

"Hold on!" a voice shouted.

Liz did.

And Tom pulled her up.

AFTER THE FALLS

Tim Lurcquer started assembling his men, making arrangements from the jail as soon as he got Liz's text. He had been buried in a colossal mountain of paperwork. One-tenth necessary, nine-tenths CYA crap. There'd been incidents at the jail before, and there would be others in the future. Too little manpower, plus relics of the old regime, where the ends always justified the means. Rough justice was the end, and nobody worried too much about means. But things had changed since Tim had been holding his position, and he was proud of that.

Until now.

He took William Mercer's suicide as a personal failure, even if the man's death wasn't exactly a planetary loss. Still, it'd been Tim's job to keep the man alive through trial, and he hadn't. Mercer's victims—the children he'd terrorized, the old man he nearly killed—would never get the satisfaction of having their case heard or seeing a verdict handed down.

Tim sat at the desk they had given him at the jail and crumpled the form he'd been filling out into a ball, aiming it in the direction of the trash.

"Lola?" he called. "Could I get another C19?"

The C19 never got filed.

Liz's message came in and the miniscule letters on his screen were all that Tim could see.

They took K9 and a SWAT team from downstate, with Lurcquer mapping out three distinct sections of woods for his friend with the helo.

Landry took his orders with a flat look that spoke louder than any objection.

"Say it," Tim commanded.

"Listen, I'm the one who talked to dispatch after the call came in," Landry said. "The lady didn't sound all that sure herself. Isn't this a lot of resources to be assembling on a maybe?"

Tim snapped a new clip into his pistol. "I wouldn't doubt Liz Daniels if I were you. One of her maybes is worth a dozen men's yeses."

Fragments coming over the radio revealed when the search dog located the picked-over remains of a woman's body in a heap of refuse, wood ash, and dung. Tim was occupied at the moment. He had just spotted a disruption in the trees, a welter of twigs and branches. The helo swooped down to the place where Liz and her charges— they were small to judge by the footprints—had entered the woods.

At first Liz thought to lead everyone around by way of the falls, using the point of entry Tom had described. It would be worth something to keep the kids—especially Reid and Ally—from viewing Paul's bloodied corpse.

Liz didn't know how she could stand to see it again herself.

But they might encounter the Shoemaker's bruised and battered body, broken in the water, and that would be bad, too.

The young woman with the infant offered to gather the other women up, deliver the news, and lead them out. No way was Liz taking the children back into the encampment.

They were clustered together in a shaking clump.

Liz's arms felt blocky and wooden, not equal to the task of escorting out her small refugees. Tom and Reid worked in concert to strip the wet outer layers off the little ones, exposing them to the emerging sun.

"Come," Liz said, her voice creaky and rusted, as if it had been left outside too long.

But the difficulty was clear as soon as they reentered the woods.

The falls were some ways east of the path Liz had followed in. If they tried to find their way from this starting point, Liz wasn't positive she could keep them from getting lost.

Her dilemma must have registered because Tom spoke up.

"My—um, my fath—Kurt has a van," he said in a sprightly tone that belied his bedraggled appearance. "He leaves it a few miles away. If you start hiking from the barn."

There was a road. Had Liz known to look for a road, been able to find one in the spider's web of camp trails here in the park, how much easier this whole thing would've been.

She gazed at the wall of woods before them, then back in the other direction.

The kids looked up at her, their hair drying at odd, scruffy angles, streaks of mud on their faces and clothes, but their gazes bright and trusting.

"Mommy?" Ally said.

"Yes, Al?"

Thinking, *What happened to Daddy? How do we get out of here? Where will we find the other moms?* or any of a dozen questions Ally might ask and Liz had no hope of answering.

"Kurt was lying, wasn't he?"

It occurred to Liz that she'd never heard the Shoemaker's real name before today.

"This isn't where the world comes to an end, is it? The world—it's still there, Mommy, right?"

Suddenly, an unnatural wind ruffled the leaves on the trees, and branches began to clatter. The air around them throbbed.

Liz looked up to see a helicopter descending, like the belly of a whale.

Tim was sitting above the skids, legs dangling as he scanned the ground.

The children were also looking up, their faces wide with wonder.

"Yes, Ally," Liz told her as she began to hustle the kids together. She put her arms around Reid and Ally just for a moment to make sure. Then she raised a hand toward Tim and started waving madly. "Yes, everyone. The world is still there."

ACKNOWLEDGMENTS

Getting to publish your first novel is a bolt from the blue; it's a is-this-really-happening? moment. Getting to publish a second one gives you the great gift of answering that question with Yes.

To everyone who helped make this happen, my deepest thanks.

The usual suspects all apply, but so that these acknowledgments don't become a novel in themselves, I would ask you to please take a look at the last few pages of *Cover of Snow*. There are resources and riches there, and many people deserving of great gratitude.

Getting to work with Linda Marrow on my debut novel made me one of the happiest, luckiest writers among that happy, lucky group. Getting to do another sends the quotient soaring. Linda deserves an acknowledgments section of her own, not only for her wisdom, vision, and breadth, but also for her support, humor, and plain old sense of fun.

Dana Isaacson deserves a thousand thanks for taking care of the million details that shepherd a book into being. If I had an eye like Dana's, I wouldn't need a dozen drafts. But I am glad I don't because he sees things I am so grateful are in there.

Kim Hovey and Libby McGuire help steer the greatest ship there is.

Anne Speyer was always there minutes after I needed her, with exactly what I needed. But Anne added something else to this process. Toward the end of the book, a character arrives at Liz's house. And it was Anne who realized that she should be there. Jennifer Rodriguez, I hope, will always be at the helm of production on my books. Thanks also go to Ted Allen, who jumped in at a necessary moment, and to Pam Feinstein, whose eagle eye caught everything from a missing hyphen to a missing character trait. I never thought I could get as lucky as I did with my first book in terms of publicity, but getting to work with Michelle Jasmine makes me gladder yet. Thank you, Michelle, for your vision and excitement. The entire Random House/Ballantine team are dream-makers and have my gratitude and thanks.

My agent, Julia Kenny, brings enough belief, hope, wisdom, and calm to the table that I count on the future she envisions.

After my first novel released, I hit the road for a seven-month, thirty-five-thousand-mile book tour. Then I sat down and proceeded to list the bookstores I wanted to single out. It was an impossible task, and so I decided that rather than asking my publisher to print a gazillion-page acknowledgments section, I would for now thank all the booksellers of this country who opened their doors, their shelves, and their hearts to me and my family. I believe that bookstores are one of the most precious resources we have, and hope that I walk the walk in celebrating them. Thank you, booksellers, for celebrating with me.

Librarians and libraries are another precious resource. In those hallowed halls I became a reader and a future author. Thank you, librarians, for the work you do; thank you for taking a chance on me. Special thanks go to Stacy Alesi for magic-making.

Book clubs and book bloggers have impacted the way we read, and the way authors reach those readers. Thank you for finding my book amongst the many thousands written. Thank you for hosting me in your homes and online. Please continue to reach out, because I will always reach back.

To the reviewers who embraced my first novel, my many thanks.

There are authors who exemplify the overflowing generosity of the writing community. (Hint: The list to come also happens to be a roster of Must Reads to add to your pile.) In no particular order (except alphabetical): Marjorie Brody, Elizabeth Brundage, Carla Buckley, Anthony Franze, Nora Gaskin, Tom Gill, Peter Golden, Linda Hull, William Kent Krueger, William Landay, Allison Leotta, Jamie Mason, Susan McBride, Jennifer McMahon, Lee Mims, Rick Murcer, Richard North Patterson, Nancy Pickard, Leah Rhyne, Hank Phillippi Ryan, Charles Salzberg and the New York Writers Workshop, Joanna Campbell Slan, Karin Slaughter, Julia Spencer-Fleming, Mary Stanton, Mark Stevens, Tina Whittle, and Carter Wilson—thank you for meeting me along the way, and fitting me into your busy, creative lives.

I wrote about one group of writing kindred spirits in my last acknowledgments section; this time I'd like to take the opportunity to thank those who rallied forces to give me that feeling every author hopes for: that of walking into a crowded event room. Diane Beirne of The Woman's Club in Richmond, Nikki Bonanni and the Killer Coffee Club, Donna Fletcher Crow, Debbie Gerrish and the Women Who Write, Sandra Hutchison, Kay Kendall, Lynne Kote, Donald Maass, Liz Main, Maryann McFadden, Bill Meissner and the Mississippi River Writers Workshop, Janet Reid, Mary Elizabeth Roarke, Linda Rodriguez, Carolyn Rose, Lizzie Ross, Janet Rudolph, Carl Selinger and the Montclair Write Group, Emily Winslow Stark, Lelia Taylor, Mike Turner, Juanita Wilson, Lois Winston and the Liberty State Writers—no writer (no person) could hope for more.

A special thanks to writer and baker Judy Walters, who filled my first month of events with sweets. Both Carrie Murgittroyd and Liese Schwarz managed to make my son's birthday on the road special, with songs, kindness, and majestic cakes.

To Julie Schoerke, Marissa Curnutte, Sami Lien, Grace Wright, and everyone at JKS Communications who, instead of laughing when they heard that I wanted to go on book tour for seven months, actually helped make it happen ... thank you. Every author should find publicists who know that it's not just about publicity, it's also about heart.

The novel you've just read was revised at many points along the way. Countless rooms, closets, and nooks saw versions of this book, but a few deserve special mention. Karen Pullen, for a room at the lovely Rosemary House Bed and Breakfast in Pittsboro, North Carolina; Judy Hogan, for a wonderful dinner and lesson in farming; Ed Schneider and Rita Kempley for a fabulous pad in the heart of our nation's capital; Mary Stanton, for a condo—on the beach, no less—in West Palm Beach, Florida; Angela Menemenci, for another lavish beach house; Tina Whittle, for a writers' retreat house by the tides of Savannah, Georgia; Janis Thompson, for the darling apartment, extra bedroom included, in Peabody, Massachsetts; Marjorie Brody, for two days in the big ole state of Texas; Reggie and Matt, for a week of respite in Arizona; Dan and Lisa Schneiderman, for a home-away-from-home in D.C.; Jerry and Pam, for a night outside the Windy City; and Eileen Baldwin and Linda Beaupre, for a magical bunkie in Ontario that delivered inspiration every writer must wish for.

I believe that writers cast a net, and the life they live goes into that net. What winds up coming out in a story is a mystery vaster than anything I've yet to pen. But two people I can identify provided inspiration for key aspects of the book you've just read, and if they don't recognize themselves, then I wish to.

To Earl Staggs, the real-life Earl: Thank you for letting me use your name, your nobility, and your spirit. I know you would do as well as the one in this book. School bus drivers everywhere, you are the unsung heroes and heroines of our children's days.

And to Andrea Lekberg, of The Artist Baker in Morristown, New Jersey: Thank you for the exquisite treats, only one aspect of which did I steal for Jill and Liz (but many of which did I eat).

At the start and at the end there is always my family, my greatest gift.

My mother-in-law, Shirley Frank, offers a fine editorial eye, and bolstering just when I need it. My father-in-law, Eddie Levenson, has quite an editor's mind himself. It is he who speaks for the semicolon . . . and makes me feel all this might really happen. Lucky for me, I have another mother-in-law, Amy Small, who ushered in my debut with a literary panel and reception, and one very special cake.

Clearly, I like cake.

I would not be writing at all without my parents, Alan and Madelyn Milchman, who taught me about finding your passion and never giving up. The fact that they are expert and trusty readers is more than any daughter has a right to expect.

My brother-in-law, James Turney, gathered troops in Arizona and Oregon. When my first novel sold out in Phoenix, it was all his work, and he doesn't even live there anymore. My brother, Ezra, and sister, Kari: If the road brings me closer to you, that alone is good reason to be on it. I hope that the next book finds us all together somehow. Thanks for always wishing . . . and thanks for the reality checks.

My children are the ones to whom this book is dedicated. They make so many things possible, you'd think they weren't the kids in this equation.

Everything comes back to Josh. First trusted reader, partner in all things crazy (which just might prove our sanity in the end), expert road warrior, and soulmate. Thank you. The greatest story of all began when I met you.

JENNY MILCHMAN lives in upstate New York with her family. She is the author of *Cover of Snow* and *Ruin Falls*.

jennymilchman.com

ABOUT THE TYPE

This book was set in a Monotype face called Bell. The Englishman John Bell (1745–1831) was responsible for the original cutting of this design. The vocations of Bell were many—bookseller, printer, publisher, typefounder, and journalist, among others. His types were considerably influenced by the delicacy and beauty of the French copperplate engravers. Monotype Bell might also be classified as a delicate and refined rendering of Scotch Roman.